# THE WEEPING WINTER

THE LIGHT OF THE NORTH SAGA - VOLUME 4

• J. C. DUNCAN •

First edition June 2023

Cover design by Damonza.com

Photography by Studio Zahora

Maps by Red geographics

ISBN 978-1-915804-00-6 (paperback)

ISBN 978-1-915804-01-3 (ebook)

www.jcduncan.co.uk

# Glossary

**Adolf, Count of Schauenburg and Lord of Holstein and Stormarn:** A Saxon lord of Duke Lothair's patronage, a senior commander of the First and Second Northern Crusades

**Aeske:** Brunhild's son

**Asel:** Senior huskarl of Jarl Frode

**Aurick:** Father of Ingrid, discoverer of the sword Ljós a Norðan

**Baldwin VII, Count of Flanders:** Son of the famous Robert II, 'The Crusader'. Commander of the Second Crusade

**Baron Hugues:** Brother of Folmar, Count of Metz

**Bekkr:** Warrior of Vatnsborð

**Bertrand Lang:** The deputy assistant minister of culture for antiquities and ancient monuments

**Bjorn Lendirsson:** Swedish huskarl

**Brunhild:** A Norse slave girl in the service of Jarl Ragnvald

**Conrad:** The Count of Blankenburg. Elder brother of Bishop Reinhard, one of three initial leaders of the Third Crusade

**Dengir:** The Norse master smith at Uppsala

**Eric Firebeard:** One of Sigurd's huskarls, companion of Gunnar

**Felix Meyer:** The assistant to Bertrand Lang

**Frederick II, Duke of Swabia:** Prince of the empire, ally of the emperor

**Gjaldir:** Legendary Norse warrior

**Gotfrit:** Saxon ex-slave, then brother of the Order

**Gunnar:** Huskarl of King Sigurd

**Professor Hallsson:** Head of the history and archaeology department at the university of Lundjen. An expert on the Northern Crusades and medieval Scandinavia

**Halfar Asleson:** The curator of the Røros Museum of Norse History and Culture

**Halla:** Wife of Jarl Ragnvald

**Harald Freysson:** One of Sigurd's huskarls, companion of Gunnar

**Hartung:** Son of Count Adolf, member of the Order

**Henry V:** Emperor of the Holy Roman Empire during the Crusades

**Henry the Black:** Duke of Bavaria

**Ingrid:** Eleven-year-old girl who likes history and hates fishing. Discoverer of the sword Ljós a Norðan

**Jarl Birgir:** Ally of Jarl Harnsted

**Jarl Einar:** Brother and successor to Jarl Harnsted

**Jarl Frode:** Swedish jarl, ally of Ragnvald

**Jarl Gustav:** Swedish jarl, known as the Raven's Claw

**Jarl Harnsted:** Swedish jarl, cousin of King Eric and one of the contenders for the throne

**Jarl Ragnvald Ivarsson:** Important jarl of the Kingdom of Sweden

**Knud:** Leader of the people of Vatnsborð

**Leif Leifson:** Huskarl of Jarl Ragnvald

**Lothair, Duke of Saxony:** Contender to be the next Holy Roman Emperor, First Crusade leader

**Ordulf:** German smith from Minden in Lower Saxony

**Otto:** Slave of Ragnvald

**Otto, Count of Ballenstedt:** One of three leaders of the Third Crusade

**Roland, Sieur de Blanchant:** Acclaimed French knight of the Third Crusade and brother of the Order

**Rudolf:** Margrave of Nordmark and Count of Stade

**Sigurd Magnusson:** King of all the Norse (*Norðrikonungr*). Son of Magnus, the King of Norway

**Sigyn:** A Swedish woman, one of Halla's people

**Simon I, Duke of Lorraine:** Feudal lord of Baron Hugues

**Sir Sighard:** A commander in the service of the Order

**Sir Dietmar of Eresburg:** A leading knight of Bavaria

**Sir Hans Mettel of Oldenburg:** A leading knight of the Saxon contingent

**Tormund Five-Bones:** Seer and adviser to King Sigurd

**Vidar Junge:** Swedish warrior and huskarl of King Sigurd

# Preface

The previous book in this series, *A Forge of Frost*, told the story of the second half of the Second Northern Crusade, the Norse victory at Jönköping and the battle in the deepwoods, and then their ultimate defeat to the forces of the Third Crusade while defending the heartland of Svealand, culminating at the battle outside Uppsala.

Many of the Norse lords have fallen, King Sigurd is wounded and the army is shattered. Rather than let Uppsala fall into Christian hands, the old smith Dengir decided to burn it, and Ordulf, now given the freeman's name Gjaldir, has decided to leave with his new Norse family to fight for them, rather than return to his Christian kin.

The sword he forged for Jarl Ragnvald, Ljós a Norðan, the Light of the North, prophesied by Sigurd's seer Tormund Five-Bones to be the salvation of the Norse, has fallen into enemy hands, prised from Ragnvald's dead hand by his killer. With the symbol of their hope lost to the enemy, their leaders dead, and their army shattered, the Norse survivors and refugees face an uncertain and desperate future as they set out on the road inland, with winter and the Christians in pursuit.

Now, Gjaldir, newly free and sworn to end his life as a smith, as a tool of other men's violence, sets out on the path of a warrior, to forge his own fate and to fight for his own family and cause. He goes with the woman he loves, Brunhild, and the child that is not his, Aeske.

The Christian lords, flush with their final defeat of the Norse army, and their capture of their capital, must continue to work together to finish the conquest, or risk losing it all with infighting and struggles for ultimate power. In the Holy Roman Empire, and in the Vatican, the future course of European politics and power may rest on the outcome, and on who can clench their mailled fist on the prize and prestige of the vast but wild new northern provinces.

Can the survivors of Ragnvald's people, led by his defiant wife, Halla, find hope and shelter in the cold and mournful months to come? Or will they be consumed in the Weeping Winter?

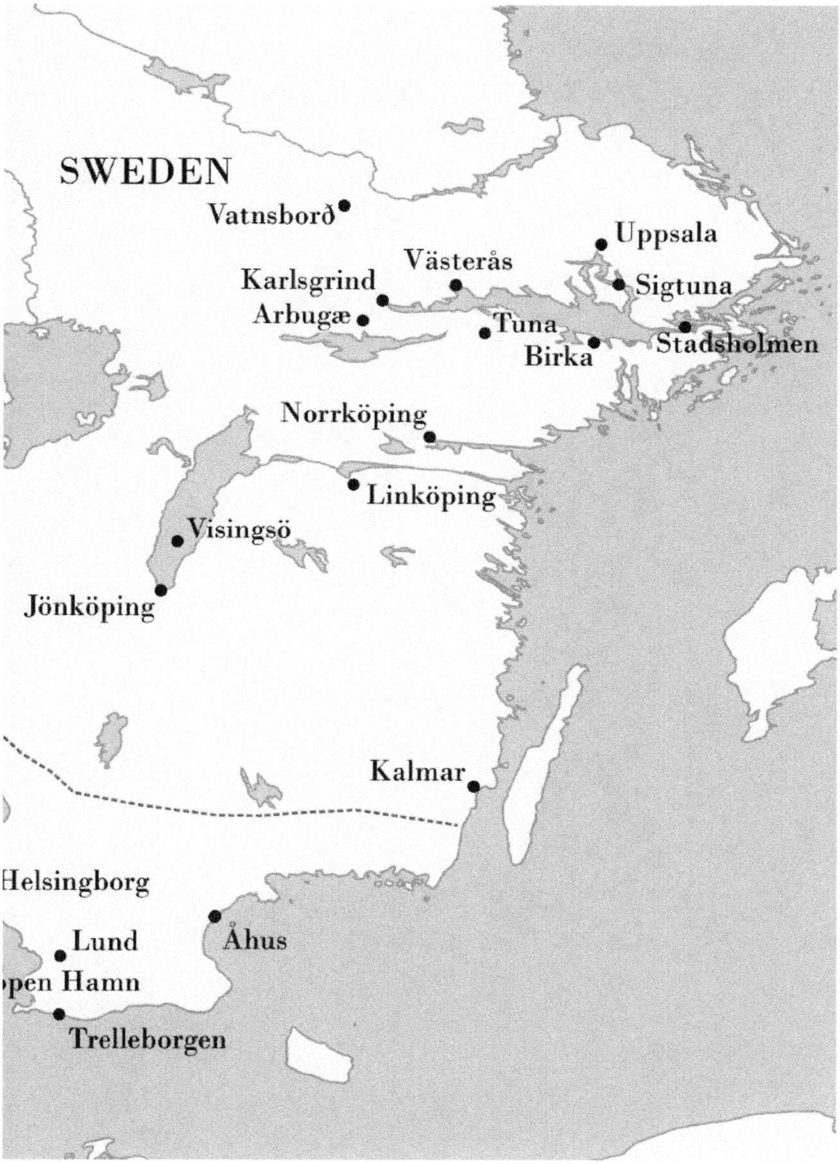


*Key named locations of The Weeping Winter*

# Prologue

## Chapter Two of the Saga of Ljós a Norðan
## by Sverre Knarlsson
## Written circa 1170 AD, Iceland

GJALDIR AWOKE, ALONE on the field of death, and did not know why he was alive. He found that his wound was healed, stitched with strange markings, and his strength was returned to his arms. He looked around, and wept as he found the bodies of his shield-brothers and companions scattered around him.

Eventually, he took up his sword and left the scene of the defeat, heading into the woods, without a thought of where he would go. After many days, wandering inconsolable in the forest, he found a band of survivors walking, leaderless, through the wilderness. The people called out to him to join them, to help them, but Gjaldir was destitute, and beyond the soothing of words, or the comfort of the company of his fellow Northmen. He left the sad assembly of the people and set to wandering once again. He walked through the woods and mountains for ten days and ten nights, eating only what he could kill, drinking only water that flowed in mountain streams, ignoring the plight of his brethren, who even now were being hunted and killed by their enemy.

Odin watched with anger and disappointment as his champion was gripped in misery and inaction. The man he had saved to lead his people was standing aside while the North bled from a thousand wounds. Eventually, one dark night, Gjaldir made his way to the top of a mountain and wept on the peak, and Odin's anger bloomed. A storm gathered from his disappointment and rage, and winds scoured the peak, and rain poured down. But yet the warrior sat unmoved on the mountaintop. The storm winds howled and shrieked with the anger of the gods, but yet the warrior ignored their rage.

Finally, shouting his curses at the sky, Gjaldir stood and drew his sword, still shining weakly in the darkness, the heart of the fallen star not yet completely consumed. He unleashed his rage on the sky and the world, and, cursing his fate, he drew his arm back and hurled the mighty sword into the abyss of darkness, before retreating to a cave to weep and rest.

Odin was enraged. He considered ending the life he had saved, but he knew the power of the blade, he knew the power of the belief it carried with the people, and, casting his eye's vision into the murky future, he knew the importance it carried, so instead of ending his fallen champion's misery, he plotted his resurgence.

When hunger finally drove Gjaldir out from the cave at the peak of the great mountain, he walked down its slopes and into the valley below. Odin, ever watching, plucked the sword Ljós a Norðan from the rocks where it lay and cast it like a bolt of lightning from the sky. The sword speared down into the ground at Gjaldir's feet, passing so close that the edge cut his face over his left eye, blinding him on that side. Standing back in shock, and blood closing his eye, Gjaldir looked around and saw nothing that could explain the sword's arrival, until he saw two ravens, Huginn and Muninn, the messengers of Odin, sitting on a branch, watching him. The warrior was at last afraid, and, when the ravens took flight and passed by him, he felt the cold wind of their passage and was drawn to follow. Taking the sword from the ground, up the mountain he followed them. The ravens would fly and then settle, watching, waiting, drawing him ever upwards. When Gjaldir reached the peak and the cave where he had spent the night, he found an old man in a cloak standing, facing away from him, watching out over the lands.

A great stillness passed over the mountain and the old man finally turned and looked at the warrior. Gjaldir was so overcome that he fell to his knees. The man had one eye, and a beard of twisted knotted silver. In his hand he suddenly held a mighty spear that Gjaldir knew at once to be Gungnir, the spear of the Allfather.

Gjaldir quailed before Odin and the old man finally spoke. 'Your sword is the hope of your people, and you must carry it in their service. Enough of your cowering in the high and low places. Have you no shame?'

Gjaldir bowed his head to the old man. 'The sword is failing, and I with it.'

'The sword is a tool for the heart that wields it. And yours is weak.'

'I am sorry, Allfather.'

'You have failed us, but my son will grant you a gift to wield against your enemy, and you will never again betray my faith and abandon my people.'

Clouds were gathering, swirling, in a vortex above the peak. Thunder rolled out across the valley. Gjaldir looked up in amazement at the clamour, the sound of Thor's arrival.

'Rise, warrior of the North, *hǫlðr* of the people, and draw your sword. Now, your fate arrives!'

Gjaldir rose slowly to his feet, pulling Ljós a Norðan from its great scabbard. The thunder was deafening now, all-consuming. The black clouds swirled ever closer and the wind ripped at his clothes and his hair. Yet he forced himself forwards, holding the sword and walking to where Odin stood, the old god unaffected by the tumult.

'Give me your swordhand,' spoke Odin over the raging storm, not raising his voice, yet clearly heard.

Gjaldir nodded and offered out his hand, Ljós a Norðan still wrapped tightly within it. Odin grasped the hand, and ripples of shock washed down the champion's arm from the touch of a god. Odin raised the mortal arm to the sky, pointing the faded sword at the centre of the spiral of clouds. Lightning was starting to sparkle in the depths of the clouds, some started lancing down to hit the mountainsides around them and Gjaldir quivered in fear, but Odin's grip steadied him.

Gjaldir could hear it now, the beat of Thor's hammer above him, each strike sending out blasts of lightning and booming thunder that drowned out the very thoughts in his head. Finally a great bolt of lightning reached down from the maelstrom and landed on the tip of Gjaldir's blade. He screamed in silent terror as he felt the wave of power run down the sword and into his arm. The sword started glowing, more than ever before. The light flowed down the core of the blade until all of its former glory and more was restored, shining in the darkness. Power kept flowing into the blade, and ripples of flame appeared around the shining core, eating at the dark surround of the blade, driving it back towards the edge as the blade drank the thunder god's power.

Finally the lightning stopped, and the flow of awesome power came to an end. Gjaldir was almost consumed by it, gasping and sagging, but Odin's grip sustained him, and kept him standing. The core of the blade shone like the brightest star in the sky. Around its core, white fire flickered and moved. Within the steel and on its surface, the smoke from the fire roiled and churned in the edges of the great blade, giving it a rim of darkness. Gjaldir was transfixed. Finally, the fire died out, but the bright core and smoking edge remained.

'The sword will still consume the souls of the enemy it kills, and thus the light will be sustained. The fire will keep it bright for as long as there is fire in your heart. If you ever betray my faith in you, that fire will die, and my people with it. You now truly carry the light of my people with you, and you will not fail me again.'

'Yes, Allfather,' said Gjaldir, raising his eyes to meet Odin's, but the man was gone, leaving him alone on the mountaintop with the blazing sword and a churning mind and the heavy cloak of destiny wrapped tightly around him.

# PART 1

## Chapter 1

# A Stone for a King

HALFAR'S MOUTH GAPED of its own accord, and he was struck by an unaccustomed speechlessness. Professor Hallsson had brought two young men in with him with a cloth-wrapped bundle, a Norse battleaxe head that their grandfather had dug up in a field on his farm decades ago. That would be remarkable enough in itself, but the axe was finely decorated with inlay and runes; runes that read 'I am Justice, the word of Sigurd Northking'.

Halfar knew who that meant, of course. The semi-mythological Sigurd Magnusson, reputed to be the only king of all the Norse, who had supposedly led the resistance to the Crusades of the early 12th century. He was a towering figure in Norse mythology, but scantly sourced in historical records. His very existence was debated by some historians, while others argued the tales of him uniting the Norse nation were fantasy, not backed up by any first-hand sources. The Christian records of the time did not mention him, and only stories in the sagas, often written centuries after his death, told snippets of his life from the Norse perspective.

But here, under Halfar's trembling hands, was an axe head that claimed, in pitted steel and shining gold, to be the weapon of the king himself.

Eventually he shook his head free of the murk and pointed two fingers at the nervous-looking young man. 'Your grandfather dug this out of a gravesite, and there was a body there. Are you sure?'

'Yes… well, I am sure that is what my grandfather said, that he found the axe and human bones when he was cutting a drainage ditch on the edge of our farm.'

Halfar clenched his fist together and felt like he could cry. 'He dug a drainage ditch through the grave?' He muttered recriminations under his breath to the long-dead farmer and lowered his head onto the fist.

'No, of course not! He re-directed the ditch well clear of the gravesite.'

Halfar looked up again, the swell of relief bursting in his chest. 'It is intact?'

'Yes. He was concerned we would get curious and dig it up, or another would find it, so he placed a large slab of stone over it. It has never been touched since.'

'Oh, thank the Lord, a sensible man. But he took the axe?'

'Yes, he did not want to put it back into the ground to rust away. It was too precious.'

'Was there anything else?'

The young man shrugged. 'He did not dig very far, just the axe and some bones.'

Halfar leaned back and blew out his cheeks, the sheer excitement of the story overcoming the anxiety and boredom of the previous weeks. He looked at Hallsson, eyes wide. 'We have to go there, surely.'

He tried to temper his excitement, reminding himself that he was no longer a part of the museum project, having quit in disgust at the government interference. He was a visitor at the university, and Hallsson bringing this axe to show him was merely a kindness between old friends. It was, frankly, no business of his at all. He gave Hallsson an earnest look of gratitude and hopefulness.

Hallsson gave his studious smile and then nodded, but he held up a hand to curb Halfar's excitement. 'Halfar, it is nearly December, and we must organise equipment and heavy machinery to move the stone, and get permissions and liaise with the government. We will have to wait for spring.'

Halfar grunted and looked away, irritated but not able to argue. It would be madness to try to dig in the middle of winter with permanent snows on frozen ground. 'We could just go and see it,' he grumbled.

Hallsson smiled. 'You will just have to be patient, it has waited nine hundred years, it can wait a few more months.'

Halfar nodded sadly. 'Okay, yes, I know, but those months will drag terribly.' He had little to do, he still could not safely return home with the threat of the so-called brotherhood hanging over him. Every time he thought of the quiet man with the calm, threatening expression in his museum, he shuddered.

He put it from his mind and looked up at the two young men still standing in the office to ask them a question, then his eyes widened and he shook his head and laughed. 'Sorry, I never even asked your names.'

The man who had handed over the axe nodded and smiled. 'I am Asbjorn, and this is my brother, Karl.'

Halfar cocked an eyebrow. 'One German name, and one Nordic?'

'Yes, our father had Nordic heritage, his family came from Norway after the war. My mother is German, so this was their compromise.'

Halfar nodded and grinned. 'I see. Well, thank you, Asbjorn and Karl, for bringing us this axe. Now.' He reached for his notebook and a pen and opened it, leafing through to a blank page, glancing quickly at Hallsson, almost asking for permission, and receiving a wry smile in response. He motioned Asbjorn to the only other chair in the small room. 'Please, take a seat, and tell me everything, from the start.'

The April morning was brisk and cold but Halfar did not notice it, bouncing with nervous energy as he stared at the large, flat-topped stone lying on the edge of the field. Professor Hallsson and his small gaggle of archaeologists, and their inevitable government minders, were standing beside him, watching with mixed excitement and anxiety as the heavy-duty straps tightened and the crane ever so slowly started freeing the big lenticular stone from the soil.

The stone was lying face down on the edge of a field, the ditch curving around it some four or five metres away. The brothers said this ground had almost been swamp when their grandfather cleared it, but now it was a vegetable field. The archaeologists' faces had grown nervous and pensive when that was revealed. The draining of the land and drying of the soil might have caused increased degradation of the artefacts in the grave in the intervening years.

The ragged stone slab itself came from the jumble of rocks above the site, a small outcrop that would once have been an island in the middle of a marshy forest, but now stood alone and stark in the middle of the family's fields, the treeline of the old forest now a few dozen metres away, the ancient woodland covering the gentle slope of the low hill that rose away to the west.

Halfar chewed his index finger with worry as the stone was ever so slowly prised from the earth. The crane, stabilising legs splayed on a mat of metal plates and plastic tiles, strained and creaked against the load.

Finally he could see clear air beneath the stone and the ground, and the crane operator gently swung the stone away to the side and laid it on the ground half a dozen metres away.

Halfar was oddly disappointed that all the stone revealed was flat, featureless earth. He knew, of course, that it would not have revealed a perfect skeleton just lying there waiting to be found, the grave itself was under a metre of earth, but it was a significant anti-climax.

He waited until Hallsson and the manager of the small team of archaeologists had inspected the depression and then sidled over to his old friend. 'So, how long until they dig it up?'

'Oh, days, I expect, you know how this works.'

'Yes, but I've never been this impatient before.'

Hallsson laughed, his grey moustache twitching as he looked at the small museum curator. 'Do you want to come back onto the project then? There will always be a place for you, you know.'

Halfar grimaced and shook his head, nodding to where deputy assistant minister Bertrand Lang's assistant Felix Meyer and another government official watched proceedings. 'I can't work with them, meddling and lying and considering the politics of everything.'

'Well, then, there will be little for you to do here. I told you not to come here for this, nothing of interest will happen for a while for an observer.'

'Yes, I know you did. But I wanted to get out of the city. And I don't want to miss anything important.'

'I'll call you when we find anything, it's only a couple of hours to get here.'

'Fine,' grumbled Halfar, having a last look at the naked patch of dirt that might or might not contain the only king of all the Norse, and then gave his friend a stern look. 'The moment you find anything, anything at all.'

'I promise,' said Hallsson with a broad smile.

Halfar was in his borrowed office at the university late one night a week later, just getting up to leave, when his phone rang. He fumbled excitedly at it to answer when he saw it was Hallsson and put it to his ear. 'Is he there?' he yelped. All week Hallsson had been silent, and Halfar had become more and more frustrated, to the point of being about to drive up there to find out.

'I don't know,' said the voice at the other end, but with no note of happiness.

'What… what do you mean…'

'Halfar, listen, I must be quick.'

'Was there a body? Did you have trouble identifying it? I could come up immediately, maybe there are some artefacts that would…'

'Yes, there was a body in the grave, but no, you can't come here, and there is nothing to see anyway anymore.'

Halfar screwed his eyes up and shook his head as he was interrupted. Hallsson sounded curt, angry.

'What are you talking about?'

'The site has been closed off, no one is allowed to come here.'

'Who…' Halfar screwed his eyes up and cursed under his breath. 'The ministry.'

'Yes. They have taken away all the finds, made all of us sign NDAs, confiscated all our records and covered over the site.'

Halfar sat down heavily. This was worse than he could possibly have imagined. 'That's criminal.'

'Technically, no, it's not. They made sure of that. They even gave us a printout of the relevant law. The finds are culturally significant and thus government property, and they are allowed to keep them secret for as long as they need to verify their history, in order to stop speculation that could be damaging to public order.'

'And how long will that take, to verify them?' said Halfar reflexively. There was silence at the other end of the line and Halfar groaned as he realised the loophole. 'There is no time limit, is there?'

'No, they will store the finds and have no requirement to publicise them if they don't want to.'

'But why can't you just tell the press? How did they get you to sign NDAs?'

'The students weren't going to stand up to the government, they have too much to lose. The ministry funds their course. They were replaced with ministry staff as soon as we uncovered the grave.'

'And you?'

'If I didn't sign it, they were going to cancel the museum project, and have me removed from post. Perhaps not immediately, but eventually.'

Halfar's hand shook with anger on the phone. 'This is madness, even for them. This is intolerable madness.'

'Yes, I admit, I am still shocked. Even Bertrand Lang seemed ashamed of it, I expect he is under severe pressure from above to quieten all this down, the government is having so many problems with the Nordic nationalist movement. They fear this will be their *Braveheart* moment, and they are weak and afraid.'

Halfar leant back in his chair and closed his eyes with a pained sigh. 'Was it even the king?'

'We cannot be sure it was the king, not yet. It was a large skeleton, but not buried with much; a seax, a brooch, armrings, some belt fittings, a shield boss, and there were some trace remnants of fabric in very poor condition. But nothing to indicate a royal burial. It may well have been his axe, but we don't know if it was the king's body. There is really nothing else to indicate it was, not that I was allowed to see, but the artefacts were confiscated before I could properly assess them.'

Halfar shook his head. 'And now we will never know. Why did you submit, why did you let them take the items away? I would never have agreed.'

There was a pause. 'I know, and you were right, all along.'

'Well, it's too late now.'

'No, it's not,' said Hallsson, and Halfar furrowed his brows, but heard a defiance in his friend's voice.

'I need you to do something for me, I need you to go to the university.'

'I'm still here.'

'Ah, good. Go to my office and get my keycard for the museum.'

'What? What are you thinking of doing?' Halfar was feeling a prickle of hope now.

'Bertrand Lang is borrowing a university computer at the museum, and I know he has his cloud storage linked. I helped him set it up months ago. He supervises the museum's progress and visits a few days a month, so that's where he works when he is there. Anyway, he is here and he has all the files on his cloud storage. I can't access them anymore, but you can, because it will all sync with the laptop there, at least until he returns and clears it. He might not even know it still automatically copies everything to that computer.'

Halfar choked out a laugh. 'What?'

'Yes, he isn't the smartest man. I need you to go to the computer and copy the case file. Now, be quick, I don't have long.'

Halfar was already out of his office and trotting excitedly down the hall to Hallsson's office, which had a keypad lock. 'The combination to my door is…'

'I know the combination, you haven't changed it for a decade,' said Halfar wryly, punching in the numbers and opening the door.

'I don't have anything worth stealing, and if I changed it, I'd only forget it.'

'Got the keycard,' said Halfar, spotting it on the cluttered desk underneath the computer monitor and taking it.

'Go to the museum wing.'

Halfar felt a rush of adrenaline. 'What will happen if I am caught doing this?' he asked in a hushed tone as he hurried down the corridor and flight of stairs towards the museum annex.

'Well, we won't do anything with the file, for now. I just want us to have it, in case the moment arises.'

'Professor Hallsson, I didn't think you had this in you. Conspiring to steal government documents?' Halfar was almost giddy with fear and excitement.

There was a tense exclamation the other end of the line. 'I don't like it put like that. I'm a whistleblower, not a criminal.'

'Of course, you are doing the right thing, I was only teasing you.' Halfar exited the main department block and headed over the decorative garden towards the museum. The night was dark and no one was around as he looked furtively about the place. He was probably the last person on the grounds other than the security guards. The university was shut down for the Easter break between terms.

He headed for the back door to the museum annex, that led to the storage and office area, wedging the phone between his ear and shoulder and fumbling in his pocket for the keycard. 'Okay, I'm there.' He giggled to himself childishly. He hadn't felt this sense of rebellion since sneaking out of his house at night as a child.

He swiped the keycard and the pad beeped, absurdly and terrifyingly loudly in the darkness, and the door mechanism clicked open. Halfar went through, trying not to look suspicious, and the door swung closed behind him.

He walked down the corridor and up the stairs, finding the small back office and the laptop Hallsson directed him to. He tapped in the password he was given, and the desktop screen appeared, with the university's logo.

'Now what?'

'Go to the documents, and then to the folder named B. Lang. It will ask you for administrator permission. The folder is password protected, but I've logged you in as an administrator, so you can bypass that because…'

'Just tell me what to do!' said Halfar with an exasperated tone. 'I don't understand half of this stuff.'

'Right, yes.' Hallsson walked him through the process quickly, and then the folder was opened before him. Halfar saw a number of Word documents, a folder full of photos of the dig site, and assorted PDFs and other files.

'There is a lot here, what do I do?'

'You need to copy those files to an online storage, or a flash drive.'

'Okay, then what?'

There was a tense pause. 'Well, you need to wait until the government is certain not to release the results, or makes up some lie. If you leak them immediately, they can claim they were about to release anyway. After that is up to you. I trust you to make the right decisions. I've taken you as far as I can, and I think it's better I don't know exactly what you do after that.'

Halfar stared at the screen. 'What if I…'

'Don't,' said Hallsson tersely. 'This is up to you now.'

Halfar grumbled to himself and stared at the folders. 'Won't there be some record of this? Security camera, some sort of log on the laptop?'

'They only keep those for a few weeks and they only cover the outside of the building.'

'And you?'

'Yes. They will probably suspect me immediately. Which is why it's best I don't know what you are doing. This could be serious, Halfar. I know your disdain of the government, but they could react very badly to this.'

'Disdain is a very mild word,' said Halfar with a nervous laugh.

'Still, be careful. And if you choose to just keep the files and do nothing, I won't judge you for it. In fact, a part of me hopes you do nothing, and I never face consequences.'

'You always were a stickler for authority. This rebellion is… delightfully unexpected.'

'Stop having so much fun with this. This is serious. I'll lose my job over this, in all likelihood. Perhaps more.'

'Do you want to back out?' asked Halfar, sitting there in silence while his friend thought it over.

'No, I don't think so… They have gone too far. Someone needs to stand up to them, even if it's an old coward like me.'

Halfar smiled. 'It's never too late to find your courage, my old friend.'

'Oh, stop it. Look, I'm going now. Good luck. Cause some trouble for me.'

'Oh, I will do, I will.' Halfar pressed the red button and looked back at the computer screen, then furrowed his eyebrows as he realised he didn't have the faintest idea how to upload the files to online storage, and only a vague idea how flash drives worked. He looked around the office, moving papers and rustling through a stationery holder, until finally finding a university-branded flash drive in a drawer.

Then, feeling like the world's worst secret agent, and with a rising and illogical terror that he would be discovered in the act, he fumbled the flash drive into the USB port and started copying the whole folder across.

In a few moments that felt like minutes, the green bar was done and he wriggled the pen drive out of the laptop, closing the folder and logging out. He shut down the laptop and closed it, heading back to his office.

He returned the keycard on the way, and sat there for a while, staring at the pen drive, wondering what, exactly, he should do. With nothing set to happen any time soon, and the investigation at the dig site closed, he was faced with the dreary reality of life in Lundjen with little to do, while the museum slowly took shape, and the secrets on the drive burned a hole in his pocket.

A few days later, Hallsson returned, and they studiously avoided discussing their little secret. It livened things up for him, somewhat, the excitement of their subterfuge. But still it didn't seem like the time to do anything about it.

It was weeks before anything happened, but one morning Halfar logged into his email and found Hallsson had forwarded him a link to a news article. It was from the local newspaper near the farm, and discussed the failure of the dig to find anything of interest, quoting a 'ministry spokesman' as saying that all that had been in the hole was animal bones, and that the rumours of a royal burial were, sadly, unfounded.

'Got you!' said Halfar to himself in delight.

He opened a new email, typing in the address he had found a few weeks ago while he was deciding how to leak the files when the time came, the smile refusing to leave his face as he started writing the message.

# Chapter 2

# A Battle Won

**South of Uppsala, in the Kingdom of Sweden**

**July 1119**

COUNT CONRAD LEANED against a tree for a moment, his bloodied, clenched fist held tightly to his stomach. One of his men approached him in concern, but he shook his head and waved the man away, pushing off from the tree and gathering himself.

He was not wounded, that much at least he was thankful for. He did not know how he had avoided wounds, he had been in the line at the end, when the fighting was fiercest and most brutal, when the desperate Norse clung to their shrinking patch of forest with the tenacity of a starving dog tugging on a fresh joint of meat.

He had been there when the French knights had broken the enemy line for the final time, when the last exhausted defenders had been slaughtered, too tired, wounded and demoralised to continue defending themselves. He had witnessed carnage that nothing in his life had prepared him for, seen experienced knights knocked to the ground and churned into the morass of bodies, never to rise, or hacked into misshapen pieces by the terrible axes of the heathen foe.

He had seen the enemy collapse, cut down in such numbers and in such a small space that their bodies piled like firewood, no mercy other than the release of death asked for or given.

Now, even when not a single one was left alive in that forest, he still had to suppress a shudder at the fear he had felt in the press of that attack, when his life had hung not on his own skill at arms, but on the luck of blows that could as easily have sliced his neck, or pierced his eye, but had thumped off his hauberk, or glanced off his helm.

'My lord?'

Conrad glanced up and frowned to cover his nausea.

'What?'

'Shall I bring up your horse, my lord?'

Conrad nodded, and looked away, trying to steady his gaze. He looked away from the charnel house of the forest, out over the open ground beyond, the gentle grassy slope where the mounted reserve was still mopping up the remains of the fleeing Norse army.

Even as his own division had finally crushed the centre, the men of Lorraine and the soldiers of the Order of the Brotherhood of Christ's Light, or simply the brotherhood as they were known in the army, had broken the Norse right wing and driven its survivors back. Those fleeing enemy had fallen back towards a sizeable force of the heathen that had re-appeared from the woods on the edge of the battlefield, where Margrave Rudolf had been attempting a wide flanking march.

The mounted reserve had charged that new force, and shattered it, breaking its formation, but it had lacked the numbers to mop up the larger groups that herded together to flee the field in some semblance of order. The knights instead roamed the field seeking easier prey, which was present in abundance.

The battle was over, but Conrad felt no joy, only relief. Nothing in his life had prepared him for the scale of the carnage of this battlefield; the stench of blood and death was not overpowering, it was consuming. The sounds, blissfully hidden when the battle was raging, were only now starting to come back into his awareness. The screams of the wounded, the moans and weeping of the dying, men begging for salvation or mercy in a dozen languages, it all assailed his ears until he wanted to clamp his hands to them and retreat into himself.

He forced himself to keep walking, down the slope towards the open field where the mounted knights hunted, away from the charnel of the forest where a kingdom had died. When he no longer had to pick his way between piles of the interleaved dead, he started feeling like he could breathe again, and straightened his back, assuming without looking that whoever of his retinue had survived would be following him.

Finally he cleared the woodline and, feeling the battle fugue draining from him, sat down heavily on a fallen log and closed his eyes for a moment. Just a moment.

'Count Conrad.' A voice reached to him in the darkness. He ignored it, as he ignored the pain in his arms, and the discomfort from sitting on the hard wood in his maille.

'Count Conrad, do you have your senses?' the voice jabbed at him again, insistent and irritated. He cracked an eye to try and find its source.

He looked up and saw an armoured man on a fine horse. The man was clean, unbloodied and untarnished by mud and battle. The horse was twitchy, horses were always twitchy around the recently dead, but it was dry and showed no sweat and dirt. This man and horse had not been in the fight, he noted in a detached curiosity. He wondered why, why had they not been in the fight?

He looked up and studied the man's face. The man was Duke Henry the Black, the Crusade commander. That brought his mind into focus again with a jolt.

He struggled, ungainly, to his feet. 'My lord, I apologise, I am here.'

'I see that.' The duke pursed his lips and looked around. 'I need you to assemble a vanguard, to march immediately to Uppsala, and ensure the enemy cannot regroup there and defend it.'

Conrad baulked. 'March on Uppsala? That is twenty miles from here.'

'Yes.'

'But… my lord, their army is destroyed, and ours exhausted. We committed every reserve, we have no contingent left fit to march.'

'Their army is beaten, yes, but not completely destroyed. On their left flank they retreated in some order, with terrible losses, but several thousand marched north together. On the right several groups of hundreds fought clear of the charge of the mounted reserves, and many others in groups or alone have fled the field. We cannot stop or rest until those forces are destroyed, we must end this war here today.'

'Several thousand?' said Conrad, disheartened.

'Yes. Your victory in the centre was complete, but on the wings it was not as crushing.' The duke looked out across the field, where in the distance the mounted knights were still chasing anything left that still moved, but on flagging and slowing horses.

'So, assemble a force, whatever you can, and march on the city.'

Conrad didn't have the energy to argue. Henry the Black was not known for changing his mind, or allowing much in the way of dissent. Quite unlike his dead brother Welfard, who had been a paragon of indecision.

'What of Margrave Rudolf, has his force arrived from the flank, can we use them?'

'Margrave Rudolf is dead, his forces were crushed in the woods, only a handful of survivors have appeared, and they brought news of his death to me just moments ago.'

Conrad's stomach churned. 'Dead?'

'Yes,' said Henry, without a hint of emotion.

Conrad shook his head sadly. Rudolf had been a genial, easy-going man. In a world where everyone of note was a deadly rival, even your allies, Rudolf had managed to make being rivals seem less important than being friends. Conrad stood to benefit from his absence, but felt nothing but more hollowness.

'And Count Otto?' Otto had been commanding the right wing of the Crusader forces, that had shattered the Norse left and driven it from the field, turning his men inwards to complete the encirclement of the Norse centre, a move that allowed its total destruction in the woods behind him.

'He is alive, but wounded in the leg. He will survive but he is not able to march today, which leaves you as the last senior commander, which is why I am here, giving you this order.' Henry was getting irritated now, and Conrad nodded.

'I shall do as you command.'

Henry nodded curtly, and turned his horse to ride off without another word. Conrad sighed and looked around him, finally daring to see who of his close retinue were still standing, and being pleasantly surprised by how many were there. 'Start gathering our men, anyone still standing.'

'I don't know if we could gather two hundred men fit to fight,' said one of his knights with a scowl.

'Then we shall ride with one hundred. The commander orders it, and we will obey.' As he spoke, his page arrived through the trees leading his horse, and Conrad accepted the reins gratefully. 'Anyone unfit to ride can stay here and help clear up the wounded and our dead. That choice might enlighten some to decide coming with us is the better option.'

Roland, Sieur de Blanchant was on his own journey of pain and exhaustion. The French knight had dragged the body of his dead brother clear of the carnage in the forest, where they had broken the

Norse line a final time, where his brother had died in the moment of his glory, and where Roland had cut down his brother's killer and broken his sword on the dead man's heathen dragon-crested helm.

He refused the help of his friends and brother knights in his toil as he removed the armoured corpse of his beloved younger sibling from the field. It was his penance, his duty, his regret. Guiscard had been the younger man, but from his youth his brilliance had shone, and Roland had always walked in its light. Guiscard had been born with all the gifts the Lord could bestow. He was handsome, charming and quick witted. He had a mild temper, but a possessed a terrible gift with the sword, a man no one wanted to meet over three feet of steel.

Guiscard had been regarded by many as the finest knight in France, or perhaps even in all Christendom, and after completing his duty in the Crusade, he would have returned home to the pick of the wealthiest and loveliest young women of nobility in Northern France. He would have won tournaments and gained riches, probably ending his days as a wealthy noble, perhaps even a count.

But now Roland was dragging his lifeless corpse from the field, and weeping bitterly for his failure to protect his flank, to guard his unshielded side as Guiscard had struck down another foe. The shame of it was crushing him. In the chaos and glory of that final fight, as the two brothers broke the line at the head of a hundred of France's finest knights, he had let the joy of battle carry him away, and had let a gap grow between the two of them as he killed, a gap that could now never again be closed.

Roland finally stopped, slumping to the ground by a low stone wall in the fields where that morning the Crusaders had lined up to advance on the forested ridge. He cradled his brother's head and muttered another unintelligible apology to the pale white face.

He had never been jealous of Guiscard. He had known that he was not as handsome, not as charming or clever, that his skill with weapons was perhaps nearly equal, but his skills in life paled in comparison. He did not know how to woo a noble lady, nor hold a conversation on politics with a great lord. But this had never driven him apart from his brother, if anything it had drawn them closer. He had been protective and proud, caring and loyal. He would inherit the bulk of his family's lands and wealth and want for nothing, and his brother would have more keenly needed the other talents with which he had been bestowed.

But now that life was over, and Roland knew he could never return and look their poor mother in the eye.

He tried to lean back against the wall but the unfamiliar sword belted to his waist was tangled and he angrily wrenched it aside, pulling it around to his front and finally looking at it. It was the weapon that had killed his brother, Roland had taken it from the body of the enemy warrior to replace his own broken sword, and had not had the heart to discard it in favour of a good Christian weapon, of which there were hundreds lying abandoned on the field.

He looked at it now in earnest as it lay across his lap in its ornamented scabbard. A strange serpent lay in carved bone along its upper portion, the mouth open, teeth bared and snarling, a single red gemstone for an eye glaring at him accusingly. He shuddered as he remembered the single piercing blue eye of the dead Norse warrior who had wielded it, even in death staring reproachfully at him from inside the ruins of his ornate helmet, the other eye lost to the fury of his hacking blows.

He thrust the scabbard away and let it fall to the ground beside him, limp on its brown leather belt. He would be rid of it shortly, as soon as he found a good weapon to replace it. It would not do for him to go without a sword, even for a moment. Having a sword and being prepared to carry it in service of his lord and his king was the essence of his warrior duties. So he convinced himself he kept it merely because he had to, and pressed it from his mind.

Sighing, and knowing his penance was only just beginning, he pulled himself to his feet, and set about continuing the awful task of dragging his brother's maille-clad body back to their camp where they had shared their last meal together that morning.

Two days after the battle, Reinhard, Bishop of Halberstadt and co-founder and Grandmaster of the Brothers of Christ's Light, stood on the low mound outside Uppsala and stared at the smoke that still drifted from the ruined city, deep in thought.

The fires in Uppsala had been dying down when the vanguard of the exhausted Crusader army arrived the day after the battle. The Norse had abandoned the city and razed it to prevent its capture, and not a living soul was in sight anywhere around it. The Crusader army, too battered and reduced to continue, had set up camp on the bank of the river that led to the city and settled in to lick its wounds.

Half the army had been killed or wounded in the battle, the numbers of the dead were beyond counting, beyond the ability to deal with. The knights and men of note were receiving proper burials, ministered to by Reinhard's overworked Order priests, but the common soldiers of the Crusade were lucky if their bodies were even collected to be burned, rather than just stripped and left to rot on the field with the enemy.

The army had moved camp from the battlefield the next day because to remain beside that vast field of bodies would be simply to invite disease and ruin. As many as twenty thousand corpses, although none knew the true number, were rapidly starting to decay in the late summer heat. All but the strongest-stomached looters would give that place a wide berth for months or years to come.

A captured Norse man, too old or too tired to flee with the rest of his people, had told Bertrand, Reinhard's ever-present assistant, that this mound and the gently smoking ruin atop it had been the fabled temple of Uppsala, the seat of the Norse gods and the worship of their heathen practices.

Reinhard had been annoyed to find it had already been destroyed, he had hoped to make something of a show of it, a symbolic destruction of the old ways to make way for the new. But now there was no symbol to destroy, and no people left in the city to witness it. He had come north with the army to witness its victory, to use it to cement the power of the Order, and to raise a church in the captured city and begin the conversion of its people to the true faith.

That was the purpose of his Order, ostensibly. To bring the light of Christ to the pagan Norse. It was the purpose that gave them their name, and gave him his power. In the service of the Lord, and with a charter sealed by the Pope himself, almost all things were possible, almost all actions acceptable, in service of that cause.

Reinhard did not know what to do now, now that the great prize of Uppsala was gone. He could have been furious or lashed out in frustration, but he controlled his temper. He prided himself on his self-control, because it showed discipline. And discipline was dear to the Lord.

'We shall raise a church here anyway,' he said, finally, nodding his head.

Bertrand raised an eyebrow slightly, which for the plain-faced monk was a rare display of judgement. 'For what flock?'

The man had a point, there was little point in a church without a local population, in a normal situation. But this was not a normal situation.

'We will rebuild the city, or another one nearby. Regardless, it is a powerful symbol, to raise a church in the ashes of their heathen temple. Even if they don't see it, they will speak of it across all the province, and they will know the superiority of our Lord.'

Bertrand crossed himself and nodded. 'As you say, your excellency.'

'Nevertheless, we will not stay in this place, for I will be needed elsewhere.'

'Where shall we go?'

Reinhard didn't answer that. Truthfully he was not sure. With the swift campaign to capture Uppsala, many other towns and cities in the area had been left aside until now, still held by the enemy. They may have won the battle, the war even, but where he could travel and the lands they controlled was extremely limited.

They could return to the south, to their base in Lund and the broad farmlands of Skania, but most of the population there was converted, or at least cowed, and there was little to be done other than to relax in comfort and enjoy the fruits of victory.

But Reinhard had never in his life rested and enjoyed the fruits of a victory, it was lazy and gluttonous, and if there was one thing he hated above all others, it was gluttony, either of the mind or body. Each victory was merely a stepping-stone to the next one, and at the moment, he was unsure what the next one should be.

'We shall return to the camp and I shall convene with Grand-steward Hugues, to determine the remaining strength of the Order, and decide on the proper actions.'

It was about as vague a pronouncement as Reinhard ever gave, and it pained him to do so, but Bertrand simply nodded and stared blankly at the ground, impassive as he always was. 'As you say, excellency.'

## Chapter 3

# A Battle Lost

MANY OF THE people of Uppsala slowly scattered on the march west from the ruins of their city. There was no one place that they could all go, and families, often just women and children, headed off to places they knew, or distant kin they had who might take them in.

Halla kept her people together as much as possible, the loyalty they had for Jarl Ragnvald holding them together, even as his fate was unknown. They kept on the well-travelled road that circled west along the lake, passing towns and villages, finding at each that the news of the defeat had preceded them, and finding a land full of fear and mourning. Every settlement had sent its youth to the battle, and each had just found out that few, if any, would ever return.

The black shade of misery lay across the lands like a blanket of mud, suppressing everything. In each town the refugees were received with blank eyes and mild suspicion, and the people spent their valuables for whatever food the inhabitants were willing to sell, and in each settlement some from the column stayed behind, finding a house, a family, a relative willing to take them in for silver or for charity, even for servitude.

After four days on the road, slowed by wagons and children, the first survivors of the battle caught up with them, arriving at the rear of the column and causing a brief panic at the sudden approach of hundreds of armed men, followed by a rush of hopeful people running to find if their husband or son or father had returned.

Gjaldir watched glumly as barely a handful of the people were reunited, and felt sick from the misery he saw as the people of Uppsala realised these defeated warriors were mostly men from the west and south of the lake, not those who had marched with Jarl Ragnvald from their own lands.

The misery was punctuated by a single glimmer of relief when Halla came to meet the leader of the band, and found herself buried in the embrace of her brother, Jarl Frode.

'Oh, brother, you live. By the gods, you live.' She pulled away from his arms a fraction and looked him in the eye, the question unspoken.

Jarl Frode shook his head just once, and Halla grimaced, looking away, but otherwise not showing her loss. 'I'm sorry, Halla. We were separated. Ragnvald and your people were surrounded, barely a handful escaped.'

'You… you did not see him fall?'

'No, but I know him, as do you. He would not have laid down his sword.'

Halla nodded and drew a sudden breath, a single exclamation of sorrow, and put her hand to her mouth to banish the sound. 'What do we do now? Are they following?'

'No, the Christians marched to Uppsala, but they do not march down this road. Not yet. It can only be a short time before they do.'

'What will you do?' asked Halla, holding her brother's arm firmly. 'Will you return to your lands to the west, gather more men…'

'We were headed to Västerås, and then home, and I have no plan beyond that. There are no more men to be gathered from our lands, nothing more I can ask of them.'

'Then where will the army gather, where shall we meet them? Where does the king go?' Halla spilled the questions like apples from an autumn tree and Frode tried to calm her and shook his head firmly.

'The king is missing with whoever remains of his men. There is no army, there will be no gathering. Each lord that lives will look to his own now.'

'The king is gone?' said Halla, horrified.

'He was wounded, his men fought their way off the field carrying him. I don't know where they went. The end of the battle… It was chaos. I was with the king and several thousand men near the end, but the Christians caught us in the open, disorganised, and a charge of their knights scattered us to every direction. Me and my men went one way, ran into the woods with everyone we could save, the king's men took him north, cutting their way free.'

'Then we must find him!'

Frode sighed, the fight visibly gone from him. 'To what end? You haven't seen them, Halla. We can never raise another army that could challenge them. Never. It is futile.'

Halla let go of her brother and looked at him in horror and disgust. 'You would surrender? And see our people as their slaves, after all we have been through? After all we have lost?'

Frode furrowed his brows. 'Do not speak to me of loss, sister. It was I who stood on those battlefields, who watched my friends fall and our people slaughtered. I know of their loss, and I don't want to see what happened to them happen in my lands, to what is left of our people.' He calmed himself and paused before continuing. 'I do not know yet what we will do, but I hope perhaps we can make some kind of peace. There are still vast lands they have not conquered; perhaps, like Norway, we can agree with them to live on our own terms, if we swear to lay down our arms and…' He coughed and grimaced, as if the words caught in his throat. 'And agree to be subject to their laws.'

Halla shook her head in horror and backed away a step. 'I cannot believe it. I cannot believe you would give up.'

'What would you have me do?' shouted Frode in frustration, as dozens of people turned to see the cause of the commotion.

'Fight!' shouted Halla back at him.

'And sacrifice what is left of our people? Have us wiped from the land?'

'It is better to die than to be their slaves!'

Frode just scowled at Halla and waved her away.

'It is what Ragnvald would have done, if he was here. But he would not…'

Frode stared at her aghast and hissed, 'Not what?'

Halla cursed to herself and looked down at the ground.

'Not what, Halla? Say it.'

'He would not have run from the battle.'

The siblings stared at each other for a few moments, Frode's face twisting in anger at the shamefulness of the accusation, Halla's slowly softening as she regretted her words.

'So simple for you to speak such humiliation to me, a woman of a rich household who does not have to back her words with steel. I stood by your husband my entire life, he was my friend before he wedded you, and I stood by him when we retreated from a fistful of battles. He was a brave man, but not a fool. And he would always try to spare the lives of his people when the situation was unwinnable.' He jabbed a finger in her direction. 'I forgive the words you speak in ignorance, but not the spite that they carry.' Frode turned and stormed away, the men he had arrived with falling in behind him, leaving Halla cursing herself in the road, an apology that was too late dying on her lips.

Gjaldir stood in awkward shame at having witnessed the encounter, and like most of her people standing there, looked away from their lord's wife as she stood alone in the roadway.

Finally she sighed and spoke up. 'We will also go to Västerås.

We need somewhere to rest, and it is the only town this side of the lake that could hope to accommodate us, if they are willing.'

People looked around at each other uncertainty, but there were few other options, and Västerås was the next town on the road, so the column shuffled back onto the road, and set off after the mass of warriors who marched with Jarl Frode, who did not look back, but waited with his men to escort the people to the city.

As the tail of the column set off, Gjaldir leant into the back of the cart that carried what they had saved of Ragnvald's valuables and heaved, as another man goaded the wizened old mule that pulled it, and they resumed its slow plod westwards.

The city of Västerås was in the domain of a jarl who had died in the great battle, and the people had not convened to raise another. So it was some time, and some invisible internal wrangling, before the town opened its gates to admit the column of defeated warriors and refugees that waited for half a morning outside its paltry walls.

They were not, Gjaldir noted, walls meant to defend against an army, merely to keep animals in, and to deter raiders and thieves. He was fairly sure he could climb them in a handful of heartbeats. The top would be barely level with his hands if he were to stretch them above his head.

The town of Västerås had perhaps five thousand people. It was the largest town on the north side of the great lake of Lǫgrinn, apart from Uppsala itself. A few hundred defeated warriors, and perhaps a thousand refugees, was more than it could accommodate easily, even though many of its own warriors were dead and other families had already left to move west, fleeing the inevitable advance of the Crusade.

So some of Halla's people had to set up a makeshift camp in the fields outside, not a hard thing in the fine late summer weather.

Over the next three days, more and more stragglers of the defeated army arrived. Alone, in small groups, and one crew of Norwegians who marched in with shields and weapons and some semblance of pride, and claimed that they had been with the king after the battle.

Some of Uppsala's missing warriors arrived, only a handful of shocked, weary and often bloodied survivors, a tiny portion of the hundreds who had marched to the battle. News of each brought more pain than joy, as those whose hope was briefly kindled only to be crushed vastly outnumbered the few joyful reunions.

By the fourth day, no more survivors were arriving, and the people started to accept that all who could reach them had already done so. Perhaps one in twenty of the force Ragnvald had left with to march to battle had survived and made it to the town, and none of them had been with him at the end, being those who had been wounded and forced to fall out of the line, or those who had been driven from the field before the end, before the centre of the Norse army had been surrounded.

On the fifth day, three longships arrived in the town's broad harbour. Jarl Frode went down to the docks with a hastily assembled band of warriors to see whose ships they were, wary that it could be more of the traitorous Danes who the Crusaders had used to force the passage into the Lǫgrinn before the battle.

But as the ships arrived near the docks, it was clear they were not enemy, as standing in the prow was the recognisable figure of Jarl Gustav, the Raven's Claw. The old jarl had a ruined left hand, thumb twisted and scarred, permanently bent back at an angle, spread like the claw of a bird. It was an old battle wound, and the source of his name. He disembarked with a hundred of his men. He and much of his warband had missed the battle. They had been in their lands south of Lǫgrinn, defending the passes that led through the Kolmården, the great natural wall of ragged rocks and forest that defended the southern border of the Svear.

Gjaldir and the other warriors stood aside as Frode came and embraced him warmly. 'It is good to see you, you old goat. I thought you would never return from the south.'

'And I am glad to find you here, Jarl Frode. I did not know what to expect, I have been going from town to town on the lake, trying to find the king or anyone who knows where he is.'

Frode frowned. 'Well, you won't find him on the lake. Some of his men are here, they say he went north with just a few of his huskarls and closest followers.'

'He is at least alive then?' said Gustav.

'Apparently, although we do not know more. Who else did you find?'

It was Gustav's turn to look grim. 'No one, a few scattered survivors, towns full of weeping women and children. Birka is deserted, I don't even know where they went, the town was simply empty.'

Frode shook his head despairingly. 'And what of the south?'

'Well, we still hold the passes through the Kolmården, although mostly because the Christians do not attempt to attack us. One of my scouts made it all the way to the ruins of Norrköping. He said there was barely a hundred enemy there. Their entire force must have sailed north to join the main army for the battle, and we didn't even notice.' Gustav sighed sadly. 'Not that it matters now. Soon they will advance on my lands from the north, and we cannot stop them.'

Frode nodded. 'What will the rest of the southern jarls do?'

Gustav shrugged. 'Mostly they will go home, bury their swords and shields, and work the land and whatever water they can reach. There is no more stomach for the fight after the news of the battle. Some said they wanted to continue to resist, but there is no agreement about how. That is why I am trying to find the king, before it is too late, to get some orders from him, some instruction to pass on, to unite those of us who are left.' Gustav shook his head slowly again and looked at Frode. 'But I do not know where to look for him. What do you plan?'

'Honestly, old friend, I have no plan,' Frode said as he chewed his lip. 'There are ten thousand Crusaders somewhere down the road, maybe more. And we have five hundred warriors, six with yours, and a wall that wouldn't stop an angry goat. What can we do? I have considered… everything.'

'Everything?' Gustav cocked an eyebrow.

Frode murmured and then looked around at the loose assembling of their men, and others from the town who were watching. He gestured towards the centre of the town. 'Come, let's go to my house, and away from gossipers' ears. We can discuss our options.'

Frode led Gustav into the mid-sized longhouse he had managed to acquire, left empty by a family who had fled west. He had not sent for Halla, the two had barely spoken since the argument on the road, seeing each other only at the frequent meetings with the town's elders, who were increasingly concerned about how many refugees were staying in their settlement, and how long they would be staying there, eating their way through the town's food stocks. The refugees paid in silver or valuables or traded whatever possessions they could, but as one of the local leaders kept saying, his people couldn't eat silver that winter, nor could their food supplies sustain so many people for the long cold months.

Frode gestured to Gustav to sit, and the two men exchanged what they knew; of the battle, of the Crusaders, of the situation of other surviving jarls and any forces that might still be willing to join them.

The image the discussion painted was bleak. There were still a number of the southern jarls with their forces intact, but most had already shown they were unwilling to continue the war, presumably hoping to make an agreement with the invaders that would allow them to keep their lands.

'It is what I was also considering,' said Frode with a healthy dose of shame.

Gustav nodded. 'I understand. I don't hold it against you.'

'You still wish to fight?'

Gustav laughed mockingly. 'I never wished to fight in the first place. But I am too old to carry on, too stubborn to give up. My people are also divided, the ones with me are the ones who want to continue, not as an army, but as raiders, Vikings in their own lands. They are too proud, too young and angry, to lay down their weapons.' He shrugged. 'And I will not abandon them. As long as they want to fight, it's my duty to lead them, even if Sigurd is truly absent.'

'Is there not another who can lead them?'

'My son, but I will not let him die in futility. My life means nothing to me anymore, time comes for me as surely as any spear, but he still has a future perhaps, and I intend him to live it.'

'So why not tell all your men to go home in peace, if you cannot find the king?'

Gustav appraised Frode for a moment, thinking over his answer. 'The ones who come with me, they will never accept peace. If I leave them in my lands, they will likely bring death there, and all this despair will be visited on my kin.'

Frode sat back in shock. 'You mean to keep the fight away from your lands, even if it means your own death, and those who follow you.'

Gustav wagged a finger almost in shame. 'No, I will not cause their deaths, they have made their choice. I will try everything to keep them alive, and to keep my lands clear of the violence.'

'By leading them far from home,' Frode said.

'Yes,' Gustav replied bitterly. 'I have left orders with my people, if I do not return within three weeks, they are all to lay down their weapons, and make whatever peace the Christians allow.'

'And you do not expect to return.'

'I do not. If Sigurd had been here, maybe something could have been done. Perhaps all together we could… perhaps we could have at least forced some favourable terms, kept a little of our own lands. But now it is too late.'

The two men sat in uncomfortable silence digesting this, and one of Frode's men came into the house. 'Lord, the town elders wish to speak to you.'

Frode looked up. 'Me?'

'Both of you.'

Frode looked at Gustav. 'This won't be good.'

They walked out of the house and found the leaders of the townspeople, their lawgiver and the dead jarl's wife, with dozens of townspeople gathered around, talking in hushed tones. Halla was there, as were a scattering of the warriors. There was no hint of violence or threat, but everyone looked uneasy.

Frode and Gustav waded through the thin crowd and approached the lawgiver, who looked at them apologetically.

'What do you wish to speak of?' Frode asked.

'My lord, we have great respect for you…'

'Make your point, before either of us age further,' Gustav said with a sigh.

The lawgiver grimaced, but stopped. 'As you wish, lord. We must ask you to leave. There are rumours of Christians in the woods to the east, and you cannot defend this town. We intend to open our gates and be at peace.'

Frode looked at Gustav, who nodded nonchalantly, and at Halla, who was furious. 'I once saw King Sigurd, your king, burn Norrköping to the ground for asking the same thing.'

'We know, lord. But we also know he spared the people. When Kalmar resisted the Christians, they burned the people in their town. It is a poor choice, but if you choose to burn us out, perhaps we will at least have our lives. If we harbour you, the Crusaders will not have the same mercy.'

Frode stared at the man and then nodded in defeat. 'I will not burn your town.'

'I might,' Halla spat, and Frode turned to glare at her.

'You will not.'

Halla ignored him and he turned to the lawgiver to continue. 'I accept your demand, we will leave, so that you can make your peace.'

The lawgiver and the people around him visibly relaxed in relief, and Frode looked around at the sullen and defeated faces of his warriors. They were no longer welcome in their own lands, with their own people. The fear of the Christians was making outlaws of them, and it crushed a part of his soul, the shreds that had not died in the fields outside Uppsala.

Frode turned to Gustav to speak quietly. 'Will you sail again?'

Gustav thought about it and nodded. 'Yes, I will not abandon the ships here, I will sail along the lake to the next town, and meet you there, Karlsgrind.'

Frode nodded. 'Good. I know it well, it is near the eastern edge of my lands.'

Gustav nodded. 'Then I will see you there.'

Frode turned to his sister, weathering her icy stare. 'Will you and your people come with us, west to Karlsgrind?'

She didn't speak for a moment, and then gave the slightest shrug of acceptance. 'I do not seem to have a choice.'

'Some of your people could stay here, I am sure there are empty houses.'

She shook her head. 'No, we will not be divided further.'

Frode was frustrated, the town could take some people in for the winter, but he saw no chance of arguing the point. 'Then we will leave at dawn tomorrow.'

'Tomorrow?' said the lawgiver with a frown. 'Not today?'

Frode gave the man a gaze that told him not to push his luck. 'It is too late today, and we must pack and prepare. Tomorrow.'

The lawgiver also saw the pointlessness of arguing. 'As you say, Jarl Frode. Tomorrow.'

## Chapter 4

# Servants of Self

'YOU ASKED FOR me, my lord?' Reinhard said with an unforced smile, peering into the interior of Duke Henry's modest command tent.

'Yes, thank you. Please, take a seat.' The duke gestured to a row of plain stools, where Reinhard saw that Grandsteward Hugues, Count Conrad, and Count Otto were already seated and looking at him impatiently.

Reinhard had not actually intended to be late, he often was late just to make others feel his power, but on this occasion he had merely been occupied up on the hill where the ruins of the pagan temple stood, discussing with his master stonemason the dimensions and key features of the new church that would replace the charred wood and debris that was already being cleared by work parties of surly locals.

Reinhard nodded obediently and walked to the remaining empty stool with only a hint of hurry. It would not do to be seen to rush to the command of another.

'Now that we are all here,' the duke gave Reinhard a flickered glance, 'we can discuss the plan and conduct of the campaign from now on.'

'The Crusade is complete, is it not?' asked Reinhard innocently.

Henry gave him an annoyed stare at the interruption, but nodded. 'Yes, the Crusade itself has achieved its objectives, but the conquest of this province, and the subjugation of its people to ensure its calm and peaceful governance in the future, is not. There is work yet to be done.'

'What forces will remain? Will the men of the Crusade not return home?'

'Some, yes. Many of the French, the Italians and some of the Germans will leave. But those lords who are being given lands here will remain, and others of their allies too. Count Otto and Count Conrad and all their forces will remain, as they have been granted large holdings.'

Reinhard turned to the two counts and nodded, smiling broadly. 'A fair recompense for your service to the Lord.' Otto returned the nod, but Reinhard's brother Count Conrad ignored him, as he had since the moment Reinhard entered the tent.

'Yes, now please, to the matter at hand,' said Henry with impatience. 'Our scouts report the part of the enemy force that retreated north has taken to its ships and fled. We suspect they are returning to wherever they came from in the far north, far enough away that it does not concern us.'

'That is good news,' mused Conrad.

'Indeed. However, the parts of the enemy army that retreated west have gathered together, the size of the force is small, but my concern is they will form the core for a new army to gather.'

'How many?' asked Otto, leaning forwards.

'Hundreds, maybe a thousand.'

'A very small force.'

'Yes, but if they join up with the enemy in the north, or new recruits, large enough to be a significant problem.' Otto nodded sagely and leant back stiffly. He fidgeted in his seat, his injured leg stretched out in front of him. The injury was not too serious, but Reinhard noted it was clearly causing him constant pain.

'With the men we lost, injured or dead, and those that are returning home, we have ourselves a greatly reduced army to continue the campaign. Conrad, the latest numbers?'

'Around six thousand men fit to march and not leaving, or needed elsewhere.'

'Including the Order's troops?'

'Yes.'

'Uh, Duke Henry, if I may,' Reinhard spoke up politely.

Henry sighed and looked at him. 'What?'

'We have not discussed the disposition of the Order's resources, now that the Crusade is over.'

'Disposition?'

'Yes. Our forces are meant to maintain order, protect our congregations, guard the people – not go on campaign. We were happy, of course, to make an exception to support you in the capture of this city, but our ranks were sorely depleted, and our men must return to their duties.'

Henry looked at him and his eyes narrowed slightly. 'And if you remove your men, and we have insufficient forces to finish the enemy, they may return and wipe out those garrisons and congregations of yours.'

Reinhard put his finger to his chin and considered this. 'Hmm, yes. I see that it might be better to stamp out the embers of these heathens now, before they take flame again. Do you agree, Grand-steward?' Reinhard looked at Hugues for an answer.

Hugues looked at the bishop and then back at the duke. Reinhard and Hugues had discussed this moment in advance, of course, knowing that their forces would be requested, and knowing that they would need to extract a price for their inevitable concession. 'We will need more men.'

Duke Henry shrugged. 'From where?'

Hugues looked at the ground in thought for a moment, and then back at the duke. 'The forces that are going home, you cannot compel them to stay, but perhaps some could be encouraged to join the Order, swelling our ranks.'

Henry sat back, considering it. 'What encouragement?'

Conrad finally looked at Reinhard, narrowing his eyes suspiciously. 'The Order already has enough men to fulfil its assigned garrisons and duties. What would it do with more, and why would any want to join now, given that they could have of their own volition at any point?'

'A fine point, and well made,' said Reinhard, closing the jaws of the logical trap and turning to Henry. 'We will need to offer more, expand the responsibility of the Order to new lands, and create a requirement for capable knights and good Christian men to join, to govern those lands. And, of course, the funds to allow that.' Conrad stirred in anger as he saw how his question had been twisted, and he looked to Henry to protest, but the duke waved him down.

'What lands, Reinhard? Which good Christian lord, having just completed his duty to the Crusade, should we now tell has to forfeit his well-earned earthly reward? And do not pretend to me that they will be happy purely with God's grace, as you know better.'

Reinhard's animated expression dulled as he considered this problem, and he puzzled over it. Then Hugues leaned over to whisper in his ear, and Reinhard nodded, a sad smile returning to his face. 'Ah, yes, the Grandsteward has it exactly. I had not thought of it, due to the great sadness of the loss, but wasn't Margrave Rudolf, God rest his martyr's soul, going to be given broad lands in the west past the lake, lands that indeed are still out of our control? Could the Order not be granted those lands, and with them pay for and attract new members from those who would otherwise be going home?'

Otto stirred now from his preoccupation with his leg, and looked around in concern, meeting Conrad's eye and seeing his worries mirrored there. 'My lord,' he said, turning back to address Henry. 'Those lands are Duke Lothair's to distribute. It was him who granted them to Margrave Rudolf, and he who will decide how to divide them.'

The implication was clear: Otto and Conrad expected their lord to divide those lands between them, and had suddenly woken up to Reinhard's plot to steal them from under their noses. Reinhard could hardly hold himself back from a look of gloating to have outmanoeuvred his brother, but he did not show any outward sign of it.

Henry looked at the agitated counts and the two masters of the Order and contemplated it for a moment, before addressing Otto. 'The charter of the Order, and my position as leader of the Crusade, allows for land to be granted to their control at my discretion.'

'The Crusade is over,' grunted Conrad, trying to control himself.

'Actually, I have not formally declared it so.'

'It has achieved its objectives!'

'Yes, and I intend to declare it over shortly. But have not yet done so.'

'This is outrageous,' muttered Conrad angrily, then he waved his finger at Henry. 'If you allow Reinhard to blackmail you for land with the threat of withdrawing his support, I can do the same. I can simply refuse to apply my own men.'

Henry sighed. 'Yes, I suppose you could. And then I would inform the emperor that Duke Lothair's forces refuse to finish the campaign, threatening the peace of his new province, and the emperor would lean on Lothair, and you would receive a stern letter telling you to comply,' Henry admonished the count. 'It would take a month, and your reputation would be harmed, and we would be delayed until spring, when achieving the same objectives would cost you more of your men, angering your lord even more.' Henry looked at Conrad icily as he described the outcome, and Conrad bristled.

'Leading by threats and accepting being blackmailed?' he snapped at Henry. 'After all we have done for this campaign?'

Henry nodded at the man. 'Yes, I will do what is required. However,' he turned on Reinhard, 'I tire of your machinations. Your Order is there to serve, yet its every service seems to be contingent on gains and increase in power.'

'My lord, I just…'

'Silence!' Henry held up a single finger. 'Do not interrupt me.' Reinhard, utterly unused to being spoken to like that, swallowed his temper quickly and closed his mouth. 'Now, let us all step back from threats and anger and squabbling, lest it threaten the very victory we have shared.' Henry took a calming breath and leaned back to compose himself. 'We are all gentlemen here, and can behave and treat with each other accordingly. We will come to an arrangement that suits all.' He turned to the furious noblemen. 'Count Conrad, Count Otto, I suggest we split the lands that were assigned to Rudolf between you and the Order. I will ensure Lothair assigns part of them to you, and in return, you do not make a fuss over me granting the rest to the Order, for our need for manpower is real, and new lands and opportunities for securing them in God's name will certainly attract more recruits. You still gain more lands than you first expected.'

Conrad looked at Otto and his expression softened. Otto gave a slight shrug and then a nod. Conrad met Henry's eye again. 'In principle, yes, depending on what division.'

'Good. I propose this. Conrad, you take all the lands south-west of the lake that were to be granted to Rudolf, and the Order takes all the lands to the north-west. A clear delineation can be made at…' He clicked his fingers in the air, trying to recall something. 'Conrad, what is the name of the heathen town that lies at the west end of the lake?'

'Arbugæ, I believe you mean. It was to be the centre of Rudolf's grant.'

'Exactly, Arbugæ. Its rents and income shall be divided between the two halves, between Conrad and the Order. Count Otto, you extend the boundary of your lands here westwards, taking some of Rudolf's allocation, ending at the river that runs north from the lake.' He looked up at them all with a stern gaze. 'That is the end of it, are we in agreement?'

Otto and Conrad murmured to each other, before reluctantly accepting. Reinhard, still silent from the admonishment, nodded mutely.

'Good. Conrad, take your forces south of the lake and take control of all the lands there that we have not yet reached. Otto and Hugues, recruit who you can from those who would be leaving, and those who are lightly injured but will recover, and do the same in the lands to the north. Your force will be smaller, but we believe the larger intact enemy forces lie south of the lake.'

'We split our army?' asked Conrad.

'Yes. If we stay together, you may merely end up chasing them around in circles as they recruit and strengthen. Better to strike now everywhere, to achieve quick submission before they have a chance. Any that resist you can drive westwards, on both sides of the lake, and meet together to crush whatever you have driven before you. We only have another month or two of good weather, and we must be finished by then and ready for winter. Our Danes will see to the islands on the lake itself.'

Conrad considered this for a moment and nodded. 'It is a risk, but I see that it may be the best course.'

'Excellent. Now, there is one more question, we promised that if the Norse fought us any further, we would burn that settlement that resisted to the ground. They denied us that at Uppsala, and we do not wish to look weak. A reminder of our promise is required, the scale of it is all that is to be determined.'

Otto looked uncomfortable. 'If we burn many more towns, we will have nothing and no one left to rule.'

'Correct, but if we appear weak, or that we will not follow up on our threats, that is also a great risk, is it not?'

Conrad and Otto nodded their acceptance. 'Perhaps, a limited display of our resolve? A single punitive act for the resistance at Uppsala?' Otto said.

'What do you have in mind?'

'A single town? Somewhere notable.'

Henry nodded. 'That might be acceptable.' He looked at Reinhard. 'Your methods have proved to be very effective at compelling captured settlements into submission, I suggest we continue along those lines.'

Reinhard smiled thinly and nodded. 'Thank you. May I make a suggestion?'

'Go ahead.'

'The enemy will be watching us carefully, trying to decide if they should fight or submit. It is important we show we are not weak, but equally it is important to show we can forgive, and that if they are willing to submit, to us and to the Lord, they can enter into our fold. We do what we have been doing before, we offer each town the sword or the cross.'

'And if they all choose the cross? How will we make our demonstration?'

Reinhard shrugged knowingly. 'It is always possible to find some contravention, it is merely a case of looking hard enough, and wanting to find it.'

Henry tapped a finger on the table. 'Fine, show mercy to towns that submit. But then find a contravention somewhere, and soon.' He pressed a finger down on the table for emphasis. 'I want these people to know the cost of resistance, and I want it to be severe.'

'As you will, my lord.'

'Good. You are all dismissed, my lords, except the Grandmaster, I wish to speak of the construction of the church.'

Counts Otto and Conrad rose and bowed briefly, and,

followed by Hugues, left the tent, leaving Reinhard and the duke alone together.

Reinhard smiled slyly once the others had gone. 'That went well,' he said cheerfully.

'Yes, I hope I didn't go too far with my threats, I still need their support,' replied Henry with a nod.

'No, my lord, it was as you planned. A stern rebuke to me, and a curtailing of my requests, made it seem like taking half the unclaimed land was the height of reasonableness.'

Duke Henry looked up in annoyance. 'It *was* the height of reasonableness.'

'Yes, of course,' said Reinhard nonchalantly.

'Reinhard, I needed to give your Order that land without it causing a permanent rift, I did not do it to boost your fraternal rivalry or deliver you a victory. And I needed to be sure you would react correctly, that is the only reason I prepared this with you. I am not taking sides. I need them as much as I need you. Do nothing to endanger that. Do you understand?'

'Perfectly,' said Reinhard, looking suitably chastened.

'Now, you have some recruiting to do, I need your forces to be capable of securing the lands I will grant to you.'

'I will find a way, as always.'

'I don't doubt it. I will have the document and orders drawn up and announced, I am sure some of the lords who plan to leave will object, but those objections will be muted. It is politically very difficult to object to the work of the Lord.'

Reinhard bounced slightly on his toes, and a genuine smile crept across his face. 'Yes, my lord. It certainly is.'

## CHAPTER 5

# SERVANTS OF GOD

TWO DAYS LATER, the call for men of the Crusade who wished to stay and continue the work of the Lord was made, along with the proclamation that the Crusade was completed, that all who had participated in the glorious victory were cleansed of their sins and could return home in the grace of God. Reinhard held an open-air service for the full assembly of the Crusade, blessing their efforts and bestowing upon them the thanks of the Church.

After the service, which he believed was particularly rousing, he waited for the volunteers of the faithful to present themselves at the front, and be inducted as brothers of the Order.

His mood turned from self-satisfaction to glum disappointment as it became clear how paltry the number of volunteers was. He kept smiling, and appeared welcoming to all those who came to the front of the field as the crowd dissipated, but it was less than half of what he had hoped for.

He stole a moment and took Hugues aside. 'What is wrong? Why are so few willing?'

Hughes shook his head sadly. 'Most of these men are exhausted, and after the battles this year and last, feel they have done their service. The mood in the army is more of relief to have survived, than exhilaration. They feel the task is complete, and our charter prevents us from outright offering them pay or rewards for joining. I'm sorry, but I was never hopeful that many would want to continue, for only reputation and the opportunity to fight some more.'

Reinhard chewed his lip in frustration. 'Perhaps we should not have been so clear that the Crusade has been a success, made them feel they have a duty to complete it.'

Hugues shrugged again. 'I think it would have made little difference.'

'Hmm. Well, we work with what we have. Is it enough?'

Hugues looked around at the several hundred who had gathered to join their ranks. 'We will have to make do, and also continue to recruit from home. There are many who missed the Crusade and would seek to cleanse themselves in God's service yet.'

'But those men will not arrive soon.'

'No, but if this war drags into next year, we will need them.'

Reinhard was unable to conceal his shock. 'You think this will continue another year? We crushed them, their army is lost, their city in ruins. How can they continue to resist?'

Hugues smiled at him sadly. 'I have been in this war since the start, and what it has taught me is never to underestimate the stubbornness of these people. It may be years before this province is completely pacified.'

Reinhard opened his mouth in horror, his usual self-control cracking. 'Years!' He looked around to make sure no one was listening. 'I don't have years, I do not intend to spend years here in this wretched place.'

'Well, if you think that, remember the men also think that. The more motivated and resolute we can keep them, the more we will recruit, and the faster we can end it.'

'So that I can return home successful.'

'So that *all* of us can return home successful,' said Hugues drily.

'Hmm? Yes, of course, that is what I meant.' Reinhard scratched his forehead and sighed. 'Well, our Lord does love to test us, and we must prove ourselves worthy. Let us go and walk among these men, and make them feel the purpose we need to instil in them, before we lose those who are unsure.'

The volunteers had drifted into several groups based on nationality and class, the knights and the commoners, and Hugues had Sir Sighard gather them all together, knights and men of nobility on one side, and the common men on the other. Sighard went to examine the common soldiers, to separate those who he deemed worthy, and Reinhard went to meet the several dozen knights and squires personally.

He introduced himself to each man, pressing his years of experience flattering and endearing himself to young ambitious men of the nobility into service. Brother Bertrand followed them along, noting each man's name and title on a scroll. They reached a man, who, unlike the others present, was not talking to his peers, but standing silent among them. He was finely but simply dressed, well kempt, and had a strange sword buckled to his gilded belt. Reinhard was instantly interested.

'And you are, good sir?'

The man bowed properly and crisply, which pleased Reinhard. 'I am Sieur de Blanchant, your excellency.'

Beside him, Hugues turned around and took notice.

'Roland?'

'Yes, my lord.'

'It is a pleasure to meet you, Roland, and a greater pleasure to have you join our brotherhood.' Hugues beamed, and Reinhard looked at him in mild confusion.

Hugues turned and explained. 'Sieur de Blanchant is a knight of great renown, regarded among the finest in France. He personally led the charge that broke the enemy centre at the battle.'

Roland bowed his head slightly, without showing any pleasure. 'You honour me, my lord, but I was not alone, many shared that moment of glory… Some who do not live to hear the accolade. I merely tried to do my duty.'

'Good man, well spoken,' said Hugues slightly awkwardly, surprised by the man's tone and response. Others were watching them now and Roland was clearly uncomfortable.

'Tell me, what is that strange sword you wear?' said Reinhard, peering at it. He had realised with confusion that it carried some of the pagan symbols, and on the scabbard was, of all things, some kind of pagan serpent or foul creature.

The knight glanced at his sword as if he had forgotten it was there. 'Oh, I…' He paused and coughed into his hand lightly, gathering himself and clearly fighting some strong emotion. 'It is the sword that claimed my brother's life. I claimed it from his enemy after taking my vengeance.' Roland shrugged. 'My own sword was broken, and I have not had the chance to replace it.'

Reinhard looked confused. 'There must be many good Christian blades that… well, that are available after the battle. A brother of the Order cannot carry the symbols of the pagan gods on his person.'

Roland muttered under his breath, shook his head and apologised. 'Your excellency, I am sorry, I had not thought of it. Of course, it is inappropriate. I shall replace it immediately.' He unbelted the sword and looked unsure what to do with it, but Hugues reached out to take it, curious to see the intricate carvings himself.

'Do not apologise, my son. I know that it must have held meaning to you,' said Reinhard sympathetically. 'The Order will of course replace it.'

Roland nodded graciously. 'Thank you, my lord.'

Reinhard and Hugues spoke to each of the nobles, and then addressed the small crowd of common soldiers, blessing them and thanking them for their enduring service to their Lord, then Hugues gave them their instructions, to report the next day to the Order's camp, which was adjacent but separate to the main army's.

The two men set off for the short walk back to the Order camp themselves, following Sighard and the dozen or so brothers who had come with them.

'So, you have sent scouts west, along the road?' Reinhard asked.

'Yes, they still have not found any armed resistance, and have been able to travel though small towns and villages unopposed. The people mostly fled in their path. They are currently scouting the next major town, Västerås, it is the first one they have encountered with a wall. I hope to receive reports on that today or tomorrow.'

'Good.' Reinhard looked at Hugues, as they passed through the gates of the camp and then laughed. 'Why are you still carrying that?' The baron was holding the heathen sword Sieur de Blanchant had relinquished.

'Oh, I found it interesting. I wanted to inspect it. And then… well, I wasn't just going to drop it in the field, I'll get one of the men to pass it off to the armourer here.'

Reinhard gestured to it. 'Let me see, I find their scratchings and symbols so strange.' They had stopped as a workgang of captured Norsemen were returning from clearing the ruins and passing through the gates behind them. A sullen and dirty group, guarded by armed men of the Order. The two stood in the road, and the soldiers ushered the captives to pass around them.

Hugues passed over the sword, and Reinhard was surprised by its weight, he had thought it would be heavier. He had hardly ever handled a sword, not since he was a lot younger, but this one had looked broader in its scabbard, and yet did not feel weightier. 'What a strange and terrible beast,' he said, gazing at the carved bone serpent with amusement.

'Yes, it is somehow quite captivating,' said Hugues.

Reinhard turned the sword over. 'And look, more on the guard.

Such bizarre people. I wonder what all the writings say.' Reinhard pointed at the Norse script on the front of the guard.

'I don't know, there are more on the blade.'

'Really?' Reinhard grasped the hilt and drew the blade, seeing the gold inlaid runes in the steel. He let out a little guilty gasp. 'Oh, I see why dear Roland didn't want to part with this, it's quite beautiful.' He turned to look behind them. 'Bertrand, do you know what this says?'

The priest leant over and peered at the sword with a furrowed brow. 'It appears to… well, it's not clear, perhaps "Light the North", although it is difficult to say, the Norse use different structures to their words and you have to infer what the…'

'Yes, yes, no need to bore us with that babble, Bertrand,' said Reinhard, and the man instantly stopped talking, without a hint of offence showing on his dour features.

Reinhard took a last look at the sword. 'Well, we can certainly recover the gold from it.' There was a commotion next to them, and Reinhard looked up to see one of the captured Norse had stopped as he was passing them, and was staring at him with a look of horror and outrage. An Order soldier tried to chivvy the man along but he was immovable. Reinhard's brows furrowed. 'What is wrong with that man? Get him moving along,' he snapped.

The soldier apologised and grabbed at the man more forcefully with both hands.

Quick as a fox, the Norseman ducked into the soldier's grasp and elbowed him in the stomach viciously, doubling the Christian over and grabbing at his sword.

Reinhard froze in panic as the Norseman drew the soldier's sword as he was incapacitated, then locked eyes with the heathen as the captive bellowed in fury and raised the blade, advancing towards him to attack.

Reinhard stumbled a half step back, dropping the scabbard he was carrying in horror as the heathen crossed the half-dozen steps towards him and swung the stolen sword down in a great arc towards his face.

Reinhard was knocked bodily aside as Baron Hugues stepped into the attack with a shout, drawing his own sword and cutting directly upwards with it, knocking the Norseman's sword off course and sending it arcing harmlessly through the air between the two masters of the Order.

The heathen recovered quickly, and even as Hugues reversed his wild parry and tried to hammer the pommel of his sword into the man's face, the Norseman headbutted him, shattering Hugues's nose, sending the Frenchman staggering back, blinded, and crying out in pain and alarm.

The Norseman did not move in to finish his armed opponent, however, he looked at Reinhard once again and bellowed in rage, raising his sword once more to attack. Reinhard remembered in that moment that he was himself holding a sword, and had once been trained as a child to use one, and he let out a cry and raised the blade limply to defend himself from a sweeping cut at his right side.

The impact of the two blades shocked his hand and knocked the sword from his grip, the dropped weapon thunking painfully off his robed side and clattering to the ground, leaving him completely defenceless.

Reinhard raised his hands in desperation as the sword came for a third swing, but the heathen sighed and drooped as Sighard's sword lanced into his chest from the side, then the knight put his left arm around the heathen's neck and threw him to the ground, pulling his sword free and brutally thrusting it into the downed man's face.

Reinhard was gasping and trembling, rooted to the spot, blinking and mumbling as he realised that he had, in fact, not been cut in half as he expected. He barely saw as a dozen men of the Order pummelled their way into the column of captured Norsemen, battering them to the ground, seeking any others who might be a threat.

He saw but didn't register it as Sighard beat the face of the soldier who had lost his sword into a bloody pulp with the pommel of his own weapon. He stared at his hands again, turning them over and disbelieving that they were still attached to his body.

Then, as the shock flowed out of him, the anger followed. Anger at being attacked, anger at how badly he had reacted, anger that he had lost his self-control. He prized his self-control above all things.

'Who was that man?' he screeched, pointing at the dead Norseman, even as two of his men tried to escort him away, weapons drawn, seeking any sign of more threat.

Reinhard resolutely stood his ground. 'I said, who was that man!'

He pointed at Bertrand, who was himself looking more flustered than Reinhard had ever seen him. 'Find out! Why did he try to kill me? Are there others?'

Bertrand nodded nervously and spoke to the cowering captives, Sighard kicking them and threatening with his blood-slicked sword to elicit a reply.

As Bertrand was questioning them, Hugues walked over, one hand clamped to his nose, his eyes and mouth a rictus of pain. He waved at Reinhard with his free hand. 'We must go, there might be more. Sighard! Take ten captives and bring them for questioning, keep the rest under guard. Fuck me, my goddamn nose. That bastard.'

'Yes, my lord,' boomed Sighard, rattling off orders to the growing group of soldiers that were gathering around the surrounded captives. Bertrand pointed at a few and ten of them were dragged off, some kicking and protesting, while the rest were herded into a corner.

'Come, let's go to my tent. I need to find the fucking doctor.' If it wasn't for the seriousness of the situation, and his racing mind, Reinhard would have admonished Hugues for the profanity, for if there was one thing he hated above all others, it was profanity and taking the Lord's name in vain. But such was the rush of stress draining out of him, leaving him feeling slightly giddy, that he let out a short, manic giggle as he realised he had never heard the mild-mannered baron swear before.

Some time later, after a profusely apologetic Sir Sighard had come to report everything was under control, and after Huges had returned from having his nose set, eyes bloodshot and face red and swollen, Bertrand finally returned from his questioning.

'So?' said Reinhard impatiently.

'It appears it was not a planned attack, your excellency. In fact, it seems likely the man had no idea who you were, most of the captives didn't.'

'Nonsense, Bertrand, why would he try so hard to kill me?'

Bertrand nodded patiently. 'It was difficult to understand at first, but it was because of the sword,' he said, nodding as if that made sense.

Reinhard was infuriated. 'Because of the sword? What on earth do you mean?'

'Well, it would seem that it is some sort of holy relic of their people, they believe it was a gift from their gods, given to them to help them defeat us. Apparently, this man who attacked you was a warrior captured in the battle, and that sword had belonged to his earl. He was so angry seeing it in your hands that he… well.' Bertrand broke off, feeling no need to explain what had happened.

Reinhard calmed slightly, his mind clearing and racing through the explanation. 'A holy relic?'

'Yes, apparently so.'

Reinhard put his finger to his lips and thought for a moment, trying to work out what to do with this information. 'And where is the sword now?'

'I have it,' answered Sir Sighard, 'it is in my tent.'

'Good. Store it somewhere safe.' Reinhard turned again to Bertrand. 'I want you to spend the rest of the day and tomorrow talking to more of the Norse, whoever is captured, or in the nearest farms, or whoever you can find. Find out how widespread this belief in this holy relic of theirs is, and anything else you can about it.'

'As you wish, excellency.'

'Good. Oh, and Sir Sighard, take the ten men who were questioned and hang them outside the camp. Make it known it is punishment for the attack.'

Sighard nodded. 'It will be done.'

Reinhard nodded to himself. 'Good.' Then he looked at Hugues, who was sitting with a face of pure anger. The French baron looked at Reinhard and winced. 'I'm sorry about your injury, my friend. But perhaps some good will come of this yet.' Sighard turned to leave but Reinhard brought his hand up and snapped his fingers at the knight. 'And Sighard, bring me that sword.'

Two days passed before the forces of the Crusade were ready to march again. The army was splitting into four parts. Counts Conrad and Otto were taking their contingents south, across the lake, to clear the southern bank and occupy the rich lands there. Many of the other Crusader lords, those who were not to be given land, were going home with their men. A third part of the forces, primarily the men of Bavaria, were staying near Uppsala with Duke Henry, to fortify the camp and garrison the area. That left only the Order's troops.

The men of the Order who could be spared from other duties were going to march west. Before they left, Reinhard called his senior brothers for a meeting, for what might be the last time that many of the brothers were gathered in one place, before they would be spreading out into garrisons and sent to secure captured towns.

Hugues arrived well before the others, so that the two masters could agree what would be said, and what commanded to be done. Reinhard liked to give Hugues, supposedly his equal in rank, and the commander of the military forces of the Order, the brothers militare, as much say as possible in such matters. It was partly because the man's much greater experience in military matters was genuinely useful, but also to keep him mollified and prevent the by now very clear fact that the real power rested with Reinhard from causing undue resentment.

A hound could not be kept on too short a leash, nor directed too closely in how to kill a stag. Sometimes, to avoid being bitten, or simply becoming tired of all the howling, it was important to let the beast have its freedom, and let it believe it was doing what it had itself decided to do.

Hugues arrived and inclined his head, making his pleasantries with his usual grace and civility, an effect largely ruined by the extent of the bruising and redness around his broken nose. Reinhard greeted him warmly, the picture of friendship, and gestured him to a chair at the head of the long table.

The table was long and set for twenty men. It was simply laid with plain tableware, and dressed with a single long white tablecloth, embroidered with the golden crosses of the Order's banner as its only concession to decorative pomp. Reinhard worked hard to keep a culture of restraint and discipline in all the Order's doings, *for discipline was dear to the Lord.*

On a side table lay the Norse sword, their holy relic that caused to much trouble two days previously. Standing beside it, as silent and still as a statue as he always was when not required to speak or take notes, was Bertrand.

'Brother Bertrand, a pleasure as always,' said Hugues drily. 'Do you have anything interesting to tell me about that from your enquiries?' He gestured to the foreign blade.

Bertrand raised his eyes in a glance to Reinhard, seeking permission, and Reinhard nodded subtly. It had been his intent to start the meeting on another topic, but there was no harm in letting Hugues indulge his interest first. Reinhard suddenly worried he was being too soft, allowing Hugues to get too comfortable, and he frowned to himself. Usually he enforced his will relentlessly, but in the past few days, he had been far more open to Hugues making decisions. He noted to himself that he must stop that going too far, lest it get out of control.

'Yes, my lord. I have learned a good deal about this sword, this supposed pagan holy weapon.'

Hugues smiled. 'You do not sound impressed.'

Bertrand shrugged. 'It is blasphemous gibberish, my lord. I feel embarrassed repeating it.'

'Well, I shall only ask you to do it once.' Reinhard smiled to himself at how much the pious monk detested the Norse religion. Reinhard himself found it rather interesting, even if it was all childish nonsense, stories for simpletons. Brother Bertrand would do whatever he was commanded, and learning their language and their ways was a key task, it gave Reinhard many advantages, but the man did not pretend to be happy about it.

'Thank you, my lord. Well, I found several people who claimed direct familiarity with the sword, and most others had at least heard of it. The man who assaulted you and his excellency the bishop so grievously was a household warrior of a man named Jarl Ragnvald, the original owner of the sword. He was captured after the battle, and apparently regarded it as such a great stain on his honour to see a Christian carrying his dead master's sword that he was compelled to try and kill you.' The monk shrugged apologetically. 'I do not understand it, but that is what they say.'

'I see. It was a matter of honour? Nothing to do with who held the sword?'

'Yes, that is how it seems.'

'And what is so important about it?'

'Well, they claim it was a gift from one of their false gods, whom they call Odin, who is known by the pagan tribes in the north of our lands as Woden.'

'That is the same god?'

Bertrand winced at the term but nodded. 'The same false idol, yes. The people familiar with it all told slightly different stories about its origin, some say it was forged by Thor, another false idol, others by a dorf... I'm afraid I don't understand what a dorf is, some sort of nonsense creature of which they have many, I could inquire more...' said Bertrand, making clear he absolutely did not wish to.

'It does not matter.'

'Very well, what they all agreed on is that the sword is linked to a prophecy.' At this point, Bertrand picked up a single leaf of parchment from a stack of them on the table, more of his prodigious notes. 'That as long as a Norseman, brave and true, wields the sword, their people cannot be defeated. That is their prophecy.' He shrugged again. 'Oh, and one other thing of note; many of those questioned agreed that the sword was reputedly forged by a Christian slave, although who exactly is not clear. Several names were used.'

Hugues nodded, now deeper in thought. He turned to Reinhard. 'A fortunate discovery, one we can use to our advantage.'

Reinhard sputtered. 'Fortunate! My dear man, it is beyond fortune for this to have fallen so neatly into our hands. No, no, this is the work of our Lord, I feel it absolutely certainly. He has delivered to us victory itself with this object.'

Hugues narrowed his eyebrows a fraction. 'In what way?'

Reinhard looked surprised, concealing his irritation at being questioned with his enthusiasm. 'They are doomed by the words of their own prophecy! They think that as long as one of them has the sword, they cannot be defeated. And by reversal, the fact that we now possess it signifies their very defeat!'

Hugues's brows rose a fraction. 'Yes, I suppose that could be claimed.'

'Will be claimed, my dear man, will be claimed. Because we shall claim it, loudly and frequently, so that all who live in these lands know it, that they are defeated and that we are triumphant.'

'Hmm, hearing it will not be enough.'

Reinhard nodded. 'Of course, we shall keep it, display it, put it in a fine reliquary and allow any who come by to gaze upon it.'

Hugues shook his head slowly. 'It will not be enough.'

'What?' replied Reinhard, taken aback.

'It is no good letting those who come here see it, they are not the problem. We must show it to those who are not yet convinced of their defeat. This must travel at the head of our army, to be presented at every town and village. They will only believe if it they see it.'

Reinhard stared, dumbfounded. *Why did that not occur to me?* He was furious, he started to wonder if the attack had not addled his senses in some way, and resolved to address that later.

'You make a good point, Brother Hugues. Yes, perhaps that is best, that it travel with the army.' He strode over to the sword. 'We shall have this pagan gibberish removed, of course.' He pointed at the bronze guard and pommel. 'And replaced with a plain cross guard appropriate to our Order. And that gaudy scabbard, that will be replaced too. We cannot have the Order bearing the symbols of paganism.'

Hugues stood and went over to the sword too, lying on the table beside the scabbard. He picked it up and contemplated it, turning it over in his hands. Then he looked at Bertrand. 'You say this sword is recognised by the Norse. Have so many of them seen it?'

Bertrand shook his head. 'Few have actually seen it, they have merely heard stories of it and some descriptions of what it looks like.'

Hugues nodded and turned to Reinhard, carefully sheathing the sword and holding it out towards the bishop. 'If you replace the scabbard, and the hiltwork, how will people recognise it? How will they know what it is, and believe that what we say is true?'

Reinhard scowled. 'What we are saying will be the truth, delivered by God's messengers.' He knew he was wrong again, Hugues had once again seen the matter clearly, which he himself had missed in his excitement, but he was beside himself at being corrected twice in one meeting. 'And the blade is unique, they will recognise it from that. It is inscribed with the name.'

'True, but you cannot see that when it is sheathed, and the letters are small and the scabbard can be seen much more clearly. I think it must appear to be the sword that they expect to see, in every way.'

Reinhard grumbled and stared at the offending article, unable to find an argument. 'It is disgraceful for us to carry these blasphemous things with us,' he muttered, weakly.

'Not as a display of our strength and victory.' Hugues tried to mollify him by offering a concession. 'Perhaps we could deface it in some lesser way. Carve some scripture into the back of the scabbard, or emblazon it with a golden cross.'

Reinhard grabbed at the offer. 'Yes, yes, I will think of something suitable.'

'Good.' Hugues drew the blade again and looked at Bertrand. 'What was it called? Light the North? What does that mean?'

'Ah, my apologies, that is incorrect. Their language is base and simplistic, you have to infer and deduce meaning from their basic wording to get the true…'

'Answer the question, Bertrand, we don't need a lesson on your insufficient grasp of linguistics,' Reinhard said, taking a little of his anger out on his assistant.

Bertrand nodded without showing a hint of offence. 'Of course, my apologies. It is called "The Light of the North". They say that the blade is supposed to represent that, but they all had a different explanation of how. Something about the centre being made of starlight, of being surrounded by fire. Really it was all nonsense at that point. Every one of them said something opposing to the others.'

Hugues smiled and pointed at the sword. 'The centre portion is brighter than the rest, perhaps that is what it means.'

Reinhard let his excitement creep over him again. 'Yes, do you not feel the hand of the Lord at work here? We, the Brothers of Christ's Light, delivered the main weapon of the enemy, which is called the Light of the North?'

Hugues looked at Reinhard with a soft smile, and to Reinhard's relief he simply nodded. 'I cannot dispute your thoughts on that.'

Reinhard continued in an animated voice. 'We are here to bring the light of our Lord Jesus to these lands, to bring these people into his flock. We are ourselves the Light of the North. This weapon is the symbol that our cause is true and correct. That bright core of the sword, with flames around it, that is the light, burning away the darkness in these lands. We are that fire, we are the light in this dark place!

'In the great Crusade to the Holy Land – blessings be upon those brave men who undertook it – they captured the very spear that pierced our Lord, and Adhemar of Le Puy carried it in battle, inspiring the men and leading them to victory wherever he rode. This can be to us what the holy lance was to them! Rallied behind this weapon, our forces will be resolute and steadfast.'

Reinhard had to curtail his excitement briefly, to maintain his composure. But Hugues was nodding more and more vehemently. 'I see it, Bishop. I do.'

'Excellent!' Reinhard clapped his hands, the anger of earlier washed away. Then he stopped. 'It remains then only to decide who should carry it.'

Hugues looked up and shrugged. 'Surely there is only one?'

Reinhard smiled back. 'Quite right, yes. He won it, and didn't you say he was a fine knight?'

'Perhaps the best in all of France,' said Hugues.

'And he is the man who brought us the sword. Yes, he shall be the one. We will have to give him an appropriate command, of course, one befitting this great honour.'

'I can arrange that.'

'Excellent. Bertrand, go and make sure that he is summoned for the command meeting.'

'As you say, excellency.'

## Chapter 6

# A Relic to Rule

Reinhard looked down the length of the table in devout silence after his prayer finished. Behind each chair, a brother knelt on the rush-covered floor with his hands clasped together on the backrest, and his forehead pressed into his hands.

He left them there for a moment longer than strictly necessary, allowing the period of his total control of them to linger and ensure it was felt.

'In nomine Patris et Filii et Spiritus Sancti, Amen,' he finally intoned, making the sign of the cross over the table.

'Amen,' the kneeling group intoned in reply.

'Rise and be seated.'

There was a quiet shuffling as the senior brothers of the Order, both the brothers ecclesiastical – the priests who oversaw the major parishes, and the brothers militare – the armed portion, rose stiffly to their feet and pulled back their chairs to sit.

Reinhard allowed them all to be seated and waited until each man was still, and each man was looking at him. When he was satisfied, he finally allowed a thin smile to pass his lips. 'Thank you all for coming, my brothers. It is a momentous day, and there is much to discuss.' He felt Hugues stir beside him, the man expected to conduct the military portion of the meeting first, but Reinhard held a hand out and placed it on his shoulder gently but firmly, restraining the man in his seat. 'If you don't mind, I have a couple of small matters to attend to first.'

Hugues mumbled acceptance and nodded, lowering down back into his seat.

Reinhard smiled in thanks and removed his hand. He was worried he had let the man feel too much power earlier. *It's important to remind you of your place.*

'I have received word from our Holy Father himself,' Reinhard announced with great solemnity. It was not strictly true, the letter was from a cardinal in the papal palace, who dealt with such matters of administration, but he was fairly sure the decision originated from Pope Pascal and it was important to keep the image of closeness to the papacy alive.

'The first bishopric has been created in the lands conquered by the Second Crusade, the Bishopric of Lund.'

There was a murmur among the robed priests around the table. This was both good and bad news. A bishop would be appointed from outside the brotherhood, and would exert the power of the Church over the new bishopric outside the structure of the Order. However, it was recognition that the Order had succeeded in creating a congregation worthy of that structure, and in such a short time. High praise indeed.

'Do not worry, my brothers, it does not mean our humble mission in those lands is complete. Far from it, we are asked to continue our work in the towns and villages around Lund, and to establish parishes and give services to bring more into the fold. Additionally, those of us freed up from our duties there will establish new churches here, in the far north, and continue our fine work, which the Holy Father commends with great enthusiasm.'

Reinhard saw many of the faces brighten at this. Personally, he hated the idea of being displaced from his relatively comfortable existence in Lund, which had required a great deal of work to create, to be moved up to the cold north. But he also knew that for many of these brothers, among the most devout and fanatical, or desperate, in Christendom, the opportunity for arduous, and most importantly, visible, hardship in service to the Lord would be very welcome. Those who brought these pagans into the fold would make names for themselves within the Church, and, later in their careers, might eventually gain a bishopric themselves, or, if events allowed, even the vestments of a cardinal.

'I would also like to thank my brothers in the Order militare, without whom our work would have been impossible.' He looked down the side of the table where the tabarded knights and nobles were seated, and bowed his head generously. 'You were not mentioned specifically in our Holy Father's thoughts, but I am sure he knows of the greatness and goodness of your work.' He turned to Hugues. 'Would you like to continue?'

Hugues gave a strained smile and nodded, once again moving his chair back to stand. He stood awkwardly for a moment, expecting Reinhard to take his seat, but Reinhard did not and Hugues betrayed a flash of irritation and then addressed the table anyway as the bishop stood next to him, smiling softly.

'Tomorrow we will begin the next part of our campaign. Our Order has been assigned lands to the west to pacify and govern, lands on the wild edge of this pagan kingdom, from a town called Arbugæ and extending northwards for a hundred miles. To reach those lands, we must pass through and subjugate a number of towns and settlements along the northern edge of the great lake, where it is known that survivors of the enemy army have taken refuge.' He paused to look around solemnly at the gathering.

'We do not know the extent of their remaining forces, or if they even intend to continue to resist, that is part of what we must determine. So we will march as if for war, with full scouting, with vanguard and rearguard, and patrols to maintain the road behind us.'

This pronouncement did not appear to trouble the men present. The mood in the army had been of relief that the war seemed over, but these men were men who had chosen to continue the fight, and they were not intimidated by the idea that they would again be marching to war. Many of them actively sought it, and the opportunities it presented. Reinhard smiled to himself inwardly. These men were the hard edge of the Christian sword, the very most fanatical and committed.

Hugues looked at the man closest to him on his side of the table. 'Sir Sighard. You have proven yourself repeatedly with your handling of the conquered peoples, with a firm hand on the rein and the lash. You will stay here while we are gone, and be responsible for the security of this vast new conquered land, and of ensuring its people stay peaceful and comply with our requirements of them.'

Sighard bowed his head. 'As you order, it is my pleasure to serve, my lord.'

'Good man.' Hugues moved his eyes down the table to the next seat. 'Brother Hartung, your time to assume a command has arrived. You have proven yourself as a fine squire, and earned your spurs in the great battle, fighting in the ranks of the Order where all could see your courage and resolve.'

The young man beamed at the praise, his pride glowing in his cheeks. Ever since the death of his father, Count Adolf, the boy had been living in the shadow of his defeat, and in concern that his father's lands would not be passed to him by his liege lord, Duke Lothair. He had joined the Order, at Reinhard's provocation, to prove himself in battle and in service, to make a name for himself and to ensure that Lothair saw fit to entrust him with the county of Schauenburg, and perhaps other lands besides. Reinhard had promised, in return for his service, to prevail on Lothair to do so, a promise that he might even keep, so loyal and useful had the boy proven himself. He was now among Reinhard's most devoted followers.

Hartung looked at Reinhard and the bishop nodded his head in approval, only brightening the boy's smile. *When you are a count, I will have a powerful ally under my leash.*

Hugues continued. 'Hartung, you must learn the ways of command, and will come with me as my second, and my aide-de-camp.'

Hartung's smile expanded from ear to ear, and, in his excitement, he stood and bowed to the baron. 'Thank you, my lord. It will be my honour.' Hugues waved the boy down into his seat with a nod. It had not been Hugues's idea to start giving the boy command, he had done so at Reinhard's request, a favour traded for... Reinhard stopped his train of thought, unable to remember what the favour he had agreed to do in return was. *No matter, if it was important he will remind me. But then, if I forget, he will be insufferable, and less likely to agree to the next one.*

'Brother Dietmar.' Hugues inclined his head to the knight, Sir Dietmar of Eresburg. A vassal of Duke Lothair, he had been the knight Hartung squired for, until he earned his spurs, and a loyal follower of Count Adolf before, and after, his defeat and death. 'You have proven yourself a great teacher and mentor, and a leader of men. I would be pleased if you would come with me, to command a hundred, and ride at my side.'

Dietmar smiled graciously and bowed his head. 'I am pleased to do so.'

Reinhard regarded the German knight with curiosity. It seemed apparent to him that Dietmar had joined the Order only to stay with his squire, presumably at the orders of the dead Adolf, but now the boy was no longer his charge, the knight had not gone home, and seemed to be an enthusiastic member of the Order. Reinhard considered the options. Perhaps the man was simply very devout, and wished to stay for his own reasons. Or perhaps his goal was still to watch over Hartung, driven by some leftover loyalty. Reinhard considered interjecting to reassign the man somewhere else, but it would shame the man without obvious reason. In any case, it was probably in his interest to have a capable fighter protecting Hartung, if indeed that was his aim. Reinhard dismissed the matter as minor, and moved back to wondering what it was he was supposed to have done for Hugues.

Hugues continued down the table, reeling off assignments and commands as Reinhard searched his mind for what it was. *Ah, of course, to write to the archbishop praising Hugues's contribution to the Crusade, and asking his support for the cause of Lower Lorraine.* Baron Hugues's entire purpose on these Crusades was to garner favours and support from the great lords of the empire, and hopefully the current or future emperor himself, to back his lord's claim to Lower Lorraine and to allow it to be merged with the Duchy of Lorraine proper, to act as a quasi-independent state, instead of a plaything passed between the Holy Roman Empire and the kingdom of France.

Lower Lorraine had been in turmoil for years, its ducal title passed between different families as each in turn ended up on the wrong side of internal wars, and made enemies of the winner. The latest being the deposed Duke Henry of Limburg, who had betrayed the emperor by backing Duke Lothair in his rebellion of 1114, and had his title and lands stripped in response when Lothair made peace, the terms of which did not include protecting his former allies.

The deposed former duke had escaped captivity and was running amok in the duchy, raising support and undermining the new duke; Godfrey, who was weak, helpless and barely recognised by his supposed vassals, many of whom were openly more loyal to France. Hugues, and his brother Folmar, the Count of Metz, regarded this chaos in their neighbouring duchy to be deliberate, aimed at keeping the region weak, to allow it to be a pawn and a buffer in the endless struggle between the Empire and the Kingdom of France. Their primary concern was that one or other would snap it up as a concession, and that the chaos and exposure would weaken the Duchy of Lorraine proper, putting it next in line to be undermined and eviscerated, its corpse given as a token to whoever won the next intercine war.

So, that was why Simon, the Duke of Lorraine, his loyal vassal Folmar the Count of Metz, and Folmar's brother, Hugues, were so invested in the Crusade. A great victory for them here might gain them an ally who would either prevent the ruin of their duchy, or perhaps even allow them to be the ones who received the ruined corpse of the Duchy of Lower Lorraine, finally re-uniting the region into a power that could steer its own destiny, a permanent buffer between the great rivals.

Reinhard truthfully didn't care about Hugues's motivations, only that they were extremely important to the man, and that thus he would do almost anything to succeed. That desperation made him manipulatable, deliciously so. The man would tolerate humiliation, subservience and degradation as long as he was convinced it helped his greater cause. So Reinhard would write a glowing letter to whomever Hugues pleased, and Hugues would continue to run the military wing of the Order, whose every move served Reinhard's own ambitions.

Reinhard almost chuckled to himself as he thought about it. Both men needed each other equally, yet he had taken near total control of the partnership. *It was almost too easy.*

'Bishop Reinhard, do you agree?' Reinhard cursed himself and smiled, looking over at Hugues, trying to recall what was being said while he had been thinking.

Not remembering, but certain whatever it was was something he had agreed to previously, he nodded. 'Yes, of course.'

'Excellent, then it will be done.' Reinhard nodded again, infuriated that he didn't know what he had just agreed to. It threatened his control of events, and he chastened himself for allowing his attention to wander.

'Now, onto our final matter.' Hugues looked at Reinhard

expectantly, and Reinhard this time knew what was being spoken of. Reinhard nodded and clicked his fingers at Brother Bertrand, who had been standing at a simple lectern behind them, taking notes of the decisions and appointments made during the meeting. The priest laid down his quill and, with a great deal of solemnity, recovered a white linen-wrapped bundle from the side table, bringing it to Reinhard.

The bishop held the bundle carefully, showing it to the assembly and waiting until there was perfect silence, and all eyes were upon it. Then Bertrand untied the cord that bound it, and peeled the fine white cloth aside, revealing the pagan sword. Reinhard held it up, dramatically, hands outstretched, silent and watching the faces of the men who sat down the sides of the table. There was some confusion, and not a little consternation, as everyone at the table got a good look at the sword. Only a handful of them would recognise it, and none of them would know its meaning.

Reinhard smiled gently, and lowered his arms, which were aching from holding the blade aloft. 'Brothers, we have in our possession the greatest weapon of the enemy, a holy relic said by their heathen priests to be a gift from their false gods, believed by their people to be the symbol of their struggle.' Puzzled faces around the table turned to surprise and curiosity, and there was complete silence as Reinhard paused.

He was not a man for sweeping rhetoric, he disliked speeches, he disliked raising his voice or trying to make himself heard. When he spoke, he spoke quietly, and he knew he would be heard, because he always knew those he was speaking to would know better than to make him shout. But he allowed a tremble of excitement to enter his voice on this occasion, allowed the timbre and pacing to rise slightly, allowed the volume to reach out further so that men at the far end would not have to slow the breath in their nose and lean forwards just to hear him.

'They had a prophecy for this weapon, as absurd as it was

blasphemous, that as long as a faithful Norseman held this weapon, they could not be defeated. But instead!' He paused and looked around the table. 'Instead, our Lord has led this great weapon into our hands, a symbol of their defeat, a symbol of our superiority. Instead of blessing their hands with victory, it has become the very herald of their doom.

'It has become clear to me, through prayer and contemplation, that this blade was not the product of some foul magic of their twisted creed, but inspired by our Lord himself. Indeed, I am told that the hands that wrought it were Christian, a good man of our lands, taken into bondage, and who our Lord chose as a conduit for his revenge on the offences of our enemy.'

Reinhard nodded to himself vigorously, a tear springing unbidden into his eye, unplanned, but welcome in the moment. His hands still clutching the sword, he allowed the tear to roll gently down his cheek for all to see.

'This sword was always intended for our hands, meant to give the heathen false hope, and then crush it in the glory of our saviour, for as we humble brothers are the guardians of Christ's light in these lands, so this sword is the embodiment of that light itself.' Reinhard drew the sword suddenly, and with a flourish, something he had practised repeatedly earlier, and held it up for all to see the steel.

'Inscribed in the blade, in their heathen tongue, is the proof of this: The Light of the North it is named, the bright light of its core is us, shining irrepressible in the darkness of this land. This sword was given to us by the Lord as a symbol of the light we carry, and every heathen who sees it will know the truth, that they have been defeated, and that it was by the will of our Lord that it is so, and that we are his weapon among them!' Reinhard finished with a rising voice and a flourish, and Sir Sighard did exactly what Reinhard had hope he would do, the relentlessly devout Bavarian knight rising to his feet and crossing his arms on his chest.

'Deus le Vult!' he cried, staring at the sword in wonder.

'Deus le Vult!' joined in the rest of the table, at first ragged, and then together as they all rose to their feet. Reinhard beamed at them as he felt the heat of the passion from so many of the brothers, and felt his eye flicker in irritation as he noted the few who joined in half-heartedly, with sceptical looks in their eyes. *I will deal with them when the time is right.*

Before their cries of devotion could die out, Reinhard held up his hand for silence, and the brothers quieted, waiting for his next proclamation.

'There remains only one question: which hand should wield the symbol of our Order.' He allowed his gaze to wander around the table, and saw the intensity with which Roland, Sieur de Blanchant, was staring at the sword. The knight's eyes snapped up as he realised Reinhard was looking at him. 'I should never have taken this from you, Sir Roland. I did not recognise it for what it was. It was a while before the Lord opened my eyes, and showed me the truth.'

'It… it was yours to take in the service of the Order, Grand-master, as is everything I own, even my life if it is required.'

Reinhard smiled gently. 'I believe you when you say it, Brother Roland. But why? Why are you so sure of your service, so soon after joining our humble Order?'

Roland answered without pausing. 'Serving the Lord is my only desire, penance for my failings as a servant and a knight.'

Reinhard narrowed his eyes slightly. 'Penance for what? What failings?' Then he stopped himself. 'No, a question for later, in private, perhaps in confession.'

Roland shook his head. 'I am happy to answer it, so that all may know it, and know the magnitude of my debt.' The knight paused as his cheek muscles rippled with emotion. 'I failed to protect my brother, who was struck down by that sword. On the Lord's name, I promised my mother I would protect him, and in the Lord's sight I have failed to uphold that promise. I will never return home until I have atoned for it, or paid with my life.'

Reinhard smiled sympathetically. 'My son, you are not to blame, this was the work of our father. Your brother was called to him in glory, and through his noble death this great weapon was delivered to us. You will not serve his memory with your death, but by being the hand that wields this blade in our Lord's service.' Reinhard turned the hilt of the Light of the North to face the Frenchman.

Roland trembled and shook his head briefly. 'I am not worthy, it is not my honour to claim.'

'My son,' said Reinhard, switching seamlessly into French, 'the hand is called to duty, and the heart must follow the path,' before continuing in German. 'It was always your sword, the Lord put it in your hand, and no mortal can separate you. You will bear this beacon of our faith, and your brothers will walk beside you in its light.'

Roland, struggling to compose himself, nodded just once and Reinhard beckoned the man to come and kneel before him, before he did anything to embarrass himself. Reinhard was worried the man might be proving too emotional. He had hoped for a more stoic response. But Roland was well versed in court, and he walked over with dignity, knelt with a demure flourish, and Reinhard felt reassured that the man had the self-control he desired.

Reinhard placed the hilt of the sword in Roland's hand and raised two fingers to begin the familiar gestures. 'Let us pray.'

## Chapter 7

# The Pursuit of Peace

'WE ARE BEING followed.'

Frode turned his head to look at Asel, one of his huskarls, who had run up from the rear of the column. 'By who?'

'Four men on horseback, Christians. Four have been spotted, anyway, but there may be more.'

'Shit. For how long?'

'Since we left Västerås, I think. They must have been watching the town.'

Frode thought about this and turned back to look, but saw nothing in the scattered trees behind them.

'You will not see them from here, they are careful, but I have had men loiter behind and conceal themselves, and they have spotted the scouts.'

'I wonder how long they watched the town, and how far behind their army is. Asel, take a scouting party back, go through the woods away from the road and watch the road and the city. Send word to us of what you see. It is only one day's march from Västerås to Karlsgrind; if their army is coming, we will need to leave immediately.'

'Yes, lord.' Asel turned and loped off back down the column.

Frode was furious with himself for not patrolling around the city while they had stayed there, and for not leaving men to watch it when they left. The anger with his lack of experience being the sole commander of an army gave him intense pangs of sorrow. He had always marched at Ragnvald's side. Ragnvald would have scouted properly, would have anticipated this.

But his old friend was gone, and the fighting heart of the army with him. 'Continue the march, do not let us become separated from my sister's people.'

Karlsgrind was not so much a town, but a collection of villages clustered together along the western bank of a river that flowed south into Lǫgrinn, the great lake at the centre of the Svear kingdom. The river was broad enough for two ships to pass alongside and it continued north for sixty miles, though a chain of lakes, until its source beyond a large lake deep in the wildlands.

Karlsgrind, the karl's gate, got its name from this river, which was the only way to travel north-west by ship, and the best way to get to and from the hinterlands, where hunting was rich, and precious minerals and stones could be found. Many Svear karls and freemen would go on expeditions for one or the other every year. All of them had to pass through the narrows of the river here, looked over by the loose town.

Along the river, stretching north-west across the wooded and farmed lowlands, and then into the low hills and deep forests of the interior, were a succession of smaller and smaller settlements. The river was the artery of the whole region, and all the lifeblood of trade and people flowed back and forth along it. It was the gateway to the hinterlands and a natural trading post.

So Karlsgrind was always a busy place, its long single dock on the riverbank always packed with ships, loading or unloading, heading upriver or leaving to go out into the great lake, to go to any of the twenty towns and cities that surrounded it. The market that spread along the riverbank was always bustling with traders and farmers, and the wealth it generated for so many, and the rich farmlands around it, meant that it had long been regarded as sacrosanct in war, inviolable in any squabble or battles between jarls.

In fact, so precious was this town to so many that rival jarls would stop their conflicts to pursue any who dared to threaten the peace there, let alone raid or destroy it. So Karlsgrind had no wall, and its people raised sheep and crops, and became fur trappers and hunters and settlers of interior lands, not warriors.

When the column of refugees arrived, they were carried across the river by the boatload and welcomed into the town. It was the price for being immune to conflict, the town was bound by tradition to welcome all who came, and to ease their passage wherever they chose to go.

Frode met with the town's leaders once they had disembarked from the final boat to cross. He knew this area and its people well, and was warmly received. A few miles outside the town to the west, at the edge of the farmland that surrounded it, his own lands began. Beyond that was the town of Stenköping, and beyond that his own home, and the largest settlement in the region, Arbugæ.

'It is good to see you alive and well, Jarl Frode,' said Svein, the town's lawgiver, with a genial smile. He did not call himself jarl, for political reasons, but in Karlsgrind he was the man who made decisions. 'We did not know if anyone would return, my heart is glad to see and your men alive.'

Frode smiled bitterly. 'Only some.' Then he frowned and looked down the empty river. 'I had expected Jarl Gustav to be here, he left Västerås by ship, and it is an easy day's sail.'

Svein shrugged. 'The wind on the lake is in the west, and he will be rowing into it. It will take him until nightfall.'

'Hmm, I am sure you are right.' Svein knew those waters better than any, and there was no sense in arguing.

'Come, let us go and eat, you look like you could be hungry.' Frode nodded uncertainly, still gazing out over the lake. 'Don't worry, we will save some for Jarl Gustav and his men.'

'I could eat,' said Frode, tearing his eyes from the quiet river. The sun was already low, and despite the distance by water being three times what it was across land, and the wind being against, he could not shake the nervousness he felt. There was a clash coming to its conclusion with Halla, and he had wanted Gustav there to be the voice of calm. *It can wait until tomorrow.*

Svein packed Frode, Halla, and all their huskarls and most important followers into the town's generously sized hall. Again, for political reasons, he did not live in it and call it his own, due to the unique status of the town, and he sat at a long table with the rest of the town's leading men, with no distinction other than his seat was in the centre. Despite this, everything gravitated around him, and Frode and Halla sat opposite him as honoured guests, their host having guided them to sit together, oblivious to the rift between the siblings.

The meal was not spectacular, there had been no warning to prepare some great feast, but the food was abundant and all of his people throughout the rest of the town were being fed as much fish, bread and baked vegetables as they could want. A wealthy town sitting in some of the rare rich farmlands in the north was always a good place to be a guest.

Once the food had arrived, and the mead was flowing, Svein nervously turned to the subject he had clearly been eager to address. 'So tell me, Jarl Frode, what do you intend to do?'

Frode looked at the man with a raised eyebrow. 'We do not intend to fight in your town, Svein, if that is really what you are asking.'

Svein gave a hollow laugh and waved with his knife. 'No, it

was not what I meant. I just want to know what will happen. Will the Crusaders come here, and what will you do?'

Frode felt Halla's anger simmering beside him, and, trying to dodge the confrontation, reversed the question instead. 'What do you intend to do, when the Christians come? What will this town do?'

There was a pause as Svein looked around the table, gauging the reaction of those present. 'We have always been a place of peace and trade, Jarl Frode. I think we would maintain that.'

Halla half hissed her disapproval and fixed Svein with a frown. 'I see this town is still full of strong young men, while every other hall in the land is filled with the weeping of widows.'

'Halla! We are guests here,' said Frode.

'The niceties of guest tradition do not concern me, brother. We all fought to defend these lands, yet I see here people who were not willing to bear their share of the burden.' She leaned in towards Svein. 'Your people were always neutral in conflicts between Norse, it is no reason to fail to stand in the line against the invader.'

Svein's mouth drew into a pressed line at the grievous insult, but he refrained from a counterattack, which would only make him look foolish. 'Our people are not trained or experienced in war, but some did go, and most did not return. We have our widows and fatherless children here too.'

Halla stood and spat on the table, and the room fell to silence. 'Not trained? I saw fishwives and boys of twelve summers take up weapons, were they trained? How foolish you are, the Christians do not care for the traditions of your town.'

'Lady, I ask you not to speak that way in our hall,' said Svein, his voice finally carrying his anger.

'Or what? Would now be the time you are finally willing to defend yourself? You were too cowardly to fight the Christians, your men don't know how to wield a weapon, and you are in a room full of my people, men who have survived only by their skill and courage.' She sneered at him and Svein glowered in return. Frode put a hand to his forehead and growled.

'Enough. Be seated,' said Svein, with surprising conviction, flicking his eyes to Frode. 'This is unacceptable, we welcomed you into our hall, fed you, greeted you as friends.' He looked back at Halla. 'Do not threaten me here, your brother and jarl would not permit violence.'

Halla laughed, slow and dry, and mocked the man with her eyes. 'My brother is not my lord, and he has already chosen the path of submission. He would not fight me any more than you would.'

Svein looked taken aback at the bitterness of her words, and realised he had drastically misread the situation. 'You are not together? But you arrived as one, what…'

'We arrived on the same road, at the same time, but my people are not his, my people are those who wish to continue the fight, who will continue until the last Christian is driven from these lands. His people,' Halla pointed at her brother, fingertip hanging a handspan from Frode's face, 'are going home, to await becoming slaves in their own lands, as you do.'

Halla put both her hands back on the table and resumed glaring in silence. Svein turned to Frode and, for once, did not know what to say. 'I am sorry that it has come to this,' he finally choked out. 'But we cannot defend this town, and we cannot abandon it. If you intend to fight, you must leave.'

Halla turned her hands up and looked dramatically around the hall. 'And go where? To my brother's lands?'

'You know I cannot allow that unless you change your intent,' said Frode with a look of pain.

'You would exile me, brother? Like this, in front of these strangers?'

'No! I did not want to do it like this at all, I wanted to talk to you alone, to show you reason, to convince you to bring your people to peace and safety in my lands, our lands, where our family has lived for lifetimes. But NOT if you bring this lost war with you.' Frode clenched his fist and thumped it on the table as he talked, and his face was full of misery.

Halla looked at him as if struck, and then shook her head again. 'Then my people will find somewhere else.'

'When I was young, I travelled north up this river many times, going hunting with my father. There's good land up there, wild but good,' said a familiar voice behind them. 'I think you could lose an army up that river, or find a place to live, whatever you required.'

Halla and Frode turned to see Jarl Gustav and a dozen of his men standing at the back of the hall by the open doors. Frode gave the jarl a smile of exhaustion and relief, and Gustav grinned in return. Halla looked on impassively, eyes fixed on the Raven's Claw.

'You made it, I was starting to worry you would miss the food,' said Frode, rising from his seat and meeting the old man to clasp his arm and grip his shoulder in greeting.

'I could smell the food from ten miles away, but we had some trouble on the journey.'

Frode frowned again. 'What trouble?'

'The Christians are on the lake, well, their pet Danes are, anyway.'

Frode cursed. 'How many?'

'We only found one ship, a small knorr, and ran it down and captured it. They didn't put up much of a fight. But we put questions to what was left of her crew at the end, and they were just a scout. They say a fleet of twenty longships is on the lake, going town to town, clearing us up like spring mice in a barn, taking any ship they find, killing any who resist. The Christians told them they can go home once every warship on the lake is burned or captured.'

'And no one fights against them?'

'Aye, the people of Birka did. Eight ships, every warrior they and the villages around them had left, they met the Danes in the lake and gave battle.'

'What happened?'

'They lost, and Birka is gone, burned to the ground and every one of its people lie slaughtered in the ashes. So these Danes said, anyway.'

There was a dour muttering in the room as the words struck home. None could have imagined this in their lifetime, that they would be hunted on their own lake, their mighty warfleet reduced to scattered survivors, hunted by their old enemy: the Danes. The ancient town of Birka, once a seat of kings, gone. The shock in the gathering was physical.

'So what will you do?' asked Frode, nervously.

'Well, we can sail home. Twenty ships is a lot, but it's a big lake, I am sure we can sneak past them. And then, when we get home, we would be faced with the same question, and the same argument you two are having here.' He looked at the siblings chidingly.

Halla turned up the corner of her mouth, resolute despite what she had heard. 'There should be no argument, any true Norseman will continue the fight, the people of Birka showed us the example of what is honourable.'

'To what end!' said Frode in fury and hurt, turning on his sister. 'When all of our towns are ash, and all our people in the ground, will you be happy then?'

'Perhaps, yes! And you talk as if defeat is certain, why?'

'Because it has already happened, Halla! I was there, I was there for all of it! I know your pain, but we are already defeated, and adding the bodies of your few remaining people to the boundless ranks of the dead will do nothing to salve your anguish, only create more.'

'Those are the words of a cowa…'

'ENOUGH!' Gustav shouted, with a voice that boomed through the hall, shocking Halla to a halt in the midst of her fury. Gustav looked at the two with sadness and shook his head. 'You achieve nothing by fighting each other, there are few enough of us left as it is.' He held up his maimed hand as Halla opened her mouth to speak more words of anger, and such was his presence and command that she was stilled. 'You are both wrong. Frode, the fight is not yet over. The battles are lost, but it is far from certain that the Christians can rule here forever, if the land and the gods and enough of the people resist.' He pointed his finger at his fellow jarl, who looked away in shame. Halla looked triumphantly at her brother.

'But Halla, you are wrong to mock him. Not all the people can fight, and if they did, there would be nothing left to fight for, just twenty towns burned like Birka, and any victory would be hollow. It is good that some will make peace and maintain the towns and farm the land, for if the Christians ever leave, we will have saved something worth having. But for now, with their army marching, and the lake lost to the Danes, those of us who will fight must run and hide, and bide our time, and preserve our strength while the enemy bleeds theirs. With our army defeated, and our towns surrendered, most of the Christians will leave, and take their Danish pets with them. And then we shall come down from our hiding places, and we will fall upon them, and we will have a chance then, a chance to reclaim our lands with some of our kin still breathing within them.'

Halla glared at the rebuke, but her posture relented slightly, and she gave a curt nod. 'So, you think I should go up the river with my people and hide?'

'Yes.'

'If the aim is to hide, why not just disperse in these lands, bury your weapons, pretend to submit, and, when spring arrives, resume the fight? Why subject yourselves to winter in the wilderness?' said another of the town's elders.

'Because some of us will not live under their rule, even for one day. Do you truly trust them not to kill us anyway?' Halla retorted.

'We were followed when we left Västerås, the Christians know this force exists, and they will come for us, it is only a question of when. You cannot hide in these lands without them finding you. My own warriors can return home, and live amongst their families, give up weapons as the Christians demand, and make fair claim to have chosen peace,' said Frode. 'They will hunt you, and they will find you, and when they do you will have to choose submission or death.'

'And that is an easy question, for we will never choose submission,' said Halla, restraining herself from spitting the words in anger.

'Which is why you cannot come into my lands,' said Frode with finality.

'So, the only option for those who wish to stay free is to run, to hide,' said Gustav. 'And in the north seems the best option. When the Christians learn that those who oppose them have gone into the hills, they will not look so hard for enemies in these lands, and the people here have a greater chance of survival.'

'Do you really believe that?' said Halla with exasperation. 'Do you really trust the Christians not to kill every man of fighting age, or to simply burn every town where one is found? Are you so foolish?'

'If we choose peace, and surrender our weapons, the Christians will allow us to live. They have made this clear in every town they reach,' Frode said, his face screwed up in pain at the shame of it.

'You are fools for believing that,' said Halla, shaking her head. 'They will seek revenge for us resisting, and I will not kneel before them and await their judgement.' She turned away from her brother. 'We will go north, and trust ourselves to the land and the winter, rather than Christian mercy and servitude.'

'It is a hard life up there,' said Svein, finally speaking again now that some of the tension was gone from the hall. 'It is no place for a great mass of the old or weak. Only the stoutest of people can survive the winter in those lands.'

'We are much tougher than you imagine, we old women,' Halla said with contempt.

'I see that,' said Svein with a hint of a smile. 'But I do not think you can take everyone.'

'It would be better for some to remain anyway,' said Frode.

Halla gritted her teeth at the thought of losing even more of her dwindling following, but saw there was no choice.

'And we can fill the bilges of those ships with tools and food,' said Frode.

'From where? We do not have enough,' asked Halla.

'This is still a market town, is it not?' Frode said, looking at Svein, who nodded. 'Then we will buy what is needed, and if that leaves this town short, we will replenish it with supplies from my own lands. That is acceptable, Svein?'

Svein nodded and smiled. 'We will be pleased to help.'

Halla still refused to acknowledge Frode's assistance, but she did at least refrain from further argument.

'If we are to return from hiding to fight in the spring, I will need a leader of men.' She looked around her remaining warriors, sitting in uncomfortable silence at the long tables. 'I cannot be your jarl, so who will lead you?'

'You can be our jarl, Halla. We would follow you without question,' said Leif, standing and looking at her with his hands in his belt.

'I thank you, Leif, but I know little of war or battles, and I am too old to learn to fight. In any case, if we are to gather support next year we need a war leader, someone with a name and respect, someone who can gather recruits and persuade others to join us. Will you do that, Leif, would you take up my husband's place?'

Leif blew out his cheeks and shook his head apologetically. 'I will fight for you whenever you require, and lead the men in battle, but I am no politician or governor.'

'Then who?' said Halla, scanning the room. There was silence, as her men looked around nervously. Those who might have been leaders had died in the battle, or, like Leif, simply couldn't bring themselves to take Ragnvald's place.

Halla looked along the tables, but few would meet her eye.

'It does seem like an awfully long way to go back home, now that I think about it. And those Danes on the lake, it would be tiring killing our way through them.' Halla flicked her searing gaze to Jarl Gustav, who looked back with a sly smile. 'I would be honoured to lend my name to your cause, and I'm sure my crews would be welcome in the winter, and in the battles beyond. We are up for it, aren't we, boys?' He turned to the dozen who stood behind him and they barked and spoke their assent.

Halla gave Gustav a stern look. 'You would be my jarl? I would happily pledge myself and my people to you, if you come with us.' Her spine stiffened as she spoke, and the distaste that she felt with having to swear to a new lord, an outsider, was on plain show.

'Jarl? No. No, I would come as your friend and your supporter. I am more than happy to let you lead your people, they are yours, not mine. But I know a little of war, and the leading of men in battle,' he said, giving the lie to the understatement with a cheeky grin that wrinkled his lined face. 'If you can make use of that, then it would be my pleasure to help.'

Halla slowly smiled, the first time she had smiled in the hall, and she nodded graciously to the old man. 'I would like that, very much.'

'Wonderful!' said Gustav with a boom in his voice. 'Let us all be friends again, for we all have so few friends left.' He strode up to the table and embraced Halla and then Frode warmly, although the siblings still stood apart from each other and Frode avoided Halla's eye. Then Gustav looked across it at Svein. 'Now, I have a hundred hungry men, and I hear you have some food?'

## Chapter 8

# The Last of the Loyal

GJALDIR WAS SITTING on the bank of the river in Karlsgrind, lost in his own thoughts, when he heard footsteps arrive, and turned to see who was coming. He smiled when he saw it was Leif.

'Ordulf, I thought an ox was stuck on the bank, but now I see it is just you.'

'Gjaldir,' he said with a smile to the huskarl.

'Sorry, yes. Gjaldir.'

It hadn't been long since he had been given his freeman name by Ragnvald, perhaps only two weeks, but already he felt the old name was part of some distant past. His new name was a gift from a great man, the man who had saved him, made him famous and then freed him. His mind quietly erased the memory that Ragnvald had also captured him, enslaved him, treated him like property, and once abandoned him in favour of a sword. Those things he did not think about anymore, the painful parts of his history cast aside like so many broken blades.

'So, what will you do?' Leif asked, sitting down on the bank next to him.

It was the day after they had arrived, and word had spread through their people that they had two choices: go west with Jarl Frode, to settle in his lands and try to live in peace with the Christians when they came, or go north along the river with Gustav and Halla, to find somewhere to live for the winter, deep in the inland areas, in the hills and lakes and forests.

Gjaldir smiled. 'I swore to go with Halla as a warrior, to serve her, and that is what I will do. I am a Norseman now, and I will uphold my oaths.'

Leif chuckled and punched him lightly on the shoulder. 'Look at you, our little Christian, taking our ways to heart.'

Gjaldir laughed. Leif's relentless mockery did not bother him, the warrior and he had once saved each other's lives, and the huskarl was the closest thing he had to a true friend.

'I am no longer a Christian,' he said casually.

'Really?' Leif looked surprised. 'How can you cast aside your nailed Christ, do you not believe he is real? I could not cast aside our gods.'

Gjaldir chewed his lip and shrugged. 'I am not sure I ever really believed what we were told by the priests, but everyone was a Christian, I was not even aware there was a different way, so I never questioned that I was too. But here, I have learned of Odin and Thor, and heard him working his anvil, and no one has compelled me to believe, yet I feel drawn to them.'

'Truly?'

'Truly. Why are you so surprised? We have spoken of this before, and you explained to me that I could hear Thor in the storm, and see Odin's wisdom in our leaders, and test the fruits of Frey's bounty in the fields.'

'Yes, I explained it, but I didn't expect a boneheaded smith like you to understand it, let alone believe it!'

Leif leaned back as Gjaldir gave him a friendly punch in return, one that nearly pushed the smaller man over as he laughed and tried to block it.

'Well, I am glad that you are coming with us, but you must go and see Halla, she wishes to speak to everyone who is coming north, and make sure they are put to best use. It will be a hard life, a hard winter, and we must all be used to our best extent. Come.'

Halla was holding court near the dock, Bjorn standing with her, watching from a respectful distance as others supervised the loading of the ships that would take them upriver. There was room for over five hundred people, if they loaded every ship to the brim for the three-day row upstream. It would not be comfortable, and the ships would be so laden that they would sink in even moderate wind or waves on the lake, but with their masts stripped out and left behind, their ballast reduced, and navigating the calm waters of the river, five hundred would fit into the seven ships. Three of Gustav's, and four they had bought from Svein's people for a chunk of their remaining wealth.

'If you keep them, the Christians will take them from you,' Gustav had told the man, and Svein had grumbled and protested, but eventually given in and agreed to sell.

Gustav's hundred warriors would join the hundred surviving fighting men of the battle who had chosen to go north with Halla. Frode and most of his men, and the rest of the warriors, hundreds of them, would go west. Some of Halla's people chose to go with him, unwilling or unable to go into the hinterland for winter. The ones who would go north did so out of loyalty, or out of refusal to accept living under Christian rule or to be subject to the whims of the conquerors who had razed Kalmar and Birka.

Leif waited until Halla was finished talking to a local merchant, negotiating for a hundred sacks of grain, and then stepped forwards, jerking his thumb back towards Gjaldir. 'Gjaldir has decided to come north with us, lady, if you'll have him.'

Halla looked at Gjaldir without a hint of warmth. 'It is possible a swordsmith will become useful later, you would be welcome.'

Gjaldir swallowed nervously. 'My lady, as I said before, I am no longer a smith.'

Halla screwed up her brows. 'You have forgotten the craft in two weeks?'

'No, I, um… I swore an oath never to forge another weapon, and to take up arms to defend my people instead.'

Halla's mouth twisted in distaste. 'A swordsmith who refuses to make weapons? What use is that to me? You wish to be a warrior, do you have any training or experience at all?'

Gjaldir was hurt at the question. 'As you know, I have killed men before.'

Leif looked at him, confused. 'Men? I saw you kill one, in the fight at the hall, what others did you kill while you were a slave?'

Gjaldir tensed and gulped. He had been referring to the men he had killed in the fight in Halla's hall, where treacherous guests had tried to take revenge on Halla for a feud with Ragnvald. But Halla had sworn him to secrecy for his involvement, for it was against the law for a slave to wield a weapon, even in defence of their masters, and questions might have been put to him that would have revealed what had happened to Halla in her bed, where the traitor Sten had pinned her down with a blade to her throat, and would have abused her so terribly, if Gjaldir and Brunhild had not intervened.

So, to protect his life, and her honour, he had kept his involvement in that fight a secret. He quickly fumbled an answer to the huskarl. 'Sorry, my speaking of the language is still not perfect, I meant man, not men.'

Leif nodded, accepting the explanation. 'Regardless, killing a man with a thrown hammer, and standing in the shieldwall, are not the same thing. Can you not be a smith also? What manner of oath did you swear, were there witnesses?'

'Yes, Dengir was there, and I cast my hammer into the forge, and swore I would never make another weapon as long as I lived.'

Bjorn whistled and shook his head. 'You cast the sign of Thor into the fire as you made this oath? That is a serious matter, a man should never break such an oath, or face terrible consequences.'

Even Leif's eyes widened. 'Yes, an oath to Thor, in front of a witness, it is a powerful thing.'

Halla sighed in frustration. 'So, a smith who cannot make a weapon, and a warrior who does not know how to wield one. What use can you be to us?'

Gjaldir was taken aback, and looked at Halla with hurt in his eyes, and saw not a shred of sympathy in her gaze.

'Well, he is a strong lad, he can help with all sorts of tasks, and he can be taught to fight. He has proven he is brave, by spring we will make a warrior of him. I bet he can fell a tree or cut logs like no other.' Leif looked at Gjaldir with a smirk. 'If you can swing a hammer, you can swing an axe, yes?'

Gjaldir mumbled his agreement.

'Good,' Halla snapped. 'You are now Gjaldir the woodcutter, that will indeed be useful. You may come with us.'

'Thank you, my lady,' Gjaldir mumbled, and Halla waved the two of them away, beckoning to the next people who were waiting, a warrior and his family.

'Why does she dislike me?' moaned Gjaldir as the two men walked away a distance towards the dock.

Leif laughed. 'She doesn't hate you, she is simply doing her duty. She is the lord now, and the lord can have no weakness, no favourites. Every one of her people is her responsibility, and she is about to lead them into a hard life. She does not have time to care for your feelings. Although, if you wanted thanks, you could have given her something of value, to pay the locals for equipment and provisions for our journey. But I know a recent freedman like you would have nothing to give.'

Gjaldir bristled at this, his pride pricked. 'Well, I did have…' And then he stopped himself with a quiet curse.

'You did? Did what?' Leif looked at him quizzically.

'Nothing.'

'What, a few pennies? What did you have? And how did you lose it?'

'I had a bag of silver and gold, as big as your head,' replied Gjaldir, bridling at the questions.

Leif laughed. 'As big as my head? When?'

'Dengir gave it to me, when I left.'

Leif's smile faded. 'After the battle?'

'Yes.'

'What did you do with it?'

'I gave it back, I refused it,' said Gjaldir, sticking his chin out even as his pride faded and he started to feel foolish. Refusing the silver had seemed like the right thing at the time, he had been wealthy once before in his life, and the silver had brought him nothing but trouble, and nearly led to his death.

'You had a fortune, and you gave it back? Did you not think we might need it? That it might be useful on this journey?'

Gjaldir huffed and tried to think of a retort, but the truth was no, he had not thought of using it for others, and he looked away in shame.

Leif sighed in genuine irritation. 'You are a strange man, Gjaldir. Are all you Christians idiots?' And he looked away to the river.

The argument was prevented from continuing when they saw a single small boat, one the locals used to ferry across the river, going to the far bank, where two dozen armed men had appeared and were waiting at the small dock there.

'Who are they?' asked Gjaldir.

'I don't know, but ours, not Christians.' Leif set off down to the dock with Gjaldir following, and they stood in silence and waited as the men were brought across in two groups.

The lead man in the first boat got out and strode up to Leif, his face drawn. 'Asel!' exclaimed Leif, his excitement at seeing it was Frode's huskarl fading as he saw the man's expression, which was dark indeed.

'Leif, good to see you. Where is the jarl?'

'He is in the hall.' Asel grunted and started to walk off, but Leif caught his arm. 'Tell me, what troubles you? My lady must know.'

'Frode will tell her.'

'They are not saying much to each other. Asel, save us the time and tell me now.'

Asel thought for a moment and then nodded. 'The Christians are at Västerås, a thousand of them, armed for war.'

'Shit.'

'Indeed.'

'Are they coming this way?'

'Not yet, but certainly they will. Their patrols are already on the road behind us. I expect they will come soon.'

As the two men spoke, the second boatload of men was coming across.

'Who are these men with you? You left with so few, and come back with so many.'

Asel looked uncomfortable. 'They are Norwegians, survivors of the battle.'

'Norwegians? Are they Sigurd's men?' Asel gave a strange look and Leif pressed him. 'Do they have news of the king?'

Asel did not answer, and Leif peered at the approaching boat, and then his eyes widened as he recognised the man who stood in the prow. 'Gunnar!'

He scanned the rest of the boat and could not make out who else was there, and looked at Asel in excitement. 'Is the king with them?' He knew Gunnar would never leave Sigurd's side.

Asel shook his head once. 'The king is dead. These are his huskarls, those who remain alive. Do not ask them what happened to the king, they will not say. Only that he is no longer alive.'

Leif felt the news as a physical blow, and he did not resist as Asel removed Leif's hand from his arm, and walked off up the bank towards the hall, to relay the news to Frode.

Gjaldir stood in awkward silence as Frode struggled with the revelation, and then walked the few steps down the bank to meet the boat as it arrived, and Gunnar stepped stiffly from the bow onto the boards.

Leif stopped in front of Gunnar, and the Norwegian gave him a look of recognition and a curt nod, then turned to help his men and their equipment out of the boat.

'Gunnar, I… Is it true?'

Gunnar turned briefly to Leif and dipped his chin once, then moved past without talking, heading up the bank, the rest of his Norwegians, twenty or so, following behind in a glum procession.

Leif looked at Gjaldir and then turned to follow them without a word, hurrying over to where Halla was still talking to a small queue of her people. Gjaldir considered following, but Sigurd had not been his king, and apart from a brief interaction, he had never met Gunnar. So he stayed down on the docks, secretly hoping someone would give him something to do.

Frode was seated in the hall with Gustav, talking to Asel, when Gunnar came into the hall. Having only just heard that the man was alive, and that the king was not, Frode stood and gave the king's champion a look of mixed relief and sadness, and waved him over.

Gunnar walked over and nodded to Gustav and Frode, and then looked around the hall at the scattering of other warriors who were there.

Frode caught the hint and raised his voice. 'Clear the hall.' Warriors looked up in surprise and annoyance, but then men got to their feet and walked out in groups, muttering and looking back in confusion.

Just as the last were leaving, Halla arrived in the doorway, breathless, and forced her way through the gaggle without ceremony, Leif on her heels.

'Is it true?' she said in a strained voice.

Frode looked up irritably, and gestured to the last of the warriors who were leaving to hurry, and they closed the door behind them.

'Well?' Halla demanded.

'We haven't spoken yet, come, sit with us,' said Gustav.

Gunnar did not speak as Halla rushed to join them, only looking at Gustav and Frode uncomfortably. 'Anything you can say to us you can say to Lady Halla. She is Jarl Ragnvald's widow,' said Gustav.

Gunnar nodded slowly and composed himself. 'King Sigurd is dead,' he finally said, voice heavy with sadness.

Halla moaned softly and put her head in her hands. Gustav grimaced. Frode just nodded thoughtfully. 'What happened? How did he die? I saw you carry him from the field, but we were separated. Where did you go, and how do you come to join us here?'

Gunnar stared at his hands for a moment. 'We took him into hiding in a village. The Christians came and we were forced to leave, to go into the woods. The king died some days after. I have sworn to say no more about it. We all did.'

Frode looked taken aback. 'Why?'

'Because the Christians will hunt for him, and our silence will protect him in death, as we failed to protect him in life. I will never speak of it again, and do not ask me to. Those are the final words any of us will ever speak of the death of King Sigurd Magnusson.' Gustav looked around the group, and they could see the finality in his cold eyes.

Gustav and Frode looked at each other and Frode shrugged. There was nothing more they could say.

'Shall we tell the people?' asked Frode.

Gustav thought about it for a good time, and then nodded. 'They will find out anyway, better to hear the truth from us, than gossip from a dozen mouths.'

Halla did not speak, did not look up, and Gustav put a

comforting hand on her shoulder. 'This is not the end, we knew that he might be gone.'

'With Sigurd gone, who will fight for his kingdom?' She looked up suddenly. 'Who will be king?'

'No one,' said Gunnar. 'The king forbade it, the title died with him. There will not be another king of all the Norse.'

Gustav looked at Gunnar. 'I understand. Raising a new king now would be a futile gesture. What will you and your men do?'

Gunnar looked out towards the door, and then back at Gustav. 'They are going home.'

'You have given up?' said Halla with a tinge of anger. 'Why did you come to join us?'

'I did not know you were here. We were headed for Lake Vänern, where the rest of the survivors of our forces are gathering, and from there, they will go home before winter sets in again.'

'The rest? How many of you survived the battle?'

'A little under a thousand men of Norway escaped with Jarl Steinar.'

'A thousand! We have not seen them, or heard from them. Why did they not stay with the king?'

'The king ordered them to leave, he could not travel, and he bade them return home. It was his final order. It is no surprise you have not seen them. They left immediately and marched hard, with orders to stop for nothing. They went through the woods to the north, not along the road. They will be ahead of us by a week or more.'

'A thousand men! Oh, what we could do with a thousand men, why did they leave?' gasped Halla.

'They left because the king ordered them to.'

'But why?'

'I did not question my king, he wished for them to return home, and save Norway if they could.'

'Won't the man who has made himself king of Norway, and his Christian friends, prevent them?'

'Perhaps, but with such a large, battle-hardened force, Steinar might be able to make an accommodation with them. He is a shrewd politician.'

'I can't believe the king gave up on us.'

'The king gave his life for you,' snapped Gunnar, but there was little anger in his voice, perhaps more shame. 'Perhaps one in five of all the Norwegians who stood in battle outside Uppsala survived to go home. My people have given all that they can for Sweden.'

'I'm sorry, Gunnar. My sister does not question your honour, she only mourns for what is lost.' Halla shot Frode a foul look, but did not argue. 'You keep saying "they". What of you?'

Gunnar nodded and stared at his hands again. 'I am not going with them.'

'Why?' Gustav asked. 'Did your king not order it?'

'My king gave me no instruction, only Steinar.'

'Then why not go home with them? Are all your men going?

'Most of them. I think a few will remain if I do. I have not told them yet what I intend to do. In truth, I was not sure until now. I did not know if there was anyone left to continue the fight.'

'You would continue to fight, when all your countrymen go home?'

'Yes.'

'Why?'

Gunnar looked at Halla and his eyes could not meet the intensity of her stare. 'My family are all dead and I was not there to protect them, or die alongside them. I was not there because I was here protecting my king, and I failed that also. I have failed in every duty, and have nothing but shame to return to. I cannot go back to Norway as the huskarl who lost his family and his king. I will stay here, and continue the fight that has taken everything from me, and everyone I cared about.'

'You would stay here to get revenge?' asked Frode.

'Revenge is for stories and fools. I will stay because if I can save even one family, one warrior, from the ravages of this war, then my life will yet have some meaning.'

'We are going north, Gustav and I, with nearly two hundred warriors, and three hundred of my people. We will survive the winter, and in the spring, we will start to take back our home. Will you come with us?'

Gunnar looked at Halla and Gustav, and nodded. 'I will. But I will not swear to your service, Jarl Gustav; my lord will forever be Sigurd, and I failed him and am unworthy to give my oath to another.'

Gustav nodded. 'I understand, and it is not required. We will need no masters or lords where we are going. But an experienced warrior and leader like you, I would be glad to have by our side.'

'Then it is done. I will speak to my men, I expect most of them to continue west, to join the rest of our people, but will you take any who choose to remain?'

'Yes, of course. You will all be welcome. We have some Norwegians with us already, scattered survivors of the battle who joined us on our journey here.'

Gunnar looked surprised and then frowned. 'Would you allow them to leave, and go with my men, if they chose to?'

Halla grimaced, every warrior was precious, and she had not hoped to lose more than she gained with Gunnar's arrival. But she could not force them. She shrugged. 'It is their free choice, I cannot take the unwilling.'

'That is good of you, lady. Thank you.' Gunnar stood from the table and walked out of the hall, leaving the rest glum and silent, pondering the fate of the people now, without the mighty Sigurd to lead them.

# Chapter 9

# Voyage of the Valiant

THE NEXT MORNING, the ships were packed and ready to depart. The host of warriors and refugees split into two, the far greater half to march west with Jarl Frode, to go home and lay down their weapons, to accept whatever peace the Christians chose. The lesser part to go north, up the river, to make their own fate in the cold embrace of the hinterlands, to trade comfort for a chance at freedom.

Gjaldir was surprised to be invited into the largest boat by Leif, the ship that would carry Halla and her closest warriors and followers. He did not ask why, he merely collected his belongings and unfamiliar weapons and made himself space in the bow, out of habit. Leif looked over and chided him. 'Gjaldir, on a bench, you are a warrior now and you will carry an oar as well as a shield.'

Gjaldir blushed and nodded, shifting his stuff to an empty space below a bench, and sitting down, unsure of what to do. Other warriors were helping people find a space in the increasingly crowded boat, in the bow or stern, or along the centre where the sail would normally go.

As the packing went on, and warriors started passing out oars,

Gjaldir saw Gunnar arrive on the dock with three warriors in tow. The former king's huskarl went over to Halla and Leif and looked at the ship. 'These men wish to come with me, all good warriors.'

Halla looked over the three warriors, wearing their weapons and carrying tied bundles of their maille and belongings. The three men had that quiet air of confidence and experience that she had seen with many of the senior warriors in Ragnvald's crews.

'They are welcome, Leif will find you benches,' Halla said without much consideration, turning to attend to another matter, while Leif stepped forwards and clasped the first man by the arm. 'Vidar, good to see you again, you wily worm. How did you survive the war?' asked Leif with a grin, slapping the beardless, long-haired Dane and smiling.

'No man had the skill to kill me!' said the man in reply with a broad grin. Vidar had been declared the champion at the siege of Jönköping, after defeating Gunnar in a mock duel with axes, by speed and trickery that had left the king speechless with shock, and earned himself a place in the king's bodyguard.

'No man had the luck,' growled Gunnar. 'Half a dozen times he should have died, but Hel won't take him.'

The old huskarl pointed at the other two men. 'The red-haired one is Eric Firebeard Lokinsson. And no, the name is not because of the colour of his hair, it is because he was dragged from a burning building at København behind the king, with his whole face on fire.' The man with the scraggly red beard smiled and nodded, and Gjaldir saw that the man's face bore the scars of the fire, and his beard was patchy from it.

Gunnar jerked his thumb at the final man, who had a thick, short-cropped black beard and who did not appear to be paying any interest to Leif, staring at the river instead. 'And this is Harald Freysson. Don't be offended by his ways, he has no humour or way with people, he manages to anger every man who speaks to him, but a better warrior in the shieldwall you will not find. Best not to speak to him unless it's giving orders.' Harald did not even acknowledge the introduction, and Gunnar just shrugged it off when Leif raised an eyebrow.

'Well, I am glad to have four warriors like you to come with us. I will find you some benches.' Leif started shuffling men around in the crowded ship, to get two benches together for the Norwegians. Gjaldir ended up sitting one row behind the four men, near the bow, next to a Svear warrior he did not know. Leif sat two rows behind him, on the first bench in the bow.

The Svear warrior looked at him suspiciously as Gjaldir fumbled with the oar he had been passed, and struggled to get it through the oarhole and seated. 'Have you done this before?' the man growled.

'Uh, no,' said Gjaldir sheepishly.

'By Odin's shaft, swap. I will take the first seat, and you watch me carefully before your turn.' Gjaldir was sitting on the outboard end of the bench, nearest the water, and he got unsteadily to his feet and climbed over the swearing warrior as others shouted at him to sit down. Finally, the warrior got control of the oar and Gjaldir sat feeling useless as everyone else settled.

Each bench sat two people, the one nearest the water would row, and the one inboard would wait for the order to swap. Like that, the ship could be rowed all day and the crews remain relatively fresh. In the smaller ships, with less space, there would only be one man on each bench, and those ships, though faster and more agile under oar, would have to stop to rest their crews.

The ship was shoved off from the bank and Gjaldir watched as the rowers aligned their oars and sat ready with them resting in the water, before Leif shouted to pull. The ship was already pointed in the right direction, so they were off upriver immediately, with the other ships pushing off and following them in an uneven column. There were not enough experienced rowers to man all the ships, and two of them became tangled and spun around in the channel in a crescendo of clanging wood and shouted curses.

Eventually the ragtag fleet arranged itself into some semblance of order, and followed Halla's boat upstream, beginning the long row against the current into the narrowing channel.

Jarl Frode leant against a building, with his huskarl Asel standing moodily at his side, watching his sister's fleet leave.

'You would rather have gone with them?' he asked.

Asel grunted and did not look at him or argue. Frode sighed. Asel was a proud man, and deeply wounded at the thought that they would surrender to the Christians while others still fought. The idea had been too much for some of his men, who had chosen to go with Halla instead of going home to their families. Frode had had no choice but to let them go, or risk dissension or even rebellion.

He recognised that there were advantages to allowing those who opposed him to go, and he hoped they would help keep Halla safe.

'There were not enough ships for us all anyway.'

'We have could have marched.'

'And the Christians could have followed and caught us. Enough, the decision is made, the fates will decree the rest. It is time for us to return home, to our families, and to peace.' Frode pushed away from the wall wearily, and turned again to check the opposite bank. There was still no sign of the Christians there, neither scouts nor army, but he knew it would not be long.

'Let's finish the preparations to march, we will be in Arbugæ by sunset if we leave now.'

Arbugæ sat alongside its own river, nestling in the elbow of a broad bend. The river ended at the western tip of Lǫgrinn and wound its way westwards following a broad plain of rich farmland. The river did not go so far west as the river at Karlsgrind went north, nor did it reach the wildlands of the interior. It originated at a lake just thirty miles inland, but it allowed Frode and his people to travel the length of his lands with ease, from the lake to the west, down to Arbugæ and then on into the great lake of Lǫgrinn, and from there the access to the cold sea beyond.

This river was the old traders' path to Norway and Denmark. From the lake, traders could disembark and go south to Lake Vättern, and Jönköping, and from there to Scania. Or they could go west, through the sparsely populated hills and forests that littered the land to the north of the Tiveden, the great forest on the border between the old kingdoms of the Svear and the Geats.

Finally, following that path they would come to the rich and ancient lands of Värmland, bordering the north shore of the vast Lake Vänern. From there, they could sail down the lake, a distance so great it would take four days under oars, or two in a good wind, to reach the far end. Or they could continue west, taking the hard overland road to Anslo and Norway, the route the Norwegian survivors would be taking.

In times gone by, now just stories barely remembered by the skalds and the old men, the kingdoms of Sweden and Norway had fought battles on Lake Vänern when it was frozen in winter, in the days of heroes and giants, before the Norse started looking outwards across the sea for new conquests.

And so Frode's lands, and his home of Arbugæ, were the gateway to the entire west, and all who wished to travel overland to Norway or Skania would travel through them. It could have made him a powerful and influential man, if he had wished it, but it had never been in his nature.

Frode had been a warrior, when required, but he never relished battle as his brother-in-law Ragnvald had done. He had spent his life carefully avoiding starting conflict, making powerful friends while himself never appearing powerful enough to make anyone feel threatened. He had gone to war alongside Ragnvald to honour their friendship and family bond, and in the recent Crusades, to fight for his people and his king, but he had always wished only to return home to peace. He was not a Viking, and his desire was to govern, not conquer.

Now, as his defeated warriors marched the final miles back to those quiet places where he had grown to manhood, and where he had taken over his uncle's title when the old jarl died childless, he hoped they would find peace. But he knew the storm followed them, as surely as night follows day, and Frode shivered at the anticipation of the darkness it would bring.

## CHAPTER 10

# TRIAL BY FIRE

REINHARD STARED AT the river in quiet contemplation as Hugues conferred with his senior men. His finger drummed on his saddle pommel in quiet irritation at the delay. Finally, he broke his intemperate silence.

'How long will it take to send for ships?' asked Reinhard.

'There were a few in Västerås, my men secured them, they are on the way. But we will have to spend a day scouting the far bank before we cross.'

'Why?'

'Because I don't want to watch the first hundred men across get massacred by whoever is hidden in or behind those buildings.'

Reinhard furrowed his brows. 'We haven't seen any armed men. Do you think they are still here?'

'You wouldn't see them, so I don't know if they are here, but I intend to find out before we cross.'

'It won't matter.'

'What?'

'You won't need to.'

Hugues's face darkened and he stared at Reinhard with anger

brewing. 'I thought we were clear you would not be interfering in military matters.'

'Hugues, I am not,' said Reinhard with a chuckle.

'It is my decision when we cross, and how.'

'I know, I'm just anticipating your mind will change.'

Hugues stiffened in anger. 'None of your games, you won't change my mind.'

'Be calm, my friend, I won't, but they might,' Reinhard said with an infuriating smile, pointing across the river.

Hugues turned to follow the outstretched finger, and saw that a dozen of the townsfolk on the other side were crewing the lone boat that lay alongside the dock. They were quite obviously unarmed, and most were older men. Not a threat.

Hugues stiffened and Reinhard stifled a childish expression of glee at the baron's obvious fury at having lost his temper. The Grandsteward turned away from Reinhard and waited for the boat to get underway from the dock and cross the river, not going down to wait for it on the water's edge, perhaps feeling it would make him look petulant.

The boat slowly rowed over, doing everything it could to make clear they meant no threat, and as the boat reached the dock on the eastern bank below the masters of the Order, three of the occupants carefully climbed out. There was a middle-aged man, still healthy looking and spry, with a good head of neat hair and fine clothes, and two older men. All three hesitantly walked up the hill, trying to look calm and confident, but clearly intimidated by the silent, motionless ranks of white surcoated soldiers arrayed above them.

Hugues had thought it ridiculous when Reinhard suggested they train the Order soldiers to stand motionless in ranks whenever ordered, as if guarding a king's table, but it was for moments exactly like this that it was done, and Reinhard saw the effect on the faces of the heathens as they warily approached the silent ranks. A few hundred armoured men in their bright surcoats and golden crosses, standing motionless in the sun, was an impressive and intimidating sight indeed.

Finally, as the men looked thoroughly unsure what to do, Hugues clicked his tongue and walked his horse over towards the tiny delegation, stopping and staring at them in silence as Reinhard followed with considerably less grace.

The middle-aged man smiled and bowed low, in a reasonable attempt at the German style, and spoke some of his people's babbling language.

Beside Reinhard's horse, his interpreter waited patiently. The man, Gotfrid, was a full brother of the Order, a Saxon soldier who had been captured by the Norse in a raid a dozen years ago, and kept as a slave in the Norselands until the Crusade freed him. He had been all too willing, desperately willing, to join the ranks of the brotherhood and serve God in the Crusade against his erstwhile masters.

'This is Svein, he is the leader of the town we see on the other side of the river, which is called Karlsgrind. He welcomes us, and says that we are free to cross and enter the town and will not be resisted,' Gotfrid relayed.

Hugues nodded to the interpreter. 'Make him the offer,' he said, referring to the choice of the sword or the cross. There was a brief exchange and the nervous man nodded.

'He chooses the cross, my lord. He… it is complicated, but he says this town has, by tradition, always been owned by no lord, and takes no sides. It offers free passage for anyone, and protected in its status by the consent of those around. He is very happy to allow your priests into the town, and will provide what they need. But he is concerned about the demand for weapons, they have almost none, just what is needed for hunting and cutting wood. Because this town does not take sides, they do not need weapons.'

Reinhard raised his brows at the development. *An unarmed Norse settlement? What next, an honest market seller?*

Hugues was clearly not sure how to react to this, or even if he should believe it, and sighing inwardly, turned to Reinhard. 'What do you think?'

Reinhard pursed his lips and thought for a moment. 'It's too ridiculous to be a lie. We would find out in a few moments of questioning if it was.'

'Hmm, we should do the questioning anyway.'

'We should.'

Gotfrid waited politely for them to finish talking, and addressed them again. 'Svein asks if you have any ships, it will take a long time to ferry your army with his single boat.'

Hugues looked at the town, and the length of the dock, and looked carefully at Reinhard. 'Perhaps add why there is only a single boat in a town this size, with a dock this size, to your list of questions.'

Reinhard's eyes did a rapid scan of the far bank and widened a fraction. 'Yes, good point, we will do, but not until we are across and in control. When will our ships arrive?'

'I don't know, I would guess not in time to cross this evening.'

'Well, shall we make camp?'

'Yes.'

The ships arrived shortly afterwards, the half-made camp was rapidly broken and the Order began to cross the river, one hundred men at a time, fully armed and armoured. The leading groups fanned out into town and made sure the banks and nearby buildings were safe, ignoring the locals.

When Dietmar, leading the crossing, was happy it was safe, he waved the second wave across.

By darkness the whole force, and its baggage, was safely across the river, and setting out a new camp in the bare fields to the west, as Hugues and Reinhard ordered Svein to gather the town's elders and leaders in the hall where they were seated in a group on one side of the hall. He looked around the seated group, who were looking nervously up at the armed men who casually surrounded them, and nodded to himself in satisfaction. The atmosphere was just right. *They must learn quickly that they are not in control.*

Gotfrid laid out Reinhard's demands, that the hall and the space opposite the hall be given over to the Order to build a church and chapter buildings, removing or re-purposing whatever buildings currently stood there, that whatever weapons they possessed be turned over, and that the town's leaders swear fealty to the Order.

Faces fell in the group of townsfolk at the demands, but Svein quietened them and gritted his teeth, nodding his acceptance, before asking Gotfrid something.

'Svein asks, with what he calls respect, that the town's traditions and status as a neutral territory be respected, and in return, he offers total loyalty and support for the Order, and that there will be no trouble allowing Christianity here and all that you have requested will be done without argument.'

Reinhard frowned. This town marked the very easternmost border of the Order's gifted lands, and would be permanently under their control. Västerås and the other towns they had passed through on their journey would be given over to Duke Lothair, to grant as fiefs to his followers.

But Karlsgrind would be run by the Order, and Reinhard had no interest in their notions of neutrality or traditions of independence. Quite the opposite, he saw it as a serious problem. There would be no special treatment in the lands of the Order, and no reason for the town's special status to continue. It was a problem he had not yet decided how to address.

'Ask Svein what he means by neutrality but loyalty. They cannot be the same?'

Gotfrid listened to the nervous man for a while. 'He says that this town does not have a lord, and does not take sides in war. That is their neutrality. But in return, as loyalty, they will provide workers, food, a tithe of their wealth to support the Church.'

Reinhard found himself considering the offer for a moment. Truthfully it was reasonable and fair. But if one town received special status, others would believe they could too. He could make a counteroffer asking for more, such as some men to fight with the Order... *But we are not here to bargain, we are here to be obeyed.*

So Reinhard ignored the question, and responded with another. 'Where are his ships?'

The question visibly confused Svein, and then worried him. 'He says they went up the river.'

'Why?'

There was a sudden conference between the locals at this question, hissed words and nervous looks. Reinhard noted that with interest and then stamped it out quickly. 'Sir Dietmar, silence them.' The quicker you got answers to difficult questions, the more honest they tended to be, or easier lies to unravel.

Dietmar and his men shouted at the locals and, despite the words not being understood, the intent was, and the hall quickly fell to stillness.

'Ask the question again,' said Reinhard softly. 'If he is loyal as he claims, he will answer instantly and honestly.'

Gotfrid nodded and turned to Svein, having a short conversation before turning back. 'The enemy survivors and fleeing civilians that passed through here, they split up into two groups. Most of them went west, heading home, the rest of them went north up the river, in his boats.'

'Did they steal these boats?'

'No.'

Reinhard stared at Svein with a scowl. 'How is providing boats to my enemy neutrality?'

Svein's answers were getting increasingly worried, and the man was sweating and waving his hands animatedly. 'He sold them. He says he would do the same for us, or anyone. All are free to travel the river or buy and sell what they choose here. It is a market town.'

'So he would provide us with boats, to chase the fleeing army north,' said Reinhard with a smile.

Svein's face fell, and he shook his head dumbly at the interpreter.

'Oh, he cannot? I see, it is because he has already given his ships away, and thus cannot give us equal treatment. We were pursuing our enemy, and were a day behind, and now are unable to continue the pursuit, because of Svein. Is this loyalty and neutrality?'

'He apologises, he will give you more ships, when he can find or buy some.'

'Which will be when?

'He does not know.'

Reinhard smiled and nodded. 'So he has helped our enemy escape us, and wants to have special privileges?'

Svein broke into a frenzy of apology at that accusation, the group around him looking increasingly nervous. The Norseman finally got up from his seat and knelt on the floor, speaking earnestly and quickly to Gotfrid.

'He says it was a terrible mistake, he did not know that you would want to pursue, he is not a man of war, but a trader. He promises that no such thing will ever happen again and begs your forgiveness.'

Reinhard looked at the kneeling man, and then at Hugues with a questioning glance. Hugues did little but turn down the corner of his mouth, this was Reinhard's territory and the baron had no interest in getting involved.

Reinhard let the man apologise and worry a little longer, milking the moment, before giving his judgement. 'I will forgive you, but in payment I will require compensation. Thirty men, to help us subdue this province. And out of respect for that neutrality, I will only require those people once.'

Gotfrid relayed the order, and Svein nodded in relief as Gotfrid translated. 'He is very happy, but he is not sure what use thirty of his people will be to you, there are no warriors here.'

'I did not say I needed warriors, only that I needed his people.'

'Then he agrees.'

'I did not ask his agreement, I merely told him what was going to happen.' Reinhard turned to Dietmar. 'Leave thirty of them in the hall, bring the rest outside with Svein and all of your men too. I do not care which thirty are left inside to help us. Gotfrid, tell the thirty to sit here and wait for my instructions.'

Dietmar nodded, and shouted the orders, while Gotfrid explained in Norse. There was confusion and reluctance as the Order soldiers divided the crowd and left the greater part, the thirty, sitting confused on the benches, and shepherded the rest out, into the night.

Svein and the remaining locals stood in a loose group chattering quietly to each other in nervous confusion while Reinhard wanted for the last Order soldiers to leave the hall. He beckoned Svein over and the man walked over, the picture of subservience. 'You will remember this day, and not break faith with me again. We do not tolerate those who defy us, or give aid to our enemies.'

Svein nodded emphatically as Gotfrid spoke. 'He says he will not.'

'Again, I was not asking him, I was telling him,' Reinhard said, turning to Dietmar and ignoring Svein. 'Have your men bar the doors from the outside and surround the hall. Then burn it.'

'Sir?' asked Dietmar, shocked. Reinhard scowled at the man and took a step towards him.

'We said that any town or settlement who resisted us, we would burn their homes, with them inside. I am doing them a great mercy by only burning this one.'

Someone in the Norse group understood their language, because there was a sudden outpouring of panic, and an old man stepped from the group towards Reinhard and addressed him in broken German. 'Lord, you said we were forgiven! That you needed those thirty to help you subdue the area!'

Reinhard looked up in surprise. 'I did. And *you* are forgiven. And those thirty *will* help me. Their deaths will serve as a warning that all will hear, that there will be retribution for any acts of help to our enemy, and no tolerance for disloyalty. I said I only needed them once, and I spoke the truth. After this, their service to me will be ended.'

The man gaped, horrified, but Reinhard snapped his fingers at an Order soldier and signalled him to take the man away with a wave. He turned his eyes on Dietmar, who had still not given the order he had requested. 'Brother Dietmar, is there something you do not understand?' he said icily.

'Your excellency, I… they are old men and… This is not right.'

Reinhard took a step towards the fully armoured knight, who was half a head taller than him, and smiled with a sharpness that conveyed no humour at all. 'You took an oath to obey, I am deeply disappointed. I will not waste time with threats on a man of your reputation. You are dismissed from your command.'

Reinhard stepped past the appalled knight, looking at the soldiers arrayed around, eyes settling on one. 'Brother Roland, are you ready to give more service to the Lord, and perform his work on this earth, without question or doubt? You, surely, of all people, will not turn your back on your duty. Will you take your fallen brother's place?'

Sieur de Blanchant stood forwards, hand on the hilt of his holy sword, and nodded nervously. 'Yes, Grandmaster.'

Reinhard felt Hugues's anger as he ran roughshod over their agreement not to meddle in the military affairs of the Order, but he didn't care in the slightest. There were times to conduct the gathering of power and times to assert it. 'Then carry out the duty that the Lord requires.'

Roland composed himself for a moment and then stepped

forwards, pointing at men and sending them off to all sides of the building, getting others to secure the doors.

Reinhard stood and watched the men barricade the doors, heard the muffled cries of alarm and pounding from inside, and felt Hugues come to stand next to him, the anger coming off the man in waves.

'Was that truly necessary?' the baron hissed.

'Yes. It sends a message, and we needed to clear this hall anyway to build the church. Duke Henry told us he wanted a clear statement of intent made, I think this will suffice. Those who were allowed to leave the meeting will spread the story, and all will know what becomes of those who help men who still resist us.'

'That, as you know, is not what I meant. Don't pretend to be a child.'

'Oh, you mean with Dietmar and Roland? I felt the need in the moment, and it had to be decisive and quick, for the same reasons. The word will spread that any disobeying of orders will not be tolerated. If I had taken the time to confer with you it would have shown nothing but weakness.'

'And instead you made me look weak, word will spread of that too,' said Hugues bitterly.

'Only if it appears we are not in agreement, so I suggest we don't allow that to happen,' said Reinhard with a glimmer in his eye, as the first torches were run along the outside of the thatch.

The furious baron did not argue further, and stalked away, unwilling to watch as the flames caught hold and the cries from within the barn become panicked and loud, and the people in the square were forced to watch, cowed and weeping, by the ring of stonefaced soldiers.

Reinhard watched as the wood of the roof took light, rubbing his thumb over the worn surface of the crucifix that hung around his neck. The old timbers crackled and shivered as vast swathes of thatch roared and the glare and heat of the flames made men shield their eyes and back away around the perimeter of the doomed building.

Reinhard smiled and looked on as the flames soared and the walls began to burn, as the shouts became screams of horror and pain, and as the hasty barricade at the doors failed when a roof beam crashed through it from above.

He did not react when several smoke-wreathed figures, coughing and swatting at their hair and clothes, ran out into the square, to be cut down by waiting blades.

He clasped his hands in prayer as a final figure, clothes alight and head encased in fire, staggered from the doors and fell drunkenly to his knees.

His lips moved in quiet recital, the screams and cries of the watching Norse preventing his words from carrying to anyone else in the firelit scene. 'And by his fire we will cleanse, by its light he will be seen – and by its fury they shall know our name.'

## CHAPTER 11

# THE WORD OF LAW

SVEIN WEPT SOFTLY in the corner as Reinhard sat, picking at a torn fingernail, trying to smooth its ragged edge.

He had not participated in the questioning himself, of course. As a senior man of the Church he was above such things, but Gotfrid the freed slave had no such compunctions, and Svein, already reduced to a weeping mess by the burning of his hall, had been a veritable fount of information.

'Is there anything else you want to know, Grandmaster?' Gotfrid asked.

Reinhard chewed it over and then shook his head. 'No, I think that is sufficient.'

'What shall I do with him? I can make it quick, dispose of the body.'

Reinhard wrinkled his nose in distaste. 'No, no need. Let him go back amongst his people, let them see him and his despair, the man who caused the death of so many of his friends. He serves as a good warning. We will not have trouble here again.' Reinhard stood and offered his ring for Gotfrid to kiss, and the man dutifully did so. 'Well done, my son. You have served the Order well. The information you pulled from this poor wretch will save many lives, and further the cause of the Lord. I thank you for your service.' He allowed the thrilled man a beaming and beneficent smile, and left the small house, mulling over what he had learned.

Eventually, when he was sure of his conclusions, he went to find Hugues. The thought of having to now persuade Hugues filled him with displeasure. The rift between them was growing, and Hugues was still too useful to do without, so he would have to manage the man, while not allowing him to interfere in his goals. In any case, it was time to move on, west towards their final destination in Arbugæ.

Baron Hugues looked up as the mounted man cantered down the road towards them. The man reined in beside them and nodded his head to Hugues. 'Grandsteward, there is a man on the road ahead, a mile outside the town. He says he is the commander of the forces we are pursuing, and he wishes to speak to you.'

Hugues looked surprised. 'Have you scouted around, there is no ambush?'

'A mile in every direction, he is completely alone.'

'Disarm him and bring him to me.'

'He carries no weapons.'

'No weapons?' Hugues paused. 'How strange. Well, bring him anyway.'

Reinhard looked over at his companion, who had barely spoken to him in the three days since the burning of the hall at Karlsgrind. 'Do we wish to speak to him? Normally we do not let them speak before we have made our…'

'I don't ask for your opinion on this military matter. It is a meeting of the commander of our force and the commander of theirs, under the auspice of peace. It is the traditional way of doing things and that matters,' said Hugues sharply, kicking his horse into a trot and leaving Reinhard fuming behind him.

It was not long before he found the group of wary vanguard knights escorting a lone Norseman back down the column. Hugues stopped, and brusquely ordered the troops on the road to halt, indicating the knights should follow him with the captive, off the side of the road and into the field beside it, out of earshot of the main body of men.

He looked the man up and down and saw nothing exceptional. A well-dressed man in middle age, a well-groomed brown beard and a head of hair that was starting to recede. The man looked completely calm. *No, it was more than that. Dejected.*

Hugues clicked his fingers at Gotfrid to translate. 'Ask him who he is.'

'I am Jarl Frode, ruler of these lands that you are entering, and the commander of the force you are pursuing,' said the man in passable French, stunning Hugues for a moment.

'You speak my French? Why?'

'I have family in Normandy, I spent much of my youth there.'

Hugues nodded in understanding. There was still a strong lineage of Norsemen living in northern Normandy. They had come first as raiders, then invaders and settlers three hundred years before, but now were their own separate duchy, ostensibly within the kingdom of France but in practice independent and now with their own conquests abroad.

'That is well, I tire of speaking through another man. So, tell me, Earl Frode, why you have come to meet me, alone.'

'I have come to tell you that you will face no resistance in these lands. I wish to make peace. The war is lost and we will submit to your rule.'

Hugues felt a surge of delight inside, but kept it from his face. 'And where is your army?'

'I have sent them back to their families, those who were left alive.'

'You sent them home? How can you surrender your army to us if you have sent them home?' said Hugues, his mood tempering.

'I cannot,' said Frode simply.

'Ah, I see, that is your purpose. To avoid surrendering them to me.'

'Yes. My scouts saw the hall burning at Karlsgrind, heard the screams. I do not know what you would do with my men, so I scattered them to every corner of these lands.'

Hugues looked at the man intently, seeing little defiance in his eyes. 'I could track them down, village to village, questioning with steel and threats, and I would find them.'

Jarl Frode nodded sadly. 'You could, and I have heard that such acts are not beneath you. But you would not find them all, and you would have to destroy this land, tear it apart, to achieve it. I think that you have come to rule, I see that you have done what you believe is best to achieve submission. So, I offer you an alternative path, one that will not require such violence, and result in a much calmer, more peaceful, and more productive land to rule.'

Hugues sat up a little in his saddle, suddenly wishing Reinhard was there to consult with, but not willing to lose face by calling him over. 'I see. Tell me your suggestion.'

'We will accept your rule, your religion, and your army. There will be no violence from my people to yours, nor will we tolerate in our lands any who wish to continue violence against you. My men piled their shields and spears before they went home, and we will surrender them to you. I hear that is what you require.'

Hugues remained impassive. It sounded like complete capitulation, but he wondered that there must be some price to pay for such total submission.

'In return, I ask that you forgive all those who have fought against you, and let them live in peace, respecting their property and their lives. They will fall under your rule and pay your taxes and we can have an end to this war.'

Hugues nodded slowly and leant forwards, staring the man in the eye. 'And what of you, Jarl Frode? What do you expect?'

Frode drew a deep breath, and his nervousness was obvious. 'If you require my death, to spare my people, I will accept it. But I would suggest that it is better if you let me continue to govern as your vassal. I know these lands and these people, and they like me and respect me. I will be able to manage them far better than you could.'

Hugues snorted. 'It sounds as if you wish to merely continue your life as if no war had happened, and merely pay us some taxes and pray in our churches. Do you think we came all this way, suffered all we suffered, and achieved all that we have achieved, just for some taxes and some prayers?'

Frode had the decency to shake his head. 'No.'

'Here is what will happen, Earl Frode, for we do not negotiate with those who continued to fight after we demanded surrender, we simply say what will be, and do not tolerate those who refuse.' He dragged out the last part of that sentence as the threat that it clearly was.

'You will not govern, in our name or yours. Your time as earl is over. That is the consequence for fighting this war and losing. For three hundred years, your people have abused ours, you speak of your family in Normandy as if you do not know how they came to be there, by the constant massacre and destruction of the French people who once called it their home. We are here to end that threat forever, and thus your people will become ours.'

'I understand, I…'

'I am not finished. You may have piled some weapons, but it will not have been all of them, so you will send messengers out and you will recover the rest of the weapons and armour your men took home, and if we are not satisfied that you have done so, we will take actions that you will regret. If you truly expect peace, your people have no further need for steel. If you are compliant, and helpful, I may let you retain some small figment of your power, as a bridge between my Order and your people, not as earl, but as a local bailiff.'

'A bailiff? I do not know that word.'

'An enforcer of the law. You claim to know your people, that you will not allow violence in these lands, so that may be your task, to help ensure that.'

Frode nodded, downcast.

'Now, we will march into this town, and we will select what buildings we require for our Order. We will be establishing this town as the new seat of our government in this region and you will get whatever people reside in those buildings out, without fuss or trouble, and if you succeed in this small task, and the gathering of the rest of your people's weapons, then maybe, *maybe* I will consider leaving you as bailiff and forgive your participation in the war against us and forget your missing men,' Hugues finished, looking at the man with a grim smile.

'Now, these men will escort you as we proceed.' With that, he pulled his horse into a turn on the spot, and trotted back to the column.

When he reached it, Reinhard and Dietmar and Hartung and the other senior members were waiting to hear his news.

'The man is called Earl Frode, he is the commander of their army, and he has surrendered to us, with the usual terms,' he said.

'Where is their army?' asked Dietmar.

'It has dispersed.'

'Dispersed?' said Reinhard, his brows narrowing as they so often did, which got Hugues's pulse pounding immediately. 'An army that has dispersed can re-gather, can it not? Should they not be surrendering to us?'

'It will not be necessary,' replied Hugues, waving the concern away. 'They are defeated, they know it, and they have gone home to get away from the war. I have received guarantees from Earl

Frode, or the former Earl Frode, that they will cause no trouble, nor provide resistance.'

'Guarantees? What guarantees?' Reinhard said in a concerned voice.

'I will not discuss this further now, it was a military matter,' said Hugues, barely containing his anger at Reinhard so publicly questioning his decision.

'Later then,' said Reinhard with disapproval written wide on his features. 'Because this is not our normal way.'

'Bishop Reinhard, you should worry more about the task at hand of bringing these repentant people into the Church, and less about military threats. We treated previous towns differently to send a message, so that we would not have trouble later. It worked, this is the last major area we needed to subdue, and they have surrendered without a fight. There is no one else left to scare into submission, and nothing to be gained by provoking trouble that does not exist. Now, I will explain the military considerations further in private, if you wish. For now, we will proceed into town and make sure our terms are enforced.' Hugues turned, not caring how the bishop reacted to the scolding, and gave the order for the column to continue the advance, trying to ignore the surprised faces of the men who had just watched their two commanders squabbling.

*Damn that man, I wish I had not let him come.*

'Continue the march, Sieur de Blanchant,' Hugues shouted to the French commander. He used the man's feudal title because he knew it infuriated Reinhard, who wanted all the Order's members, even the military ones, to forgo their ranks and simply be referred to as 'brother'. But old habits died hard, and out of earshot of their leader, most of the knights in the Order still used their proper titles.

'Yes, Grandmaster,' replied the knight, standing in his stirrups and shouting his orders to the head of the column.

Arbugæ was a relatively pleasant town, Hugues thought, as they processed through the narrow streets with a hundred of Roland's soldiers to guard them. It was perhaps the best built and least noisome of the towns they had marched through. The whole settlement was built into the elbow of the river, surrounded by fields and pastures, with a faint line of low hills visible to the north, and a more rugged wooded slope on the southern bank.

The town did not have a central square as such, the hall of Earl Frode was built right onto the riverbank, adjacent to a generous dock, and the lane that the hall opened up on ran right along the riverfront, with a broad gap between the hall and the other buildings, creating a long and wide space filled with boatsheds, fish racks, small barns and stores, and a lot of open space.

He saw at once the advantage of having the hall next to the dock. It could be used to control and observe comings and goings by river, and also be a means of escape or reinforcement in case of trouble.

The hall was not the long, low, hull-shaped construction of many of the buildings, but a two-storey building with stone for the lower walls, a rarity in the towns they had passed. He imagined being right next to the river allowed for easy supply of stone for building, compared to many of the other towns.

Outside the hall, along one wall, were carefully propped rows of spears, axes, swords and shields. Not dumped in a pile as they had often seen, but neatly and carefully arranged. *The difference between an army that believes it is defeated, and one that still has pride.* Hugues worried about this as he looked at the cache. Pride could be dangerous, and a people who did not believe they were truly defeated could not submit, or at least could not stay that way.

'Sir Roland, have your men count those weapons, and tell me how many warriors you think they would arm.'

He turned back as the knight sent a half-dozen men to perform the task, and for the first time since entering the town acknowledged

Reinhard's existence. 'We have reports of four hundred armed men coming this way. I do not believe that is nearly enough equipment.'

Reinhard looked at him impassively. 'And what shall we do about it, shall I interrogate your pet Norse lord?'

'No, you are welcome to make your inquiries with the people, but that man is my prisoner and is not to be harmed. He is more useful alive and unharmed, for now.'

Reinhard urged his horse towards Hugues so that they could speak more quietly. It was an ungainly process, that would have humiliated any nobleman, but Reinhard did not care what his horsemanship looked like.

'Our agreement is that I manage the land we capture. You have captured it, let us end this unseemly arguing.'

Hugues took a deep breath and gently shook his head. 'Our agreement was that in towns we captured you would manage affairs for the purpose of imposing the authority of the Church. In all cases, we knew they would be given over as a fief for someone to govern. We never said that you would become governor of our own lands, a position of unparalleled power, and one you are not, as a member of the clergy, best suited for.'

Reinhard's already sallow face frowned and Hugues saw the tension in his temple. 'So, you would claim the governorship of this area.'

'Why not? I am of sufficient rank, and have plenty of experience governing my own lands, which you do not. In any case, you still have the vast task of converting this entire country, and the ones conquered before, and building and maintaining the network of churches and congregations and the priests that fill them. Your focus does not need to be on the separate task of governance.'

'Ah, you would relegate me to the lesser role. Do you not also face the enormous task of maintaining security for the entire region?'

Hugues shook his head, barely looking at Reinhard. 'No, the other forces of our allies are covering much of it, and it seems the war is truly over.'

'Over? What about the army that fled north, along the river? You have to hunt them down and destroy them, do you not?'

Hugues thought about it for a moment. *If I go after them, it may take months, and when I return, Reinhard will be in total control. If I remain here and send most of the men under another commander, who do I trust to be more loyal to me than to Reinhard? Roland? Hartung?* It was an intractable problem. Reinhard had ruthlessly courted most of the Order's senior leaders, and humiliated the only one, Sir Dietmar, who Hugues had felt he could rely on. His authority dangled by a thread, he could not risk leaving, nor detaching from his men.

'No, we will not pursue the fugitives north this year. There is no need,' he said dismissively.

Reinhard gaped in genuine surprise. 'No need?'

'No, why would we? They are fleeing north into uninhabited lands, we control the town they left from and the river through it. They are a few hundred men, who will be too busy trying to survive to bother us, and winter may finish them anyway. Why commit our men to another pointless winter campaign in the forest, searching the vast north for a few starving refugees?' He shook his head. 'It would be foolish to even attempt a pursuit. Even Count Baldwin would have known that. No, the important thing for our troops is to remain in these lands, garrison them strongly, and make sure all the people see our strength. Once we have secured this as our base, and if the enemy survives the winter, then we can go and finish them off at our leisure.'

Reinhard flared his nostrils with barely contained anger and gave Hugues a look of pure spite before jerking on his poor horse's reins and leaving without another word.

Hugues smiled as the furious bishop walked his horse away. *You can't have everything your way.* But despite the brief elation of the victory, he immediately felt the worry of knowing Reinhard, and knowing that a response would be severe. The man wasn't one to let go of any power that he felt he needed.

With the smile fading, he went back to the men counting weapons, and waited while they finished, in his mind already planning additions to the hall, which he had decided would be converted to his home and headquarters. If things got really bad with Reinhard, he might greatly benefit from having a home with a dock attached.

He paused his musings as he saw Roland walking over to him. 'Perhaps two hundred men, Grandsteward. But there are more weapons than shields, and hardly any armour at all.'

Hugues sighed. Frode had said his army had dispersed throughout the entire lands, and it was no simple matter to search dozens of miles in each direction looking for maille. Especially since the very person who would be best for that was Reinhard's pet bloodhound, Sir Sighard.

Nor could he do nothing, as Roland would surely tell the bishop of the paucity of the surrendered cache. He sighed and rubbed his head. 'Choose ten houses and search them, you know the method. Find someone to make an example of, and then we shall have another collection.'

'Yes, Grandsteward. It will be done.'

# Chapter 12

# Search for Sanctuary

GJALDIR'S HANDS WERE rubbed raw from rowing all day upriver, although they were much better off than many of the others who were new to the activity. Years of wielding a hammer and tongs had hardened his fingers, but his palms were a new sore point, and a line of blisters had formed in the meat of them. He sat by a fire, having enjoyed a good meal with several of the other warriors, picking at the blisters in the firelight.

'You shouldn't do that, it will only make them worse tomorrow.'

Gjaldir looked up and saw Brunhild gazing down at him with a reproachful smirk. He grinned back at her and waved her away. 'What do you know of rowing a ship?'

'More than you, that is clear. Even the children know not to pick apart their blisters.' She shook her head at him, as she so often did when she was exasperated with how ignorant he was.

'She is right,' said Bjorn, piping up unhelpfully and humourlessly. 'You will only make it worse for tomorrow.'

'See, as I said.'

Gjaldir reluctantly stopped worrying at the raw and inflamed skin and sighed. 'Whatever you say, but you did not come over just to tell me that. Come, sit by the fire with me, where is Aeske?'

Gjaldir had been relieved and delighted when he found out Brunhild was being brought north with Halla. Some of the other thralls had been sent with Frode, some had been freed, some had simply disappeared in the chaos, including Otto, Aeske's father. The German thrall had probably slipped away to go to the Christians, abandoning his son to return to his people.

But Brunhild had stayed faithful to Halla, going with her as her personal attendant, all while nursing her young son, the boy who Gjaldir had once believed was his, only to have that joy stripped from him. He despised Otto more than ever for abandoning his child, but was quietly grateful that it gave him the opportunity to take his place.

'I left him with some of the other mothers, we take turns. And anyway, I can't leave you alone for too long, in case you do something stupid and don't have anyone to point it out to you.'

Gjaldir smiled ruefully. He couldn't deny that had often been true. Then Brunhild looked around with indecision at the small circle of warriors. 'But I can't stay, I… have water to fetch and some other chores.'

'They can wait,' said Gjaldir, beckoning to the ground beside him, not understanding her reluctance as she eyed the warriors.

'It's okay, girl. There are no slaves and masters here in the wild, just people. Sit with us, we do not mind.' Bjorn motioned Brunhild to the empty space and none of the other warriors looked concerned.

Gjaldir cursed himself for not having realised why Brunhild had refused. In their old home, a slave would never come to sit with a warrior or freewoman. Brunhild smiled and nodded her thanks nervously to Bjorn. Gjaldir was in wonder how the brusque, confident woman who spoke to him with such a sharp tongue was so meek around the other men.

'Gjaldir is only half a real Norseman anyway, so it is he who is lucky be to be allowed to sit with us real warriors,' added Lief in jest, getting a round of chuckles from the other seated men.

'I'm twice the size of you!' said Gjaldir.

'That is true. And yet, despite that, you are still only half the man!'

The men burst out laughing, even the usually taciturn Bjorn. Gjaldir felt the prick of his hurt pride worming into his insides but laughed along anyway as Brunhild sat and gave him a long raised eyebrow. 'Don't worry,' she said, putting a comforting hand on his shoulder. 'I have seen him bathe, and you are indeed twice his size…' She paused and looked at the huskarl in the firelight with a wicked smile. Leif put his hands up in mock outrage and Gjaldir grinned at him triumphantly.

She grabbed his ear and wiggled it like she would a child. 'But he is right, boy, you are not yet half a man. A big spear is worthless to a warrior who doesn't know how to use it.'

Leif howled with laughter and rocked back to lie on the ground as Gjaldir tried to swat away the hand that was painfully holding onto his ear, his deep blush unseen in the firelight.

'Someone give that girl a drink,' said Leif, giggling and wiping the tears from his eyes as he sat back up and looked at Gjaldir, who was shaking his head and soaking up the jests in the best spirit he could muster. These were battlebrothers, men who had fought and killed together, and he was coming to realise that having the status of a warrior, and being one of them, were a long way apart. Probably the only reason he was accepted at this fire was that he and Leif had once also fought together, in the chaos of the attempted assassination in Ragnvald's yard. It was a bond that Gjaldir felt with no other living man. And as he looked up at Leif ruefully, he saw the big blond-haired man give him a nod and a wink, and his heart lightened a touch.

Brunhild accepted a proffered mug of watered ale gladly, and shuffled over to sit next to Gjaldir, close enough that their hips touched and shoulders rubbed, and the brief shiver that sent down his spine melted his annoyance away in a moment. She raised her horn mug towards him and he thunked them together and sighed. 'I'm so glad you came to visit.'

'Good. I wouldn't want you to forget me.'

'How could I?' he said, with a sarcasm he didn't feel.

The two of them settled in together in the chill evening air, soaking up the warmth of the fire and looking out over the lake. It was a magical moment in the chaos of war. The other warriors chatted in low voices around the flames, but he felt like they were alone together for that brief stitch in time, with nothing but the cold of the blazing stars, and the heat of her body and the roaring fire.

'Gjaldir,' she whispered, leaning into him. 'I must go, Aeske needs to be put to sleep.'

'What, won't the others do it?'

'Maybe, but they won't thank me for it.' She emptied her mug and rose smoothly to her feet, smiling at him and walking off as Gjaldir frowned after her.

He suddenly realised that all the warriors were staring at him in amused silence.

'Oh, my poor lad. You have it bad for her, don't you,' said Leif with a chuckle.

Gjaldir blushed again and tried to look nonchalant. 'It's not like that.'

'It fucking is,' said another man with a knowing grin.

'It can't be like that,' said Gjaldir, frowning and lowering his voice. 'She is a slave.' He trailed off, not needing to explain to these men what that meant.

'Fate will leave things that way, or it will not. Only time will tell,' said Bjorn, with no trace of humour.

Gjaldir looked at him and pursed his lips, unsure what to make of it. 'Why does it have to be fate, not my actions, that decide her future?'

Bjorn shook his head. 'No, you do not understand, fate is not a rune set in stone, it is a twisted road with many turns and branches. The end point is decided by the Norns, but how you get there is down to you, that is your duty as a man, to find the best path, even if it is the hardest. Your path may lead to her, or it may not. But how that happens can be decided by you.'

Leif nodded. 'Bjorn is right, even if he is just saying what Jarl Ragnvald used to say, but in three times as many words, and less cleverly.'

Gjaldir nodded as he remembered what the old jarl had once said to him, after the assassination attempt. He repeated the words out loud. 'A man is his word and his wyrd. The gods may decide the path of a man's life and its destination, but he alone decides how he walks it.'

Leif smiled. 'Exactly his words. He liked to say that.'

'Many times,' said another warrior with a sad nod.

'Too many times, if anything,' said Leif with a smile. 'But he lived by his word, and he died by his wyrd, and he walked the path he chose to get there.' The men all nodded in silence and were lost in their thoughts. Leif stood. 'Come, it is time to sleep. In the morning the river continues.'

The next day, Halla stood in the stern of the lead ship and pointed at the eastern shore of the long lake they were rowing along.

'Is that the village?'

It was the second day of their voyage north, and they had not seen a substantial settlement since midway through the first. The shores of the lake were thickly forested, and seemed untouched by the hand of man, but as they turned a corner, a small village came into sight in a clearing in a broad, deep arm of the lake.

'Yes, that is Vatnsborð. Hidden in this bay from the main lake, only those who know it is here can find it easily,' said the steersman, a local from Karlsgrind who had decided to come north with them. 'Do you want to land there?'

Halla looked at it for a moment and nodded. 'Yes, we have come far enough, I doubt they can follow, even if they wished to.'

'As you wish. We can land there, the lake is rich with fish and the land around is good for hunting.'

Halla smiled coldly. 'It sounds suitable.'

The seven ships pulled slowly towards the small village, making sure not to show any hostile intent. The village bustled with activity as the occupants armed themselves and arrayed in a respectable shieldwall on the central beach, men and women with bows standing ready on both sides, between fishing boats, sheds and fish-drying racks.

The steersman shouted to the boats behind, and they all headed to the narrow, pebble-strewn beach, eyeing the defenders nervously, but not raising a weapon or shield to cause any provocation.

Halla examined the village. It was a simple place, low, turf-covered houses well insulated against the winter, fish racks heavy with fish, and pens full of sheep. A few small ships were drawn up on the shore, which had no dock. None of them were bigger than twelve oars and they could simply be dragged up each night rather than leave them in the lake.

They reached the shore and more armed men were standing warily around, eyeing the oncoming ships with distrust.

Gustav leapt down from the boat with surprising agility and stopped, and he waved to the nearest group. 'I am Jarl Gustav, of Svealand, we are not here for violence. Can I speak to your jarl?'

One of the men watching waved at the others to remain, and stepped forwards.

'There is no jarl. My name is Knud. I am the leader of this village, when one is required. Why are you here, with so many warriors?' The man squinted as he stared at the ships behind Gustav. 'And so many people.'

'We were driven from our homes by the Christians, and we are seeking a new place to live.'

'And you chose to come so far, onto our lake?'

'We chose this *because* it was so far, beyond the reach of the invaders.'

The man looked unconvinced, eyeing the ships nervously.

Halla decided it was time to intervene and waved urgently at Leif. 'Help me down.'

'What, no, this is too dangerous, this might still come to violence.'

'That is exactly why I must go, they will not think an unarmed old woman is a threat.'

Leif murmured his dissent but did what he was told, helping Halla out of the bow and onto the stony beach, following her up to stand with Gustav as Knud watched.

'And this is your wife?' Knud asked.

Gustav laughed a deep, amused belly laugh. 'No, this is the leader of these people.'

'I thought you said you were the jarl?'

'Yes, but of lands to the south, not of this woman or her followers.'

The man looked even more confused, but he fixed his eyes on Halla. 'Then I should be asking you, what do you want here?'

'A place for my people to be safe,' said Halla, for the simple truth seemed the best option.

Knud nodded slowly. 'We hear of the foreign invaders, and of the great battle. You are not the first to flee this way, although you are by far the most numerous. Tell me, will they follow you?'

Halla bit her lower lip for a moment, but decided the truth was still the best path. 'It is possible, but I do not think it likely. This is a hard place to get to, and there is nothing here for them to desire.'

'I see. So why should I shelter your people, who are equal in number to my own, when the enemy might come here looking for you?'

'Because if they come, they will not care if you shelter us or not. You will be subject to their violence and their rule. If we are here, we can help defend you, if we are not…' Halla shrugged, the rest did not need to be said.

'A convincing argument, Halla of the Svear. But we do not have the houses, the food, the clothes or the tools to shelter you.'

Halla smiled and waved at the small fleet behind them. 'We brought everything we need, or at least, almost everything. All we need from you is your agreement for us to settle with you, or even near you, and we can help each other.'

'If you have everything you need, you could settle somewhere else.' Some of the locals loudly grumbled their assent at this, nodding and looking at each other.

'And then, when the winter or the enemy comes, we will be separate and weaker.'

'We are ready for the winter.'

'And we are ready for the Christians,' Halla said with a soft smile.

Knud thought this over for a moment, and then turned to the men behind him, having an animated discussion. Finally, he turned back to Halla.

'Come, your men can eat and rest here, on the beach, and let us talk properly before we decide.'

Gustav smiled at Halla and they did as they were invited, the pair of them walking through the village behind Knud and into a low longhouse, with a smoky, darkly lit interior. It was simple but very skilfully built. The wooden frame was finely hewn and solid, and the inside well organised and arranged, with long, smooth-topped wooden chests lining one wall, and a compact firepit in the centre.

They were all directed to sit and Knud asked one of the women in there to bring dried fish and porridge.

The men exchanged guarded pleasantries while they ate, and then Knud put down his own bowl and gestured to Gustav. 'Now, let us come to understand each other, so that I can put the minds of my people at rest. We are not used to large bands of outsiders here, let alone those so heavily armed.'

Gustav nodded carefully. 'I can tell you we are no threat to you.'

'Desperate people are always a threat.'

'But we are not desperate.'

'Not yet, perhaps.'

Gustav scowled. 'You do not know me, so I will not take offence at that, but I am known as a man who avoids violence where violence seems inevitable, makes alliances between enemies, brings peace where none thought it possible.' He held up his disfigured hand. 'This was the last time I tried to solve a problem with violence before trying to solve it with words. A lesson I have never forgotten.'

Knud's eyes flicked to the clawed hand and gazed at it with curiosity.

'He is called the Raven's Claw, as much for his wisdom as for that injury,' added Halla.

'Well, that is good to know, Gustav the Raven's Claw. But the only reason you pose for me allowing you to settle with us, to overwhelm our town with your numbers, is that the Christians might come, but you, Halla, believe they will not come. So then I do not find this very convincing.'

Gustav wagged his finger at the man. 'I do not think you understand the nature of the threat these Christians pose.'

'Perhaps, but you also do not understand us, if you seek to take over our lands.' Knud smiled. He seemed to be a cagey man before, but his face was now open and honest, without mocking evident in his tone. 'We have lived in these lands all our lives, we know all of it like we know our own wives. You are southerners, used to riches and comfort. Do you know what winter will be like here, when you arrive this late in the season, with nothing prepared?' Gustav stiffened at that.

'Nor can Christians surprise us here. We knew your ships were coming long before you arrived today, we would spot an army marching overland sooner than that. If the Christians come, we will see them, so why do we need you?'

Gustav met the man's gaze and searched his eyes. 'The question, Karl Knud, is what you will do once you discover them?'

'We have faced raiders and invaders who wish to take this village and we have survived them all. Some are buried here, some are forever lost in the woods, their bones picked by the crows. If they are too many, this village would be empty long before a single Christian set foot here, we have places to run and places to hide and places to trap and fight.'

Gustav nodded, a tinge of relief on his lined old face. 'I am glad to hear that, but do not underestimate this enemy. We did, we thought our lands impregnable, thought our people's will unyielding, and we were shown to be wrong. If they want to, they will reach this place, however hard it may be, however much you bleed them. We beat them half a dozen times and they just kept coming back, stronger and stronger than before. They have turned some of our own people on us. They could sail up this lake in ships steered by Norsemen, and you would have little time to flee, however well prepared you are. And if you don't flee, you will give them what they want, one way or another.'

Knud looked at Halla. 'If what he says is true, then I ask again, what do you hope to achieve by coming here? You bring women and children, to build a settlement, why? Why not remain in the south? Why bring your people north with this jarl and his warriors?'

'We could not leave these people behind, or they did not wish to be left behind. Each has their own reason to fear the rule of the Christians. I myself will never be subject to their rule, or their cruelty. We think it is better to survive the rigours of the winter in this place, than to become the slaves of the invaders.' Halla glared at him, putting all her intensity into the stare, and Knud did not appear either insulted or intimidated.

'Very well, you have made your position clear. We will discuss it and then tell you our decision.'

Halls bridled at the dismissive tone. 'How long will that take?'

Knud shrugged. 'As long as it does for our people to have agreement. As I said, I am not the jarl here.'

Knud stood and guided them out of the door. Gustav's face was dark, and Halla was holding in her annoyance. They walked back to the beach where fifty or so of their people had come down off the ships, and were in a wary but peaceful stand-off with the locals higher up the shoreline. They were relieved when they saw Halla and Gustav return.

'Do you think they will let us stay?' Halla asked Gustav quietly.

Gustav grumbled and shook his head briefly. 'No, and I would not either, in their position.'

'No, I do not feel it either. Well, at least perhaps they can help us find somewhere suitable.'

'Perhaps.'

They reached those of Gustav's warriors standing around on the beach and talked about their next move, planning where they would go, and how they would find somewhere. For a long time, they stood there, waiting, until suddenly there was movement in the village and Knud re-appeared at the head of several dozen people, not all of them armed, some of them old.

Halla looked up defiantly as Knud approached at the head of the little delegation. 'You may stay.'

Halla was almost stunned to silence. 'What?'

'We have decided that it is better you are with us here, than elsewhere. We will show you an area outside the village where you can build your homes, and we will help you where we can, as long as it does not endanger our own survival.'

Knud touched his hand to the handle of the seax he had at his waist and nodded. 'I swear it, we shall be friends to you, as long as you treat us the same.'

'Good!' said Gustav, recovering from his surprise much faster than Halla. 'Now, is there any chance you have some ale? We have not had ale for weeks, and we can pay.'

Knud grinned, the first time Halla had seen him do so. 'Of course. And friends do not make friends pay for ale.'

The ships were rapidly unloaded of the most crucial supplies. They took with them what was needed immediately. Warm clothes, axes and woodworking tools, cooking utensils, and a good portion of the grain and dried meat and fish. A team of ten men took a sled with six grindstones and wrestled it ashore and through the village. Those grindstones were precious, made from a stone that was not readily available in this area. Hard and coarse enough to grind grain thousands of times, but not so brittle that it would break into thousands of shards that would get into the flour and make the bread almost inedible.

At the back of the pack was the most valuable cargo they had brought from Karlsgrind, taking up most of a ship. Ten crates of hens with a pair of cocks, and five goats. There had been six goats, but one had panicked and broken free of its tether and jumped overboard, drowning before it could be recovered. Its carcass was being carried and would make a good meal for fifty people but its loss was a serious blow.

They had not brought any pigs, they were too heavy and awkward to bring on the ships, and they would be able to hunt wild boar instead, but the goats would give them precious milk, and, if they were lucky, the single male would allow them to build a small herd over a couple of years.

Knud took them through the village and out to the far side, beyond the fields and a line of trees. There was a broad area of flattish ground beside the lake, and next to a small stream running into it from some low hills to the north-east. The stream water ran fast and clear, and various of Halla's men pronounced it to be good water.

Most of the warriors were, or had been at one time, farmers, fishermen or hunters. And after a short meeting, it was announced that the land was good, high enough not to flood, with soil good enough to farm. Halla smiled at Knud and thanked him.

With their journey at an end, the people were divided up into groups with different tasks, and soon the land was a hive of organised activity.

Twenty warriors were sent out to scout the lands around for game trails, paths, and dangers. A large group was put to work clearing the area around the site of trees for building. There was not time to prepare and season the wood in the proper way, which would take several years; they would build longhouses of greenwood, low and stout, layered with wicker and earth bank walls, and thick grass-covered roofs.

To house the nearly five hundred people would require dozens of these houses, and each would require dozens of trees felled, cut to length, prepared into timbers and planks, and then mountains of soil and cut grass slabs. It was a huge task, and Gjaldir was assigned to the group that would fell trees.

He went with one of Gunnar's men, the cheerful Eric Firebeard, who put a long-handled wood axe over his shoulder like it was born to be there, and took four of them into the woods to search for good trees. Eric was unrepentantly joyful about the task, and about sharing his knowledge.

'We will make pillars first, corner pillars need the older trees, slow growers, gnarled and tough. Ash if we can find it, oak would be ideal but there is none of that up here, I think. Birch will do, or spruce.' He looked at the men following him with a grin. 'Can any of you tell an alder from an ash?' Several men nodded derisively at such a basic question, but Gjaldir just looked on awkwardly.

'Ah, the Christian boy doesn't know.' He grinned and walked over to a small tree with light smooth bark, picking one of the yellowing autumn leaves off it. 'This is alder, see, the leaf is shaped like an oar blade, with spiked edges. Ash leaves are normally narrower and more pointed, like a spear. Although sometimes it is the opposite, and you have to recognise the bark. Ash is the king of woods. Not as hard as oak nor as strong, but more flexible and hard wearing. Alder is not as good, but acceptable for what we need, and more common up here.'

'We used ash for axe handles and tools,' said Gjaldir, trying to redeem himself.

'Exactly, but then how can you not recognise it?'

Gjaldir shrugged. 'I never saw the leaves, just the wood.'

'Well, you'll learn fast, or you'll be sent to cut earth.' Eric looked at him intently. 'You recognise mud, don't you, boy?'

Gjaldir didn't react beyond a tightening of his cheek muscles.

'Good, good to know you would be a useful turf cutter if you are shit at this. Come, let's find some ash. I think there is a group over there.'

Gjaldir laid his axe over his shoulder and set off after the cheerful Norwegian. *Was ash the pointed one, or alder? Shit, I don't want to be a bloody turf cutter.*

## Chapter 13

# Building a Future

IN TEN DAYS, Gjaldir learned how to recognise a dozen species that before had just been trees to him. He learned how to judge the age and know which firs were good for planks, with long sections without knots that could be easily split, and how to find good strong timbers for rooflines and pinnacles. He proved to be a natural with the axe, being able to throw powerful, accurate strokes under the guidance of Eric and the others, cutting trees so that they fell untangled by others, lying flat on the ground so they could be cut into sections for carrying back to the burgeoning village.

The first houses were already complete, and more were being erected every day. The wood cutters and the carpenters could provide wood for three or four houses each day, and then two groups were putting the frames together while others made wicker from saplings and branches and yet more did the thankless task of mixing mud and sand for the walls.

The villagers of Vatnsborð mostly kept their distance, the two groups separated by the narrow strip of fields and trees, but Knud did send a few men to help, and to show them how best to make houses in these lands. Once the timber frames of the low buildings were erected, and the mud-packed wicker walls in place, each side would be built up with an earthen embankment and finally a stout roof put over the top, to be covered with turf with grass already in it. In the south of the country, such houses would be thatched or tiled with bark, but in the cold north, and lacking any crops for thatch, the roofs were painstakingly covered in squares of cut turf laid on top of rough overlapping planks. The living grass would bond it all together in the spring with roots growing between all the sections, leaving a waterproof, insulating layer that would stay warm inside, even in the depths of winter.

Game was scarce in the surrounding woods this late in the season, apart from the last of the winter boar, and some deer. Elk would appear soon, coming down from the hills for the winter, bringing with them their following packs of wolves, but none had been seen yet, although their calls had been heard.

A group of sailors had bartered with the villagers to borrow two small boats, and they went out onto the lake and fished in the deeper waters in the centre, bringing back fish to dry on the racks that were appearing along the shore.

Everything in the new village was going as well as could be expected, perhaps better, even the weather was holding warmer and longer than normal, and it appeared they would be able to get enough buildings up before the snows came, even if they were very basic and rushed.

One day, a man appeared from his village with a gaggle of people in tow while Gjaldir was out splitting logs on the edge of the village. The man waved at Gjaldir. 'Knud told me to bring them to you.'

Gjaldir looked at him in confusion. 'To me?'

'Well, to your people. You are the first one I found, so now I have delivered them.' With that, the villager simply walked off, leaving Gjaldir looking at the huddled group in perplexity. He turned to where Eric was staring in curiosity from further past the trees.

'I think we need Jarl Gustav,' said Eric.

'Yes.'

'Well, go get him then,' said Eric with a grin. Gjaldir rolled his eyes but did not argue. Leaving Eric watching the nervous group, he headed into the village to seek the jarl.

Jarl Gustav was in the centre of town, and nodded when Gjaldir explained what was happening. He grabbed a couple of his men and they armed themselves, then they followed Gjaldir back to the edge of the village. When they got there, he looked over the group of strangers. 'Who are you? Why are you here?'

'We are from near Västerås. We left our homes ten days ago. The Christians said we all had to accept their ways or be punished. We cannot betray our gods, so we fled in the night.'

'Near Västerås? Why would you come so far north? How did you expect to survive here?'

'We heard that there was a group coming up here that was living free, and still following the ways of our gods, and we came looking.'

'Who did you hear about us from?'

'We passed near Karlsgrind, and found some others who were also on the road, and they saw you come north. They are with us now.' He pointed vaguely at the column.

'But how did you find us out here, in this vast land?'

'We followed the river and the lakes, expecting you would have to be somewhere, or at least hoping to find your ships. And then they found us in the forest.' He jerked his thumb back over his shoulder towards Vatnsborð.

Gustav's eyes closed and he muttered under his breath for a while before speaking again. 'So much for this place being hard to find. I will take you to Halla, she is the leader of this town.'

'Thank you.'

'Do not thank me yet, I do not know what she will choose to do.' That warning silenced the man, and he nodded.

'You will give us your weapons now,' said Eric, with a warning growl.

The man looked torn, and glanced at his companions. There were at least eight of them there with weapons, and they could probably take on Gustav and the four men with him, but then what? What would they do, they had nowhere to run. The leader bowed to the inevitable and quietly told his people to disarm.

Gjaldir left his axe with Eric and cautiously approached to collect their weapons in a heavy, awkward bundle. As he walked among them, he came face to face with Tormund, and stopped in surprise.

'What are you doing here?'

King Sigurd's seer did not look surprised at all, only a ghost of a smile creasing the corner of his mouth and eye. 'I did not know, until now.'

'Speak sense. What are you doing here? Why aren't you with the king's men, your people?'

Tormund did not betray a hint of sadness. 'The king's voyage was ending, his men saw no use for me, and I no use for them. I wandered the forest, feeling nothing, searching for understanding, until I found this group and felt the guiding hand of Odin bonding me to them. So I followed them, and now here I am, and here you are, and his mystery is once again revealed to me.'

Gjaldir shifted the weapons in his arms again. 'You think you were brought here to find me?' said Gjaldir, remembering how irritating the seer's ramblings were, but also remembering how he could not draw himself away from them.

'Not to find you, no. To be here with you. To guide Gjaldir, the man who binds stars in steel, but does not understand the message. I will show you the meaning.'

'The meaning of what?'

'Yes,' replied Tormund with a smile. 'That will be the question.'

'Ah, enough with you.' Gjaldir set off following Eric, leaving the infuriating seer behind, although his mind was still full of the man's words.

'You found us just by following the river?' said Halla in horror.

'Well, no. We had almost given up, our food was nearly gone, but then some men found us and brought us in,' said their leader. 'Without that, I think we would never have come here.'

The new arrivals were standing in a tight group outside the biggest of the new buildings, watched by the handful of wary-looking warriors.

Halla scowled. 'That was still too easy. Can we move again?'

Gustav shook his head. 'Not before winter.'

'Then we just wait to be found and killed?' Halla said scathingly.

Gustav didn't rise to the barb. 'We have no choices here. Even if the Christians can find us, they would need a good reason to do so. Why would they come this far? We are nothing to them. And as Knud said and this group proved, his people would see them coming long before they found us.'

Halla didn't stop scowling. 'I still don't like it.' Then she looked at Eric and Gjaldir, as if she had forgotten they were there. 'Take them and find them a house, or a place to build one.'

Eric nodded cheerfully. 'Of course, Lady Halla.' He waved at the group. 'Come on, let's go.'

Halla went back to her conversation with Gustav as Gjaldir reluctantly left with the refugees.

'Gjaldir.' Gjaldir looked up from the axe he was sharpening on a whetstone and saw Leif coming his way.

'Yes?'

'You are coming on a trip with me.'

Gjaldir looked confused. 'Where?'

'You want to be a warrior, well, we are going scouting, you will learn many things.'

'Scouting where?'

'South and east, three days' walk from here. We need to know the land around us. Bring food for five days, your weapons, your flask, and warm clothes and some rolled blankets. No tents, we travel light.'

Gjaldir felt a prickle of excitement. 'Why me?'

Leif put his foot on a split log and looked at him appraisingly. 'Do you want to know the truth?'

'Yes, of course.'

'Because you are not very important, and scouting is dangerous. Perhaps we will find Christians, perhaps we will find a bear. We will need someone who is fat and slow and can be left behind in either case.' Leif kept his face serious, but his eyes were glinting with amusement.

Gjaldir gave Leif a look that would wilt a thornbush.

'Also, you wish to be a warrior, so you must learn how to move over ground quietly, how to spot danger, how to see signs and marks of men's passing, how to cook food on the smallest possible fire and which wood and fire methods make the least smoke. And a hundred other things. Few people understand how little of being a warrior is about fighting, you will start to learn that.'

'Then I will come.'

'It wasn't a question. We leave at first light.'

Gjaldir nodded and went back to his axe. He would have plenty of time to prepare before darkness fell.

Once he had finished his work for the day, he went back to the house he had been assigned to. He didn't sleep there, most of the warriors still slept in tents and makeshift shelters outside while the women and children stayed inside, but he left his possessions there to keep them out of the rain and mud.

Brunhild was there, feeding Aeske, and Gjaldir went over and sat down next to her on the rough, new-cut bench. 'He is bigger every day.'

Brunhild smiled. 'He is fat and healthy, everyone says so. A good boy.' She wiped Aeske's mouth and lifted the boy up so that his feet were on her leg. 'He is starting to try and walk now.'

'Already?'

'Yes, he is over a year old, some can walk already at his age. But with everything that has happened, well…' She shook her head with a worried expression. 'He has not had much chance. But now he is learning.'

'He will make up for lost time, I am sure,' said Gjaldir confidently.

'Here, you can help him, hold him under his arms, let him take the weight on his legs, and then move him, he should move his feet with you. When he gets better, we support him less, and less, and then finally he walks on his own.'

Gjaldir was fascinated. 'How long does that take?'

'How long?' Brunhild laughed and wiped her eyes with mirth. 'Really, you have never seen a baby grow before?'

'Never,' said Gjaldir, too happy to be upset at being ignorant. 'I had barely seen a baby until I came to the North, I never lived with one.'

'That explains many things about you. Well, it will take him weeks to learn, maybe months. But you can help.'

'Good, I'd like that. One day I will teach him to use a hammer.' Brunhild's smile became more forced, and Gjaldir felt her unease. 'If… you want, and I am still nearby.'

'Of course, it would be good. Now, I have to wash, be careful with him, he likes to fall on his nose, and I don't want him to be as ugly as you.'

Brunhild walked through the packed house and out of the door and Gjaldir smiled at Aeske, who smiled back gleefully, arms waggling and grabbing at his tunic sleeves. Gjaldir lowered the boy down to the ground and let his feet hit the dirt, and then felt the child take his own weight, and then a wobbling, unsteady step.

Gjaldir smiled broadly, like it was a great victory, and then the boy took another and Gjaldir beamed and lifted the child up to replace him and start again. He had come into the house to tell Brunhild that he was leaving, and that he did not know when he would return, but he had quite forgotten that, lost in those bright, happy brown eyes.

They set out the next morning, ten of them, Leif and Bjorn and seven other warriors Gjaldir did not know, mostly Gustav's men.

The advantage of him not knowing who they were was that they did not know who he was, although he got strange expressions when he told them his name. Gjaldir was not a normal Norse name, and everyone recognised it.

'You are the Christian smith?' said one, an eyebrow raised.

'Yes, he is the one who made the sword Ljós a Norðan. I heard he was here with us,' said another.

'Are you, is it you?'

'Yes,' said Gjaldir awkwardly.

The man furrowed his brows. 'Then what are you doing coming with us?'

'He is no longer a slave or a smith, he wants to be a warrior, and he is coming with us to learn the ways,' Leif said, over his shoulder from where he led the group with Bjorn.

'Does he speak?' said the stranger, directing this to the Svear warrior.

'Yes, I do,' said Gjaldir indignantly.

'Then why does he speak for you?' said the man, indicating Leif.

Gjaldir just shrugged.

'I ordered him to come with us, so I want it to be clear. He is one of us, and will be treated as such.'

The warrior looked at Gjaldir dubiously. 'You have any skill with that axe?'

Gjaldir shrugged. 'I killed a wolf with one once,' he said, pulling the wolf's tooth out of his tunic to show.

The warrior was unimpressed. 'Was it tied to a tree?'

'No.'

'Then why the fuck would you fight a wolf with an axe? Are you stoneheaded?'

Gjaldir scowled. 'Because I had no other choice, I had to kill the wolf to save a friend.'

The warrior raised his brows and nodded. 'Then it was a good kill, I commend you. If the wolf had its own shield and spear, then I would consider you a warrior too.'

'He has fought warriors before,' said Bjorn, and Gjaldir sighed inside, worrying how Bjorn would tell that story. 'He knocked one down with a throw, a second one he avoided after a clash of blades, and the third one had him beaten in two blows.'

'Oh, really, in two blows? Then why is he alive?'

Bjorn turned and gave a rare smile. 'Because I was the third, and I spared him.'

That got a round of laughter from the men, and Gjaldir gave Bjorn his best attempt at a scalding look, which only widened the man's smile. 'He is easy to tease, it is our favourite feature of his, but in his credit, he is brave and abnormally strong and fast. If he lives long enough, he will be a dangerous man.'

'I was dangerous already,' said Gjaldir defensively, and that provoked another round of laughter. 'I stopped your attack,' said Gjaldir to Bjorn, with a little more venom than he intended.

Bjorn wagged his head from side to side slightly. 'Through luck, not skill. Being lucky does not make you a dangerous man. It makes you a lucky man in the past, and unreliable in the future if you rely on it.'

'I killed your friend,' said Gjaldir, referring to the man who face he had crushed with a thrown hammer, and who had never woken from the blow.

'True, you would be dangerous with a thrown axe, no doubt. But not in a close fight.'

'I put Leif on his back, the day we met.'

'I was not there for that, but I hear Leif was trying to catch you, not kill you. If he had been trying to kill you, you would be dead. Is that not true, Leif?'

Leif nodded without looking around. 'You have never beaten a man in close combat, a man who is trying to kill you.'

Gjaldir shook his head in irritation at the Norse warrior, feeling his definition was unfair. Ragnvald himself had told Gjaldir that if he had been a freeman he would have been accounted an *ulfdrengr*, a wolf-warrior, a killer of a wolf and a man in combat, eligible to wear its pelt in battle. He never dared lay claim to the title, but he always held in his heart that it was his and always wore its tooth around his neck.

The men's jokes and laughter moved on to other things and Gjaldir stewed in silence and annoyance at the back of the column, ignoring them as they ignored him. Halfway through the day, they stopped at a stream to drink and rest and Bjorn nodded his head at Gjaldir. 'You are still annoyed, why? I spoke the truth.'

Gjaldir looked back at the warrior and tamed his angry tongue. 'You discount everything that I have done. I was an untrained man, a slave with no weapon but a hammer, yet I beat Leif to the ground, I killed a man with a throw you yourself praised, and I faced you and other warriors in combat and did not run or die.'

Bjorn nodded. 'I do not contest any of those things, but none of them make you a warrior, as I explained.'

'What do you know of fighting?' said the stranger, who had still not introduced himself.

'I spent many years fighting, with my hands and feet. Competing with the other men and boys of my town, I was the best.' replied Gjaldir with a confident sneer.

The warrior was unmoved. 'Show me.'

The man got slowly to his feet and stretched his arms, loosening his shoulders.

'Easy, lads, we can't afford any injuries,' growled Leif.

The challenger shook his head. 'No bad blood here, the boy is here to learn, and I am merely making a demonstration.'

Leif looked at the two men and nodded his assent. 'If you break him, you carry him.'

Gjaldir smiled slowly and got to his feet too, eyeing the warrior up. He was older, perhaps nearly at his thirtieth year, but still looked strong and in good shape. Gjaldir saw no obvious injuries or stiffness in his movements.

Gjaldir rolled his shoulders twice and grinned. It had been a long time since he had fought on the patch at Minden, in the area of beaten earth behind the alehouse where the boys and young men of the town had gone to drink and show off their strength and skill in bouts of wrestling and grappling, but he felt confident he remembered the ways.

The other warriors spread out and let him and his opponent have a circle, there was no jeering or jokes, just seasoned killers watching with professional interest.

Gjaldir started circling to his right, and the man matched his movement, body lowered in a fighting stance. Gjaldir kept both arms forwards and saw the other man prepared differently, his left arm out in front, and his body twisted, his right arm back. It would give him a better position to strike from, but Gjaldir did not mind, he had always been able to take a punch and win in the grapple.

He made a feint forwards and the warrior barely flinched, just kept circling. Gjaldir closed the distance and swayed side to side, trying to pick his moment to go for the grapple.

The warrior made the first move, darting in and shoving Gjaldir with his left arm, keeping the distance open. Gjaldir grabbed for the offered arm, preparing to use it as a lever to bring his opponent down to the ground. But his opponent shrugged the arm back and flashed a strike with his right that Gjaldir couldn't avoid, taking it on his ribs with a grunt.

He managed to get the opponent's arm on the second attempt and locked it, suffering another pair of sharp blows to the ribs and one to the side of the head in return. The blows hurt him, but with one arm locked, they lacked full power.

The warrior gave up punching him and tried to fight for his arm, the two men tussling and scrabbling, until finally Gjaldir's superior height and strength won over and he twisted the man over his hip and thumped him to the ground. He smiled and let the man get cautiously to his feet. 'You see?'

'I do see. Come at me again, and you will see also.'

Gjaldir clapped his hands together once and advanced, confident now that he had the man's measure of strength and reach. This time, the warrior kept both his hands forwards, mimicking Gjaldir, and they both jumped in together, and Gjaldir got a good grip on his right arm, and his opponent got a good grip with his left. The two men strained and wheezed and Gjaldir slowly forced the man's arms apart, bringing their heads closer and closer together. It was easier than he expected, he had thought the man was stronger, perhaps the first fight had hurt hi…

The knee to his groin was completely unexpected, and it knocked the life right out of him. The headbutt to the side of his head as he sagged killed his senses and left him swimming in pain, and then he was on the ground with a steel arm around his neck, and gasping for breath as his lungs tried to howl in agony but could not.

He felt the warrior's lips pressed against his ear as he wheezed on the ground. 'And that is why you are not dangerous, oh champion of your town. You learned to fight with rules, in war there are none. When a man is trying to kill you, he will do anything, anything at all. And there is no use being stronger than him when he is wiggling a blade in your ear, or tearing your guts from your belly. Have you got the killer spirit in you, boy?'

Gjaldir couldn't answer, he could barely whimper. Pain was washing over him in waves, his head rang like a smith's anvil, and he could not muster the strength in his arms to do anything about the arm around his neck. Then the arm was suddenly gone, and he was rolled over onto his front as the warrior sprang to his feet.

Gjaldir half crawled and dragged himself to his knees, one hand clamped to his stones, groaning as other warriors clapped his opponent on the back and congratulated him. The man stepped past him to go back to his discarded weapons and Gjaldir sprung to life, swinging a vicious kick at the front of the man's leading leg, tumbling him with a curse and causing him to fall nearly into Gjaldir's lap.

Gjaldir rolled over, still nauseous with the pain, and got a knee on the man's shoulder and both hands under the opposite arm, wrenching it back and trapping the warrior face down in the dirt, with all his weight on the man's left side, and his right arm completely in Gjaldir's control.

There were angry shouts from the men around and he grinned at them through the pain. Then he let go of the warrior's arm and drunkenly levered himself to his feet, leaning down to look at his opponent. 'And that is why I am dangerous, because men always think I am not, that I am helpless or beaten.'

The astonished man looked at him from the ground for a moment, nursing his twisted shoulder, and then smiled slowly and reached a hand up. 'I am Halfdan, a warrior from Tuna.'

Gjaldir grabbed the hand and helped pull Halfdan to his feet. 'And I am Gjaldir, who was once a Christian slave in Uppsala, and now am a warrior.'

His opponent gave him a thump and a wry smile, and Bjorn gave Gjaldir a deep, slow nod. 'Being able to fight through pain is a great skill.'

'What pain?' said Gjaldir with a grin, even as his eyes swam and his stomach convulsed, and he feared taking a step towards Bjorn in case he toppled.

'What pain! Hah! By the gods, there is some fire in you,' said Halfdan, clapping him on the shoulder and nearly toppling him. 'You were right, lad, we'll make a warrior of you yet.'

Leif walked over, not looking amused. 'Are you two finished? Good. Let's continue, we have a long way to go before we can return home.'

The little column started off again, Gjaldir once more at the back, but feeling a little less maligned than before, even as he nursed his aching head.

The next day, the group was moving south-east towards the rising sun, when the lead man spotted something and called out quietly. They all stopped and crouched in the undergrowth, quiet, looking out all around them.

Gjaldir saw nothing in the trees and scrub around them, and then finally they all stood and moved up to see what the scout had found.

There was a disturbed patch in the vegetation ahead of them, and dark bloodstains on a faint game trail that went through the trees.

'Perhaps the work of wolves, hunting.'

'No,' said Leif, leaning down to inspect something, picking up a bloodied, torn scrap of clothing. 'Not wolves.'

That got everyone on edge.

'Whoever fought here, this is not old. Yesterday at most, probably this morning. We will spread out, search for the one who did the bleeding, they cannot have lived long. Three groups. Go no further than two hundred paces and then meet back here. We need to know who did this.'

Bjorn nodded to Halfdan and Gjaldir, and the three men headed eastwards in a loose line, moving slowly and carefully, and stopping frequently to look and listen.

They had been searching for a while when Gjaldir saw it, an

arm, lying on the ground sticking out from behind a felled tree, the rest of the person concealed behind the trunk. He stopped and gestured wildly to the others, his heart thumping. He pointed and Bjorn came over to him and saw, nodding, and signalling Halfdan to go around the other way, they advanced on the tree.

As they got closer, it was immediately apparent the person the arm belonged to was dead. Not least because the arm was no longer attached. The body lay a short distance away, blood everywhere, flies already gathering over the cavernous hole in the stomach. Gjaldir felt quite nauseous as he stared into the cavity inside the woman's body. For a woman it undoubtedly was, despite the horrific injuries.

'Wolves?' asked Halfdan quietly.

'Possibly,' said Bjorn, with a surprising degree of relief. 'It is not our concern. This is not the work of raiders or Christians.'

'Who was she?' asked Gjaldir, unable to take his eyes away. 'What was she doing here?'

'A refugee? Perhaps there are others who were with her. It doesn't matter. Whatever did this is gone.'

'No, it isn't,' said Halfdan nervously, and at that moment Gjaldir heard it too, a subtle crunching in the undergrowth nearby.

'Bear!' shouted Halfdan, and Gjaldir sprang up from the ground in panic as a mountain of brown and dark fur rushed from the trees, roaring and huffing, stopping to rise to its hind legs in front of the men.

Gjaldir snatched his axe from the ground and scurried backwards in shock, completely unsure what to do. The beast was massive, far larger than the captive one he had once seen in the square in Minden. Its paws were the size of his head, and tipped with claws like eating knives.

'Stay together!' shouted Bjorn as the small group backed away from the beast. Bjorn had a spear, Halfdan an axe, and Halfdan closed up with Bjorn, letting the spearpoint hang between them and the bear.

Gjaldir saw he was alone, and made a sudden rush to return to his fellows. The bear, perhaps spooked or threatened by the sudden movement, dropped to the floor with a great roar and charged.

Bjorn shouted and thrust the spear, catching the bear in the shoulder with a solid thump. The bear hardly seemed to notice and swatted both man and spear away with a single swipe of its paw, Bjorn crashing to the ground with a curse and a thud.

Halfdan tried to protect the fallen man with his axe but the bear was fast, and it snapped its jaws at the warrior, going for his face, and Halfdan managed to get the axe haft into the toothy maw instead, being knocked to the ground as the bear clamped its teeth down on the wood, crunching it, and putting a single huge leg on the man, pinning him to the ground as he shouted in pain and fear.

Gjaldir ran at the bear and drew his axe back to strike, a high-pitched yell of fear emanating from somewhere deep inside him. But the bear heard him coming and turned its muzzle from Halfdan, who was ineffectually beating at its head with his fists. Being confronted with that scowling face put Gjaldir off his stride and the axe missed its intended mark on the animal's neck, instead thumping into the shoulder, digging into the fur and eliciting a roar of outrage.

As the bear turned from Halfdan to deal with this new attacker, there was a shout from the other side. Bjorn had risen to his feet, unsteady and weak, and jabbed his spear into the bear's flank.

Attacked from two sides and with the weapons digging into its flesh, the bear's roars became more wild and panicked, and it backed away a step, turning this way and that, backing away from the painful bites of the spear, allowing Gjaldir to haul Halfdan to his feet.

'Run!' he shouted.

'NO!' shouted Bjorn back. 'Attack it! Drive it away!'

Gjaldir was utterly unwilling to run back into the range of those enormous, lethal paws, especially with his paltry axe, but

Halfdan picked his own weapon up and together, they advanced on the beast, shouting and waving their axes, and the bear turned sideways, shuffling and howling at them, before it finally turned and loped off into the trees, leaving only the indignant sound of its cries behind.

Gjaldir panted and stared after it, shocked they had survived. Bjorn was groaning and leaning on his spear, the other hand clamped to his side. 'I think it broke my ribs,' he moaned.

Halfdan looked unscathed, and he walked over to support the other man. 'Come, let's go to the others before it returns.'

Gjaldir went over to Bjorn's other side and they started walking back towards where Leif had left them, Gjaldir nervously looking back over his shoulder frequently.

'You still aren't a warrior, Christian,' said Halfdan with a frantic giggle as they stumbled away. Gjaldir looked at him and saw that the warrior was grinning like he was moon touched.

'I should have let the bear eat you,' replied Gjaldir, but then he laughed too as the fear and the stress flowed out of him.

'She wasn't going to eat me. She was already full. She just picked the strongest and best man to be her mate.'

'You are as ugly as her, perhaps you are right.'

Only Bjorn, wincing and panting as they hobbled away, didn't seem to find the situation very funny.

## CHAPTER 14

# NOT ONE STEP BACK

SIR HANS HELD up his hand. 'Halt!' he shouted, and the thirty mounted men in the small column stopped their horses on the road. They picked up on his tension quickly and immediately put their own eyes on the road ahead and the forest to either side, hands on weapons, ready.

Ahead of them a fallen tree blocked the way, and Sir Hans was suspicious. The forest on both sides of them was relatively dense and close to the road, it was an ideal ambush spot. He chewed his lip for a moment. He could not retreat from a fallen tree, not with the army behind him expecting him to clear the path, nor could he blindly walk into what could be a trap.

He pointed at two squires at the head of the column. 'Go, investigate the tree, tell me if it is cut or just fallen. Keep your eyes out, and stay on your horses.'

The two squires, young and eager to prove themselves, cantered the two hundred paces down the road to investigate, while his more experienced men spread out a little and got their shield and swords to hand. It really was a perfect ambush site; hemmed in on both sides by the forest, and with no room to charge.

The army behind them was Count Conrad's forces. Hans had returned to Saxony for the winter, the whispers of disgrace and cowardice harrying him in the Crusade, and his duty to return and see that what was left of Adolf's men made it home forcing him to leave.

He had told a tearful Hildewa of her husband's death, and promised her what he had once promised Adolf; that he would keep their son Hartung safe, and quietly accepted her fury that he had not brought the boy back with him. Hans had travelled back to the North in the spring, and pledged his service to Count Conrad, who had been glad to take on an experienced knight and battlefield commander. The whispers of cowardice and disgrace had not gone away, and Conrad had put Hans in the ranks without command, to prove himself once more before men would be willing to follow him.

Hans had fought in the third and final line at the battle outside Uppsala, accounting himself well in the final collapse of the Norse army, and earning enough respect from Conrad's men that he could be given a small command again.

So Hans came to be in command of one of the scouting forces that preceded the army, tasked with clearing the road of any small warbands of the enemy, and reporting back on any larger force as the army advanced.

The army of Conrad had cleared their way along the southern bank of the great lake, burning a town on an island to the ground after a brief but bloody ship fight, and then faced off against the Norse forces who had been blocking the passes to the south, and had missed the battle outside Uppsala.

That force had simply disappeared, shattering, either through intent or through loss of leadership, and they had been fighting occasional skirmishes with groups of enemy warriors ever since. None of the towns had resisted, they knew the price of resistance by now. Södertälje, the first town at the south-east of the lake, near

Birka, had surrendered its walls without a fight. Then had been Strängnäs, whose people mostly fled after seeing the fires of Birka on the horizon, leaving the town empty and silent when Conrad's forces arrived.

The next major town along the coast was Tuna, the largest and most important town in the area, and the one where Conrad intended to set up his feudal seat. These were his lands by gift of the emperor, and Tuna was the key.

The two squires came cantering back down the road and reined in. 'It's rotten and broken, not cut. No sign of any Norse there.'

'Good,' said Hans. 'Move on.'

The party carried on towards the fallen tree and Hans guided his horse around it and stopped on the far side. Only one horse could pass at a time, and he watched the road ahead intently, still wary of a trap, but saw nothing and was satisfied. He turned to look back, watching the men passing the tree one at a time and glanced at the trunk, then furrowed his brows. The trunk was indeed rotten, but on this side, hidden from the way they had come, the trunk had been cut. He swore and reached for his sword. 'AMBUSH!'

He needn't have shouted, the first arrows flicked from the trees, just a handful, but several horses were hit and panicked, and in moments the space around the fallen trunk was a chaos of screaming, kicking horses and shouting men.

These men, knights and squires all, were veterans of the Crusade, hardened men not prone to panic or indecision, and weapons leapt into hand and horses that were still unharmed were turned to face the treelines even as the first charging Norse warriors burst through, and his seasoned horsemen roared their challenge and kicked their horses into action.

There was no time for orders, none could be heard above the melee. Ten of his men were on his side of the tree, and twenty on the other. The horses barely got moving before the enemy were amongst them. Hans saw the first knight ripped from his horse even as he speared a Norseman through the face. Ludorf went down gargling blood with an arrow in his chest and slumped from his horse beside Hans, who powered his mount past the dying boy and stood in his stirrups, bringing his sword down savagely at the head of the first warrior to reach him.

The man tried to block with his spear shaft and the defence extended his life by moments, at the cost of most of his hand, carved from the wooden shaft it was gripping by the sliding steel blade. Hans pulled the sword back and spurred his mount, trampling the screaming man down as he moved to cover the left side of a squire who was gamely fighting three enemies, even as one punched a spear into his unprotected flank.

Hans roared in frustration as the squire dropped his sword and grasped pitifully at the iron embedded in his side, and Hans lanced the tip of his sword into the warrior as he passed, a foolish strike that left the sword embedded deep in the body and meant it was ripped from his hand.

Suddenly unarmed, he turned his horse sharply and felt it stagger as some unseen blow stuck it. He risked a single glance around him to assess the situation and saw that nearly half his men this side of the fallen tree were down, but that the larger group on the far side were faring much better, pushing back against a smaller group of foes.

There was a group of Norsemen in front of him, backs turned as they fenced with spears at a group of four knights, who poked back with their own weapons as they gave ground. Hans threw caution to the wind and simply charged his mount into them, the injured animal screaming in fear and pain and slewing, thumping into the melee sideways and starting to roll as its right-side hooves were fouled by a corpse.

Hans kicked from his stirrups and went with the fall, letting his right knee bend and buckle as it hit the earth. He rolled over his shoulder, using the speed of it to help power to his feet the other side, and he yanked his dagger from its sheath at his belt as he rose.

The two Norse nearest him, staggering from the horse barging into them from behind, turned in confusion and stared wide-eyed at the snarling, maille-clad man who leapt at them with only a dagger. Hans knew he had no choice but to close with them. To fight an axe and shield with a dagger at full distance was to die. He leapt on the closest man before he was ready to defend himself, grabbing hold of the half-turned shield and yanking it to the side. Dagger held point down, thumb over the pommel, he hammered it into the warrior's unarmoured chest even as he ran into him, screaming into the shocked face and feeling his enemy's gasping breath in his ear as he ripped the dagger from his chest and let the man fall to the ground.

He turned into a crouch as fast as he could, knowing the other man would be striking, and an axe skimmed off his shoulder, giving him a painful thump but leaving him unharmed. He swung the dagger backwards, a brutal strike that went under his opponent's ear and through his neck. It was a lucky blow, not aimed, but luck matters as much as skill in a melee.

Hans tore the dagger from the neck and saw that the four knights had used the opportunity to clear the enemy that had been corralling them and one of them jumped from his horse and grabbed Hans. 'We must climb over the trunk, now!' Hans turned and saw that the rest of the ten who had been with him were down, a dozen enemy finishing them off on the ground and readying for the next fight. He and the four at his back were trapped, horses backed into a corner by the trunk and the low branches of the trees behind them.

Hans had a sudden memory of the ambush at the fjord in Denmark, how his men had been swarmed by enemy warriors, fought valiantly and skilfully, but been slaughtered nonetheless. And how he and a single companion had cut their way free and fled. He had never overcome the shame of that, worsened by his humiliation after the lost battle in the forest the year before, when he had retreated from the field where Count Adolf died.

He would not flee from this fight. He could not – never again. He shook his head at the man and fumbled to put the dagger back in his belt, picking up an axe from the ground beside him, then ripping his famous steel-faced helmet from his dead horse and jamming it onto his head. 'No,' he snarled through the steel. 'We hold here until the others get through, get the others off their horses and form on me.' The knight looked astonished, but then gritted his teeth and nodded. The man, like all knights, had trained from birth to be a warrior, and to accept that death in battle might one day be his duty. He was not going to argue.

The four men got into formation with Hans, swords low and ready, just as the Norse gathered themselves to attack again.

For a moment, the two sides stared at each other, heaving air into their lungs, and then the Norsemen charged.

It was not a good charge, it was not even particularly complete, some of them had to climb over a dying horse, and another slipped on a body, but half a dozen Norsemen hit Hans and his men in a ragged group and instantly the world was all blood and chaos.

Hans put his axe into a body and took a counter blow on the top of his helmet, sparking light into the back of his eyes and staggering him. He pulled the axe back with a wet squelch and started hacking in front of himself with it. There were bodies in the press all around him, someone was clinging to his left arm, someone else was raining weak blows on his head and back.

The helmet saved his life five times in as many heartbeats, but it, and the blows to the head, robbed him of his vision and hearing and he was fighting by touch. He swung and swung with the axe and felt it bounce off wood, thunk into maille, and sink into flesh. Then suddenly a hand grabbed the haft and it was ripped from him, and the point of a spear or sword stabbed into his ribs, not hard enough to penetrate his maille, but enough to hurt like a lance of fire, and he recoiled from it.

The man clinging to his left arm used that moment of unbalance to shove him to the ground, and suddenly he was on his back with a screaming man on top of him, a warrior who was battering his helmet and shoulders with the pommel of a sword he was too close to use the point of. Hans struggled to fend the attacker off with his left arm as he scrabbled for his dagger with his right.

Desperate fingers searched under the rim of his helmet, trying to rip it off to expose his face, but they slipped on mud and blood and all that filth flicked into Hans's mouth and he choked, shouting and writhing and kicking as the man bore down on him.

Finally, he dragged his dagger free and he jabbed it into the side of his opponent, but the man was also maille clad, and from that close range the broad bladed dagger did nothing but anger the Norseman, who gave up hammering at his helmet and instead shoved a hand under the rim of Hans's metal facepiece, closing heavy fingers around his throat and squeezing.

Hans's left arm was trapped, entangled with his opponent's right, and the fingers wormed their way ever further around his neck, even as he clamped his chin to his chest to stop them and stabbed wildly with the dagger, trying to find a weak point, feeling the rising tide of panic starting to suffocate him even as the wriggling fingers attempted the same end.

He became ever more panicked as the fingers finally got a good hold and closed with horrifying strength, the pressure on his windpipe making his head throb and his eyes stream as he choked and gasped, heaving lungs trying to draw more breath through his closing throat.

He tried everything in his desperation, with more and more panic and less and less control. He tried to roll, but a body was wedged against his. He tried to buck, but the armoured man was far too heavy. He kicked and flailed with his legs but to no effect.

As his vision was starting to black out, his scrabbling leg hooked around behind the left leg of the man who was killing him, dumping him on his hip, and he put all his remaining strength into a roll, not managing to get on top, but instead ending up lying alongside.

It was enough, he reached down as far as he could with his dagger and brought it up, point first, between his own body and the Norseman's, and his hand went up underneath his enemy's hauberk and jammed into soft flesh. His opponent screamed in agony but somehow kept hold of Hans's neck while he grabbed at Hans's dagger hand with his other arm.

The two men fought over the dagger, locked together on the ground, even as Hans stabbed it up again and wriggled it. This time the man screamed like a dying pig and let go of Hans's neck, putting both his hands on Hans's dagger arm, slippery from the mud and blood, and wriggled and wailed as Hans killed him.

Before the man's feeble wails had finished, Hans, gasping for breath, helmet askew on his head and slick from head to toe with blood, rolled back off and tried to get to his feet. Being on the ground in a fight meant death. He knew this instinctually, and despite the screaming voice in his head begging him to just curl up and breathe, he scrambled to rise.

As he got his first foot underneath him and rose to one knee, he got a glimpse of a spear coming his way, with a Norseman behind it aiming at his chest.

He twisted his body and wildly parried with his left arm, knocking the point past his side. He clamped the spear in his left hand and under his arm against his body, and as the enemy yanked it back, powered off his right leg and stood, springing at his half-seen foe.

The man was helpless, far too close to use his spear even if Hans didn't control the other end of it, and he made the mistake of trying to wrestle for the spear instead of dropping it, and Hans drove the point of his dagger at the warrior's face, seeing it bury itself in the man's eye and lodge in the bone, barely a finger's depth in.

The man howled, a low, guttural sound, and to Hans's shock did not fall. He dropped the spear and flailed wildly at Hans, twitching and jerking, as if he no longer had control of his limbs. Hans was knocked as another pair of wrestling men barged into them and he jammed his fingers into the back of his enemy's hair and pushed on the dagger with all his strength. It slipped a little deeper and he wiggled it from side to side, feeling bone crunch and flesh part, and suddenly the howling went silent and the twitching stopped and his opponent fell like a sack of flour.

Hans's helmet was now completely askew, and one of the eye slits rammed with mud and gore. Despite the danger, he pulled it off his head and looked round furtively as he yanked the dagger from the dead man's eye. There was utter carnage around him, barely a handful of men of either side were left fighting, and he turned his attention to the two men wrestling behind him, hardly able to tell who was who, both were so caked in filth.

'Say something so I know you!' he shouted, as he blinked and tried to shake his vision back into focus.

'It's me!' shouted the blurry figure on the right, and Hans wrapped his arm around the head of the figure on the left and slashed at its throat until it stopped resisting, letting it fall to the ground without even looking at it.

The man he had saved turned to help a comrade who was fighting on the ground behind them and Hans staggered drunkenly towards the only other figure that was still standing, a Norse warrior judging by his shield, who was cursing and clamping a hand to a nasty leg wound.

The man saw Hans coming and shouted in panic, trying to get his shield up and retreat at the same time. Hans caught the shield and ripped it from his grasp, and was so devoid of breath he could barely pursue as his wounded opponent staggered away.

Hans aimed a blow at the retreating back but barely scratched it, and he stumbled, reaching out to grab anything to keep himself upright, and getting a handful of the man's tunic.

The wounded Norseman stumbled and fell as Hans tugged on the heavy garment and Hans fell to his knees, still holding the clothing, and stabbed his dagger into the back of the warrior's calf, pulling it out and stabbing down again as he crawled forwards over the shouting, wriggling man. Again and again he stabbed down, into thigh and arse and back and ribs and finally the thing that had tried to run simply shook and burbled and Hans stopped, the last of his strength and willpower leaving his arms. He sat slumped against the dying body of the man who had tried to run, and ignored its shakes and whimpers. He was beyond caring.

He felt the shivers run through his body, and his arms and legs went limp, and a boy with a spoon could have killed him at that moment, but his eyes were finally clearing and he could look back over his shoulder and see that the fight was over.

A single one of his companions, wounded, looking shocked and confused, was standing desolate in the carnage, and dismounted men, his men, were streaming around the fallen log with weapons out and eyes wide.

One of the Bavarian knights came over to Hans and dropped to one knee, holding out a hand to steady him, and the man tried to check Hans for wounds but in the state of him it was impossible. 'Where is the wound?'

Sir Hans did his best to shrug. 'I don't know there is one. Just help me up.'

The knight dragged Hans to his feet and put a shoulder under his arm, helping him limp back towards the fallen tree, skirting the dozens of strewn bodies before letting him lean against the trunk. His men cleared the area and chased the few surviving ambushers off, before sending a man back to the main force to bring reinforcements.

The only other man who had survived the fight this side of the tree on his feet, the Bavarian knight he had briefly spoken to, was sitting on his haunches in silence, staring at the ground. Hans had been in many battles and smaller fights, but nothing compared to the intensity and desperation of what had just happened.

The men were walking to and fro, collecting weapons and clearing the bodies, men that he had mostly only met a few days ago. They gave him a wide berth, and the looks they gave him, seeing the scene of his fight, varied from awe to hostility.

As he watched, there was a commotion as a living Christian, knocked senseless and limp, was found half buried under a horse and two bodies. They heaved the dead animal off his leg and dragged him free, and Hans grimaced as he saw the limb was twisted and broken. His second in command, a solid West Saxon knight called Matheus, shook his head and ordered the crippled knight to be carried away. Then he came over to see Hans, his expression grim.

'Ten dead, seven wounded.'

Hans sighed and nodded. Over half of his force.

'Three times as many of them, give or take. Not enough.' Matheus gave Hans an angry look. 'Why didn't you retreat with those who could? Those men would still be alive.'

Hans was too tired to be angry, he just met the man's eyes with his own unrepentant stare. 'And so would the enemy. They would have escaped and taken a story of victory, or held us at this tree long enough to bring reinforcements. And everyone would hear that we fled while men fought and died.'

The implication of cowardice softened Matheus's glare. 'I have heard…' He stopped and decided against it.

'You have heard that I have fled battle before?'

Matheus nodded once.

Hans tapped his finger on his gore-caked chest. 'Never again.' He looked at the bodies of his men who were being carefully collected and carried away. 'They died well, and through their deaths we were victorious, and because of their valour men will remember them, and our enemy will hear of their bravery and their violence, and fear to meet us again.'

Matheus looked at him with discomfort, but could not argue with the sentiment. He looked around the carnage again and spoke without looking back. 'I understand that you wish to prove you are not a man who flees, and you have made your point clear. But men do not gladly follow those who are reckless with their lives.'

Hans gave a single dry snort of derision. 'I do not care if they are glad, only that they fight when it is required, and do their duty.'

Matheus stood and walked away, leaving Hans sitting against the trunk in silence, staring at the forest in the distance.

## Chapter 15

# The War Within

BARON HUGUES STORMED into the building Reinhard was using as his quarters, brandishing a rolled sheaf of parchment, with a look of pure anger on his face. Reinhard was surprised by the dramatic entrance, but he tried very hard not to appear so, flicking a casual look up to see what the commotion was.

It was three weeks since they had arrived in Arbugæ, and the weather was rapidly turning. The days were cooler and the first frosts had appeared on the colder mornings. Reinhard spent most of his time in that building, praying, meeting with clergy and brothers of the Order, and writing orders to the ever-increasing number of parishes he was responsible for.

He found the work increasingly irritating, but not as irritating as Grandsteward Hugues, who became ever more confident, and was imposing his authority on a tediously regular basis.

'This is your doing, isn't it?' snapped Hugues, waving the offending parchment like it was on fire.

'My dear man, what are you talking about, and please, would you do so less loudly?' Reinhard said, looking up.

Hugues gritted his teeth and slapped the paper down on Reinhard's desk. 'Duke Henry asks that we send half of our forces south for the winter, he is concerned the locals there are restless, and with the forces of the Order concentrated in the north, that there is risk of rebellion and discontent. He wants the Order to reinforce the major towns in the south to ensure peace, and asks that I see to it personally.'

Reinhard made a dismissive gesture. 'I do not understand the problem, it seems perfectly sensible to me. Is it not true that we stripped every man possible from the southern provinces to come north?'

'What? Yes, but that is beside the point and you know it. Don't play the fool with me. He could have sent anyone, but he sends me.'

'I still don't understand the problem,' said Reinhard innocently.

'Oh, you…' Hugues clenched his fist and bit back another angry outburst as Reinhard remained utterly unmoved.

'Count Conrad is still mopping up resistance south of the lake, on his way here. Count Otto's men are clearing through the coast north from Uppsala, trying to find the remnants of the army that reportedly fled there from the battle, we are the only ones who have already secured the lands we were assigned. Pardon my ignorance, but I don't understand why this has angered you so much.' Reinhard looked back down at the letter he was writing and dipped his quill again, just putting the finishing touches to the last line.

Hugues's hand appeared over the desk and snatched the letter away, Reinhard looked up, the corner of his eye twitching slightly as Hugues slowly and deliberately tore the sheet in half. Reinhard felt his own anger blossoming in his chest as the product of half his morning was ripped into pieces in front of him, but he did not let the emotion cross his face.

'That was rather childish,' he said, managing to keep his tone even. 'Bertrand will have to write that again now.'

Hugues turned and tossed the pieces of parchment at the quiet priest, who stood immobile at his own writing lectern, and turned back to Reinhard.

'You arranged this, so that I would be gone for the winter, so that you could take over here.'

'That is a bizarre accusation,' said Reinhard, reaching for a new sheet of parchment. 'Duke Henry does not take strategic advice from me. In any case, Duke Henry is not our lord, and you can refuse his order if you wish, so it would have been a stupid plan even if it had been me who set it in motion.'

This made Hugues visibly doubt himself for just a moment and the conflict showed in his face. It was all Reinhard could do not to just laugh at him. *Of course it was me, you simpleton.*

Hugues pushed the doubt aside and stood up from the table, left awkward and toothless.

'Will you do as he asks?'

'Of course I'll do as he asks,' snapped Hugues. 'He may not technically have command of us but as you fully know, nor can we afford the rift caused by refusing him.'

'Then leave whoever you choose behind as your second, and they can make decisions in your stead.' Reinhard dipped his quill again and started rewriting the letter, carefully recalling exactly what he had written before. *I wonder who he will leave behind? Who does he trust most? Sir Dietmar is in disgrace, Sir Sighard is my man through and through, Roland is too devout to be reliable, Hartung is practically my ward. I have every one of his senior men under my thumb, one way or another.*

Hugues grumbled and turned and ground his fist into his side as he stood there with his hands on his hips, but he could not, or would not, find any threat or blackmail to use against Reinhard, and eventually he just let out an exclamation of frustration and left without saying another word.

Reinhard allowed himself a small laugh of pure delight after the door closed, shaking his head as he chuckled. It was prideful, to celebrate such a victory – and the Lord did detest pridefulness – but he could not help himself. He got control of his pleasure and returned to the letter, feeling much better about having to re-write it now, he almost considered dictating it to Bertrand, but some letters were best written in your own hand, especially those written to the Pope.

Reinhard was surprised to find who Hugues had left behind from his senior men, the answer being almost all of them. He took half of the Order's forces and left most of the senior officers behind with Reinhard, ostensibly to guide and advise him.

Reinhard at first was confounded, but then he realised with a burst of admiration that it was really quite clever, making the best of a bad situation. Hugues had left all the men Reinhard had so carefully cultivated behind, giving Hugues the opportunity over the winter to groom new leaders, loyal to him, and to do so far from Reinhard's influence.

He had also not left any of them in charge, leaving Reinhard in the position where he would have to decide who was responsible for what, risking pitting one against the other, possibly even losing the carefully built loyalty of one or more of them in the process. It was so clever and unexpected a solution to the problem he had created that he was not even annoyed. He respected a good opponent, and Hugues, for all his failings, was still capable of challenging him from time to time.

The problem was soon present in the flesh when Hartung requested an audience with him. 'He said that, he said he was "requesting an audience"?' Reinhard asked Bertrand.

'Yes, your excellency,' said Bertrand.

'And he knows I am here.'

'Yes, he is waiting outside.'

'Hmmm.' Reinhard pressed a finger to his lips as he thought about it. 'I have not decided what to do, but I cannot really send him away.' Reinhard sighed. He hated having conversations he wasn't prepared for, or didn't already know the outcome of.

He was still trying to plan the meeting when Hartung arrived, and the boy flawlessly made the required gestures of respect and then sat in the seat Reinhard gestured to.

'Good morning, Brother Hartung, what can I do for you today?' Reinhard asked pleasantly.

Hartung was practically jittering with nerves, or perhaps excitement, it was hard to tell. Either way, it was the angst and impatience of youth on full display. Reinhard hated impatience, *for patience is dear to the Lord*. He did not allow his disapproval to show on his face, and smiled warmly at his young petitioner.

'Well, Grandsteward Hugues has left me in charge here, it seems.' He sounded rather unsure about that part, although he tried to sound confident.

'It seems? Is it not clear?' replied Reinhard with feigned confusion.

'Well, I was, as you know, his second. And that never changed, although it seems during the rush to leave, he has not pronounced, exactly… or perhaps clearly, who indeed is in command of the forces left behind.'

Reinhard waved his hand nonchalantly. 'A minor oversight, I am sure he simply trusted his officers to sort the matter correctly themselves.'

'Perhaps, but… well.' Hartung ground to a halt and looked unsure, perhaps even ashamed. 'It seems that a couple of the other brothers see it differently, and are not inclined to accept that I am, in fact, in command now.'

Reinhard raised his eyebrows. 'Oh, really? Why? If you were second, it makes sense.'

'Exactly!' said Hartung, trying hard to keep the whine out of his voice. 'But their claim is that I was his second only in his command, and now his command is gone, and that it should be a case of seniority who takes over here now.'

'Are you not senior?'

'Well, that... that is also not clear. If Lothair had decided on my father's titles, and given them to me by now, then it would be me, yes. But at the moment, technically speaking, I am a newly belted knight, not a count, and others would take precedence by rank and experience.' The admission clearly hurt the boy, who physically squirmed in his seat.

'Well, then why don't you let them take command, and agree to some compromise.'

Hartung's face fell, and Reinhard's mind raced through the obvious request the boy was going to make, and tried to weigh if he would agree to it, and if he would then follow through with that promise.

'That would not do. I... You see, I need to make a name for myself, to guarantee my lord Lothair's support. I cannot do that if I am humiliated by having my intent to command questioned, even refused.'

Reinhard nodded slowly and his eyes widened. 'Yes, that would be difficult indeed.'

'So, Grandmaster, I was hoping you could intervene. Your ruling on the matter would be respected, I am sure.'

Reinhard feigned surprise again and looked at Hartung as if internally debating the decision he had already made. 'Well, it is not my responsibility, the command of the troops here. Not my business to interfere in,' he said, telling the lie with profound tones of regret.

Hartung looked deflated and annoyed. 'But you have assigned command before, at the meeting in the camp at Uppsala, and on the field, where you removed Sir Dietmar and replaced him.'

Reinhard shook his head. 'Different matters, my boy. The decision at Uppsala was pre-agreed with Grandsteward Hugues, and the one in the field was a matter of insubordination that required instant action. Quite different, you understand.'

'I see. Well, could you not put in a quiet word for me? I am sure that even if it is not officially your decision, anyone in the Order would take your advice. I would really be most grateful, in the future.' Hartung made the bribe-laced promise clumsily, and Reinhard drank in his desperation, but knew that he had no choice but to agree, or risk losing the boy.

He let Hartung sit and worry for a few moments longer, allowing the gravity of the decision to weigh on his features, before slowly nodding his assent. 'I suppose that in this one case, I can make a small intervention for the good of the Order's interests. It is best that we do not have squabbles for the leadership, and I can see your case for it makes sense. I will speak to a few brothers – discreetly – and see what can be done.'

Hartung's face dissolved in relief and he smiled, standing and bowing. 'Thank you, Grandmaster. I will prove myself worthy of your efforts.'

'I know you will, my son, you are an asset to the Order.'

Hartung kissed Reinhard's ring when he proffered it, and then bowed flawlessly again and left with a spring in his step.

Reinhard tapped his nose for a while as he thought about his next move. It was complex, he had to pressure the right people in the right order, to ensure this did not cause him more problems than it solved. He decided to start with the easiest one first. He clicked his fingers at Bertrand. 'Ask Sir Sighard to come and see me, and once he has left, ask Sieur de Blanchant, and then… No, I will decide the rest later.'

'Yes, excellency.'

'There are two notable men still refusing outright to accept this, and others who are undecided, waiting to see which way the wind blows.'

Reinhard had spent two days pressuring the senior knights and officers of the Order to accept Hartung as the commander. He had faced stiffer resistance than he expected, finding even Roland hard to persuade. 'He is not respected, and he has little experience,' the man had said, warily.

Nor had he been able to provide a particularly convincing reason for his sudden interest. To the Saxon knights, he had played on the fact the boy was probably going to become count soon, emphasising the benefits of being seen supporting him. To the devout ones, he had hinted that it was divine inspiration, that the Lord had a plan, an argument that had swayed Roland. To others, he had said that the young man would only be a figurehead, with the power lying with those around him.

One by one, he had won over most of the officers, but he needed to decide how to handle the other two. Sieur de Blanchant was there, his support was essential. The sword made him a figurehead of the truly devout, and his skill at arms and reputation made him well respected by most of the rest. Sir Sighard was there, he was Reinhard's most dedicated follower and had backed his decision without question. It was the sort of unflinching loyalty Reinhard craved, and he had been rocked to the core how much his influence had slipped with the others.

Sir Dietmar was also there, called to advise him. To Reinhard's surprise, the soft-spoken German knight had agreed to help him, despite Reinhard's public admonishment a few weeks before. The knight was resolute in supporting Hartung's best interests, and in trying to remain on the fickle young man's good side, and perhaps he simply saw supporting Reinhard in this as serving both interests.

Other than that, support had been weak and hard to pin down. Perhaps it was the result of men seeing him arguing with Hugues, or perhaps it was a lack of recent effort, but his untouchable standing within the Order was in danger, and something would have to be done to rectify that. Opposition to his decisions or wishes could not be allowed to fester or spread.

'Who are they?' asked Sighard.

'Brother Jean, and Brother Andretti.'

Andretti was one of their handful of northern Italian knights, and he had poured scorn on the idea of being commanded by 'that German child'. His opinion wasn't so important, the number of men who looked to him, mostly the Italians, was small.

Jean de Valais, a noted French knight, was a different problem. He was a commander of a hundred, and well regarded by the French members of the Order, although disliked by many of the others for his repeatedly proven distaste for non-Frenchmen, who he regarded as inferior soldiers and gentlemen.

Jean was far too proud to take orders from Hartung voluntarily, and had demanded written agreement from Hugues to do so. Reinhard knew that sending a request to Hugues for mediation was pointless, and if he simply waited until Jean did it, the response was certain to be carefully calculated to make the situation worse.

No, something had to be done about it, and be done quickly.

'Can they be ordered to accept it?' asked Sighard.

'No, I don't have the authority to do that.' *And if they challenge me, it could destroy my power. After I have been refused once, I will find myself questioned at every turn.*

'Perhaps they can be encouraged with some reward or offer,' said Sighard uncertainly. The man was not subtle, which pained Reinhard, and he was not particularly bright, but he valued the big man's loyalty more than anything else.

'No, that would not be acceptable.' *If I am reduced to bribery, every order will be accompanied with a conditional refusal, conditional on giving favours.*

'Well, I could...'

'No, threats will not work. And if any knight of this Order can be cowed with mere threats then they should not wear our emblem.' Reinhard drummed his fingers on the tabletop, flirting with the only answer he could see, but knowing how extreme it was.

'This debate threatens the whole integrity of the Order here,' said Dietmar with a grimace, and Reinhard could have kissed the man for saying that, unprompted and so well timed.

'Indeed, Brother Dietmar, indeed.' Reinhard snapped his fingers and nodded. 'You have it exactly correct. That is an offence to this Holy Order, ordained by God through his representative on earth, our Holy Father. The sabotage of our Order will not be tolerated.'

Dietmar frowned. 'I did not say sabotage.'

'You did not need to,' said Reinhard with a serious nod. 'It is not in my power to order a resolution to this issue, but it is my absolute authority, granted by the Pope and by Duke Henry, to maintain order in these lands, and to maintain discipline in this brotherhood.'

Dietmar and Roland frowned and looked at each other. 'You mean to punish them?'

'I mean to make an example, that undermining our success and unity will not be tolerated. Sir Sighard, take ten men, your most reliable, and seize Brother Andretti. Take him to the front of the hall, strip him, whip him, and tie him to a post. Let all see what becomes of those who oppose the brotherhood, even from within.'

Dietmar sputtered in horror. 'You cannot do that!'

'I certainly can,' said Reinhard with a cautionary look.

'Grandmaster, if I may, a knight cannot be subject to corporal punishment. His body is inviolate, other than by the use of weapons in battle, or in a legal duel.' Roland leaned in, his face drawn. 'He can be executed, or fined, or stripped of his lands or titles by his king or his liege lord, if his offence deserves it, but he cannot be beaten or whipped like a commoner. Never.'

'He is not a knight, he is a sworn brother of this Order, and he is not in Italy, he is here, in the Order's lands. There is no law here but God's law, and the rules of this brotherhood. And I judge both,' Reinhard said sternly, and Roland backed up a fraction and his fingers were clenched until they shone white.

'This will go very badly, Sir Andretti will not accept this.'

'His acceptance is not required.'

'His men will not accept it.'

'Then they are liable to join him! Do you see, even the notion that he opposes me is insidious. Already you feel many more will do so. This is not a brotherhood of equals, this is not a travelling court of a king, this is a Holy Order of brothers sworn to a sacred duty, who have no choice but to follow it. If any question that, they need to be removed, like diseased animals are cut from the herd. If Andretti's punishment reveals those who are not true, good! We will strip them of the Order's badge and exile them home in disgrace, if that is what they choose. In any case, there are not so many of them.'

Reinhard stopped his diatribe and carefully wiped the spittle from his lower lip, and calmed his temper, returning to a neutral expression. 'There has been enough talk of disobedience. How can we enforce our will on the conquered people, if we cannot enforce it within our own ranks? Did our saviour not teach us, before we remove the speck from our brother's eye, we must remove the log from our own?'

Roland breathed heavily for a moment and then nodded. 'It is written that is his word, yes.'

'Then we will follow it. Before we can cleanse this province, we will cleanse our own ranks, and we will start with the troublemaker Brother Andretti.'

## Chapter 16

# A New Order

THE RIVER AT Arbugæ was not wide, but it was too deep to ford, and Hans and a half-dozen of his men left their horses on the south bank with the rest of his party and were ferried across by a boat they called from the far bank. There were some buildings on the south side, tucked in between the forested hills and the water, but most of the town was on the north bank on the flat land beyond the river.

Conrad's army had captured Tuna without a fight, and cleared their way through the towns and villages all the way to reach Arbugæ, and now were spreading out to garrison key towns and set up winter quarters. Hans and fifty men had been assigned, at his request, to stay in Arbugæ for the winter, as the town was nominally the border between Conrad's and the Order's lands.

Conrad had left an assistant, a dour-faced administrator who regarded Hans and his soldiers with practised distaste, to deal with matters of governance and represent Conrad's interests. Hans's job was to help the Order maintain control, patrol the local area, and to defend the town if it was attacked. But the Order was quite capable of doing all of those things, and Conrad had made clear the real reason for his presence there was to keep an eye on the Order's activities, and maintain Conrad's presence and claim in the town with a visible garrison.

Hans and Matheus disembarked after the brief crossing on the dock next to the largest building on the riverside, a large stone-walled hall with the Order's banner flying proudly from both gable ends. There were additional walls for a new building being added to one side of the hall, with three courses of stones already in place.

There was quite a crowd around the front of the hall, Order soldiers and townsfolk, and Hans walked around to see what had drawn them. As he rounded the corner, he saw that a naked, bleeding, shivering man was tied to a tall post rammed into the earth in front of the main building, right at the side of the broad path that ran along the riverside.

He squinted at the man, and thought that he did not look Norse, which piqued his curiosity. As he stood and stared, a familiar voice spoke up from his left, and he turned to see Sir Dietmar stopping next to him.

'Sir Hans Mettel, by God, I am surprised and pleased to see you here!'

Hans smiled at his friend and embraced him. 'Sir Dietmar, I heard that you had joined the Order, but I did not know where you were. I am happy to see you are well. Tell me,' he jerked his head at the prisoner tied to the post, 'what is happening here?'

Sir Dietmar's eyes flicked to the man and his smile faded. 'Come, best not to speak of it here.'

Hans caught the trepidation in Dietmar's voice and felt the pang of worry. The whole atmosphere was off. He followed the knight away down the riverside path a little and Dietmar stopped and leaned in close, keeping his voice down. 'That is Sir Gennaio Andretti, a knight of the Order. Or at least he used to be a knight of the Order.'

Hans was horrified. 'That is a knight? Who tied and beat him?

This is an outrage.' Hans's eyes narrowed at Dietmar. 'Why have you not released him?'

Dietmar looked away in shame. 'Believe me, I wish I could, but there are too many fanatics there, and in the ranks of the brotherhood, who would cut us down if we tried.'

'What are you talking about, what is going on?'

'A power struggle, it is ugly. There was nearly a mutiny three days ago, when the order for this punishment was given. Many of the knights of the Order opposed it. Some of them were stripped of their status, others were expelled, two of the more vocal ones disappeared in the night, only their weapons and blood stains were found on the riverbank in the morning.'

Hans's mouth opened in shock. 'They were murdered?'

'We don't know. The men on guard that night in that area say they heard nothing, saw nothing, but… well, those men are among the fanatics.'

'They murdered brothers of their own Order?'

'It is possible, but I have already said too much.'

Hans choked back his surprise, putting a hand on Dietmar's shoulder. 'You are afraid to even speak of it? Where is Baron Hugues, who can put an end to this madness?'

'Baron Hugues has gone, Grandmaster Reinhard is in charge here now, and he is ruthlessly enforcing his power. This is all part of that.'

'Then who is in charge of the Order's soldiers? Not the bishop, surely.'

'No.' Dietmar looked at Hans with a mournful expression. 'Hartung.'

'Hartung, he is allowing this?'

'Worse, he is actively supporting it. The bishop gave him the position, and the boy is his faithful devotee. They are inseparable now, and Hartung does anything his master requires.'

'How… how did it come to this?'

'I am sorry, my old friend, it is my fault. I helped the bishop promote Hartung, I did not understand what it would mean. I thought…' Dietmar looked away for a moment, shaking his head with regret. 'I thought it would keep me close to him, but after I opposed this punishment, Hartung took that as an attack on him, he will no longer even allow me in his presence. The bishop is considering exiling me, and I have no path to repairing the situation, none that I can see, anyway.'

Hans's stomach churned at the pain on the honourable Dietmar's face. Dietmar had always been a straightforward and considered man, and that was a great strength as a military leader, but made him vulnerable to the machinations of power and politics.

'It is not your fault, you behaved as you believed was correct.'

'Regardless, I have completely failed. Our lord's son is lost to that monster.' Dietmar looked at Hans. 'Perhaps he would speak to you?'

'I doubt it, when I left last year he would barely look at me. Reinhard's claws were deep in him, even then.'

'Then why are you here? How did you come to return?'

'Hildewa sent me, to try to bring her son home. She is struggling to retain control of her lands, already other lords are petitioning Lothair for parts of Adolf's domain, and she needs him there to press his own claims.' He did not add that his own status and future were also at stake. Whoever claimed Adolf's lands would also be Hans's liege lord. He did not know if Hartung was even someone he should be supporting at this point, but he was still bound by his promise to Adolf, and he would see that through, no matter what.

'Reinhard has convinced him to make a name for himself here, and that he will then have a stronger case when he returns home.'

Sir Hans scowled. 'A name made by whipping belted knights? That will hardly help, nor will it matter what reputation he makes if his lands are already gone.'

'Well, he cares about that, he wants his father's titles, perhaps you can convince him that he needs to go home to lay claim to them formally.'

'Yes, well, I have a letter to him from his mother, and I will at least pass that to him.'

'Good, hopefully he will see sense.'

'Or we will have to find another way.'

Dietmar stiffened and gave Hans a concerned glare. 'What do you mean by that?'

Hans shook his head. 'I don't know yet.' He took another distasteful look back towards the bloodied Italian knight, and waved at his men to join him. He had to secure quarters for them, and organise the reconnoitre of the surrounding lands.

Reinhard's nose twitched as Sir Sighard went on. 'Seven of the Italian brothers left in the morning, they piled their surcoats in the street and trampled them into the mud, for all to see. My men cleared them away as soon as they heard about it, but not before a number of the locals had seen it. I expect word has spread throughout the town by now.' The knight sounded almost apologetic, which was rare.

'I see. And what of the others, what other traitors lurk in our ranks?'

'It is hard to say, Grandmaster. There are some who have secluded themselves from the rest of us, they still perform their duties, but they do not speak to outsiders, and I know they harbour great resentment.'

Reinhard was furious. He was furious with the Italians who had abandoned him, furious with the knights who had ridden away in broad daylight a week ago, furious with the other brothers who whispered in dark corners that he was losing control, that he had gone too far. It was two weeks since Sir Gennaio Andretti had been cut down from the post where he had been whipped. He had been a thorn in Reinhard's side ever since. The man refused to repent, refused to leave the Order in disgrace, and Reinhard was too worried about the consequences to either exile him or punish him further.

He was also furious with himself, not for going too far, his mind would not consider that as a possibility, but for not predicting the results. He had spent his life imposing his will on clergy, functionaries, weaklings, easily flattered lesser nobles and defeated Norse townsfolk. He had never before had to tyrannise veteran soldiers and veteran knights, and he had simply miscalculated how hard that was, and how obstinate they would be.

*It was not a mistake per se, merely a miscalculation of the reaction.* He had thought that after the humiliation of Andretti, most of the rest would fall into line, but it might perhaps have weakened his position further. The locals would smell the weakness, he was sure of it, and that army that had dispersed in these lands would recover their courage and come after him. *Why couldn't these troublemakers see that? Why didn't they understand that their actions helped the enemy?*

'Grandmaster?' Reinhard looked up and saw Sighard looking at him earnestly.

'Yes?'

'What do you wish me to do?'

Reinhard tried to appear confident as the unfamiliar feeling of terror dug into the pit of his stomach. *I have no idea how to solve this.* The realisation was physically painful. He had never before found a problem he could not threaten his way out of. Killing Brother Andretti would do nothing more than make a martyr of him, leaving him alive made him a constant reminder of his opposition to Reinhard.

What he needed was a distraction. Something to focus the Order on an external enemy. He needed to find a Norse enemy and fight them, and, if no enemy could be found, he needed to create one.

'Sir Sighard, I am concerned about a revival of the Norse armed resistance, in this period of difficulty. We must pre-empt this threat. We never cleared out the defeated army that dispersed in this area, we never made a full accounting of their weapons and armour; a serious mistake. We must make efforts to do so now.'

'Grandmaster, winter is almost upon us.'

'Exactly, exactly why we must do this now, before we are unable to do it for months, giving the enemy time to lay their plans.'

Sighard looked confused. 'I have seen little evidence of armed Norsemen since we arrived.'

Reinhard waved the retort away irritatedly. 'You do not hear everything that I hear.'

'As you say, Grandmaster.'

'I wish for you to arrange expeditions, to the local villages and towns. Search them for any signs of an armed resistance, for any evidence of warriors present, and deal with those found with the utmost severity. Do you understand?'

Sighard nodded dutifully. 'I do understand, Grandmaster.'

'The utmost severity! We must crush this potential rebellion in the cradle, before it has time to spread in the spring. Send out patrols of fifty men, at least four of them, spread these troublemakers of ours amongst them, and let them focus their attention on God's work, not on their own selfish grumblings.'

'It will be done, Grandmaster.'

Sir Hans cupped his hands and blew on them, before showing them again to the fire. He had just spent hours with half a dozen other men caring for the horses in the makeshift stables they had constructed at the edge of town. The buildings were rough, but they were shelter, and they kept the horses out of the wind and the snow that lay on the ground most days.

His men had settled in uneasily, billeting on the edge of town to stay away from the internal strife of the Order's soldiers in town.

They had patrolled the area and visited local villages, but had not been attacked, nor sighted armed Norsemen more than a couple of times, in both cases just small groups spotted moving through the woods.

They knew armed bands of the enemy still roamed the land, but they were keeping a low profile, and attacks on the Christians were currently rare. He supposed that everyone was settling in somewhere for the winter, no one could hope to survive it living rough in the woods. He remembered his last winter in the North, at the siege of Jönköping, where men had frozen at their posts and been found stuck to the palisade in the morning, or simply died in their blankets. He shivered at the memory and inched a little closer to the fire.

Footsteps crunched behind him and he turned to see who was coming. 'Sir Dietmar, what are you doing out this late? Come to the fire.'

'Sir Hans, I am pleased as always.' Dietmar came over to the fire and sighed in satisfaction as the warmth hit his face. 'Your men told me you were seeing to the horses.'

'Yes, we take turns, I take mine with the rest.'

'It is good to do so.'

'Yes. Anyway, is there something wrong?'

'Ah, well… always.'

'You are still having troubles?'

'I am still in disgrace, if that is what you mean.'

Hans gave him a sympathetic smile. 'Well, you will always be welcome in our quarters.'

'I thank you for that, but it is not why I came. Reinhard has ordered a series of expeditions, in force, to the local villages. He says it is to root out armed Norsemen, look for signs of rebellion, and search for hidden weapons from the scattered army that came here.'

'Now?' said Hans. 'In this weather?'

'Yes.'

'He is insane. And in any case, what armed Norsemen?'

'You have seen some, haven't you?'

'Well, yes, a couple of pairs of them, perhaps they were just hunters, no threat to us in any case. There is no army out there, no threat other than in his imagination. What is he thinking?'

'Well… He has assigned many of those who are opposed to him to these expeditions, all under the command of men loyal to him,' Dietmar said, with heavy emphasis.

'Oh, for…' Hans shook his head in frustration. 'He is sending you out to hunt ghosts, merely to keep you busy?'

'Something like that, I assume. Idle minds have more time to conspire against him, and idle tongues to gossip and complain. Or at least, that is what I suspect is his reasoning.'

'Well, you have my sympathies, I assume you are going on one of these, an outcast such as yourself cannot be left out.'

'Yes, but don't be too happy for me, Reinhard has requested you send some of your men too, to foster cooperation between the Order and Duke Conrad's forces.' Dietmar gave Hans a dry smile, which Hans did not return.

'Why on earth would I agree to that, sending my men on these pointless missions?'

'Because it will likely be easier than the consequences of refusing.'

'I am not afraid of that scoundrel.'

'No, perhaps not, but who supplies your food?'

Hans stilled and then swore. 'He wouldn't.'

'I am not sure there is anything he wouldn't do, and abusing his power to make your life here miserable would be the least of it. I suggest you agree, go along, be cold for three days and come home. We won't find anything significant anyway. It's all just a show.'

'Fine, I will do it.'

'I am assigned to the group going west, there is a village in the next valley. I think you should come with that one, Hartung is leading it.'

Hans looked at him intently. 'You have been sent under Hartung's command?'

'Yes.'

'I'm surprised he is giving you that chance to spend time with him.'

'I think, at this point, he knows there is little I can do, perhaps he even hopes it will make it worse. Anyway, that is what I am ordered to do, and I don't feel like a whipping today, it's a bit too cold.'

Hans laughed at the dark humour. Dietmar almost never joked. 'Perfect weather to sit on a horse for three days achieving nothing, however.'

'True enough, but we will endure it.'

The column of fifty men set out the next morning. A cold wind was blowing and light snow fell persistently from before dawn. The road was well worn by horse, foot and cart, and easy to follow even with the ankle-deep snow, and the drifts that piled under the sunken verge.

Hans led five of his men, and Hartung commanded a small band of Order knights and squires and men at arms on horseback, with thirty or so footsoldiers following on. Hans was perfectly polite, and accepted the boy's nervous commands without issue or resistance. He had seen Hartung twice since he arrived, once to deliver the letter from his mother, which had elicited little response, and once at a feast in the Order's headquarters that he had been invited to.

He had tried to wheedle from Hartung his thoughts on returning home as his mother wished, but the boy had been evasive and irritated by the questions. Worried about alienating him, Hans had not pressed further. Nothing would happen until spring, and there was no sense in applying too much pressure too quickly. He was sure a better opportunity would present itself, perhaps even on this march.

They brought a Norseman with them, the local ex-ruler called Frode, who had been the earl of these lands. Hans was fascinated to find out from Dietmar that the man had been a senior leader of the Norse army throughout the Crusades, as far back as the campaign on the island of Sjælland, and all through the siege of Jönköping and the battle outside Uppsala. He was curious to speak to the man, to perhaps learn something about his past enemy, but the deposed earl was dispirited and quiet, barely speaking unless required, and only spoke in halting French. He looked thoroughly reduced and defeated.

The short day was already darkening when they reached the village they were headed to, and with the help of Frode, they attained shelter for the men and horses without having to spend a miserable night in tents or around fires. They evicted half a dozen Norse families from their homes for the night, who moved in with neighbours, and settled down into crowded Norse houses. Hans's men brought their own rations, but he noted with distaste how some of the men of the Order in his house rummaged through the locals' food stores, carelessly discarding what they did not want.

The needless sabotage rankled him, but he had no authority to stop the men.

The next day was as dim as the one before but the snow had stopped falling. The men were roused from the warmth of their shelters and gathered in the centre of the village. Hartung had had his horse brought, so that he alone sat on one, and could look over their ranks.

'Gather all the people here, tell them once they are here my men will search the village for weapons. Frode, talk to them and have it done peacefully, or my men will do it by force.' Hartung gave the order in German, he did not speak French well, and another knight translated it for Frode, who nodded leadenly and walked off into the buildings.

Hans stood there for some time waiting for something to

happen, and for a good while nothing did, then people started trickling warily into the space from all around, others going around the buildings behind them, entering and rousing the people within. Hans counted the Order soldiers while this was happening, and realised at least half a dozen were missing. He mused over that as the roundup of the locals, several hundred, continued.

Finally, Frode walked over to Hartung. 'This is everyone except a few who are too sick to move.' Hartung nodded at the translation and sat up in his saddle.

As Hartung talked to the man, hooves could be heard coming into town and eight Order soldiers, the ones missing from the gathering, appeared between two buildings, and there were gasps of horror and anguish when the locals saw that they were driving prisoners before them. There were five men, all of fighting age. Some were bloodied and injured, one was prone and unmoving and had been dragged there on his face and chest, leaving a smear of blood and mud behind him.

'We caught them sneaking out of the village and into the woods to the west, as you expected,' said the lead knight, dismounting and backhanding a struggling prisoner to the ground. The knight reached up behind his saddle and untied a wrapped bundle and dumped it on the ground where Hartung could see it. He leant down to unwrap the cargo, revealing a sword, a bundle of axes and a bag of spearheads. Two other men brought a pair of maille hauberks and half a dozen shields strapped together in a stack.

Hartung looked at Frode furiously. 'What is this then? I thought your people would obey our laws?'

Frode looked deflated and shook his head. 'I am sorry, I ordered them to surrender their weapons, but my people are proud. Please, they can learn, if you give them time.'

'Oh, they will learn, but they have no time.' Hartung turned to the knights. 'Tie nooses, we will hang them.' He pointed at the crowd. 'And bring me their families.'

'Their families?' asked Frode dumbly.

'Yes, their families. They would have known about these weapons, they are just as guilty. We understand that many of your men are willing to die, but are they willing for their families to die with them?'

Dietmar finally broke his silence, moving quickly over to stand in front of Hartung. 'You intend to execute their families?'

'Yes.'

'You cannot do this.'

'I can, it is the order of the Grandmaster. An example is to be made, and from now on, all families of traitors are guilty, and are to be punished accordingly.'

'That is outrageous, the men with the weapons must be punished, but women and children? This cannot be allowed, this is not right, this is not Christian.'

Hartung simply looked away from the outraged Dietmar and waved at some of the men guarding the crowd. 'If the families refuse to step forward, seize fifteen, three for each criminal, I don't care who.'

There was a wave of fear and shouting as the crowd worked out what was happening, and then Order soldiers were bodily hauling people out of the panicked mass. Women, old men, boys, even a young girl, were hauled out and thrown to the ground, where they huddled together in fear as the armed men stood over them.

Hans watched with rising horror and a sense of dread at what was happening. The fifty Order soldiers suddenly looked very thinly spread, many of them trying to control the angry and frightened crowd, others standing with Hartung and the captives.

Sir Dietmar finally decided to act. He walked over to the small group of the condemned. 'Enough! Back away!' he shouted at the soldiers guarding the captives, who looked at each other but instinctively moved away, well used to the tone of authority, and unwilling to argue with a knight.

Dietmar stood over the group of Norse and calmly stared at Hartung. 'I will not allow this.'

'You will do as commanded!' Hartung looked around, his face red with fury, and finally he pointed a finger at Dietmar. 'You would defend our enemies? TRAITOR!' he screamed.

'These are not our enemies,' Dietmar replied. 'But by your actions you will make them into that.'

'I am your commander, I ORDER you to stand aside!' the boy said, his horse whinnying and sidestepping, ears pinned back as he felt and heard his master's anger.

'You are a boy, unfit to lead. I had thought better of you, it is my failure and shame that you have turned out to be such a failure of a knight. There is no honour in this, no justice, your father would be ashamed of you.'

'How dare you? How DARE you!' shouted Hartung. 'You defend these filth, you who would not defend my father? You will stand your ground for our enemies, but you fled the battle and left my father to die! These people killed him, they took everything from me, and YOU, you of all people, would side with them over me?' Hartung was struggling to control his emotions, and Hans saw that the accusation had landed hard, and Dietmar was reeling.

'Seize him!' shrilled Hartung, but no one moved to obey. Most of the soldiers had their hands full, and the knights behind Hartung looked uncertain, many looked outright disgusted.

Dietmar looked at Hartung sadly and shook his head. 'I decline to be subject to your justice, I have seen what that means. I am Sir Dietmar of Eresburg, I was knighted by Duke Lothair himself, and my person is inviolate, I cannot be taken or harmed unless on the orders of my liege lord, or by force of arms – if any are willing to try.'

'Then that is your decision,' said Hartung with spite. Hartung pointed at the men who had backed away from Dietmar. 'Seize him, or be condemned with him. We will take him to Grandmaster

Reinhard for judgement and punishment, you can guard him or you can join him.'

The four soldiers finally made their decision, and advanced warily on Dietmar, who turned to the advancing soldiers and drew his sword. He pointed it at them and the first one stopped and looked around nervously to check his fellows were with him.

'Dietmar!' Hans shouted, as he saw his friend draw, and he moved to go and join the man, but a hand clamped onto his and he turned to see Matheus looking at him. 'If you go, we will follow. Do not throw away your men's lives for this, we cannot win here by force.'

Hans looked at Matheus in anger and struggled to pull his hand away. 'No!' a proud voice called, crisp and clear. He turned to see Dietmar looking at him, holding out his hand. 'This is not your fight, Hans.' The German knight smiled and shook his head. 'Not this time, old friend. Someone must see the truth of this, and someone must continue our duty.'

Hans shook his head and snarled in rage, but his struggles against the hands that held him lessened. A few of the Order soldiers ran over to corral him and his men, both sides eyeing each other and gripping the hilts and hafts of their weapons. He saw Dietmar return his attention to the soldiers and calmly set his grip and stance, and two of them summoned the courage to try and take him.

Dietmar whipped his blade up from a low guard, almost casually, and knocked the spear of the left man aside, then lashed the raised blade back in a vicious backhanded cut that half severed the second man's raised sword arm and ripped out the side of his face in a spray of splintered bone and blood and teeth. The grievously injured soldier screamed and reeled away, blood pumping from his wounds, and Dietmar pivoted and struck the stumbling spearman down with a crunching blow to the temple that killed him before he hit the ground. Dietmar's back foot had not even moved.

Hans felt a thump of hope in his chest as Dietmar stood there and slowly cleaned his sword on his red-spattered surcoat, before resting the point on the ground and looking at Hartung with disgust. 'You send peasants to bind me, Hartung? Did I really teach you nothing?'

Hans looked around and saw the reluctance of any others to step forwards, and saw the restive crowd of Norse that so greatly outnumbered their captors. For a moment, he envisaged that crowd breaking loose, and him and his men fighting their way to Dietmar, and then to escape.

But two of the knights behind Hartung looked at each other and walked past the young commander, who was frozen on his horse in rage. Dietmar eyed the two men as they approached. 'Which of you will be first, brothers? At least you are belted, and know how these things are done.'

One of the knights stopped and rested his hand on his hilt, and the other drew. Nothing flashy, he simply put his sword into a low guard in front and advanced carefully into range. Slow, deliberate, a seasoned killer.

Dietmar moved into his own stance and the two men attacked and struck together with no preamble. Dietmar got the inside of the bind as their swords met and he thrust the crossguard into his opponent's chin, knocking him off balance. He used the time gained to step around the man and, hooking his blade around the knight's neck, he grabbed it with his free hand on the other side, leaving the edge resting against his opponent's throat, locking his head in a sharp steel embrace.

The knight froze, eyes wide, knowing his death had already happened.

But Dietmar did not pull back on the blade, even as blood was starting to trickle across it from where the keen steel bit into the soft skin. He looked at Hartung and held his victim there while he gave his old squire a look of pity.

'May God forgive you, my boy. Because I cannot.' Then he let go with his left hand and spread his arms, holding his sword out from his body. His shocked opponent, released from the blade, twisted and brought his own sword up again to strike, and Dietmar never stopped staring at Hartung until the knight whipped the blade around and cut him down where he stood.

Hans's mind swam in shock and anguish as his friend fell, and he screamed and ripped at the hands that restrained him and headbutted the Order soldier who tried to hold him back. Sound and feelings deadened and merged into one wave of hatred as he clawed to get free, to get to the murderer who was pulling his sword free of Dietmar's dying body.

But the hands would not release him, and the rage would not leave him, and he was borne to the ground, kicking and cursing and swearing death on them all.

He did not hear the shouted commands. Did not see as the Order soldiers moved to the captives, or as the steel of their weapons struck cowering flesh, or as the crisp white surcoats of the Order were spattered red once again.

# PART 2

## Chapter 17

# The Pain of Pride

**Spring 1120**

'SOON WE WILL have to fight the Christians again. Halla has asked us to train you to be ready. Some of you have fought before, some of you have never held a spear, it does not matter, we will tell you everything you need to know.'

Gjaldir stood in the cold morning, shield in one hand, a spear shaft in the other, and listened as Gunnar spoke. The town was emerging from a long, tiresome winter. It had not been as severe as the winter before, during the siege of Jönköping, which the locals had said was one of the worst in memory. But here in the wilderness, frequent snows and intense cold had still restricted life to a pattern of tedium and chores.

Gjaldir had spent much of the limited daylight each day, other than in the worst weather, felling small trees and splitting firewood for the insatiable fires that kept every longhouse warm. They had managed to build enough houses before the worst of winter came, and then the ground had frozen and more work was impossible until the spring thaw, which had yet to happen.

But now the days were warmer and longer, and despite the still biting chill, the people were beginning the preparation for a season of building, hunting, and if required, defending their settlement.

So Gjaldir stood in rows with about fifty other inexperienced men who wished to be counted in the shieldwall, and listened as King Sigurd's old champion spoke.

'There are three types of fight: the shieldwall, the broken shield-wall or open fight, and the duel. You must learn each to be an effective warrior, for many of the skills are shared. Fighting in the wall is the simplest, but requires the most discipline, and we will do that last. First, we will see who among you has the instinct and the heart, and teach the basics of weapons and shields.'

Gunnar walked down the line, separating them into groups of five or six, and sent each group with an experienced warrior. Gjaldir was in the last group, and Gunnar took them himself. They moved over to a clear area of ground at the edge of the forest, near the stony lake shore.

'Which of you has fought with shield and spear before?' Gunnar asked. Three men nodded. 'And with axe or sword?'

Gjaldir was tempted to say he had, but he knew the one brief fight he had had with Bjorn's men was mocked by the Norse warriors, and he kept quiet. Gunnar looked at him. 'You, Gjaldir the smith, you have never fought? I thought Eric said you claimed to be an *ulfdrengr*.' Gunnar eyed him suspiciously.

'I do not claim that. My jarl said that if I had been a freeman I could, as it is true I have killed a wolf and a warrior in combat. But I killed the warrior with a thrown hammer, not in a close fight as you were asking. I have never fought with a shield and spear.'

'Ah, I see. A thrown weapon can be powerful indeed, in the right situation, but is not advisable in most fights. Here.' Gunnar pulled his axe from his belt and tossed it to Gjaldir. 'Hit that tree.' He pointed at a tree some twenty paces away.

Gjaldir caught the axe and felt its weight, looking at Gunnar but not seeing any mocking or contempt. He turned his body to an angle and judged the distance to the tree. Then he cocked back his arm and swung the axe hard, letting go and watching it swoop towards the target, rotating in the air. The weapon glanced off the side of the tree, hitting it handle first, and spun off into the grass.

Gjaldir looked at the axe, embarrassed, as a couple of the other men chuckled.

'This is why we don't often throw our weapons in battle. That was a useful axe, and now you do not have it, and the enemy does.' Gunnar walked over and picked up the axe, returning it to his belt. 'I believe you when you say that you have killed a man that way before, I have heard the story told. But that is the lesson, a thrown weapon is very unreliable, sometimes it kills, sometimes it doesn't, in both cases you no longer have the weapon. It is only useful in very limited circumstances.'

'Like what?' asked one of the other men.

'When you are defending a wall, or if you have two weapons and are being charged by two opponents. Or if your shieldwall faces a larger mass of poorly armoured enemies. In those situations, a thrown weapon could be an advantage.'

He hefted his spear shaft, which, like all of theirs, had had the killing tip removed. 'Now, we will start with the spear, it is the chief weapon in battle, and the first you must master.'

Gjaldir returned to the longhouse bruised and battered, his arms aching and his lip bleeding. Using a spear had been utterly alien to him in a way that using an axe never would be. The strange positions he had to hold the shield and spear in had used muscles he did not normally use, and he had tired quickly, his shoulder becoming numb and exhausted from the work.

Time and again Gunnar had made them practise attacks and defences he had demonstrated, simple thrusts with the spear and parries with the shield. Gjaldir had been no better at it than the others, and a missed block had let a blunt wooden spear shaft strike him in the mouth, splitting his lip and leaving blood in his mouth for the rest of the afternoon.

As he entered the building, Aeske tottered over with a squeal of delight and latched himself onto one of Gjaldir's dirt-streaked calves. 'Jaldir!' the boy exclaimed, and he ruffled Aeske's hair in return, a broad smile cracking across his tired face.

'The warrior returns, and it looks like whatever you were doing went badly,' said Brunhild, appearing behind her son and giving Gjaldir an amused look up and down.

Gjaldir shrugged, a movement which elicited a wince of pain from his shoulders. 'It went… It was more difficult than I expected.'

'Outside?' asked Aeske, still clinging to his leg with one hand and pointing back out the door with the other. Gjaldir had been taking Aeske out and helping him learn to walk, then start to run and play during the spring whenever he had time, as Brunhild was busy for almost all of the day. The boy had loved it and grown very attached to him in those months.

'No, not now,' he replied, and Aeske's face fell. He turned to his mother, looking crestfallen, hoping for a different answer, and she sighed.

'I will take you,' she said, looking almost as exhausted as Gjaldir.

'Outside!' Aeske squealed in delight, bouncing at the knees.

'Yes, outside.'

Aeske let go of Gjaldir's calf and rushed past him, waddling off out the door at an impressive speed for such unsteady legs, not waiting for his mother to join him. She managed one knowing glance at Gjaldir on her way past him as she followed her son out the door.

The spring and early summer continued in the same pattern, an endless, exhausting litany of work and training and chores. Gjaldir learned how to handle a spear and shield, and then an axe and shield, and finally crude wooden swords. Whenever Gjaldir thought he was beginning to know their ways, Gunnar brought in experienced warriors to spar with the new men and Gjaldir would find himself on the receiving end of beatings and humiliation, only rarely punctuated with moments of triumph.

As the weeks passed, he began to truly realise how little he had known before, and each revelation gave him false confidence that hid the next nasty surprise from his eyes, but as time went on, he became more and more often the equal of the warriors brought to spar with them, even beating some handily.

He was the master of everyone in his training group. It had reached the point where many were reluctant to face him in sparring, as his speed and strength and blooming skill were hard to contend with. He finally began to believe that he was ready to move on from the training, and fight with the men who were already starting to go out on raids back down to the south.

That was the case on a fine May morning, as he pummelled aside the shield of his opponent, a young farmer from outside Uppsala called Lefnir, who had spirit but not enough skill or decisiveness in combat, and struck him a nasty blow to the shoulder with his wooden sword.

The man reeled away with a curse, and threw his weapons to the ground as he nursed his shoulder and Gjaldir smirked, looking around the group and grinning, enjoying the moment and the feeling of power it gave him. He had always enjoyed physically dominating other men, ever since the fighting on the patch in Minden in his youth.

Gunnar walked over and looked at Lefnir in annoyance, then cast his stare on Gjaldir, who was still grinning haughtily. 'You think you are done here, Gjaldir?'

'I think these men no longer challenge me.'

'Really? Because I think you have only just begun to learn.'

Gjaldir couldn't resist a chortle at that, although the look on Gunnar's face when he did somewhat quelled his outburst. He waved a hand at the group. 'I can beat any of them, and many of the experienced warriors.'

'It is true, one on one, in a fair fight.'

'Yes.'

'You think that makes you ready?'

Gjaldir frowned slightly. 'Does it not?'

'What about an unfair fight?'

Gjaldir paused, confused. 'Well, I don't know, it depends...'

'Let's find out,' said Gunnar, pointing at two of the other men. 'You two, fight him together, now. Don't stop until he is on the ground.'

'What?' Gjaldir barely had time to react, and his protest died on his lips as two of the men, who he had often beaten down, grinned and advanced on him with their wooden weapons.

Gjaldir got his shield and sword up and glanced nervously between them, unsure what to do. He had never fought two men before. He had not decided what to do before two weapons started hailing blows down on him. At first, he caught most on his shield and sword, but the first one that got through and hit his head confused him momentarily and he lost track of both his opponents, taking a welter of hits before someone tripped him and put him on his arse, to a patter of laughs from the rest of the group. He had not even touched them in return.

Gjaldir scowled as the two men backed away, nodding and laughing to each other, and he jumped to his feet.

'Again,' said Gunnar, without a hint of emotion, and the two men got their weapons up and advanced once more, grinning and spreading out to trap him.

Gjaldir decided the best thing to do would be to attack one

quickly, and then turn and deal with the other, so he charged the man on his left and hacked wildly at his shield, trying to force it aside to get a winning blow at the man's head. But the man simply covered and blocked, not giving him an opening, and after two blows the second man landed his own weapon on Gjaldir's shoulders from behind, then a jab in the ribs, and then a glancing attack to the head as he ducked and tried to turn.

As soon as he took his eyes off the first opponent to deal with the second, the first counterattacked and Gjaldir went down under a welter of strikes again, driven to one knee, wincing and cursing. The laughter rang around the group once more.

He got his breath back and pushed himself to his feet, staring angrily at Gunnar. 'This is impossible.'

'In a real battle, it will happen often, where one man faces two. Especially for a man like you, who does not care if his comrades are his friends. Men like you will often find themselves alone in battle. Will you be ready?'

Gunnar pointed at the two men who had bested Gjaldir. 'Now try against me.'

The two men looked at each other nervously and nodded, advancing on the old huskarl the same way, as Gunnar nonchalantly picked up a shield and wooden sword. They attacked together, and Gunnar sprang back, letting them foul each other's path and end up shoulder to shoulder, and then jumped back in with a crash, shield on his shoulder, sending the first man sprawling backwards and turning a backhand blow on the second's shield, forcing him to raise it hurriedly and following up with a thrust to the stomach that drove the wind out of him.

Gunnar casually advanced on Gjaldir as his two opponents recovered and Gjaldir fumed. 'You see, you have much still to learn. You are the better of Lefnir when you are fresh, and unwounded, and on even ground, and one on one. But battles are not fair, and you must learn to fight when it seems impossible to win, when you are tired, or wounded, or have lost your shield or your friends, when blood closes one eye or you have to hold your sword with the wrong hand because the other hangs from a thread of sinew. You must fight when you think you cannot, when you think you are beyond the ability to stand or when you think you are already dead.'

Gjaldir looked at the huskarl dumbly as the man's speech became ever more animated and the distance between them closed.

'Can you? Can you do that?' Gunnar asked, his face burning with an intensity that made Gjaldir doubt everything he thought he knew.

'I… I don't know.'

'Exactly! Because you have not experienced it. You think because you can beat a smaller, less skilled man in a fair fight that you are ready to be a great warrior. Now let us see you beat him in an unfair fight. Drop your shield.'

Gjaldir hesitated for a moment and then threw the wooden boards aside. Without any warning or preamble, Gunnar attacked, a series of quick, vicious, efficient strikes with the edge of his shield and his sword that Gjaldir was unable to ward off.

The rim clattered into his nose, blinding him, the tip of the sword dug into his ribs, winding him, then a hard cut hit his sword arm, numbing his fingers, before three or four more battered his body and arms as he was driven back, trying to cover his head and avoid the stinging wood.

As quickly as the blows started, they stopped, and Gjaldir swayed and groaned as the pain from the strikes blossomed and radiated. He could barely feel his fingers and his legs were wobbling. He shook his head and held his nose, trying to clear his vision.

'Now can you beat Lefnir?' he heard Gunnar say.

Gjaldir just had time to blink away the blur from his eyes and see Lefnir advancing with a wolfish look on his face. *Shit.*

Lefnir beat him into the ground, twice, until Gjaldir simply couldn't rise, before Gunnar called them to stop. The rest of the group laughed and joked at his expense as he lay there taking long slow breaths and groaning. Then Gunnar told them the session was over and sent the rest of them away, standing over Gjaldir as he lay on the ground.

'What did you learn?' the huskarl said, squatting down to look at him.

Gjaldir gritted his teeth and levered himself up on an elbow. 'That I am not ready for real battle.'

Gunnar raised an eyebrow in surprise. 'Really? Good. What else?'

Gjaldir grimaced, wondering what other concession the man wanted to extract from him. 'Not to disagree with you.'

'No, you can disagree with me; as long as you can back it up with actions,' said Gunnar evenly. 'The other lesson I hoped you would learn today was why it is stupid to humiliate those of your comrades who you see as weaker than you. You think you are a better fighter than them, and you are right. But instead of using your superiority to raise them up, to teach them, to help them, you simply use it to humiliate them and make them feel weaker. You attempt to rise up by standing on their bowed shoulders. You may be the best warrior among them, but you are the very last one I would put in the wall beside me. Think on that as your bruises heal, think on why you took pride from beating lesser men and rubbing their faces in the defeat. Think of how that will make them think of you in return.'

Gunnar got up without reaching out a helping hand to Gjaldir, a gesture whose meaning he felt the full weight of, and strode off without another word, leaving Gjaldir on the ground angry and ashamed and feeling the pain of the truth in those words more than of the beating he had taken.

Gjaldir was not called for training for a few days, and he carried on with his carpentry work as best he could, and consumed his time with chores and with playing with Aeske. He saw other groups of men training together, including his, and felt the sting of being an outsider more than ever. He felt some shame for how he had treated the other warriors in training, but they did not understand what it was like to be him, to be a Christian, an ex-slave. All he had tried to do was prove himself with his strength, was that not the Norse way?

He wandered down to the lake shore that afternoon and stood on the stony margin, absent-mindedly skipping stones across its calm surface as he brooded. He did not hear Leif approach until the stones behind him crunched and the warrior's cheery voice spoke up in his ear. 'Gjaldir, you are not training? I thought you wanted to be a warrior.'

Gjaldir tossed a stone aside and sighed. 'I am not wanted there.'

'Nonsense.'

'I was not called for it,' Gjaldir spat.

'You are not a child, you do not have to wait to be called. Simply go there and join them.'

Gjaldir tensed, thinking of how that would feel, crawling back after several days' absence, to see their looks, to feel the humiliation. He shuddered.

'Did anyone tell you not to go?' continued Leif.

Gjaldir shook his head slightly and remained silent.

'So, you can just return.'

'And what will they say?'

'I don't know, I don't care, and neither should you. What does it matter?'

Gjaldir screwed his face up and looked at the older man, who had an infuriating grin on his face.

'You don't understand.'

'Ah! I see, what don't I understand?' asked Leif innocently.

'What it is like. Everything is so easy for you, you are one of them, you don't have to prove yourself.'

'And what are you proving, by being down here alone, throwing stones at water?'

Gjaldir scowled, but could not think of an answer.

'You are not proving that you are strong, or wise, or brave, or calm, or anything good. So yes, maybe I don't understand.'

'They will never accept me.'

'Maybe not. Certainly in the past, no. But these are strange times that have brought us all together, and this sulking doesn't help.'

Gjaldir rounded on Leif and felt his anger rising, infuriated that the warrior was still smiling and calm. 'How are you always so happy? Do you give a shit about any of this? Is everything a joke?'

'Why are you always so angry with those that try to help you?' countered Leif, tilting his head inquisitively.

'Why am I angry?' said Gjaldir, his face blushing red with the heat of his rage, his fists clenching and his heart hammering. 'I was taken as a slave, beaten and bound. I was kept with the animals and used like a dog. My master valued me less than the sword I made for him, and only once he was done with me released me, refusing even to let me go with him. The woman I love had a child with another man the second I left her side, and despite all I have achieved, making the axe of the king, and that stupid sword everyone thinks is magical, I am constantly humiliated and made to feel small. But the very instant I prove myself at anything, I am brought down again by those who are jealous of me. I live with people who see me as nothing more than a stupid Christian and hate me for everything, no matter what I do.' Gjaldir trembled as he let the anguish and pent-up injustice flow from him.

Leif did nothing but raise an eyebrow and his smile remained. 'Poor Gjaldir the wronged, how hard it must be for you. Tell me, do you think you are the only one who has had a hard life, who has suffered injustice?'

Gjaldir thought about where they were, and how they had all got there, but waved the man away. 'You have all just experienced real loss for the first time, but for me this has been my life for years, and nothing has changed. You all still have each other; when I lost my home and my family, none of them came with me to build my new life, I did that alone.'

'I bet you felt alone at home, didn't you?'

Gjaldir stiffened, and his eyes flicked away from Leif for a moment.

'Ah, yes, there it is. Some men always make themselves alone. You say nothing has changed, and that is true. And nothing will change until you change it. You were alone at home, you were alone on the Crusade, you were alone as a slave and now you are alone as a warrior. It is always that way because that is the way you wish it to be, and it is you that causes it. It will remain like that until you change, because the world around you will not.'

Gjaldir sneered and shook his head. 'So what do you know of it, you who has always been so content, so happy and carefree. What do you know of being alone?'

Leif's smile cracked just a little, and he nodded very slowly, looking out over the lake and staying silent for a long time before finally speaking. 'Have you ever met my family? My brothers, my cousins, my father, my wife?'

'No.'

'It is because they do not exist,' said Leif, the smile still there, but pained and stretched. 'I lost them, I lost my father, my friends, my home, my love… everything, many years ago.'

Gjaldir deflated, embarrassed. 'What happened?' he asked quietly.

Leif looked back at him and bit his lip, the smile gone. 'I never told anyone, but I think that does not matter anymore.' He looked at the ground and pushed a stone with the tip of his shoe, deep in thought. 'I was the son of a jarl, destined to take his seat. But my uncle murdered him and took everything.'

'How… how did you live?'

When Leif's eyes returned to meet Gjaldir's, they were hollow and dim, the eyes of a different man. 'I ran.'

Gjaldir was stunned. 'You ran?'

'Yes, I left everything behind, my wealth, the woman I loved, my family, my friends, and I ran. I ran until I reached a place where no one could know me, and then I came to be in Jarl Ragnvald's service.'

Gjaldir's eyes widened. 'Did you take your revenge?'

Leif shook his head slowly. 'No.'

'But how did Ragnvald accept that? Isn't it required, doesn't honour require that you have revenge?'

'Yes, but my father ordered me to run, and I did. I promised myself I would return and take revenge, and I kept the anger burning, and I plotted and waited, and as the years passed, I felt nothing but hatred and shame and it hollowed me out.'

The warrior looked at him. 'I never told anyone, not even Ragnvald, because I didn't want them to know my shame, that I had failed. But they all felt it, sensed something was wrong in me, I was vicious and spiteful and always trying to prove I was the best to make myself feel better. Then one day I heard news that my uncle had died, killed by some other lord who had taken his lands. I went back to my home and it was gone, everything had been burned to the ground and the people killed or scattered. There was nothing left of my old life to save.'

Gjaldir recoiled as the last words escaped Leif like a whisper. 'I'm sorry.'

Leif poked a finger into Gjaldir's chest. 'Do not be. It saved me. Once I knew it was gone, I was free of it. I left the angry, bitter man behind and became the man you see today. Revenge helps no one, not those who carry it out nor those whose behalf it was done on.

If I had returned home to fight my uncle, I would have died. If he had continued to live, I would have continued like you, angry and afraid my weakness would be known and I would be cast out. His death freed me. You must find a way to do the same, you cannot live in the past, or bear its shame and injustice forever.'

Leif clapped him on the shoulder, the pain dissolving from his face like ice melting in the sun. 'I am not happy because I have never lost anything I cared about, I am happy because I know what it is to lose everything, and am glad to have found a new life, however hard it is. You must do the same. You will be accepted as one of us when you accept that yourself, leave the past behind, and stop being such a moody, prideful cunt.'

Gjaldir gaped at Leif and then shook his head. 'You make it sound so easy.'

'It is. Stop making stones wet and go back to training. Every day you refuse just makes the journey back harder to start.'

'Gunnar doesn't want me there, he has been hard on me since the start. He wanted me to give up.'

'Don't be thick. Gunnar is hard on you because he sees your potential, not because he cares that you were a Christian slave. He tests you because he wants to know if he is right about you. He put you in his group because he believes you can be worth it. He wouldn't waste his precious time on someone he hated. He wants you to succeed, not break, so stop disappointing him and get back to work. You have a lot to learn, but he thinks you could be a good warrior, if you would only get out of your own way.' Leif shrugged. 'Of course, I don't see it, I've fought you twice and beaten you both times. I think you would be better as a wood cutter than a warrior, but your future is up to you, not me.'

Leif wandered off without letting Gjaldir see if he was smirking, the stones crunching under his feet, and Gjaldir muttered angrily to himself under his breath. He bent down to pick up another flat stone and hurled it across the lake, all power and no control, watching as it caught an edge and tumbled in a spray of water before disappearing beneath the surface.

He drew in a deep breath to calm himself and stared out over the lake. 'Fuck it.' He turned and started back up the slope, teeth gritted for what was to come.

He went up past the village, and out into the open space where the warriors were practising, dreading the reception he would get and trying not to show his anguish. Gunnar barely looked up as he approached, before flicking his eyes towards the pile of shields and practice weapons and turning his gaze back to his other charges.

Everyone was too busy sparring to pay him any attention, except for Lefnir, who was waiting his turn at the side and who glared at Gjaldir as he retrieved his weapons.

'Go on, Lefnir, show him what you have learned while he has been too busy to join us,' called Gunnar from behind.

Gjaldir and Lefnir moved out into some space and took up their guards. 'What have you been learning?' asked Gjaldir curiously.

'How to deal with bigger, stronger opponents, and use their size and strength against them,' said Lefnir, with the beginning of a small smile, angling his shield and stepping in towards him.

Gjaldir nodded curtly and settled in behind his shield, feeling a distinct rush of nerves.

## Chapter 18

# First Blood

**June 1120**

LEIF DUCKED INTO the grass-roofed house that Halla used, nodding to the small group who were gathered there talking in low tones. Jarl Gustav was there, his maimed hand hooked into his belt. Gunnar was there with Vidar and Eric Firebeard beside him, and Halla stood aside, listening as the warriors talked.

'You need me?' asked Leif, nodding to Halla.

'Gustav needs you,' said Halla gesturing to the old man.

'It is time for the first big raid,' said Gustav with a smile. 'We have discovered, from discussions with some prisoners taken on the last raid, and from some of our own people in the area, where many of the Christian stores of food are kept.'

Leif nodded, he had been on one of those raids, down the river towards Västerås. 'What has been decided?'

'Nothing yet, that is why I wanted you here. The Christians take most of the food they need from the people where they are garrisoned, and as they move about, their armies strip the land, leaving little for the people.'

Leif nodded with a scowl. 'But they do not take it as they need it, they gather and store it like squirrels, more than they require. They even bring more in from the coast. It seems they are obsessed with making huge piles of it.'

Leif looked at the old jarl. 'Maybe they are planning a new campaign, and need to build up supplies for that.'

'Against whom? There is no army left opposing them. Jarl Einar was defeated in the north, his remaining forces scattered, the Geats have been brought to heel, or so I hear, and the Norwegians remain at peace.'

'Perhaps it is just a precaution.'

'Maybe, but truly the reason is not that important. For us what matters is that all those vast stores are spread out across every town, and it does not seem all of them are well guarded. We will go to the less well-protected ones and liberate those supplies, keeping what we need for ourselves, and giving back to the people what they require.' Gustav finished with a satisfied smile.

'What is the aim?'

Gustav looked confused. 'To kill some Christians, to make their life difficult, maybe eventually to starve them out.'

'If we take food from them, they will just take more from the people,' said Leif warily.

'Maybe, but we will not have enough for the next winter here without it. We have few crops in the ground, nor are we likely to this year. We must take from the Christians, or we will starve,' said Halla.

'I see.'

'What did you expect?'

'To defend our land here, and prevent the Christians from finding us. If we need to raid for supplies then we must, but we cannot take enough to starve their army, we are too few.'

'Would you suggest we just give up? I am confused, Leif, I thought this was settled.'

'Giving up is not what I suggest, but we cannot starve the Christian forces with the two hundred warriors we have here.'

'Nearer three hundred, with new arrivals and those who have been trained,' said Gustav.

'Three hundred, it changes nothing. We cannot conduct a war with three hundred warriors.'

'Maybe not, but we can make the occupiers' lives harder, kill a few, perhaps cause them sickness and starvation in the winter.'

'Any suffering we impose on them will also be imposed on our people. The Christians won't starve while our people have food.'

'And maybe that will turn them against the Christians in large numbers, that might be the way the war is won.'

Leif looked at Halla nervously. 'It might also be the way our people are destroyed.'

'That has always been true, it is ours or theirs, we cannot live in the same land together. The longer they are here, the worse it will be,' said Gustav.

'Enough, this is already decided,' said Halla, holding a hand up to still Leif's reply. She took a step over to him and stared him down unwaveringly, then she softened. 'I know you do not have an oath that binds you to me, but this is what I have decided, and what Gustav has decided. My people need your leadership, are you with us or not?'

Leif felt uncomfortable under her gaze, and he let it drift uncomfortably long before he nodded. 'Of course.' He bit back a follow-on comment and Halla nodded graciously and turned back to Gustav.

'Please, tell us the plan.'

'Gjaldir, Gunnar wants you.' Gjaldir looked up from the trunk he was splitting as Eric walked over.

'There is training today?'

Eric grinned broadly and put his hand on the side of Gjaldir's face. 'No, my little Christian, we are going Viking, and you are coming with us.'

Gjaldir's eyes opened wide as Eric patted his cheek and turned to return to the village. 'Where to?'

'Gunnar will tell all, come now, don't keep him waiting.'

Gjaldir picked up his axe and tools, leaving the half-split log where it was, and trotted after the Norwegian.

They jogged all the way back to the village and Gjaldir for some reason was surprised not to find the warriors formed up outside the village ready to march, instead it was just fifty or so men in normal clothes milling about and chatting in small groups outside the edge of the settlement.

'It is just us? Where are everyone's weapons?'

Eric laughed. 'We aren't leaving today, blockhead.'

'Oh.'

'Just come, and listen.'

The two men joined the throng that Gjaldir quickly realised was only made up of warriors that had been recently trained alongside him, and it was not long before Gunnar appeared, with Leif and Vidar behind him. The excited and anxious chatter died down as Gunnar stood and waited.

'You are the men who I am told are ready for battle by those who have been teaching you.' Gunnar looked around the group sternly. 'We are going south, to raid a town, kill the Christians who live there, and steal their supplies, weapons and anything else of use.'

'Which town?'

'Västerås,' replied Gunnar, which started a murmur of excitement. This would be the first major settlement they had returned to.

'Just us, what, sixty new men?'

'No,' replied Gunnar. 'There will be a hundred and fifty, you are just those who have been chosen to join the experienced crews.'

'But the river at Karlsgrind is guarded by the Christians!' said one man nervously. 'How will we get past them?'

'We will not. We will leave our ships miles upriver of Karlsgrind and cross overland. We will raid Västerås and return to our ships.'

'How will we carry…'

'We will steal horses and oxen and wagons and whatever is needed to transport the supplies back to our ships,' said Gunnar, impatiently holding up a hand for silence. 'This is not a council of war, the plans are made and we do not need discussion, I am here only to tell you what you need to do. We leave in two days, clean your weapons and equipment, expect to be gone for ten days. If you don't know what to bring, find someone in your crew who does.' Gunnar looked around impatiently. 'It is not normal to take this many unblooded warriors on a raid, but these are not normal times. Listen to those who know more than you, and avoid the urge to do anything stupid to prove yourselves. Your role is to hold in the line and do as you are told. Victory is living to learn from the experience.'

Gunnar nodded and walked off with his two companions, leaving the crowd to break up into excited groups headed back to their houses. Gjaldir jogged after Leif and the other new warriors who were Halla's people. He fell into step alongside the blond warrior and leaned in. 'Do you have a spare hauberk?'

Leif looked at Gjaldir and laughed. 'For you? No. We have no spare maille fitted for oxen. No spare helmets either. You will have to find armour the old way, by killing someone your size and taking it.'

'Killing someone my size?' he asked, taken aback.

'Yes, I accept that means you will likely never get any, but we have no one here with the time and skills to make it new, and even if they did, it would make more sense to make hauberks big enough for two normal people.' Leif chuckled and turned to another warrior on his other side, leaving Gjaldir swallowing a dozen nervous questions. He had marched to war as a blacksmith and a slave, but now he was going as a warrior, and with nothing to protect him but a shield and axe that were older than he was.

Leif answered the other man's question and turned back, thumping Gjaldir in the chest. 'Don't worry, this is our way. You will kill someone with better weapons than you and take them. It would be easier if you would just make your own, but…' Leif shrugged and grinned. 'You chose this harder path.'

This didn't reassure Gjaldir at all. He wanted better equipment before he fought, not afterwards, if he was lucky and he had managed to find, fight and defeat someone his own size. But Leif was gone, chatting excitedly with another pair of warriors, and Gjaldir pushed his nerves aside and headed back to the longhouse he lived in to find and prepare his kit.

Three ships, the largest and best of their small fleet, had been prepared for the raid. Gjaldir marched with Leif and the men of Halla's people, seventeen of them, an understrength crew in the larger raiding force.

Bjorn was there with Leif, the only other of Ragnvald's huskarls to have survived. There were half a dozen other warriors, survivors of the battle or who had not been present, and then the clutch of new, unblooded men. They joined Gunnar's larger warband of Norwegians and a collection of more recent arrivals to make the crew of the lead ship. Gustav's men filled a second, and everyone left over, including Knud and a band of his warriors, went in the third.

The three ships were launched and got underway, their unpractised and unfamiliar crews unwieldy and clumsy on the still waters of the lake, a chorus of shouting and reprimands emanating from the frustrated shipmasters of each vessel.

Eventually they managed to ship their oars and put the sails up, sailing slowly down the lake as the sun rose high in the sky and the forested banks passed idly by.

Two days of travel brought the small fleet to the last small lake on the river before it wound its way down to Karlsgrind and the Christian garrison there blocking the route. Knud, the leader of the men of Vatnsborð, led them to a small channel that branched off from the lake, where they could hide the ships until they returned.

The column of warriors were now on the edge of the Christian-controlled lands. To the south, a half day's march down the riverbank, was Karlsgrind. To the south-east by the same distance overland was their target, Västerås.

Gunnar gathered his crews in once the ships were secure and waited until everyone was silent.

'Good, this is how it will continue,' he said. 'Christian patrols could be anywhere around us now. There will be no idle talking, there will be no jokes or shouts of command and there will be no fires. In these woods, sound and smell of smoke carries much further than sight ever can. We will move silently, we will make no camp, we will carry only two days' food, water, and our weapons. Leave everything else in the ships.'

The Norwegian warrior looked around the tense group and did not look impressed. 'We will march to within striking distance of the town and then find somewhere to hide and sleep for the night, while a few men scout the defences. We do not know how many enemy are there, and will not wade in blind. While it is important we scout them, it is essential they do not see us. I will gut any man who foolishly gives our position away.

'Now, we will march out, my crew first, Knud's crew second, Gustav's men last. March in single file, drop nothing, pick up nothing, we must be ghosts in this land.' Gunnar did not wait to see if anyone had any questions, his orders were clear.

Gjaldir adjusted the simple rope sling on his unfamiliar shield on his shoulder and checked the axe and seax on his belt for the tenth time. He found it helped his nerves to make sure everything was in its proper place, and the feel of weapons under his hands reassured him.

He shuffled into place a few men behind Leif, Bjorn just in front of him, and waited for the long, serpentine column to set off.

The march to the target town was silent, slow, almost funerary. There were frequent stops where scouts crept forwards to assess the land, or examine buildings or treelines or folds in the land that might conceal the enemy, but nothing was discovered.

As evening was falling and the shadows were lengthening, the head of the column led them into a dell in the woodland, hidden from all sides unless someone was to stumble directly into it and the men, without tents, fires, or even blankets, huddled together in groups in the cool evening air in near silence and tried to get some sleep.

Gjaldir lay on his side, using his thin cloak as a makeshift blanket, trying unsuccessfully not to fret about the fight that would come the next day. His body felt tired, but his mind continued to race and as the hours dragged on, he tossed and turned and fidgeted and tried to force himself to sleep, but each thought only led to the next and he ran through everything he had learned in training with Gunnar in his mind, trying to remember it all and panicking when he thought he had lost something.

He drifted off to a restless sleep but was woken what seemed moments later, opening his eyes to find that there was a hint of light in the sky through the trees. A hand was rocking his shoulder, although it was too dark to see the face. 'Up, quietly. Piss and get ready to go.'

Gjaldir mumbled his acknowledgement as the figure moved on to the next sleeping man. He sat up and looked around and saw that many of the men were already up, quietly moving around or just sitting on the ground, looking like they had never slept.

Shaking his own tiredness off, unsure if he had slept half the night or mere moments, he stumbled off and relieved himself behind a tree before heading off to find Leif and the rest of the crew.

'Gjaldir,' a voice said softly to one side, and he stopped and recognised the group standing there as men of Leif's small band.

'Where is your shield?' said Bjorn in an irritated voice, stepping forwards.

'Shit,' replied Gjaldir, cursing himself for looking like a fool. It was still lying on the ground where he had left it as he slept. He was completely unused to having it with him all the time. Embarrassed, he turned around and walked away, struggling to work out in the dim light where he had slept, with so many warriors milling about.

He found his shield, mostly by virtue of it being one of the last still on the ground, and jogged back over to the column, earning more hissed curses as his seax fittings rattled as he went.

He got back to his group with a mumbled apology and tried to ignore the disapproving looks he got being last, noisy, and unprepared. He stared at the ground as the last of the other crews got into their groups and the whole column set off.

They were near the front, and Gjaldir could see that as they left the dell and headed through the woods, the edge of the forest was not far away. The trees gave way to fields of newly sprouted barley and rye, and the whole column followed the edge of stands of trees and then a small streambed, trying to keep hidden in the more open landscape.

The town was soon visible ahead of them, its low walls and buildings silhouetted in the light of the sun that would soon rise behind it. Gjaldir squatted as the column came to a stop, anxious and confused. 'How will we get in?' he whispered to Bjorn.

The man motioned him to stay down and be quiet and Gjaldir just sat and stewed, not understanding what they were waiting for. The column compacted, men settling in low to the ground on their left and right as the whole party joined them in the edge of the thin undergrowth they were hiding in.

Finally, Gjaldir saw what they had been waiting for as a group of a dozen warriors, wraiths in the dim light, crept along the base of the wall towards the paltry gatehouse, just two platforms either side of the wooden gate that only reached the height of a large horse.

The figures grouped up around the base of the wall and then two figures were boosted over it, and then four more.

Nothing happened for an agonisingly long time, and then there were shouts and screams from beyond the wall.

'Now!' said Leif loudly, standing and breaking into a run across the open ground, the hundred or so paces that separated them from the still closed gate.

Waves of Norsemen broke cover from the scant shelter of the bushes and ran across the cleared land, weapons in hand and angling for the gates. Gjaldir, filled to bursting with nerves and excitement, hared after Leif, trying to keep up and fumbling his axe from his belt as his shield bounced on his shoulder.

As they neared the gate, it suddenly swung open, first one door and then the other, and Gjaldir saw a lanky, long-haired figure appear in the opening, beckoning to the running horde. Gjaldir recognised it was Vidar, one of Gunnar's Norwegian huskarls, and suddenly he understood why Leif was leading the charge; Gunnar and his small crew were the ones who had climbed the wall and opened the town.

Seeing the gates open and their own men within finally loosened the closed throats of the attackers, and there were cheers and bloodcurdling warcries from the warriors as they approached the gates at a run.

Gjaldir was near the front of the pack with Leif and Bjorn and the rest of their group, and they bundled through the narrow entrance, passing several bodies on the ground, and coming upon the blood-spattered group of Norwegians, Gunnar at their head, facing off against a dozen or more Christians who were just arriving from inside the town.

The Christians shuddered to a halt as the group they were facing changed from five to fifty, and they instantly began looking back over their shoulders and retreating in a huddled blob.

'At them!' shouted Gunnar, blood shining on one side of his face, waving his sword at Leif and the rest of the leading men. Leif shouted in wild joy and pointed his sword at the enemy, setting off at a jog as men jostled to get in line beside him.

The mass of warriors carried Gjaldir along as they bore down on the Christians, who were stumbling over themselves and breaking their formation as they tried to retreat.

The Norse warriors hit the enemy force like a wave breaking over a rock, and bodies and weapons were suddenly everywhere, so confusing in the dim light that Gjaldir could not tell friend from foe, holding his shield in front of him and pressing forwards as men clashed and shouted and died.

He exchanged a single confused blow with a panicked Christian before that man went down with a spear in his chest and then there was no one left fighting, just a collection of bodies strewn across the ground.

'Keep at them!' shouted Leif, and Gjaldir, heart pounding in his chest and breath ragged, recognised Bjorn and ran after him as the Norse pushed further into the town, groups breaking off and heading out into buildings and down side passages.

He caught up with Bjorn and Leif and the others as the Norse spread out and thinned, and he heard clashes and shouting all around them, although nothing faced them on the path they were on.

'This road leads to the hall where the Christians have made their fortress, where their stores are located,' said Leif, panting. 'Stay together, and push to the hall. If there are too many of them there, we wait for more to join us.'

They kept pushing forwards, passing silent houses and dark, closed doorways until the large hall came into view. The square in front of the hall was empty save for a pair of confused guards standing in front of the hall's entrance. They saw took one look at Leif's group and hammered on the door, shouting, presumably begging to be let in.

Leif ran at them and one of them bolted, the other dying with Leif's sword through his side. 'Bring an axe, get this door open!' shouted Leif, then he pointed at Bjorn. 'Go round the side, look for another way in.'

Bjorn nodded and grabbed Gjaldir and the two other warriors closest to him. 'Come with me, I'll lead, you guard my flanks.'

Gjaldir nodded nervously and put himself on Bjorn's left side, going with him as he skirted the hall and headed into the broad gap between it and the next building. No sooner had they turned the corner than three other men ran around the corner and clattered to a halt in surprise. The enemy took a moment too long to recognise who they had stumbled upon, and it was too late to run.

Bjorn hammered his axe into the first man, who barely got his shield up in time. Gjaldir set his wide eyes on the next Christian in line and stepped in towards him, pushing his shield out as far as he could to try to protect himself, far further than he had been taught, but in that moment everything he had been taught was just a confused jumble in his mind.

The Christian, recovering from his surprise first, jabbed his spear overhand at Gjaldir and missed, the shaft bouncing off the rim of Gjaldir's shield. Gjaldir, facing a spear with only his short axe, rushed forwards instinctively, closing the gap and trying to get inside the reach of the spearhead.

The Christian backed up, trying ineffectually to get his spear-point into Gjaldir's body as he went, and Gjaldir got close enough to hack at his opponent's shield wildly, cutting chunks off it, but doing nothing more than rattle the man's arm.

The ineffectual fight was brought to an abrupt close when Bjorn stepped around the Christian's shield and killed him with a single blow to the head. The warrior turned to look at Gjaldir, a look of exasperation on his face. 'What were you doing? Push into spearmen, get close, speed and fury.' He didn't wait for a reply and indicated Gjaldir to follow as he continued, the three of them following and leaving the bodies behind them.

They found another door to the hall, fresh and bright new wood against the dark old timbers of the lintel.

'Damn, a new door, thick and strong,' said Bjorn. He looked at Gjaldir. 'Time to use that axe, get through this door.'

Gjaldir nodded and moved forwards to inspect it, seeing that the planks were indeed thick, and nailed with large iron nails to the structure behind. It would take a long time to hack through to the locking bar. But he didn't complain, he set his eyes on the area around the handle and sank the axe blade in with a solid thunk, bringing it back and hammering it forwards again, chipping a chunk of bright wood away.

As he was working, they heard shouts behind them and Bjorn cried in alarm. Gjaldir turned and saw that half a dozen enemy had appeared, and he swore and turned away from the door as the four Norse faced the six enemy. 'Backs to the wall, stay together and use your shields,' said Bjon with a calmness that helped the terror that was grabbing at Gjaldir's heart.

The Christians nervously advanced and the two small groups made contact, axes and spears and swords flashing across the shields as the men grunted and cursed.

Gjaldir was next to Bjorn and he desperately covered himself with his shield as a Christian jabbed at him with a sword. He managed to strike a blow in return on the man's arm, eliciting a yelp of pain, and then Bjorn cut his opponent in the neck, sending him staggering backwards as another took his place.

Seeing the Christian retreat lifted Gjaldir's spirits, only for them to be crushed as the man to his left folded around a spear in his guts, unable to defend against the two who had been attacking him.

The Norseman went mewling to the ground, and now Gjaldir was about to be facing three, and panic gripped his arms and he stumbled backwards into Bjorn as the three enemy bore down on him.

At that moment, there were more shouts and men appeared behind the Christians, Norsemen, stopping them in their tracks. Two of them turned to face the new threat and Gjaldir was left facing a lone swordsman.

Bjorn pushed back at his opponent and the space cleared, leaving just Gjaldir and his enemy. They looked at each other nervously, and the Christian made the first attack. He pushed his shield forwards and swung across his body at Gjaldir, who got his shield in the way and let the blade clatter off, huffing nervously as the Christian re-positioned for another attack. Gjaldir thought about attacking but stopped in indecision, his opponent was armoured and carried a good shield and sword, and Gjaldir feared leaving himself open to a counter while wasting an attack on that maille.

As he was stuck thinking about what to do, the enemy attacked again, shoving his shield against Gjaldir's and trying to lunge his sword down the centreline. Gjaldir batted the strike aside with his shield instinctively and swiped back with his axe, missing by several handspans.

Again they stared at each other and the Christian made another attack. As Gjaldir calmed himself, he finally realised that his opponent's attacks were predictable and simple. He was stepping forwards and showing his planned attack long before it landed.

As the blows came, Gjaldir become more and more confident in predicting them and blocking them, until he saw that the man was about to go again for a big lateral swipe.

Gjaldir jumped forwards with a nervous cry of triumph and got inside the cut, catching it on the face of his shield even as he crashed into his opponent, sending him staggering back. Gjaldir used his forward motion to keep pressed close in and he brought his axe down over the man's shield in a savage blow that crunched into the shoulder. The maille held but he felt something break in his opponent's body, a sickening crack, and the enemy's shield dropped on a limp and useless arm.

Gjaldir brought his axe up again and hacked down, the blade thumping into the same place, even as the man tried to bring his sword up to block it.

A third blow from the axe connected with the sword but the power behind the strike clattered the sword aside and the axe blade sank into the Christian's helmet, denting it and knocking the man senseless or killing him, leaving him slumping to the ground at Gjaldir's feet.

Gjaldir looked at the enemy for a moment and howled in relief and triumph, looking around finally to see what was happening, and finding half a dozen confused Norse warriors staring back at him. There were no living Christians left in sight.

His eyes met Bjorn's and he grinned. 'I beat him! I won,' he said, trailing off as he realised how absurd he sounded.

Bjorn shook his head. 'Why did you take so long? He barely knew how to hold that sword, but it took you so long to finish I nearly had to do it for you again.'

The sounds of fighting were dying down in the town around them and the screams and shouting were changing from those of battle, to those of victors and terrified civilians.

Gjaldir swallowed and panted, using his axe hand to wipe away the sweat that was trickling into his eye. He looked around the group, deflated, and then back at the slumped body of his enemy. The figure looked small and helpless, and Gjaldir shuddered.

'Get back to the door, Gjaldir. There are more of them left inside and we need to be quick getting them out,' Bjorn said, grabbing Gjaldir's arm and turning him towards the hall.

Gjaldir nodded and headed over, calming his breath and steadying his grip for a renewed assault on the wood. *I killed him. He tried to kill me and I killed him.* He shuddered with the thought of it, and sank his axe into the wood once more.

## Chapter 19

# Hunters and Hunted

BEFORE GJALDIR COULD hack his way through the door, Leif and his warriors had breached the main door the other side. Gjaldir and the men with him heard a short, vicious fight inside the building, clashing steel and wood and screams of the wounded and dying, and then quiet fell. Norse voices were heard approaching and the door was suddenly unlocked and swung open, revealing a grinning Leif.

'Welcome to my home!' the warrior said, standing aside to let them in.

Bjorn rapped his axe on Leif's shield and smiled back. 'You are cheerful.'

'It was an easy fight, and this building is filled with treasures.'

Gjaldir went past the two senior warriors and walked into the hall. He saw that he was in the small back room, once the lord's personal chamber, but now a storeroom piled high with boxes, baskets and barrels of all kinds. Two dead priests were huddled against a stack, blood still leaking from their wounds. Gjaldir swallowed nervously at the sight and pushed past, headed through an open door and into the main room.

The space was a charnel house. Dead priests and monks were mixed with a dozen dead armed men, mostly Christians, but with a pair of Norse among them.

Most of the bodies were clustered around the doorway, and he could see that as that resistance had been broken, men had fled across the room in all directions, and been cut down as they fled, or died with their backs to the wall.

He looked at one Christian soldier, dressed in a white surcoat now covered in red, an embroidered gold cross still visible on the breast. Gjaldir walked over to the man and was startled when the body coughed and its head turned up and looked at him, the man's face white and drawn.

Gjaldir hesitated, unsure what to do. Pained eyes looked up at him and Gjaldir saw the fear and horror in them and it struck straight to his core. As he and the dying man looked at each other, a Norse warrior wandered nonchalantly over and pinned the Christian's head with his foot, aiming his sword for a finishing strike.

The Christian muttered and then blabbed, shaking his head weakly and trying to ward off the blade. But the steel was uncaring, and it jammed into his neck and was ripped free with a sucking noise.

The Norseman looked up at Gjaldir and was bemused by his shocked expression. 'What?'

'He spoke my language,' said Gjaldir absently, staring at the body.

'Oh? What was he saying?'

Gjaldir just kept staring at the dead man, unable to look away. 'He was begging for his life,' he said softly.

'Thought so. Christians are such cowards,' the man said with a chuckle, punching Gjaldir on the shoulder as he walked away.

Gjaldir felt an uncontrollable urge to vomit, and staggered out of the hall the way he had come in, passing Leif and Bjorn and ignoring their confused looks. He went straight to the man he had felled and dropped to his knees, lifting the soldier's head and looking into his eyes, breathing hard.

But the man's eyes were open and vacant, pupils wide and breath stilled; quite dead. Gjaldir shuddered and let go of the dead man's head, rocking back on his heels.

'Is he one of your people?' asked a voice behind him, and Gjaldir looked guiltily around to see Leif standing there, a sympathetic look on his face.

Gjaldir paused. 'I don't know.'

'And you killed him?'

'Yes.'

'Don't be ashamed, to feel what you are feeling. The first time is the hardest. You did well, you have bloodied your axe and killed a man in battle, steel to steel. No one will ever again be able to question that you are a warrior. But it is a hard thing to take a life of one of your own people.'

'They are not my peo…'

'Don't say it, Gjaldir. You don't need to prove your loyalty to us that way. Of course these are your people, they always will be. But you have made your choice of your own free mind, and we and the gods will respect it. It will be difficult for you, at first, but that will ease over time.' Leif paused and shrugged. 'Or it will destroy you from the inside.'

Gjaldir pushed slowly to his feet, feeling numb. 'Perhaps I was wrong to want to be a warrior. I saw how easily you all kill, how you enjoy it. I feel no joy, none at all.'

'Excitement?'

Gjaldir paused, before nodding guiltily. 'Yes, it was exciting.'

'Well, the joy comes later, if at all. For some it is the pure joy of battle, for others it is a mask to hide the horror and despair.'

Gjaldir turned and met Leif's eye. 'What is it for you?'

Leif laughed and shrugged unashamedly. 'I do not deny it, I love a good fight, and although this war has robbed me of my belief that war can be glorious, my hatred of these Crusaders, my anger at what they have done, makes killing them a task that does not trouble me, and each kill fills me with the joy of purpose.'

Gjaldir looked back at the body. 'I did not hate him.'

'No, and that will make it harder. But if you do not hate your enemy, it can be enough to love your own people, and know that to protect them you must fight, and you must win.'

Gjaldir gritted his teeth and nodded. 'I feel that in every bone in my body. These men come to destroy everything I have come to love.'

Leif clamped a hand on Gjaldir's shoulder. 'Good. Now, he is your prize, claim what you wish from his body, it is your right.'

Gjaldir looked over the smaller man, seeing that his maille would be no use and considering the helmet. But the front was dented very heavily, and blood oozed from beneath it. He shuddered at the idea of cleaning, repairing and wearing it, even if it was big enough, and having that reminder every time he put it on.

'He has nothing I want.'

'Then we will find you something else, come, we will be leaving soon, before the Christians come for revenge.'

The two men headed back into the hall, Gjaldir not looking back at the man he had killed, and as they passed into the main room, Gunnar was there and saw Leif and called to him.

'Leif, come, bring your men. We must find the rest of them.'

'The rest of them?'

'We have killed far too few. Our scouts saw over a hundred men here, yet we have killed less than half that.'

'Ah, it did seem too easy,' Leif replied with a grimace.

'The rest could be camping outside, they could be marching for help, anything.'

A new voice joined the group. 'Hey, Gunnar, hear this.' They looked around and saw Eric Firebeard shoving a terrified-looking local man towards them.

'What?' asked Gunnar.

The man looked around nervously. 'The Christians left yesterday.'

'Shit, why? How many?'

'They went to punish a nearby village that did not supply enough food, about a hundred of them,' the man said, the words flowing from him in a babble.

Gunnar stroked his beard pensively and then nodded. 'Which way did they go? Which road did they take?'

'I can show you, it goes from the east gate, ten miles, straight north. It is easy to follow.'

Gunnar nodded at the man. 'Thank you. You may go.'

'I… I can go?' the man replied, his face washing with relief.

Gunnar furrowed his brows. 'Yes, we are not here to hurt our own people, we are here for the Christians. We will take their food and their weapons and their lives. We will free these lands and return the people to the old ways.'

The man looked distraught again. 'You will take the food and leave, you are not staying?'

'Yes, the Christians' food, and no, we cannot hold this town yet.'

The man shook his head. 'You do not understand, lord. This is the food for the whole town, they take it all from us, and give us only what they say we need. If you take it and leave, we will starve.'

'Then we will leave some for you.'

'And they will take it back from us.'

'They will bring more food, they will not let you starve, they need you to work the land and give them silver.'

The man stood back and lowered his eyes. 'They will punish us for what you have done.'

Gunnar growled in annoyance. 'We must all endure hardships. Now take what you want from the food and be gone.'

The man looked around wistfully and shook his head. 'When you leave us, they will return, and we will have to answer for it. Perhaps it would be better that you killed us all.'

Gunnar shoved the man towards the door and snarled. 'You have steel, that is something you can do yourself.'

The man staggered and backed away a few steps, giving one more desolate look at the group before leaving.

'What an arserag,' muttered Eric.

'Not the welcome I expected,' said Leif.

'Ignore it, it is not our problem. Nothing changes, we take the food and weapons and anything else useful and leave. Find horses or carts and wherever else they are hiding the food, this can't be all of it.'

'What about the men who went north?'

Gunnar looked at the men. 'Yes, what about them?'

'We could set up an ambush, on the road back.'

'It's risky, they might already be returning, in fact it is certain they will return today. They have no reason to stay there.'

'True, but it is still early, they will be only starting on the road, we have time.'

Gunnar nodded slowly. 'I agree, we probably have time. But with all this food and equipment? It will take us time to leave, and we will be heavily laden for marching and setting up an ambush.'

'Burn it,' said Gjaldir, unaware he had been about to speak before the words just blurted out. The warriors looked around at him as one.

'What?'

'Burn it,' he repeated boldly. 'We can't take it all home, we can't leave it for them. Better to burn it here than to drag it through the forest and dump it in the river. Nor can we give it to the people, it will just be taken back. In fact, if we hide it, the Crusaders will suspect the locals and do terrible things to them to try and get it back. If it is burned, they will see the remains and know it is gone.'

'He is right,' said Leif, looking back to Gunnar. 'It's quicker and easier too. Pile what we don't want to take, burn it, kill the horses, break the wagons... we can do that in half the time of packing it all, and then we are free to go and ambush the returning soldiers.'

Gunnar toyed with his beard nervously. 'It is not what we intended, and it feels wrong to burn so much food knowing the people here will starve.'

'You said it, the Christians will feed them, they need them.'

Gunnar looked unconvinced, but nodded reluctantly. 'It is the least bad plan, killing their soldiers is the most important thing.' He thumped his hands together. 'Then let's do this quickly. Burn and destroy everything other than what we can carry quickly on a few horses, and destroy everything else, except our people's homes. Leave them intact. Burn the gatehouse too, we might want to come back.'

The room burst into a hive of activity as men rushed to go and tell their crews the new orders, and Gunnar gave Gjaldir a single look and a nod, and then went out of the hall.

Leif led his crew of fifty out of the town as the raiding force left the blazing piles of food and equipment behind in the town and headed out up the northern road with a dozen stolen horses in tow bearing everything they had chosen to keep.

They went up the road as fast as they could without risking exhaustion until, after just a couple of miles, Gunnar found a spot on the road he liked the look of and quietly signalled a halt. The road passed through a meadow, long and broad, where sheep were happily grazing, paying no attention to the column of armed men. If there was a shepherd boy, he had fled at the sight of the men or was hiding in the trees beyond. Behind the meadow on the left was a dense forest of pines and firs, while on the right there was a scrubby patch of woodland and bushes re-growing in an area that had been cleared of trees just thirty paces from the road.

Leif joined the other leaders of the three crews as the rest of the column went off the road into the edge of the scrubby forest to hide. Gunnar looked at Leif and the others and pointed down the road north, where the Christians would surely soon arrive.

'This is where we will ambush them.'

'This is not an ideal spot,' said Leif, shaking his head. 'This open field will give them room to move, and on this side these bushes and saplings will conceal us, but make an attack difficult to conduct with that distance to the road. They will have time to react.'

'We cannot go further and risk running into them, or their scouts if they have any. It is this or nothing. But you are right, we cannot simply jump out of those bushes, they are too far away and the enemy is too many to attack in that manner, and as you say, if they have horsemen, this field is their advantage.'

'Then what?'

'We lure them into the forest over there, take them into the trees and fall upon them, that is how we will achieve our surprise.'

'How? You will alert them?'

Gunnar sighed and gave the younger man an annoyed look that silenced him. 'Give me five breaths to explain and you will find you have fewer questions.'

Leif shut his mouth and nodded.

'They will not be expecting a large enemy force, they control these lands and have been combating raiders and thieves, they will be confident and aggressive. We will have a party of men, perhaps a dozen, crossing the field as they arrive, as if they are headed towards the town. The Christians will think they have come upon a small raiding party and they will attack them immediately. Our men will appear to panic and flee across the field into the forest beyond, where we will lie in the true ambush. If the horsemen reach us first, we will kill them while they are unsupported in those dense trees. If they are smart and wait for the footsoldiers, we will ambush them nonetheless, they will not come in battle formation, they will think they are hunting fugitives. We will crush the head of their pack and then grind over the rest until they break.'

Gunnar gave the group a questioning look.

'They might have nearly equal forces to us, if we only kill their horsemen, the rest will form up and we will have a hard fight,' said Eric Firebeard cautiously.

Gunnar nodded. 'Yes, but we will be better formed up and prepared, and they will be shocked and unsure.'

'We have half a dozen men with bows, we could have them concealed in those bushes. If the enemy form up in good order to attack us, they could wait until the best moment and attack them from behind.'

Gunnar nodded slowly. 'It takes six men out of our wall, but yes, having the Christians suddenly finding arrows falling into their backs might be worth that. It will add to their confusion and fear.' He nodded at Leif. 'Do it. We have no time for more talk, each crew send four men, fast runners, lightly armed. Leif, you will lead them, I am too old and slow.'

Leif raised an unamused eyebrow. 'Oh, good. And what if their entire party is mounted?'

'Then run quickly,' Gunnar replied, already jogging off towards his men.

Leif grumbled to himself and ran over to his own crew, looking over the nervous and excited-looking men. 'Gjaldir, Bekki, Manni – you are coming with me. The rest of you follow Gunnar into the forest over there.'

'What is happening?' asked a nervous Gjaldir.

'We will lure the Christians into the forest, and Gunnar and the rest of the boys will wait in ambush.'

'We will… what?'

'I was also doubtful, but I think it is a good plan.'

'How will we lure them?'

'By pretending they have come upon us crossing this field, and running while they chase us.'

Gjaldir blanched. 'We will stand in the open field and wait for them to come for us?'

'Yes, now come, we may not have much time. You are all young and strong and have no maille, you will run quickly and you will live. Or you won't and…' Leif winked and shrugged.

The three chosen men looked at each other nervously, but none dared try to refuse.

The chosen men of the other crews came scurrying over to join them, and Leif took them quickly along the meadow northwards to a where a low fold in the ground gave them some concealment to the road north. He looked south-west to where Gunnar was disappearing into the forest with the main force and judged the distance. 'Yes, this is where we will wait.'

'That is a very long way,' said Manni nervously.

'We will watch the road from here. When we see them coming, we will set off across the field, walking as if we feel safe. The dip in the ground will hide us for a time, we will probably be halfway across before they see us and start the chase.'

'And if they see us sooner?'

Leif shook his head. 'There is no time for doubt. Now, listen, we must be convincing. I will watch the road from behind that patch of long grass.' He pointed at a tuft on the crest of the rise. 'When I see them, I will come down the slope and we will start walking across the field. Resist the urge to look back. Be relaxed, look at ease. We need them to believe they have caught us in the open unawares. When they see us, I will cry out in alarm and we will run for those trees. Make it look panicked, not organised. Spread out a bit, but not too far so we can't gather up again. You all understand?'

The group nodded at him and Leif saw the fear in some of their eyes. 'Trust in…' Leif stopped and snapped his head up. He had heard a noise, faint but clear, a horse whinnying to the north. 'Fuck,' he hissed. He had left the road unsighted just for a few moments. He scrambled up the bank and carefully peered through the grass. His heart stopped in his chest. Visible through the waving stalks were about eight horsemen at the head of a column of soldiers, already inside the distance he had hoped to spot them in, much closer than he had planned.

Panic's cold hand gripped at his belly and he slid back down the slope. 'They are already here, start walking!' he said in a low voice, trying not to let on how much trouble they were in.

The men, already in a loose single file, set off walking across the field, horribly slowly to his eyes, and looking awkward and stiff.

He wanted to shout at them to hurry up, to run even, but he forced himself to stick to the plan. They walked towards the forest, unhurried and tense, for what seemed like an eternity but was probably only fifty paces. Then Leif heard the cry of alarm behind them.

Finally, he allowed himself to turn and look and he saw one of the lead horsemen pointing at them with their spear. The man next to him stood in his stirrups and looked for a moment and then waved his arm in the air and pointed it down at Leif like a lance. The horsemen all gave cries of excitement that chilled his blood as they were released.

Leif did not have to feign his fear or urgency as he turned to his men and shouted. 'RUN!'

The group burst into action, far too quickly and decisively, but Leif doubted it mattered. *Fuck fuck fuck!* he shouted to himself as they sprinted across the field in a loose group towards the trees, still a hundred paces distant. He risked tripping and falling to snatch a glance behind and saw the horsemen were nearly at the rise where they had been hidden. *Too close.*

The horsemen had to slow or turn aside for the unsure footing of the slope, allowing his band to eat up some of the distance to the trees, but once they were at the bottom of the dip, it would be a straight, flat run – with their prey in sight.

Leif knew in that moment they would not reach Gunnar before the horsemen reached them, but he thought they would make it to the trees. If they could get into the forest, they had a chance.

That slim chance evaporated when Bekki tripped on some unseen hole and went down with a sharp cry. Leif skidded to a halt and got an arm under the man as he struggled back to his feet, panting and groaning at the pain in his leg. Leif could only pray it was not badly hurt but half dragged the man back into a run regardless.

The rest of the group was ten or twenty paces ahead of them as he heard the hooves approach behind, and Bekki hissed and grunted with each step. Leif shouted desperately at the man to go faster as the first of their band reached the edge of the trees and kept on running.

The sound of hooves grew and grew and Leif turned to see his death coming, eyes pinned wide and mouth hanging open, his left arm still entangled with Bekki.

Bekki's leg gave out in that moment and he fell, taking Leif down with him even as the spearpoint of the lead horsemen sliced through the air where they had just been.

Hooves pounded the ground around them as Leif rolled and sprawled with Bekki in a tangle of limbs. He saw grass and sky and horseflesh and then grass again, and he hunkered down as more hooves thundered towards him. He looked up, trying to judge the moment to stand, or to try and dodge, and saw Bekki facing him, face white with pain and panic, struggling to stand.

Leif reached out a hand and shouted at the warrior to get down. Bekki looked at him in realisation of his mistake only at the moment the sword swung down and lashed into his back, splitting his skull, and sending him facefirst into the mud.

The horse passed right over Leif, its front hooves landing just next to his hand and its back legs dealing him a glancing blow to his shoulder that he barely felt in the grip of his fear. He looked for the next threat but realised with great surprise that the last horseman had passed him. Jumping to his feet, giving the body of Bekki a single hurried glance to check he was definitely dead, he ripped his sword from his scabbard and turned to look for the rest of his group.

He could see the horsemen pushing through the trees, whooping in excitement but slowed to a walk by the trunks and branches, and he saw the one who had killed Bekki reining in and turning, eyes fixed on Leif, face set in a triumphant snarl.

The Christian lined up his mount with Leif and urged it forwards with his heels, the horse springing forwards straight into a run, clods of earth flying up behind it.

Leif thought about it for half a heartbeat, stood in the open with nowhere to run, and transferred his sword to his left hand, stepping over to the body of Bekki and snatching the man's axe from his belt.

He raised the axe and twisted his body. There was no time to think or measure or aim as the big horse and the armoured rider bore down on him. He whipped his arm forwards and hurled the axe, seeing it cross the dozen paces between him and the charging Crusader and feeling a spark of triumph as it smashed into the horse's face.

The animal twisted its head to the side in pain and terror as the heavy blade tore at its skin and cracked its teeth and it turned and stumbled. Leif put his sword back in his right hand and jumped to the side as the horse careened sideways through the space he had just been standing in, the rider leaning as far back in his saddle as he could and sawing on the reins as he tried to prevent the inevitable result.

The horse went down, front legs tangled, and the rider was pitched off, slamming into the turf with an audible 'ooff' as the air was driven from his lungs.

Leif did not waste a moment seeing if the rider would rise, he just sprinted towards the forest, abandoning his shield where it lay beside Bekki's body. He reached the trees and heard shouts and fighting ahead. Through the dense trees he could see moving shapes and hear horses and men. He ran past the body of a Norse warrior and then narrowly avoided a riderless horse that was running back towards him with blood running down its flank.

He finally caught up with the running skirmish and saw the six remaining horsemen pressing his men, who were trying to run while keeping their shields up and facing backwards, which had slowed them to a jog, but he felt a burst of relief that they had organised and grouped together even as they fled.

The men saw him and one shouted out and the group stumbled to a halt as they waved at him, imploring him to reach them.

He shook his head as he ran. 'Keep running!' He knew that if they stopped, they might never reach Gunnar's ambush, they had to keep luring the Christians deeper into the woods.

The group ignored his shout, not hearing or not caring, and the horsemen milled around them, jabbing with spears and swords but unable to break into the tight group of warriors in the confines of the trees.

He was now only twenty paces away and closing fast when a horseman saw him and turned, going for the easier prey of the lone enemy. He had no axe to throw, and no shield, so he got a tree between the horseman and himself and readied his sword to defend himself as best he could.

The horseman seemed unsure what to do, and as he chose a side of the tree to go Leif darted the other way, the enemy slamming his sword into the trunk futilely as he passed, showering Leif with bark and dust. He put everything he had into his legs, pumping them as fast as he could, his lungs burning and muscles screaming, as he closed the gap to his men.

He saw Gjaldir urging him on from behind his shield and then moving to one side to leave a gap for him to pass through. He heard the hooves behind him again, a softer thump in the pine litter but growing in volume. He saw Gjaldir's face fall, and then the idiot sprang towards him, rushing to reach him before the horseman.

It was hard to know who reached him first, it seemed simultaneous. Gjaldir did not join him, he shoved Leif to the ground with his right arm, raising his shield and taking the blow that was meant for Leif on his shield with a thunderous crash as he pushed towards the mounted man.

Leif sprawled in the soft litter and rolled, seeing from his back as Gjaldir cannoned into the side of the horse, whose rider was trying to slow and turn, and *shoved* the horse off balance with a great shout of anger.

Leif watched in awe and confusion as the horse took a single sidestep from the force of the impact and skewed, its back legs running wide as it tried to regain its balance. The horse and rider saw the oncoming tree too late, and the animal thumped into it with an impact that shook the branches that hung down around them.

Gjaldir, roaring in anger, stepped over to the stationary mount as it stood by the tree and reached out to grab the rider, simply hauling the dazed man from the saddle and throwing him to the ground. Leif hauled himself to his feet as Gjaldir pulled his seax from his belt and plunged it down into the prostrate man, ending his squirming with a single blow.

Gjaldir looked around in the leaf litter for his axe, lost at some point in the confrontation, but Leif shouted at him, 'Leave it!' The others were getting separated from them, and behind he could hear more shouting, and the distinct rattle of running, armoured men. He turned to confirm his fears, and saw the main body of the Christians was arriving, plunging into the woods at a run.

'Go!' he shouted, and Gjaldir looked up and nodded, the two men running back to their band, who were still fending off the remaining, much subdued enemy horsemen.

They rejoined their group and they set off together at a run, Leif struggling to keep his exhaustion at bay as they plunged deeper into the woods. With their prey running once again, the horsemen regained their determination and two more swooped in between the trees for another attack, spearing one of Gustav's men with a curdling cry of agony. The warrior went down and they wordlessly left him as the horseman wheeled away for another attack. The first Christian soldiers were in the trees behind them and there was nothing they could do.

They pushed their tired legs up a gentle scree slope of stones and small bushes as Leif started to lose his hope again. *Where the fuck is Gunnar? Have we gone the wrong way?* They scrambled and panted and gasped their way up to the top, the sound of the pursuit growing and growing, even as the uneven and loose surface gave them sanctuary from the horsemen for a moment.

Leif hauled himself to the crest and over the top and almost fell into the lap of a warrior crouching the other side, one of a long deep line hidden all along the summit.

He fell to one knee and whimpered in relief as he heard a shout from his right, and recognised Gunnar's voice. 'Stand and charge!'

The silent warriors all around him rose to their feet as one and let out a deafening and horrible roar of warcries, passing around Leif as they surged over the crest and charged down towards the oncoming Christians.

He struggled once more to his feet, seeing the survivors of his men stopping around him, sinking to the ground or putting their hands on their knees, someone was vomiting.

Leif forced himself to straighten his back and he looked around the exhausted group. Over the small crest the sound of fierce fighting and the screams of the wounded and dying could be heard.

Leif lifted a shaking arm and pointed his sword back in the direction they had come from. 'Come on, boys, we can't leave them to fight without us,' he managed between breaths.

Some of the faces that looked back at him looked horrified or numb, but no one refused. Groaning and sucking in air as fast as their lungs would work, the nine survivors gathered their weapons and their wits, and went back over the crest to join the fight.

# Chapter 20

# Guts and Glory

As the group went back down the scree slope, they saw the carnage that was taking place at the base of the slope. The Norse were slaughtering the leading Christians, who, out of formation and having moments before been involved in a headlong chase of a few fugitives, had been swarmed by the rapid ambush.

Several dozen bodies and wounded men lay in the pine litter, and the Christians that survived were doing so only by retreating fast. Leif saw over the heads of his people as the few Crusader horsemen left in the saddle tried to regain control, shouting at their men and corralling them into a group even as they fled.

As the Norse chased them, picking off stragglers but staying together as one tight group, the Christians regrouped with more and more of their number until all of them were together, retreating almost to the edge of the forest before the horsemen managed to halt the headlong flight and get them into some sort of fighting order.

The Christians were still heavily outnumbered, there were perhaps half again as many Norse, and they were fresher and flush from the killing and the sight of their enemies fleeing, but Leif bitterly cursed the enemy horsemen for preventing a total rout. Finishing off the reforming line would be hard, bloody fighting.

Leif made it back to his crew as they faced off against the Crusaders, and Gunnar shouted up and down the line to re-form the wall, three ranks deep. Even as they did, the mounted commander opposite them urged the Christian line to form matching them, only two ranks deep, but still formidable.

Gunnar shouted out for the wall to advance, and the Norse walked forwards, shields and weapons up, howling at their foe as the gap closed.

Just before the two sides met, there was a buzz and a thump, and then more, and a scream of pain and alarm from the Christian side. Leif grinned and strained to look over the enemies' heads. In all the fighting and terror, he had completely forgotten about the archers who had been left hidden behind the Christian lines for just this moment. They had crept up across the field and were loosing shafts into the back of the enemy line from just a few dozen paces away, close enough to avoid hitting their own people, but also close enough to be in extreme danger.

The Christian line shook and shuffled back, men looking over their shoulders and the tangible air of panic once again settling in over the recently rallied soldiers. Of the four remaining mounted enemy, one was shot off his horse almost immediately, but another two turned and charged the scattering of archers, hunkering down behind their horses' heads and lowering their swords to point them like a spear.

The first horse got about halfway to the rider's target before it was hit by several arrows and slewed to a messy halt, rearing and screaming, tossing its rider like a child's toy. The second rider made it to within touching distance of his target before an arrow slipped under his helmet and killed him in mid-stride, the body limp and senseless as it toppled from the saddle, leaving the horse continuing to run across the field.

The Norse line surged forwards, seeing the indecision and panic in their foe, and they crashed into the wavering line with wild aggression, breaking it in several places almost immediately.

The man who had been commanding the Christians looked at his faltering, outnumbered line, and then at the archers who were once again flicking shafts into the back of it, before deciding the fight was lost. He shouted at his men again and again, waving his sword over his head towards the town and ducking under his shield as an arrow was sent his way.

The Christian line, already on the verge of collapse, crumbled like stale bread, and as one they turned to flee. Leif howled in triumph and joy and broke the wall to run after them, ignoring the burn in his already tired legs as he angled to overtake the slowest.

All around him, his men broke from the wall and joined the chase, many on fresher legs overtaking him, and the real slaughter began.

The last of the Christians, maybe two dozen, and their commander on horseback, managed to outrun their pursuers for long enough that Gunnar shouted out the order to end the chase. The victorious Norse shouted abuse at the fleeing men as Gunnar came over to Leif.

'Get your crew under control, we are going to the ships now. Leave the loot and the dead,' said the old huskarl in a gruff tone that took Leif by surprise.

'Now?' said Leif, furrowing his brows at the man, while the other warriors celebrated their victory around them.

'We don't know if the Christians sent help to the town, if they did, that man on the horse is going to tell them where we are and they will be here before we get ourselves in order and leave. We leave now, or we risk being overtaken by a much larger force, if, indeed, it exists. Get these men in order and get them in the forest, as fast as possible. Do you understand?'

Leif fumed at the tone being taken with him, but nodded curtly. He realised the Norwegian was right. That Christian commander had galloped off down the road, and would be at the town and summoning whatever force had arrived there before his men had finished looting the dead and swapping stories, if they were left to their own devices.

'Back to the forest! Leave the dead, leave the enemy to the crows. Carry our wounded. Hurry now,' he shouted to his men, waving and gesturing at those further away. There were confused looks, but he didn't have time to go around and explain to everyone. 'NOW!' he shouted at three men who were searching corpses for valuables. The men gave him surly looks, there were riches scattered over the field, but they obeyed. Leaving the few dead friends that had fallen in the fight for the Christians to find would earn him permanent enmity, but it was not his choice.

As the group coalesced around him on the fast walk back to the ambush site, he came across Gjaldir stripping the maille off a big Christian soldier. He was struggling to do it alone, the body was almost as big as he was and it was hard to take the heavy, close-fitting maille off the dead weight of the corpse.

'Leave it, Gjaldir, we have to go.'

'What? I'm nearly done.'

'Now, Gunnar's orders.'

Gjaldir stood up, exasperated. 'He is the only one here big enough, I'll never find another one that fits.'

Leif growled and walked over to him. 'Quickly, I'll take the arms. The rest of you, keep going.' He felt a fool for changing his mind in front of the other men, but Gjaldir had a point, and it wasn't wealth he was trying to get, but armour.

With Leif's help, Gjaldir got the maille past the dead man's shoulders and Leif pulled it free from the arms, dumping the bloody, mud-covered mess into Gjaldir's grasp and slapping him on the back. 'Quickly, catch up with the others.'

The two men jogged to catch up with the crew, Leif ignoring the filthy looks he was getting from the men he had stopped from looting. 'Get to the horses, recover anything you left behind, we will be marching for the ships immediately.'

'What are we so afraid of?' grumbled one of the men behind him.

'Being caught out like these poor fuckers,' said Leif, waving his arm at the scattered bodies around them. There was more grouching, but no one else confronted him with it.

They reached the ambush point and climbed the churned scree slope and down to where the horses and other equipment they had left before the fight was. Gunnar re-organised them into a column and they set off back to their ships.

It was almost midday now, and Gunnar was anxious to get to the ships and make some distance along the river before nightfall.

They retraced their steps through the scattered forest and open fields, seeing no one other than people in some isolated farmhouses, who fled their homes into the forest as the column passed, not risking the intentions of the large armed band.

The sun was sinking low as they reached the ships, and the men were exhausted. Leif went up the line to find Gunnar and took him aside. 'Are you sure we need to leave now?'

Gunnar looked at Leif and chewed his lip. 'It is a great risk to stay, anyone could follow the trail we left.'

'But this late? Anyone following us has marched as far as we have, if not further. Will they follow that trail into the night and risk another ambush? We could leave at first light.'

Gunnar looked back along the trail that they had come down, and then at the ships, hidden in the inlet off the main river. 'If they come sooner, we are dead. If they come up the river in ships, we are dead.'

Leif did not have a good answer to that, but he was surprised how cautious Gunnar was being. The man read his thoughts.

'You think I am being too careful, that I don't understand the reaction from the men once I have taken their spoils of victory and then their chance at rest. But we are so few, and we can afford no more defeats, no more mistakes.'

Leif nodded. 'I understand that, but some might think this is more than caution.'

Gunnar stiffened. 'Anyone who accuses me of cowardice can face me over shields, and learn the truth.'

Leif shook his head. 'No one believes you are a coward.'

Gunnar looked at him for a moment. 'The risk is too great, we leave now, we will row upriver until we find somewhere else.'

Leif sighed but would not argue any further. 'I will get my ship ready to leave.' He walked off to where his men were gathered, most sitting in the grass or even flat on their backs.

The discontent from the men when he told them was palpable, the murmuring of discontent just out of earshot constant. Nevertheless, the men got to their benches, the provisions from the horses were put in the hulls, and the horses were slaughtered. They didn't even have time to take cuts of meat from them, the bodies were simply left in the grass.

The mood of victory had completely passed, and it felt like a desperate run from defeat. But Leif knew the sense in Gunnar's words, he only hoped the man had not lost his nerve. Fear was infectious, and even the appearance of it would not be tolerated in a leader of these men.

The ships got moving in the fading light and headed out into the main channel and the long row home up the river.

Bishop Reinhard was poring over a letter he was writing when there was a knock at the door. He looked up across the room and nodded once at Bertrand, who was copying out orders on his writing stand. His assistant went wordlessly to the door and opened it to go out, closing it behind him.

Reinhard would have preferred to have an antechamber for this exact reason, to keep a buffer between himself and visitors, but the crudely converted hall he had made into his personal quarters was too small and simple for such a luxury, so he made do with sending Bertrand out to meet visitors first before he decided to let them in.

He heard the unmistakable voice of Sir Sighard outside and his dread lessened. Brother Sighard was a man of few words, a quality he greatly valued, and only came to speak to him when something was truly worth reporting.

Bertrand knew his preferences well, and the door reopened shortly so that the priest could give him a questioning glance. Reinhard beckoned crisply with his free hand and the priest stood aside to let Sighard in. The whole procedure had taken place in total silence, which was exactly how Reinhard liked it.

Sir Sighard entered and strode over to the desk, refusing a proffered seat. That got Reinhard's attention, it must be serious.

'What have you to report, Brother Sighard?'

'Trouble in the east, your excellency.'

Reinhard raised an eyebrow. 'There is always trouble, elaborate.'

'There has been another raid, much larger this time. Västerås has been sacked, the garrison slaughtered and the stores looted and burned.'

Reinhard pursed his lips, but then shrugged and shook his head. 'Västerås is not in our lands, it is Count Otto's domain.'

'True, but there was a party of our men there at the time, and some of the clergy.'

Reinhard stiffened just a touch. 'All dead?'

'Most of them, yes.'

'Hmmm, then I suppose something must be done. We can't have men of the brotherhood slaughtered without consequence, or the enemy will become far too bold.'

'They are already. Since these raids started, there has been a great increase in banditry on the roads, in our lands and also those of Counts Otto and Conrad. Small patrols being attacked, convoys ambushed. It is no longer safe for less than thirty men to travel.'

Reinhard frowned at that, it was much worse than he had believed it would become. He looked at Sighard for a few moments and then nodded. 'Thank you, Brother Sighard, for your report. The situation is serious and I will consider what is to be done about it. For now, use your men as you see fit to patrol the roads and increase our escorts.' Reinhard nodded his thanks and went back to his reports.

To his considerable surprise, Sir Sighard did not take the unspoken request to leave, and remained rooted to the spot in front of the desk. Eventually Reinhard looked up in irritation. 'What else is there?'

Sighard looked mildly uncomfortable, which was the first time Reinhard could remember that. 'Your excellency, may I suggest you release some of the garrison troops here under the command of Brother Hartung? My men are stretched very thinly, and I don't believe I have enough to contain these raids.'

Reinhard shook his head. 'No. I need the main body here in our headquarters, ensuring that we can react to any major uprising or significant threat, and to keep our main camp safe. If you are having problems with locals being troublesome, use the usual methods until those troubles go away.'

Sighard nodded reluctantly. 'As you command, Grandmaster.' The knight bowed and left smartly, leaving Reinhard troubled. The knight had never complained nor contradicted him once. The situation out in the countryside must be worse than he thought to cause it. But he was unwilling to splinter his limited forces all over the province chasing shadows, so he thought about it for a while, and then alighted on a solution.

'Bertrand, send someone to fetch our guest, Earl Frode. I wish to speak to him immediately.'

Bertrand nodded and scurried from the room without any fuss. Reinhard smiled in the silence and went back to his letter.

He had just finished his letter when the erstwhile Norse earl was ushered in, looking as prideful and miserable as he always did.

'Earl Frode, good of you to come,' he said, mocking the man for his lack of choice in the matter.

'Bishop Reinhard, what do you need?'

Reinhard waved to the chair, which he had moved further away from his desk to keep the Norseman at a suitable distance. Frode went to the chair and sat, two gold-crossed guards going with him and standing behind him in silence.

'You two may go, thank you,' Reinhard said, without looking at them. The two guards looked concerned and did not immediately move, but Reinhard turned his thunderous glare on them. 'Did you not understand?'

'Uh… yes, Grandmaster.' The two soldiers reluctantly withdrew from the room and Bertrand shut the door behind them.

'You aren't going to attack me, Earl Frode, are you?'

Frode did not bother to answer.

'Good. The same, however, cannot be said for your people, I'm afraid.'

Frode's hooded eyes perked up at that. 'What? My people have done nothing.'

'Not what I hear. Reports are flooding in of trouble on the roads, and attacks in villages. Västerås was just burned by a large raiding force.'

Frode shook his head. 'Outsiders, desperate men fleeing from other provinces. Not my people. And that large raid? Impossible for mine to have been involved, I would have heard of it.'

'No, those raiders were surely not your men, almost certainly they were your sister's mangy band of runaways,' said Reinhard with a serpentine smile.

Frode went white before his eyes as Reinhard shared his knowledge of that secret.

'Yes, the much-underestimated Halla. It seems like she has not given up and fled, as was thought.'

'I… I…'

Reinhard held up his hand for silence. 'I am beginning to wonder what was the point of our arrangement, Earl Frode. Your job is to keep your people in line, but bandits roam your lands, and must surely have support from your people to do so, or at least have been spotted by them and gone unreported. And your own family is burning garrisons and killing my priests.'

Reinhard sat back and steepled his fingers. 'Tell me, what exactly is it you do for us? Baron Hugues convinced me you were useful, but I've yet to see it.'

Frode tensed and stammered out his answer. 'I cannot prevent every malcontent, but I have kept the peace between our people much more than would otherwise be. Without me, there would be far more trouble.'

'Frode, the acceptable number of my priests being slaughtered and churches burned is none, do you understand?'

'Those are not in my control, that is not my land.'

'Nothing is your land.'

Frode gritted his teeth and took a breath. 'If that raiding force came into these lands…'

'My lands,' said Reinhard with an edge in his voice.

'… your lands,' agreed Frode, as if swallowing bone shards, 'then they would have been seen, and I would have heard, and I would have warned you.'

'How charitable. But it is not enough. I want an end to this banditry in these lands, and I want an end to the raids, and you will help me or I will unleash my hounds on that quiet village where your family are hiding.'

Frode tried to hide his shock and fear, but failed at both. His knuckles went white and his mouth pressed into a line.

'I have known for a long time, Earl Frode. I do not blame you for trying to keep it from me, but it did display a lack of judgement. I was always going to find out.'

Frode visibly shook and tried to hold down his anger, and for a moment Reinhard wondered if he had been mistaken to send the guards out. But Frode deflated slightly, and the fight went out of him. 'What do you need from me?'

Reinhard smiled broadly, feeling the warm rush of pleasure at his opponent submitting to his will. 'Better. Now, this is what I have in mind.'

Frode left the hall some time later feeling hollow. The anger and misery of the last months had worn away at his soul, but what Reinhard had asked him to do in that room was beyond his ability to abide. He thought of his family, who he had thought were safely hidden in the quiet farming village upriver, but whom Reinhard had so ruthlessly leveraged.

After the Christian had made his demands, he had left Frode with a last, chilling warning. 'Frode, I have men watching that village. If your family try to leave…' Those cold dead eyes had looked up at his without a hint of shame and then flicked back down to his papers without saying another word.

The thought of it chilled Frode to the bone. The anger, the helpless rage that his family were hostage to these men who ruled his lands.

All these thoughts and more roiled around in his mind as he stumbled back to his horse and rode home. He did not see the miles pass, he and the horse were absentmindedly following the familiar path. His whole being was occupied with trying to prise himself free of the paralysing fear and anger to try and decide on his course of action.

There were no good options. He could obey the bishop and live with his family in a world of crushing shame, or disobey them, and curse his kin to a terrible fate, without even the comfort of being there with them.

He left his horse with one of the few attendants he had been allowed to keep. The man had been his thrall, but slaves were not permitted by the Crusader overlords, so a few loyal men and women had simply stayed on, doing the same jobs in exchange for food and shelter and some paltry bits of silver.

Frode wandered into the longhouse and found Asel there waiting, staring at the fire. The huskarl looked up at him expectantly, nervously, and Frode's resolve threatened to crumble entirely.

'What did they want?'

Frode held his tongue for a moment, trying to work out how to describe it. 'Too much,' was all he could finally say. His jaw set into a rictus of hate and he looked away from the warrior before he would make an outburst. He struggled to control himself.

'What?'

'They want us to help them hunt down all these raiders, to spy on them, to betray them and everyone who is helping them in the villages. They want us to turn on our own people and be seen to be dealing with them with our own hands, to prove our loyalty for all to know.'

Asel swore softly. 'And what do they threaten us with to force compliance?'

Frode swallowed and flicked his eyes to the man. 'That they will burn the closest village every time bandits are seen, regardless of involvement, and put every living being there to the sword.' He did not mention the direct threat to his family, he did not want Asel to know the shame of his fear.

Asel choked in outrage. 'What? How can they be responsible? How can that be justice?'

'It is not intended to be justice.'

Asel stood and breathed heavily as he digested the news. 'This is not what we agreed. You said we would help keep our people safe, that the Christians would respect that.'

'I know.'

'We never said we would be their murderers, not against our own people.'

'Asel, I know! It was a mistake, I believed they could be reasoned with, that some form of peace would be accepted. What they do is madness, they are animals with no soul. I'm sorry, old friend, I was wrong to believe we could live alongside each other in peace.' He nodded gently.

Asel stiffened and his eyes widened. 'Does this mean you will refuse them?'

Frode grimaced and shook his head. 'I cannot refuse, the results would be a disaster.'

'Then what!' snarled Asel angrily. 'You will hunt and murder your own people?' Asel looked ready to launch himself at his sworn lord.

'No, I will not do that either. I will say, I have already said, that we will comply. But we will betray them and help bring an end to this mad priest and his rule.'

Asel's anger cracked and he slowly grinned. 'We will fight them?'

'Yes. How many men could we still raise?'

Asel put a hand to his chin and thought for a moment. 'I should think three hundred good men, more if we take the untrained. But weapons are scarce. Some were hidden but some have been found by the Christians.'

'Less than half the force that the Christians have in this one town, not enough for a direct confrontation,' said Frode.

'So what then?'

'We need more men, and more weapons. And we know where to get both.'

Asel's smiled broadened. 'Your sister.'

'My sister,' agreed Frode heavily.

'She will not easily be persuaded to help you.'

'No, no, she won't.'

'She may not even trust you.'

'No.' Frode looked at him. 'But she would trust you.'

Asel nodded slowly. 'Send me to her?'

'Yes, I have to stay here anyway, my disappearance would be immediately noted. I need to make pretence at complying with this order, buy some time to let you find her and help her, and secure her help for us. Combined, perhaps we have enough to win.'

'How will I gather and take three hundred men to her unnoticed?'

'You cannot, the men must stay here, I will pass word to a few we trust to be ready to raise the rest. When the time comes, we must strike swiftly and decisively.'

'So, what shall I do?'

Frode folded his arms across his chest and stared into the fire. 'Take half a dozen men you trust and go and find her. Tell her that you have grown tired of my peace with the Christians, and that you and the men are ready to rise up against them.'

'Lie to her?'

'Yes. As you say, she will not trust me, but she will believe what you say. After all, was it not nearly true?'

Asel shifted uncomfortably but did not deny it.

'So, she needs to back this plan with her full strength and belief or it will not work, and our people will suffer the consequences. You must present her with a vision she can believe in, and it is so close to the truth you will have no trouble convincing her. Given the chance to end the Christian rule here, and to show me that I was wrong and that she can save us, she will not refuse.'

Asel looked unhappy but nodded. 'I do not like the idea of deceiving her, even for this cause, but I see your reasoning is sound. So what do I persuade her to do?'

'She will need to gather strength, and I need a little time to prepare here. She should continue the raids. You can provide her information of what you know about the Christian movements and outposts. They need to capture supplies and weapons from them, and weaken and spread their forces. Then, when we are ready, we can help her sneak her army into our lands, arm as many of our people as she can, and then rise up as one against the enemy.' Frode looked at Asel with the most confidence he could muster. 'Everywhere in these lands at once, one blow, one chance at freedom.'

'And what of the rest of the country? What of the Christians there?'

'Either the people there rise with us, or we will all be destroyed. But would it not be better?'

Asel jutted out his chin and nodded. 'To die as free people, not live as slaves. You are right, Lord Frode. It is better to try while we still have strength, than to surrender to captive misery.' He stepped forwards and clasped arms with his lord. 'I am sorry I doubted you.'

Frode met his eye and nodded slightly and his heart nearly wavered. 'I am sorry too, my friend.' *I am so sorry.*

## CHAPTER 21

# TO THE VICTORS

THE VICTORIOUS RAIDING party returned to Vatnsborð in high spirits. Jarl Gustav welcomed them back, and after conferring with the leaders, immediately ordered another raid, this time sending mostly those who had not been on the previous one, giving the returned warriors the chance to rest and heal their wounds.

Gjaldir returned to his longhouse and saw Brunhild outside, hanging washed clothes in the warm summer sun. He grinned like a child and it was all he could do not to run over. She looked up as he was nearly there and his heart soared when she immediately broke into a beaming smile when her eyes met his. Aeske was sitting on a box behind her, and he saw Gjaldir too and sprang to his feet in excitement.

It was too much for Gjaldir, who burst into a jog and dropped his bundle of kit, heavy with his new maille, and stretched out his arms, leaning down and gathering the waddling Aeske in mid-stride, lifting him up into the air as the boy squealed with joy. He swung Aeske effortlessly up and planted the child on his shoulders, where his little hands grabbed handfuls of Gjaldir's greasy hair and clung on as he burbled wordless happiness.

Gjaldir looked at Brunhild, who came over and planted an enthusiastic kiss on his cheek, ignoring for a moment the fact he was unwashed from six days of travel and battle. 'You seem pleased to see me,' he jested, his grin even broader than before.

She punched his defenceless stomach lightly. 'I'm only happy for Aeske that you have returned. He likes you, and he isn't old enough to know better.' She gave him a pout and returned to the clothes as he followed, Aeske bobbing along on his shoulders.

'Jaldir!' the boy squealed happily.

'Gods, his hands are strong,' said Gjaldir, wincing as the boy tried to remove clumps of his hair as he swayed.

'Yes, he will be a strong man, stronger than you even, but better looking.'

Gjaldir rolled his eyes and reached up with the hand that wasn't clamped to Aeske's tunic to try to prise the little fingers free from his hair before it was ripped out. He felt the old, faded stab of pain that the boy was not his, as he wondered what father could sire a child so strong. But the pain was dull and distant, he had come to terms with the truth many months ago; that it didn't matter whose child Aeske was, he loved him as a father would. More, in fact, than most fathers he had met in his orphaned childhood.

He finally got Aeske's hands free and lifted the boy back down to plant him on the box where he had been before, tussling his hair and sidling over to Brunhild, snaking a single arm around her waist.

'Don't even think about it,' she said without looking round. 'What comes out of Aeske smells and looks cleaner than you do. And is that your blood?'

Gjaldir looked down at himself. 'Which bit?'

Brunhild turned her head and gave him an unamused glare. 'I hope it is the blood of a Christian at least.'

'It is.' Gjaldir paused. 'I killed him,' he said quietly, without boast.

Brunhild's expression softened for a moment and then the moment passed and she nodded firmly. 'Good. That is one less, and now the other men will speak of you with more respect, I will be less ashamed to be seen with you.'

Gjaldir grunted, confused at the mix of emotions Brunhild had shown. She looked him up and down and beckoned. 'Come on, give me those disgusting clothes.'

Gjaldir paused for a moment, looking around, but there were few other people in sight. His old habitual nervousness at being naked in front of others was hard to entirely shake. He stripped his bloodstained tunic and trousers and his leg wrappings and braies and handed them gingerly to Brunhild, who wrinkled her nose in disgust. 'Animals,' she said. 'You didn't have time to wash?'

Gjaldir shook his head in embarrassment. 'We barely stopped moving all the way back.'

Brunhild gingerly put the noisome bundle in a basket and looked back at him, standing there naked in the sun. Gjaldir was suddenly and painfully aware how long it had been since she had seen him like this, and of the feelings he had repressed in the time in between. He had accepted that she was not his, not in that way, but his body had other opinions.

'Well? I'm not washing you too, you can do that yourself!' said Brunhild with a laugh, shooing him.

'What? No, I know, I just…'

'Go on then. And come back quickly.' She gave him a mischievous look. 'I will get one of the girls to look after Aeske for a while.' He furrowed his eyebrows for a moment and then Brunhild's eyes dropped from his face down his body and flicked back, giving him a look he had not seen for a long, long time.

The understanding spurred him into action, and he nodded nervously and looked around, seeing the washtub beside the house was half full of water. He walked over, the sound of Brunhild's giggling spurring him on as he reached for the ladle and the rough homemade soap the Norse used. The water had been sitting in the sun for a while, and, mercifully, was not as cold as the lake.

Gjaldir scrubbed himself as best he could standing next to the tub, teasing the crud out of his hair and rubbing the dark stains and dirt from his skin. There was no comb there but he rinsed his hair and pushed it back across his skull, shivering as the sun's warmth did little to dispel the cold of the water.

When he decided that he had done enough, he upended the tub of brown water, knowing someone would be angry he had used it and not refilled it, but not caring, and headed to the door of the house, naked as the day he was born. He had hoped Brunhild would bring him his other clothes, they were inside, but she had chosen to leave him without.

He gingerly made his way inside and found, to his surprise, that Brunhild was the only one there, standing alone, leaning against a post where the rough woollen hanging that divided the house into two rooms in winter was tied up. She was toying with her simple rope belt, which she had undone, and was left wearing nothing but her plain linen shift, still damp in patches from the washing.

Gjaldir gulped as he looked at the way it clung to her, and at the soft intensity of her stare, welcoming and mocking him in one. He stood there in dumb silence, drinking her in while she returned his stare with easy confidence.

'I asked the others to take Aeske and play, but they won't be gone for long.' She twisted her body, slowly and gracefully, and as Gjaldir watched, transfixed, moved over to the long, broad box that ran along the wall, perching on it and inclining her head to beckon him over.

Gjaldir strode over, flushed with nerves and excitement, somehow once again being turned into the blushing maid by this woman, and stood in front of her, his knees against hers, unsure what to do.

She laughed again, not her mocking tone, but warm, silken, and she opened her knees so he could step forwards, her shift riding up to her hips as he reached her and looked down into her eyes.

'I'm sorry it's been so long,' she whispered.

Gjaldir smiled back and brushed her hair. 'Don't be.'

'I was just so…'

'I understand.'

She nodded and buried her head into his neck, kissing him gently and sending fire up and down his spine as her hands moved over his back.

'You know Aeske will tire of playing quickly, we don't have long.'

'I don't think we will need long,' said Gjaldir with a shake of his head, and Brunhild leant her head back and laughed, half choking on her mirth. He bent down and kissed her, long and firm, and she melted into his powerful embrace.

They were lying on the benchtop in each other's arms, Brunhild back in her shift, Gjaldir in his fresh tunic and trousers, when the door opened and one of the other women brought Aeske back in. 'He needs feeding,' the woman said simply, ignoring the cosy scene she had walked in on.

Brunhild looked at Gjaldir and smiled, kissing him softly on the cheek. 'I have to go.'

'Can I help?'

'No. Go, go and do whatever it is men do when we are busy.'

Gjaldir smiled and levered himself upright with a groan. He knew he should clean his equipment, it was dirty and damp and the maille was already starting to rust, but the thought irked him. He just wanted to lie there in blissful quiet with Brunhild, but she was already tending to Aeske, and they both had responsibilities.

He wandered out of the house, stretching his back and legs in the sun, and picked up his abandoned bundle of equipment. He had lost Dengir's old axe in the running fight in the woods, a loss that saddened him, but Leif had been able to find him a spare, a newer, larger axe with a fine bearded blade that he already preferred to the worn old relic from a previous generation.

He took his equipment down to the lake shore to get some sand to scrub and wash away the rust and dirt; it was a tedious chore, but the longer you left it, the worse it got.

Gjaldir smiled down at Lefnir, his old training adversary, and reached out a hand to help him up. The smile was not mocking or smug, as it once would have been. Lefnir had very nearly got inside Gjaldir's shield with his practice sword by using a deft feint and sidestep that Gjaldir had not anticipated. A few more inches of reach and Gjaldir would have been 'dead'. But his reactions had allowed him to jerk back just in time, and then slam forwards as Lefnir was off balance, knocking him to the ground.

'I nearly had you.'

'You did, it was well struck. Desperate, but well struck.'

'Desperate?'

'Yes, even if you had succeeded, it is unlikely to have been a killing blow, and you were at my mercy.'

Lefnir snorted as he stood up. 'This is not a real battle, so it does not matter.'

'Hold!' shouted Gunnar, walking over to look at them with a scowl. 'What did you say?'

Lefnir blanched. 'That this is not a real battle.'

'Why would you do something here that you would not do in battle?'

Lefnir shrugged slightly. 'Because I wanted to win for once.'

Gunnar huffed and shook his head. 'Everyone, gather.'

The half-dozen pairs stopped their fighting and came over, forming a half circle around Gunnar, who stood there with a stormy expression.

'Half of you have had your first real battle, the other half seek to prove they are ready, yet none of you are taking this seriously.' His eyes scoured the group. 'Half-hearted fights, stupid tricks, more concerned with not hurting yourself or your friends than learning anything.'

Some of the warriors looked ashamed, but others looked defiant or bored. 'Why do we keep doing this training? I have fought and killed in the wall, this battling with sticks, what is the purpose?'

Gunnar turned his steely gaze on the man who had spoken. 'You think one battle was enough? I have been a warrior for twenty years, I have fought dozens of battles and killed more men than I can count. Yet I still practise, and I still learn. Why do you think you are too good?'

The man shuffled on the spot. 'What do you expect us to do?'

'I expect to see you trying to kill your opponent,' Gunnar growled. 'I want to see him desperately defending himself, testing the limits of his speed and strength, learning from his success or failure while the weapons are wood and not steel.' He pointed his finger at the man. 'All I see from you is a boy playing at fighting. You have stood in one wall for a dozen heartbeats against a defeated enemy, and your pride blinds you. How fortunate you were, to have so easy a first battle.'

Gjaldir tensed at that, he thought his first battle had been anything but easy. He did not like hearing it mocked. But Gunnar missed nothing, and he rounded on Gjaldir. 'You disagree?'

'It was not so easy for all of us.'

'Really? I hear you killed a man in single combat, and that it took so long some men argue he died of thirst, waiting for you to finish him. Tell me, Gjaldir, did I teach you to wait so long?'

Men laughed and Gjaldir tried to control himself. 'I was merely being careful.'

'Care is good in battle. But your kin were fighting behind you, what if they had needed you? What if they had died waiting for you to finally attack?'

Gjaldir looked down and said nothing.

'And you, Lefnir, you threw yourself past Gjaldir's shield just now, only to land a half-powered strike on his chest. Would you do that to a man in maille?'

'No.'

'Our enemies wear maille, so why practise it?'

'I'm sorry, Gunnar, but I couldn't find another way. Perhaps I could have hit his arm…'

'His arm?' Gunnar shook his head. 'You had given away your footing and position, any strike you made had to be a killer, or nothing at all. Listen, because I see all of you do this. You hit your opponents on the shoulder or the leg and declare victory. I have seen a man lose his arm in a fight and still kill his opponent. I have seen a man with one leg half severed holding his place in the line. You all practise as if for a duel, where a wound can lead to victory, but we are not fighting in duels, this is war.'

He waved Gjaldir over and pointed at the empty space to his side, leaving Gjaldir standing there while he talked to the group. 'Wounding an enemy is fine, if you are ready to defend yourself from his counter. If you are not, do not strike, because your attack may wound him while his kills you. It happens all the time.'

'What if your strike kills, but his counter also kills you?' Lefnir asked.

'Then at least you have died well,' said Gunnar coldly. 'And not put the man next to you in immediate danger. Sometimes it is necessary to risk your life for the killing blow, but do not risk your life to stripe someone's arm, remember that he will have a man next to him.'

Gunnar turned again to face Gjaldir, he dropped his shield but kept his sword. 'Strike at my exposed side.'

Gjaldir hesitated, nervously watching the huskarl, but did as he was told. He stepped forwards with his shield out and aimed a blow at Gunnar's arm.

The blow never landed, Gunnar simply used his free arm to snatch Gjaldir's shield, wrenching it to one side, and slapped his sword onto the back of Gjaldir's neck, which jolted fire up his spine and rattled his teeth.

'And you are dead.'

Gjaldir shook his head to clear it and shrugged. 'I did what you told me to do.'

'Yes, I needed to show them what a fool would do. Even if you had hit my arm, I would have killed you. A shield is not there to protect my arm, it is there to protect my head and body. In its absence, do not strike at my arm, strike where it will kill. Go again.'

Gjaldir thought for a moment, settling his eyes on Gunnar's angled chest. He advanced forwards with his shield out and wooden sword hidden behind it, as Gunnar had taught them.

Gunnar reached for Gjaldir's shield again and he whipped it to the side to block Gunnar's weapon arm and lunged forwards with the blade. Gunnar caught the blade in his outstretched hand and stepped into Gjaldir, headbutting him in the chin, a blow that he only pulled at the last second, still leaving a stinging impact. Gjaldir's head snapped back and a moment later the tip of Gunnar's sword slammed painfully into his ribs. 'You're dead.'

Gjaldir rubbed his jaw and waved his arm exasperated. 'You couldn't do that if I had a real sword, you couldn't grab it like that.'

'Yes, I could, my hand would be wounded, but you would be dead,' Gunnar said, and a few men laughed.

Gunnar turned to look at the group. 'You need to strike to end the fight, not to draw blood. If you have a good position, maybe a blow to the chest or stomach will work, if you can get enough power to pierce the maille, but there are three places that are never armoured well, and will end a man instantly. What are they?'

'The head?'

'No, not always. It will bleed like a river, but the man might stay in the fight.'

'Inside the thigh?'

'A man will bleed to death in twenty heartbeats from that, but he can kill you while he does. Stop being honourable, you are close to the point but not there.' Some of the men winced visibly and Gunnar scowled. 'It is not pleasant, it is not glorious, but this is war. You must be mean, you must fight without compassion, and no man, no matter how strong or brave, will continue to fight after you put your sword between his stones. You cut a man there and his fight is over. Where else does that?'

'The eyes,' said Gjaldir, rubbing his chin to dull the pain.

Gunnar turned to face him. 'Good. A man cannot fight what he cannot see, and the horror of losing your eyes will paralyse any warrior. And every man, even with a good helmet, has to leave his eyes open. A thrust to the eyes will end any fight if it lands, and terrify your opponent if it does not.'

Gunnar looked around but did not wait for another suggestion. 'The last is the throat. If you cut a man's throat, he cannot breathe and he will panic. Eyes, throat, balls. Those are the real fight-enders. A man struck in those places will abandon a killing strike mid-swing, and a man in maille with a shield leaves all three places vulnerable.' Gunnar waved at the group to spread out again. 'Two walls, let me see you practise as you mean to fight. I want to see you put fear in your opponents, you may only have sticks but I want to see real fights, I want to see black eyes and hear choking gasps and have men limping home with one hand clamped to their groin, or you will be learning nothing.'

By Gunnar's standards, the rest of the session went far more satisfactorily. He watched them all with a steely expression, but inside he was pleased. By the time he told them to stop, Gjaldir had a nasty gash above his eyebrow, and Lefnir was still sitting on the ground, gasping for air from a blow to his throat. There were men groaning and bleeding and giving him filthy looks, and it almost brought a smile to Gunnar's face. They had needed a shock, as was often the case. Those who had survived one battle suddenly thought themselves invincible, a mistake that needed correcting.

He left the group and headed back to the hall where Gustav and Halla stayed. It had not always been like that, they had had separate houses with their closest kin, but Gustav had announced it was better if they lived together, to plan things more closely. Gunnar knew the real reason, it was a small village and the truth got around quickly, but he did not begrudge them the small slice of comfort.

The village was a hive of activity as he walked through. It was late afternoon on a fine summer's day and everyone had something to be doing. One longhouse whose frame had settled badly was being disassembled and rebuilt by a team of men, while others were re-turfing houses that needed it, getting ready for winter.

Leif was still out on a raid with fifty warriors, although they were expected back at any time. Then they would hear what he had to say and plan the next raid. So it would go on until one side cracked, or until their woefully small force was caught and destroyed.

Gunnar did not hold much hope that they would win, they were simply too few, but his heart held no space for giving in, it was not even a part of his thoughts. His king had fought to the death seeking victory, at the expense of everything, and to not follow his example would be a terrible dishonour.

He reached the biggest hall and looked inquiringly at one of Halla's warriors who was lazing around outside. He nodded back at Gunnar. 'You can go in.'

Gunnar nodded and pushed through the door, looking around and seeing Halla and Gustav sitting at a rough table in the centre of the room, talking in low tones. They looked up as he walked across the beaten, reed-covered floor towards them.

'Gunnar, what news do you bring?'

'I was hoping you had heard from Leif.'

Gustav shook his head. 'Nothing yet, but one of the hunting parties found half a dozen warriors wandering in the woods, looking for us. They are bringing them in now.'

Gunnar nodded. It was not unusual now for exiled men or those running from the Christian rule to seek them out, although it seemed worryingly simple for them to do it.

'We were discussing what the next target should be for a large raid.'

'Uppsala,' said Halla firmly and Gunnar pursed his lips.

'Their main encampment? It is very far away, and will be very heavily defended.'

'It is symbolic, our people need to know we can strike the Crusaders anywhere.'

Gunnar furrowed his brows and did not wish to argue, although he thought it was not the best idea. This did not escape Halla.

'Then what would you suggest?'

'Karlsgrind,' he said without hesitating. 'The Christians have built a fort on both banks, sealing the river and the crossing there. It is what stops us accessing the lake, and it is the route that links the east and west of their lands.'

Gustav nodded. 'That was my intent also. It is easy to reach, we might even be able to hold it, and it means we could send a ship to my lands, for more men, or to stir trouble there.'

Halla scowled. 'Surely they will expect an attack there, it is too obvious.'

'You are right that they will expect it,' said Gunnar. 'But that does not mean we cannot win.'

A figure filled the door behind them. 'The hunters have arrived with those men they found,' the warrior called out into the room.

Halla nodded. 'Disarm their leader and bring him to us.'

'Yes, lady.' The man left the doorway again and Gustav turned to Halla. 'I think it is best that we save a raid on Uppsala. If we continue to stay more locally, they might even send some forces from there to strengthen this area, leaving Uppsala vulnerable later.'

Halla pursed her lips and looked at Gunnar. 'What do you think?'

Gunnar was noncommittal. He was uncomfortable deciding the strategy, it had never been his role. He was a commander of men in battle, even leading a raid made him nervous and doubtful. 'I think it is possible.'

Halla scowled and then threw her hands up. 'Then I will abide by Gustav's decision, but I wish to see the Christians burned out of Uppsala sooner rather than later. It is a blow that may rally the North against them.'

Before they had time to discuss it further, a man was led into the room, but not a stranger as they expected. 'Asel?' said Halla in surprise, and then cautious joy. She stood and walked over to the man, pausing as if unsure, but the man smiled broadly and she went to embrace him. 'Asel, why are you here? I am pleased to see you, but what has happened? Is my brother…'

Asel's face contorted slightly and he gave Halla an odd look. 'You brother is alive, but I have left his service.'

Halla looked confused. 'For what reason?'

Asel gathered himself and looked at the others in the room. 'I have broken my oath to him, because I believe he is no longer worthy of it. Our people are suffering, the Christians kill and steal, and he does nothing, he helps them even.'

'He helps them?' said Halla in horror.

'Yes, he says it is to spare us, but you cannot save a people by allowing them to be treated as sheep, killed at a whim.'

Halla's face contorted in pain and she shook her head, looking away. 'I cannot believe he chose this path, but I saw that he was broken. The brother I knew died at Uppsala.' She sighed softly and looked back at Asel. 'So you have come to join us?'

'Yes, lady. And I come with news of our land, and a plan to free it from Christian rule.'

Halla's eyes widened. 'To free it?'

'Yes. I have the support of most of Jarl Frode's men, they are ready to rise up, and many of the people with them, if only they are given the chance. But we do not have enough weapons, or enough warriors, and Lady Halla, I am hoping you can provide us with both.'

Halla walked forwards, her eyes blazing intently, and grasped Asel's hand. 'You said you have a plan?'

'Yes, of sorts, and information about where the Christians are weak, and where we can strike.'

Halla's pinched lips spread into a thin smile. 'Tell me everything.'

## Chapter 22

# Earthly Masters

REINHARD LOOKED AT the partially built church with a feeling of moderate surprise, bordering on being impressed; a feeling he tried his best to avoid as it often led to weakness. The men he had left in charge of its construction were Bavarian stonemasons and they were making the most of the locally available stone. The mound, just outside the ruined city of Uppsala, was where the pagan temple had once stood. All signs of it had vanished, pulled down, cut up and burned, removed from existence. Just as he had ordered.

His imported stonemasons had declared the mound was stable enough and old enough to support a good-sized stone church. Despite the burning of Uppsala, he had decided this would be the most important church in the conquered lands, symbolically built on the ashes of the pagans' holiest site, demonstrating for anyone who passed the supremacy of the Christian faith.

He considered going over to talk to the masons, but decided it was a task to be left until later. The summons from Duke Henry took precedence, and he had no need to annoy the man by taking time to attend to others first.

He had not admitted to anyone that it was, indeed, a summons he was answering. His position was precarious enough as it was without the men of the Order learning he could be called to heel by the duke given that he was supposed to be above such treatment. But the practicality of the situation demanded he obey, and obey quickly.

He leaned over and spoke quietly to Sir Sighard, the commander of his escort, and the knight called out curt orders to the twenty-man mounted escort, and the fifty men and wagons that followed, to head south past the city to the main Crusader encampment.

Calling it an encampment was a disservice now. The camp was well on the way to becoming a town. Sited in what had been farmland near the river, using the old Norse docks, real buildings were springing up, the main street from the docks to the Crusade headquarters had been paved, and the headquarters itself was a two-storey stone and wood building that dominated the single-storey warehouses, barracks and stables that surrounded it. Even the ruined town of Uppsala was being partially cleared, and half-intact buildings repaired for the use of the large labour force of Norse people who worked for their new rulers.

Reinhard felt the unwelcome sensation again of being impressed with the progress, and suddenly doubted his decision to make his base in the relative rural backwater of Arbugæ, instead of here, where the true power would clearly lie. But then the same counterargument swirled in his head, that here he would only be living in the dark, deep shadow of Henry the Black, while in Arbugæ he was the lord of the land.

It was important to him, that feeling. Bishops and cardinals could be powerful, could be leaders in battle or politics, could own vast amounts of land, but could never truly be lords. That was the line drawn, they were never allowed to have all the trappings of feudal power, always their lands lay within someone else's demesne. Not here, not in the conquered lands of old Sweden, where as the

Grandmaster of the Order he was second only to God in the lands it controlled.

His mind sidestepped the falseness of that argument, even ignoring the evidence that he had been summoned by his patron and overlord. He still told himself it was a relationship of convenience. His brother and father had conspired for his entire life to prevent him having this kind of power, and nothing, not his enemies, the Norse, his family, nor even his allies would stop him achieving and enjoying that position.

The escort reached the headquarters and smartly formed a corridor for Reinhard to approach the entrance, quite the spectacle in that bustling street, which was entirely the point. Reinhard and Sighard rode down between the two lines of mounted knights of the Order, dressed in full armour and with their white and gold surcoats blazing in the sun.

Reinhard sighed in pleasure at the sight, an earthly demonstration of his God-given power. He reached the large double doors and Sighard announced him, the guards quickly opening the gates for them to ride through. They entered into an inner courtyard, so new that carpenters were still finishing the east side building, and pages came to help them dismount and take their horses. Other than the smell of fresh-cut wood and whitewash, it was like arriving at any good lord's manor in Germany. Reinhard made a string of mental notes to have something similar built in Arbugæ.

A well-dressed attendant wearing the duke's falcon crest on his tunic was waiting and he bowed to Reinhard with a precision that he enjoyed.

'Your excellency, his grace Duke Henry welcomes you, and is waiting on you in his private study.'

Reinhard nodded crisply. 'Thank you, you may show me the way. Please have food and water provided for my men, Sir Sighard here will direct their needs.'

The attendant bowed his head in acknowledgement and

gestured for the bishop to follow, heading across the courtyard to an open door that led inside the two-storey part of the building.

Reinhard followed the man through a dining hall and into a reception room, then up a set of stairs and onto a landing with a number of rooms branching off it. A guard stood at the top of the stairs, doing his best not to look bored and failing, straightening himself to a rigid poise as Reinhard approached.

The attendant walked over to one of the doors, Reinhard guessed all these rooms must be Henry's personal quarters, and knocked, waiting a few moments before entering. 'Your grace, his excellency Bishop Reinhard is here.'

Henry was sitting on a chair at a small writing desk in the well-furnished room. It was decorated and appointed in the latest German fashion. Thick, richly coloured dark red drapes and tapestries depicting hunting scenes adorned the walls, there was a pair of fine chairs near the fireplace, a small, well-carved table with two seats against one wall, and a series of shelves stacked with neatly arranged papers, books and scrolls.

Henry stood from his small writing desk, the least ornamented and visibly the most used item in the room, and gestured to the chairs by the empty fireplace. 'My dear bishop, come, sit with me. Francois, bring refreshments for the Grandmaster and I.'

The attendant bowed, left, and closed the door behind them, leaving the two men alone. Reinhard smiled thinly and took the proffered seat.

'You look well, Grandmaster, your stay among the pagans has not affected you badly?'

'A shepherd is not harmed by staying among his flock,' replied Reinhard with a hint of mischief.

'And I hear the wolves are very much among those sheep,' said Henry, turning the tone in a moment.

Reinhard pursed his lips and waved the concern away. 'There are some troublemakers and remnants, but nothing too serious.'

'The town of Västerås was sacked, the garrison slaughtered.'

Reinhard stiffened slightly and could not hide his annoyance. 'Not my lands, not my concern.'

'I do not mean to blame you, my friend, do not think it,' Henry said with a broad smile. 'We are only speaking of events.'

Reinhard stiffened, mortified that he had so easily allowed himself to be riled. He was tired from the long and unaccustomed journey, that would be why he was on edge. 'Of course, I simply mean it is beyond my control what happens in Otto's lands.'

'So it is. In any case, I have asked you here to discuss this very problem, the constant and seemingly unstoppable troublemakers and remnants, as you call them.'

'Is it such a problem?'

'Yes, we are losing men rapidly, half a dozen here, twenty there, over a hundred at Västerås. The land is huge, and the people overly prideful and violent.'

'Are we not eradicating the bandits? I hear Grandsteward Hugues has had significant success in the south.'

'That is the news I arranged to be spread, the truth is more complex.'

'Ah,' said Reinhard. 'Perhaps I had too much faith in the man.'

'I do not believe it is his fault, he has an area of forest the size of Saxony, full of an unknown number of Norse malcontents, and only a couple of thousand men. An enormous task.'

Reinhard said nothing, unwilling to give Hugues any succour, even in conversation.

'In any case, we face the same problem here, and Otto does in the north, and Conrad on the south side of the lake.' Henry looked up and stared at him. 'All, in fact, except you. Your lands seem relatively peaceful. How have you done it?'

*Ah, the crux of the conversation, and the reason for my summons.* Reinhard smiled, allowing a smug curl in the corner of his lip. 'Well, I have made a pet of the previous lord of the land.' There was no need to admit that it was, in fact, Hugues who had done that, against Reinhard's stiff opposition. Reinhard had come to see the value in the man, and used him extensively.

Henry furrowed his brows. 'You have done what?'

'We captured the earl who used to rule much of those lands, and I have bent him to my will. He helps keep the people in order. I give them an illusion of power, and it keeps them in check.' It wasn't completely true, there was still some trouble, and it was growing, but he wasn't going to let that ruin the moment.

'Hmm, interesting,' said Henry, disappointed. 'Not an option for us, all the leaders in these lands are dead or gone. We tried the old methods at first, as you know, making examples in towns. But it doesn't work as well anymore. The large towns are all appearing to be compliant, it is the men who sneak into the woods and live in all the small farms and settlements that are the problem.'

Reinhard nodded sympathetically. The idea that he was going to make any extra effort to help Conrad and Otto control their unruly pagan peasants made him want to chuckle effusively.

'The problem, as I see it, is that there are too many of them, and not enough of us. They are realising it. When we were a single army, all bowed before us, but most of that army has gone home, and those that remain have been swallowed up by the vastness of this land, which is much greater than we expected. Recruiting more lords and soldiers to come here and chase bandits in the forest is extremely difficult.'

Reinhard nodded sadly at that. Even for the Order, recruitment had slowed to a trickle, despite his best efforts to rally support with the papal hierarchy. Men at arms had flocked to the Crusade in search of glory in battle, but far fewer were willing to come and help secure the conquered lands. 'Well, then there need to be fewer people,' he said with a shrug.

At that moment, the door opened again and Francois came in with a pewter tray, two goblets, and some sort of sweet pastries that

Reinhard could smell the moment he entered the room. The smell was intoxicating and it tugged as his discipline to appear unaffected. His mouth started watering, a function of his body he had never been able to control, much to his irritation.

'Ah, excellent,' said Henry, as the platter was offered to him and he took a goblet and a pastry and set them on the small table beside his chair. 'My cook is French, and these are superb.'

Reinhard pretended disinterest, but took the pastry nonetheless, leaving the attendant to put the goblet on his small round table. The smell of cooked fruits and fresh, crisp pastry filled his nose. He took a bite and for a moment was lost in the rich flavour. It was some sort of dark berry filling, it was quite wonderful.

He forced himself to only eat half, leaving the other half on the platter with the goblet as if it was of no great importance, and picked up the silver goblet to wash the dry flakes down. The metal was extraordinarily cold to the touch, and he peered into the cup in surprise he was not able to hide, looking up to see Henry grinning smugly at him.

'Ice?' he said in surprise. 'You have ice here?'

'Yes!' said Henry in delight. 'My cook insisted on it. There is a new icehouse behind the stables, it was cut and stored in the winter and there is still plenty left.'

Reinhard shook his head in wonder and took a sip. The drink was simply water, but flavoured with lemon and some sort of herb. It was superbly refreshing on that warm day in his thick robes. He took a few shallow draughts and set the cup down next to the pastry, giving it half a longing look before turning his eyes on Henry with a subtle look of reproachment.

'What, you think I have gone soft?'

'I remember your brother,' said Reinhard, trying to sound disappointed but still savouring the taste of the lemon on his lips.

Henry laughed, shaking his head. 'I am the Duke of Bavaria, but I am not Duke Welf. If I have to be here in this cursed land, why should I not have some of the comforts my position affords me? This house, good food and drink, it is not so outrageous.'

Reinhard gazed around at the sumptuous room, feeling the sickly creep of envy. 'I suppose it is not too harmful, if carefully controlled.'

'Why would it be harmful?'

'Luxury is the pursuit of greed, it is a sin and it weakens a man.'

'We are all sinners, my good bishop. That is why we need the clergy. Now, as we were discussing.'

'The troublesome people of this land, and the number thereof.'

'Exactly.'

'You suggested there should be fewer of them.'

Reinhard sighed slightly. 'Yes, and I need not explain how that can be achieved.'

'Well, it is not so simple. As you are well aware, most of these lands and the people living within them are the demesne of other lords. My own parcel is quite modest.'

Reinhard frowned. 'Yes, why is that? You commanded the Crusade, yet you receive little reward.'

'My dear man, you know me better. I merely received my reward in means other than worthless land. What I received was far more valuable. However, it doesn't help the problem at hand. I cannot simply burn towns to the ground. The Dukes of Swabia and Saxony want to see incomes, and to see incomes they need peasants, and they expect these pagans to be transformed into their peasants. Dead people create no income.' Henry shrugged. 'So I cannot simply slaughter them openly, or I will have to compensate their lords.'

Reinhard raised his eyebrows and nodded. 'Quite the predicament. How do you suggest I help? I cannot do it for you, the Order's reputation and charter would survive even less well than you if we did.'

'Quite, as you say, it would not do. No, we need a more subtle approach, and one presents itself with all this current trouble. You see, this is why I am not interested in blaming anyone. It is not a problem, it is an opportunity, one your Order is uniquely positioned to take advantage of.'

Reinhard leant forwards a little, tapping his finger on the rim of his iced goblet. 'How, exactly?' He was nervous. He did not know what the duke meant, and not knowing what he was going to be asked in advance of it was always disconcerting. Preparation for these things was essential to proper outcomes.

'You and your Order are still largely responsible for much of the food supply to the various forces in the provinces.'

'Not all of it, not anymore. Most of the garrisons take their food from the locals now.'

'Yes, but a significant portion of it, and more importantly, the transfer of it from one place to the next.'

Reinhard conceded with a cautious nod.

'Well, my reports say that the raids are often targeting the food stores, either stealing or destroying them.'

'Yes.'

'And, if it continued, such actions could lead to food shortages.'

Reinhard suddenly saw the direction of the thread and his heart started racing. 'Yes.'

'And food shortages will, unfortunately, lead to famine.'

Reinhard's face set in a heavy frown. 'A famine the Order would be blamed for.'

Henry waved his concern away. 'No, not if we carefully and widely blamed the raids.'

'In any case, the raids are not nearly serious enough to threaten the food supply of the entire country.'

'No. You know that, I know that. But most others don't know that. Especially if we invent losses that have not actually occurred, and take food from the population to replace our own losses, and take more than we need.'

'So, if we are clear, you mean to create a manufactured, provincewide food shortage, and blame it on the raids and rebels? And you wish my Order to organise this, exaggerate it, and starve the locals while ensuring ample supply to our own troops.'

'Perfectly said, my dear man. Perfectly. I would go as far as to say take far more food than the soldiers need.'

Reinhard's brow furrowed even further. 'And this must be entirely a secret, so that you cannot be blamed.'

'Quite, I knew you would understand.'

'But then I will be blamed.'

'Ah, well, not if we skilfully divert the blame to the locals and their destructive, selfish raids.' Henry took another draught of his iced drink and smacked his lips in satisfaction. 'He really is a superb cook.'

Reinhard squirmed in his seat. The duke was setting him up to take the blame for an enormous disaster. The German dukes would not care for excuses about rebels, it was his Order's role to stop the thrice-cursed raids. He closed his eyes and steadied himself, furious at Henry, with his dread growing. Not only would the great lords of the empire blame him, but the locals would, and even his own Order would see him as weak for allowing it to continue.

'Your grace, I don't think you understand my situation. If I allow these raids to continue, and cannot explain why, I face…' He struggled with what to say. If he told Henry he faced internal rebellion he would weaken himself enormously in the duke's eyes, perhaps even making the ruthless lord lose faith in him, faith he still needed. If he did not tell him, and went through with this, the results of a rebellion could be disastrous, even fatal.

Reinhard felt the closest thing to panic that he had felt since he had been attacked with the pagan holy sword in this very camp the year before. He was trapped, and he saw no way out of it. He fell into unaccustomed silence.

'You are worried what it will look like, being unable to stop the raids?' said Henry with a sympathetic nod. 'I am sure it will dent your power and position, but I also know you will manage it. You always do.'

Reinhard realised pleading his weakness would achieve nothing here and he confined himself to a terse nod.

'Good! Then we understand what is required,' said Henry with a smile. 'And do not think that I am leaving you alone in this. I have arranged for Hugues and his men to rejoin you in a few weeks, they will keep any trouble in check, and his presence will help keep the blame shared, and the focus off you.'

Reinhard absorbed the last blow with a sickening feeling. Hugues returning would only make his problems worse, bringing with him his own men, splitting the loyalties of the Order further. Reinhard looked at Henry's vacuously smiling face and had a deep realisation that he had become expendable. He felt he could barely gather the strength to stand and make his exit.

'Oh, and it bears making clear, Hugues cannot know either. He may tell his lord, and his lord may tell the other dukes. You understand, of course. If he tries to effectively counter the raids, you must prevent it. I'm sure you will find a way to manipulate him, you always seem to do so.'

Anger and fear washed through him. He had given Henry the position he was now in, arranged and secured the path, opened the door for him, but he still needed Henry, and Henry had finally realised he didn't need Reinhard, or perhaps he had always planned to betray him. He finally managed to get to his feet. 'As you command, your grace. It has been a long day, may I go? I have to see the new church and find my rest.'

Henry did not bother to stand and waved towards the door. 'Of course, thank you for visiting with me, I hope to hear of your success in the near future.'

Reinhard nodded drunkenly. 'If I am successful, there will be no need for me to tell you, you will hear the clamour of the starving outside your door.'

'No, I will not. I am leaving for home. My position here once the Crusade ended was dubious as it was. Now I must go back to Bavaria, and my duties. I have barely visited since I succeeded my brother.'

'You are leaving?' Reinhard said, numbly.

'Yes, but I will return once you have succeeded. In the meantime, I have instructed my staff that you be allowed to use my quarters here, as and when you need. On a temporary basis, of course.'

Reinhard nodded. 'That is most generous, my lord.' Then, after mumbling his goodbyes, he turned and headed for the door, passing the obsequious attendant and the bored guard.

He stumbled down the stairs, trying not to show any emotion. *He thinks he can discard me?* He went into the yard and found his horse was not there, nor was Sighard. He looked around in confusion. But of course, word he was leaving could not have arrived at the stable yet, or wherever Sighard was.

The attendant went through the door on the far side of the yard to the stables in question as Reinhard stood there, seething with anger and his mind racing to try to work out what to do. It was not long before Sir Sighard appeared, and their horses shortly after.

'Is all well, Grandmaster?' said Sighard in concern at his vacant look.

'Hmm? Yes,' Reinhard replied, using the proffered stool to mount his horse as the stablehand held it for him. Sighard swung himself into his own saddle unaided and even that infuriated Reinhard, his mouth twitched and his temple throbbed. *He will regret betraying me.*

'To the church?' asked Sighard.

'What? No, no, there is no need. We need to return to Arbugæ, immediately.'

Sighard stammered and stopped, alarmed. 'To Arbugæ? Grandmaster, it is late in the day, I sent the men to camp, it is too late to start out again. We must spend the night here.'

Reinhard scowled and looked at the knight, and then at the sky. It was indeed getting darker. 'Then we will leave at dawn.'

'Yes, of course.'

'Oh, and Brother Sighard.' Reinhard fixed the man with a murderous glare. 'Don't make a habit of disagreeing with me.'

'No, Grandmaster, I will not. My apologies.'

Reinhard followed the man out of the gate, his horse barely under control as his whole mind was focused on how to escape the pit he was in. He wrestled to get the stubborn beast under his command again and hissed in anger. *They will all bend to my will. I will find a way, Henry. Come hell or all the fallen angels, I will find a way.*

## Chapter 23

# The First Blow

GJALDIR WIPED THE sweat from his brow as the heat of the forge lashed at him, a feeling he loved, but had forgotten in the year that had passed since he last felt it.

Halla had come looking for him one day, wearing her usual look that allowed no disagreement. 'I need a forge set up, for repairs and making. You are our only proper smith. Can you do it?'

Gjaldir's face fell and he grimaced. 'I can help set up a forge, yes. But…'

'I know, you will not make weapons,' said Halla with a lopsided frown. 'Fortunately, we don't need weapons, we need tools, hinges, nails, hoops. What tools we brought with us are wearing out and we have outgrown their number.'

'I am not a blacksmith,' said Gjaldir with a helpless shrug.

'But can you make a hammer?'

'Yes.'

'Then you are the best blacksmith we have, you will work the rest out, I am sure.'

'What about my training? I will still go on raids.' He stated it, rather than asking it, but his eyes flicked between Halla's nervously. It was some time before she answered.

'Yes, that is the promise my husband made to you, and I will keep it. Even if it is better to have our only living smith in the camp. You will take someone and train them, so if you do die in battle, we will not be left destitute. You understand?'

'Yes, Lady Halla. Thank you.'

Halla had looked anything but pleased, but she had left.

So here he was, two weeks later, hammering out a hinge, poorly, and trying to teach a young carpenter who had done a little basic smithing before and was given to him as his trainee. Truthfully, the boy was not that good. But then he was a terrible teacher, the forge was basic – more of a firepit – and their tools were even worse. He didn't have half the tools he needed, his supply of iron was small and relied on things stolen from the Christians, or recycled items.

Overall, it was not going well. He had managed to make a few hammers, a scythe, which in fact was the only thing he had done well, and some other tools like chisels and some tongs for the forge. So far, in terms of making things for the village, he had just about managed to work out nails, but lacked the proper heading tool for them and didn't know how to make one.

But Halla insisted he persist, so persist he did, much to his annoyance.

He saw Leif walking past the open shelter where the crude forge was and put down his tools, running over to the huskarl. 'Leif!'

Leif turned and grinned at the filthy, soot-smeared man. 'Gjaldir! Back to your old ways, I see.'

'Please send me on the next raid.'

'Ah, not enjoying the return to smithing, are you?'

'I am not a blacksmith, the tools are terrible, the forge is terrible, the iron is terrible, my student is...'

'Terrible?'

Gjaldir nodded exhaustedly. 'Yes.'

'The tools are terrible? I thought you were making the tools.'

'Yes, that is why they are terrible.'

Leif laughed again and nodded. 'It sounds terrible indeed. And why would I risk Halla's wrath by sending you on a raid?'

'Because she said I could still fight.'

'I see, and did she mean it, or did she just say it to keep you quiet? I am aware that you know little of women, but sometimes they say a thing hoping you understand it is not actually what they mean.'

Gjaldir faltered, but then shook his head angrily. 'I am a freeman, I came here to be a warrior, and no one can take that from me, even her.'

Leif considered him for a moment and then nodded. 'Good, I agree. And I am pleased to see the fire in you. I was worried you would seek safety in your old work and give up on being a warrior just as you were getting good at it.'

'You think I am good at it?'

'No, I said getting good, on the path, heading in the right direction.'

'Hey! I wrestled a horse for you,' Gjaldir said with mock outrage.

'Yes, and that was an enormously stupid thing to do. I hope Gunnar has taught you better since then.' Leif grinned and slapped him on the back, pulling his hand back with a frown, covered in sweat and charcoal dust. 'Well, Gunnar is taking a large raid out in two days, I am not going, it's not our turn, but I will ask him if he will take you in his crew.'

Gjaldir grinned like a child. 'Thank you, Leif,' he said, his heart rising in his chest.

'Don't make a fool of us with Gunnar, he won't accept fooling around or stupidity in battle.'

'No wrestling horses?'

'No wrestling horses.'

Gunnar accepted Gjaldir's request and two days later, scrubbed of charcoal dirt and carrying his freshly cleaned gear, Gjaldir gathered with the Norwegian crew on the outskirts of town, nervously greeting the men, of whom he knew very few. Most of them paid him little attention, but then a big hand thumped into his shoulder and he turned to find Eric Firebeard grinning at him. 'Christian!' the broad-shouldered Norwegian exclaimed. 'You are coming with us?'

'Yes.'

'Good, good. I am interested to see you fight, apparently in the last battle you fondled a horse.'

Gjaldir half choked. 'What? No, I *fought* a horse, shoved it away from Leif.'

Eric narrowed his eyes and shook his head confidently. 'That's not what I heard.'

'Who would say I fondled a horse?'

'Someone whose word I trust above a Christian's,' said Eric with a wink. 'So, you can fight with us, but try to stay away from the livestock while we are out. No one will want to eat anything you have touched, just in case.'

Gjaldir rolled his eyes at the mockery and Eric chuckled and wandered off to talk to another group of warriors, laughing about something Gjaldir didn't hear, and hoped wasn't about him.

Gunnar appeared shortly after, with Vidar and another warrior in tow. He noticed Gjaldir and strode over. 'You will be with Vidar and Harald.' He pointed at the two men. 'Do what they say, guard their flank, remember what I have taught you.'

Gjaldir gulped under the intense gaze and nodded. Gunnar strode off without another word, calling to the rest of his crew.

Vidar looked Gjaldir up and down and then tilted his head. 'Come on, follow me.' Harald said nothing, he just looked at Gjaldir once and walked away with Vidar, his jet-black hair marking him out amongst the rest of the warriors. Gjaldir followed along meekly.

Gjaldir shared a bench with Harald for most of the trip downriver but they did not share a word. Harald did not seem hostile, nor resentful, simply disinterested. He did not speak to the other Norwegians either, beyond the odd word or two. He seemed content merely to be quiet.

Once they were going, Gunnar told them their aim was to capture Karlsgrind, burn the fort there, and open the river to the lake. Also to take the large cache of food and any other valuable items they found there. Being right on the river, they could bring the ships in and take far more than usual. Gunnar hoped it would be a huge haul.

They landed the ships upriver of the town, hiding them in the same inlet they had used a few weeks before for the raid on Västerås, and the hundred or so men made camp on the bank, a fireless, chilly night after a damp, overcast August day.

The next day was no better. The weather had turned on the day they left, and men were struggling not to see it as a poor omen. Each morning was foggy, and the fog barely raised before noon. The sun had barely been seen and yet hardly a breath of wind had blown. It was the kind of gloom that got into the souls of the hardiest men, the weather of witchcraft and shadows in the mist.

Gunnar seemed unaffected, in fact he saw the weather as a good thing, the fog would cover their movement, and the gloomy, cold evenings would keep men huddled around their fires instead of keeping a proper watch. It would all help them get close to the town the next day.

In the morning, the ships proceeded carefully and silently downriver, eyes and ears straining in the fog. If a Christian ship was coming up the other way, the two ships would barely see each other before they clashed, so they rowed quietly and men stood in the prows of the ships listening to the river ahead.

Finally, they had gone as far as Gunnar dared, to within a few miles of the town, and they left their boats moored to the bank in a small bay on the river. Any boat passing on the river would see the longships, but they were well hidden by trees from anything else.

Gunnar set the men in the woods to hide and wait, and disappeared with half a dozen scouts. Gjaldir sat in the damp air and wrapped his cloak around himself as he sat in silence. The time crawled past slowly as the fog slowly lifted, and eventually he heard low voices and saw that the scouts had returned. The leaders gathered everyone around apart from some men watching the river and the forest and Gunnar explained his plan.

'The fort is on both sides of the river, and they have moored a line of barges across it, blocking the way, that were not here last time. The garrison does not look large, but the walls are high, new and strong. Now, Asel says that convoys come through almost every day, supplies, messages and travellers. None travel without twenty or more men for fear of us.'

Men chuckled in low tones at that, it felt good to know their enemy was afraid. Fear saps at a man, and seeing it in your enemy lifts the spirit.

'Now, we could try rushing the gate when a convoy is arriving or leaving, or we could try climbing the walls at night. I had hoped to go in with the ships, take the fort from the inside with a surprise attack from the river, but they have expected that, and the barges make it impossible.'

'What if we did not go in as a convoy arrives, but we go in pretending to be a convoy?' asked Vidar.

Gunnar looked at the quick-thinking huskarl. 'We don't look like Christians, we have no wagons or horses.'

'We take armour, clothes wagons and horses from one of theirs and then just walk up to the gate. We even have one who speaks their language.' Vidar turned with a grin and looked at Gjaldir, who stiffened as dozens of pairs of eyes focused on him.

'Uh, they might not speak my language.'

'You were a Christian like them, no?'

'No.' Gjaldir shook his head. 'There are men of many nations here, not all of them speak my language.'

Vidar thought about it. 'It does not matter, they will know you are not speaking Norse, it should get us close enough at least. We can hide hooks and ropes in the cargo.'

Gunnar nodded carefully. 'That could work. There might be a signal or word that convoys give to the guards, to let them know who they are.'

'Then we capture some men in the convoy and get the signal.'

Gunnar grunted his assent. 'It is better than rushing the gate while enemies block it. We shall do that. We need to find a place on the road to wait, it might be tomorrow before a convoy comes, or even the day after. Bring food, clothes and water.'

'What about the ships?' asked Eric.

Gunnar shrugged. 'It is unlikely any ships will come, there were none in the fort and blocking the river suggests they don't want to patrol it, which would be a better choice for defence. If the ships are lost, we will walk home.'

'That will be a terrible loss for further raids, and ruin our ability to carry looted supplies home,' said Eric with a shake of his head.

'Fine. Leave ten men here, they might be able to save the ships if someone spots them.'

Ten very irritated men were left behind to sit with the ships while the rest of the party set out. Gunnar called Gjaldir up to him and he fell into step by the king's old champion.

'Listen, you are key to this plan and must not die in the ambush. Stay behind me, don't do anything stupid.'

Gjaldir nodded.

'If we find a convoy to ambush, your job is to try and find someone who speaks your language, and get them to surrender before they die.'

'I understand.'

'Good.'

It did not take them long to reach the road, and they found a good area of young saplings and bushes that verged almost onto the road from where to ambush. They would camp a hundred paces into the woodland and a few men would watch the road from hidden places. When a convoy was spotted heading into the town, they would get into position and attack.

Gunnar made one thing clear to all of them, no one could be allowed to escape. They would attack in two groups, one at the front, and another behind, instead of along the flank of the enemy. It would give a harder fight, but should leave the enemy surrounded. The first target for the archers and spearmen was anyone on horseback.

The rest of that day saw nothing pass on the road apart from a single fast man on horseback, a messenger or scout. The group spent a miserable day in the trees and again the next day the sun rose and fell with nothing passing but a few riders.

Gjaldir wondered if they would wait another day, they were running out of food and men were getting irritable and restless.

Gunnar had clearly made the same judgement. 'We can't wait another day in this wood, and it's too risky for the ships. We will climb the walls tonight, when it is darkest. Everyone prepare yourselves, hand out the ropes and hooks and get into groups of ten to lift men up the walls. We will…'

'Gunnar!' a voice hissed.

Faces turned in the half-light to see one of the scouts crouch-walking into the group.

'What?'

'Convoy, on the road coming towards us, twenty men, four wagons, no horsemen.'

There was a ripple of excitement through the group and Gunnar hushed them. 'The gods are still with us. We will take the convoy. To your positions, let none escape.' Gunnar looked around and waved at Gjaldir. 'Come.'

Gjaldir followed Gunnar as the Norse filtered through the darkening trees like wraiths, as silent and just as foreboding.

Gjaldir stayed right behind Gunnar and stopped when he stopped, not able to see the road, but soon able to hear the grinding of the wagons' axles, and the clopping and jingling of the harnessed draught animals hauling them.

'Wait,' Gunnar whispered, and he sank lower to the ground, hiding behind the last bush before the road.

Gjaldir's heart was throbbing so loud he worried about it for a moment, and he peered through the dense leaves and branches, trying to catch a glimpse of the enemy, but all he saw was shadows and dark green shapes.

They heard the convoy get so close that he heard men's footsteps, and the squeal of one wagon whose axle was badly fitted or perhaps on the verge of breaking, and then the noise was right the other side of the bush.

Still Gunnar was immobile, a shadow within shadows. The moments drew out painfully before the huskarl rose and barked a single command. 'Now.'

The warriors rose from their hiding places and burst out onto the road, falling onto the rear of the column as Christians shouted in panic and men began to scream.

Gjaldir, mindful of his instructions, followed Gunnar like a loyal hound as the huskarl drove into the scattered and confused enemy. Gunnar cut down one man who had not even got his weapon up, kicking the dying man aside and reversing his sword to cut the arm off a spearman who threw it up in a desperate attempt to defend himself.

Gjaldir watched in awe as Gunnar went through the back of the escort without even slowing his pace, cutting down a third man in a precise thrust to the sternum before he charged at a fourth.

The fourth man, leading a wagon horse and without a weapon

in hand, was rooted to the spot in fear and he held up an arm, shouting for mercy.

Gjaldir suddenly realised he understood the man and desperately grabbed the back of Gunnar's belt, hauling him back. 'NOT HIM!' he shouted, and Gunnar turned his head angrily at the sudden grab and then realised why and nodded.

'Grab him, keep him safe.'

Gjaldir walked over to the man, Gunnar blocking another warrior as men went past, hunting for more victims. 'You! Come here,' he shouted, feeling stupid and unsure what to say.

The Christian looked at him, shocked and shaking, and did precisely nothing as the flood of Norse warriors went past him and the horse stamped and skittered in its harness.

Gjaldir snarled and grabbed hold of the soldier, who he now saw was nothing more than a boy, perhaps sixteen. 'Get on the ground, or they will kill you.'

The boy finally reacted, nodding violently and letting go of the horse's nose rope, sinking to the ground and huddling against the wagon's front wheel. 'You… you are Germans?' he stammered.

'Saxon. Where are you from?'

'Saxon? Why are you attacking us?' The boy looked around as the last of the convoy escort were being slaughtered as they tried to flee.

'No, they aren't, I am.'

The boy's eyes met his and he looked horrified. 'Why are you with them?'

Gjaldir sighed, it was too complicated and he didn't want to explain it. 'It doesn't matter. Listen to me… What is your name?'

'Friderich.'

'Listen, Friderich, they will have questions for you, answer them if you want to live.'

The boy nodded forcefully.

'Good.'

Gjaldir stood and looked around. It was gloomy, but he could see the fight was over, and the Norse were killing the wounded and starting to strip the bodies. Friderich looked on, horrified, but silent.

Gunnar returned with Vidar and nodded to Gjaldir. 'So?'

'He will answer your questions.'

'Good. Ask about a signal, or a word, or something that lets the fort know them.'

Gjaldir looked at the boy and asked.

Friderich looked confused and then shook his head. 'When we reach a gate, they just shout up who we are, and we are let in.'

Gjaldir frowned. 'No signal or anything?'

'Not that I have seen.'

'And who do you say you are?'

'Well, we are from Count Otto, carrying food to the fort.'

'That's it? You would just say that?'

'Yes, well, Max would say that, but he's…' Friderich stared off at the bodies around the lead wagon.

Gjaldir looked at Gunnar and Vidar. 'We say we are from Count Otto and are bringing food. And maybe that our name is Max.'

Gunnar looked at Vidar and shrugged. 'I expected something cleverer.' He nodded at Gjaldir. 'Fine, well done, we will try and find you a clean one of these odd tunics they wear and you can lead us to the gate and say you are "Max".' Gunnar pronounced the odd name weirdly, the sounds unfamiliar to him.

He waved a hand casually at the boy. 'Kill him.'

Gjaldir swallowed and looked at the boy, then back at Gunnar, who was already walking away. Gunnar sensed the problem and stopped to look back. 'Kill him, we don't need him anymore.'

Gjaldir mumbled and then looked down at the boy again, who was looking between him and Gunnar in fear and confusion.

'But…'

Gunnar took a step back towards Gjaldir, brows furrowed. He leaned in and spoke quietly. 'What did you expect? He is our enemy, we can't take him with us. If you don't kill him, right now, without argument, none of these men will ever trust you again. You said you are one of us, any of us would do it. Are you one of us?'

Gjaldir recoiled, looking down at the terrified, helpless boy, seeing himself being taken on the Crusade at much the same age, remembering being captured at the ford and kneeling in the sand, thinking he was about to die.

He froze, staring down at Friderich and just saw a boy like him who had no…

There was a wet crunch and Friderich's blood spattered his face, rending his thoughts in two. He blinked in shock as the boy slumped to the ground with Vidar's axe in the back of his head, the confused and fearful expression replaced with a slack unknowing.

Vidar bent down and cheerfully recovered his axe with a foot on the body's shoulder. Vidar gave Gjaldir a sideways glance and turned to Gunnar, who looked troubled.

'He needed to do that. They needed to see him do it,' growled the older man.

'Well, he wasn't going to do it, and it was more important they didn't see him *not* do it. Pretend it is no big issue, I don't think many were even looking.'

Vidar smiled and wandered off, leaving Gunnar giving Gjaldir a dark look.

'I'm… I'm sorry,' he muttered.

'How can I trust you to stand in my line if you won't kill my enemies?'

Gjaldir looked at him with all the confidence he could muster. 'I will kill anyone in battle, I have before. But,' he waved a hand at the slumped body, 'I remember kneeling like that, unarmed and afraid, in front of a Norseman who wanted to kill me and thought nothing of it.' Gjaldir shuddered. 'I wasn't ready to be that man.'

Gunnar didn't say anything, he just gave a shallow nod and looked at the dead boy again. 'Refuse again and you will leave us. There are no half measures here, no room for doubt, and I doubt your resolve. Now come, you still have a task to do.'

Gjaldir scowled at Gunnar's back and followed him, seeing Vidar coming back with a dark red surcoat and a helmet. 'Here, Christian, put these on.'

'Lucky they wore red,' said Gunnar, looking around.

'Mostly red, some green.'

'I will get as many of our men dressed and armed like them as we can, then we will continue to the fort. The rest of the men will follow, you lead them. Don't risk being seen, but get as close as you can. We will hold the gateway once we are in.'

Vidar nodded. 'We will get close, it is dark.'

'I will see you in the fort then.'

'Or in Valhalla.'

The two men clasped arms and Gjaldir suddenly realised both thought it might be the last time, and it dawned on him how risky this was, and that he was going to be the lead man through the gate.

He shivered and looked down at the surcoat, seeing darker patches of red in the red, and suddenly wondering if a surcoat had had two owners die in it on the same day before.

The wagons jingled and groaned and the horses, still nervous, whinnied and complained. The noises made Gjaldir want to shrink into himself. The fort was looming out of the darkness ahead. But they were not trying to be quiet, they wanted to be seen. They wanted the sentries to be aware of them for as long as possible and decide they were who they were pretending to be. A convoy of bored, tired Saxons bringing some wagons of supplies.

When they were no more than twenty paces from the gate, and it had still not opened, a man shouted down to them.

'Why are you arriving so late?'

Gjaldir waved at the men behind him to stop and his mind raced, trying to imagine he was the commander of this convoy and what he would say.

'We were delayed, a broken axle, but it was too late to make camp.'

The guard leaned over the wall and stared at them. 'We don't open the gates after dark, those are my orders.'

Gjaldir swore internally, but then puffed out his chest and tried to imagine he was a petty leader, one of the self-important bullies he had met in the Crusade's ranks. 'Count Otto said to come here, and here we are. Don't make me explain to him that some fucking gate watcher told me to go back.'

'What, Count Otto sent you himself? Four wagons of food? Horseshite, you just don't want to camp outside for the night.'

Gjaldir's mind raced. 'No, not the supplies, the messages we are carrying.' He waved vaguely back down the column. 'We have urgent messages, important ones, and they can't stay out here all night waiting, or risk the half breeds capturing them.' When he was on Crusade, he had heard soldiers refer to the Norse as half breeds of pigs and men, and hoped that was still common and would lend credibility.

'What messages?'

'How the fuck would I know? They are sealed. I've got orders to get them through, now open the damn gate. It's not dark yet, I can still see you, and you can see me.'

The guard grumbled and shouted something down into the fort and then re-appeared.

'Right, but I've had to send for the commander, you better not be lying about the messages or he'll have you strung from the gate.'

'Good, I'm glad the commander is coming, saves me going to him.' Gjaldir looked sideways at Gunnar, who was doing his best not to look worried and failing, and Gjaldir gave him a slight nod. As he did, the sound of wood scraping on wood came from in front of them and then the gate squealed open, protesting on its new, and by the sound of it, poorly mounted hinges.

Gjaldir barked a command in German and waved the convoy forwards. The warriors behind him wouldn't understand the word but the meaning was clear. He marched forwards confidently, trying not to shrink down under his stolen helmet as he passed under the gaze of the men on the wall above. He was sure they would see the hastily and poorly cleaned blood stains or notice that the men were Norse, and then he would die, very quickly.

But no alarm was raised, and no shouts or weapons came at him in the gloom, and he got through the gate and Gunnar's men came through behind him. Inside the gate was a building on one side, and an open area with horse stalls on the other. There were about a dozen soldiers in the immediate area, and beyond that were lines of tents and then the river. Beyond the river, Gjaldir could see the small fort on the far bank and the Norse town of Karlsgrind around it.

The group continued to come through the gate behind him, stopping the second wagon in the gateway as they had planned. The warriors abandoned the rest and filtered through the opening.

'Oi, move those wagons in!' said the guard.

'You told me to wait for the commander,' shouted Gjaldir back.

'I'm in command here, what is going on?' said an angry voice from in front and a man in a tunic wearing a sword appeared with three soldiers following him. He walked up towards Gjaldir with everything about him screaming that he was a knight, from his clothes to his richly decorated belt to his air of certainty and assurance.

The knight got to within three paces of Gjaldir and stopped, his face slackening from anger to confusion. Gunnar did not let it progress further than that. In a movement so sudden and violent that the knight barely got his hand to his sword, Gunnar stamped forwards two paces, drew his blade and put it through the man's chest.

The sword, a stolen Christian blade, jammed in the body and Gunnar cursed, letting go and drawing his seax from under his surcoat as chaos erupted behind them, the Norse taking the signal to attack the guards on the wall and on the ground around the gate.

The three soldiers with the knight reacted poorly to the sudden attack, and only one got his weapon out, marking him as the next one to kill as Gunnar fell on them, Gjaldir running forwards to guard his left side as Gunnar had instructed.

Gunnar killed the first man and then attacked the second, who had a spear and shield and managed to keep Gunnar at distance with the longer weapon. The third man got his sword out and charged at Gjaldir with a wild scream, all fear and no skill, and Gjaldir calmly knocked the sword to one side and chopped his sword into the soldier's neck, nearly severing it.

As the soldier collapsed, the shouts of alarm rippled through the camp, and Gunnar looked back, snatching the dead knight's sword as they retreated. 'SKALDBORG!' Gunnar roared, and the warriors, who had finished slaughtering the shocked men around the gate, clustered together and got their unfamiliar Christian shields into a tight wall.

'Oh, that is a lot of them,' muttered Eric Firebeard jovially, taking the place on Gjaldir's left.

Gjaldir looked at him in mild horror as the man smiled at the oncoming enemy, dozens of them, who were coming out of the area with the tents and the building to their right, and already organising to attack.

Eric saw Gjaldir's look and shrugged, his smile never leaving.

'Ready!' shouted Gunnar, settling down a fraction, sword behind his shield, tip up and pointing at the first group of enemy.

Gjaldir heard someone shouting orders in German to get on the wall and get above them. 'Gunnar, they are going for the wall,' he told the huskarl.

Gunnar nodded. 'Nothing we can do about that.'

Someone behind passed a spear forwards and Gunnar took it, stuffing his stolen sword into his belt.

Then the Christians, urged on by a grizzled old soldier in the front rank, charged at the Norse shieldwall.

## Chapter 24

# Holding the Wall

GJALDIR RECOILED FROM another blow to his borrowed helmet. The fight was already fuzzy and confusing. He was buffeted from both sides and front and back, his sword was gone and he didn't know where. He also didn't know when he had drawn his seax or how he had got it out past his stolen surcoat, but it was in his hand anyway.

Gunnar was panting and grunting on his right, Eric was screaming obscenities on his left, he could feel both men move as they fought, but Gjaldir could only hide behind his shield as the fury of the attack hammered at them. He tried to pick a moment to use his own weapon but he was putting everything he had into keeping his shield up and not being pushed backwards.

He steadied his mind for a moment and a glimpse of Gunnar's training came back to him. He lifted his head just a fraction and looked over the shield, seeing two Christian soldiers in front of him, the first one so close he could almost have headbutted him. The man was also not using his weapon, too pressed against Gjaldir to wield it, and Gjaldir had a moment of clarity where he realised what he could do.

He put his seax up behind the rim of his shield, point outwards, and watched as the Christian's head leaned back and then came forwards as he shoved.

Gjaldir lanced the point of the seax forwards and put it straight under the rim of his opponent's helmet, feeling bone crunch. The Christian squealed and writhed as the steel embedded in his eye socket, dropping his shield and putting both hands to his face.

Gjaldir wrenched the blade back, and had ample time to choose his spot, ramming it into the man's throat and pulling it back as he collapsed with a gurgle. The man behind stepped over his fallen comrade and came forwards, but he was carrying a spear, and in trying to bring it to bear he was already too close, pushed on by the men behind, and the tip went into the ground somewhere at Gjaldir's feet and the Christian grunted and shouted and wriggled as he tried to back away.

Gjaldir thrust at the man's eyes again and his enemy ducked behind his shield, raising it to cover his head. Gjaldir lowered the deadly blade behind his own shield and thrust it forwards at hip level, past the side of the long, narrow tip of the fabric-covered wood.

The tip of his seax sank into flesh with a thud on the second thrust and he heard a scream and a curse and the pressure on his shield went as the spearman tried to back away.

He pulled the blade out and risked another look over the top, seeing the spearman trying to retreat into his own ranks while blood gushed out of his thigh.

There was a gap as the remaining enemy gave up their wild attack and reformed nervously, looking at the bodies the Norse had left in front of their wall. But more men were arriving on their side, and they soon re-gathered their heart. Gjaldir took the opportunity to grab his sword from the ground in front of him, thankful to have the bigger weapon again.

As they were about to come forwards, there was a thud as

something hit Eric in the back, and he grunted and pitched forwards, barely getting a hand out to catch himself as he fell.

'On the wall!' shouted someone behind them, and Gjaldir looked back to see figures running along the rampart behind them, picking up rocks left on the wall for that purpose and hurling them down at the Norse.

A warrior behind Gjaldir had his arm broken by one, and another was knocked senseless, and Gjaldir felt the deep grip of fear surging as they were trapped between the rocks and the oncoming soldiers. 'Get them off that wall!' roared Gunnar, as someone jabbed with a spear at the ankles of the Christians above them.

A hand grabbed his left arm and Gjaldir looked to see Eric struggling to rise, groaning, his left arm hanging limp, shield gone. He tried to help Eric to his feet just as the Christians attacked again.

Gjaldir shouted a warning and pushed himself past Eric to get his shield out and cover the warrior's exposed back. He caught a sword blow on the shield and bounced his own off the man's helmet in a failed attempt to cut at his neck. Suddenly he was on his own, a gap between him and Gunnar, and Eric struggling to stand behind him.

He lunged his sword at a Christian that got too close and it bit through the man's maille, more scaring him than injuring him, and he earned half a pace of room. Another man jumped at him, thinking it was an opportunity, but Gjaldir leaned into the charge and jammed his weapon into the attacker's stomach as the overhand swing clattered off his helmet and shoulder.

The body went down with his sword stuck in it and Gjaldir struggled to rip it free, still half crouched as a spear came at him. He deflected one thrust on his shield, another caught a glancing blow on his helmet and the third jammed into the sleeve of his maille and tore some rings.

He shouted in terror and anger and twisted and pulled on the blood-slicked hilt of his sword, but the spear was going to come back again and he couldn't stop it.

A figure stumped past him with a roar, swatting at the spear and then headbutting the carrier viciously in the face, steel helmet crushing the Crusader's nose and smashing teeth. Gjaldir finally got the blade free and got up on Eric's left, covering his injured side.

The Norseman on his left went down under two Christians, and more were coming all the time. Not in a wall, but in a flood, desperate to get to the gate. Eric and Gjaldir were moments from being overwhelmed in the flood if they stayed.

Gjaldir stabbed and ducked, shouted and cursed as Eric jabbed at anyone in range on their right. They backed up a step and defended, backed up another and jabbed, trying wordlessly to get back to their friends.

Gjaldir ducked a spear thrust that skipped off his helmet peak and then looked up, and suddenly the Christian advance had stopped. The soldiers he could see looking past him and shouting to each other and he heard the blissful sound of battle cries from their rear. Gjaldir risked a backwards glance and saw Norsemen pouring through the gateway, Vidar at their head, and his shoulders slumped in relief as the howling warriors poured past them and fell on the demoralised and now heavily outnumbered Christians.

Gjaldir didn't join in the slaughter. He and Eric just looked at each other and laughed as their comrades pushed past them, eager to get to the retreating enemy, a laugh of pure relief and surprise at being alive, then Eric gasped and screwed his eyes shut.

The huskarl rolled his shoulder and tried to move his left arm, hissing and shaking his head at the pain. 'Not broken,' he said with a grimace, 'but it hurts like shit.'

Gjaldir saw Gunnar and smiled, relieved the man was still alive. He had not seen him since they were separated. Gunnar stopped next to Eric and clasped hands with the man. 'I'm glad you are still with us, brother.'

'I am not, I will be remembered for the rest of my life as a warrior saved by a Christian slave,' he said with a rueful grin, looking at Gjaldir.

'Don't worry, Eric, I am not a Christian or a slave, and I saved much better men than you when I was.'

Eric chuckled and put his filthy sword through his belt with his good arm. 'Thank the gods.'

Gunnar stepped up to Gjaldir and looked at him intently. 'That was a brave deed. I will not doubt your resolve again. You are truly a warrior, Christian or not.'

Gjaldir felt a warm rush of pride and nodded. 'Thank yo...'

'But it was fucking stupid,' said the huskarl, jabbing a finger into Gjaldir's chest. 'Don't ever break the wall, not for anything. You saved one man but on another day could have caused the death of ten more by leaving that gap.'

Gjaldir's mouth flapped like a landed fish and he looked at Eric, seeing no sympathy there.

'He is right,' said Eric with a shrug.

'I should have left you to die?'

'You hold the wall, whatever the price.'

Gjaldir looked back at Gunnar, hurt and appalled. 'You mean it.'

'Yes. Eric is my friend, but you risked all our lives by stepping out of the wall to cover him,' Gunnar said sternly. 'You have heart, and you fight bravely, and even with some skill, but you need to harden your spirit to be able to make the decisions needed in battle.'

Gjaldir lowered his chin and nodded. 'I will remember.'

'Good. Now, come, we still need to take the fort on the far bank.'

The fort on the far bank was smaller, wedged in between the town and the river. Its garrison stayed around long enough to pelt the Norse with arrows, but Gunnar got men to haul in two of the barges blocking the river and then they used them to cross to the other side. The two dozen men of the garrison, unwilling to defend the open riverbank and having seen their fellows slaughtered, opened the gate and fled east rather than share their fate.

It was fully dark by the time the fighting was done, and it was a cloudy and deathly dark night. Too late to go and get the ships, Gunnar had the gate closed and barred and they spent the night in the fort, eating the food the Christians had left behind for their evening meal, and sleeping in their tents.

Gunnar had them up before dawn, tired and nursing the aftereffects of the hard fight the day before. Twenty men were sent to get the ships, and everything of value in the forts was piled on the riverbank. The barges were pulled to the side and enthusiastically sabotaged, holed and smashed.

It was not long before their ships arrived and were piled with weapons, food and equipment. Then the wounded were loaded and fires were put to both forts, the half-ruined barges, and piles of abandoned equipment, even the rows of tents.

The Norse inhabitants of the town stayed well away from the invaders, although they could be seen peering between buildings or leaving the town to go into the fields. Gunnar ordered them to be ignored, unless they became a threat. Gjaldir could see they wanted nothing to do with the raiders, and wondered what the Christians had done to make them so fear their own kin.

The three ships rowed north with the bodies of the handful of warriors who had died in the battle, Gunnar unwilling to leave them to the mercy of the Christians. The enemy were left where they had fallen, or dumped in the river, drifting in the slow current as the light of the flames from the burning forts danced around them.

Baron Hugues reined his horse in as the trio of mounted men galloped down the column towards where he rode with the command group.

He had left garrisons in various important towns at Henry's direction, but he was returning to Arbugæ with five hundred of the Order's men. Despite their number, they were taking precautions, he had heard of the raids and ambushes along this road. His entire force was marching in campaign order, strong bodies of armed men at the front and rear, and riders scouting the road and protecting the wagons in the centre.

He pulled his horse off the road to let the wagons behind him continue unimpeded and the first of the three riders stopped with a flourish and bowed in the saddle.

'Grandsteward, trouble ahead at the river.'

'At the fort?'

'The fort is gone, burned to the ground, the garrison killed or fled.'

Hugues felt a rush of nerves, the fort at the river had been their intended camp for the night, and evening was rapidly falling. If an enemy army strong enough to take and destroy that fort was still in the area, his men would be extremely vulnerable in a makeshift camp by the road.

'By the Lord, do the enemy still occupy the position?'

'No, there is no sign of them, and some of the survivors of the garrison are on the far bank, although there is no boat to cross over to them. There is no immediate danger. By the looks of it, the attack happened perhaps four or five days ago, the fires are all out and the ashes cold, and the bodies are starting to darken.'

Hugues swallowed. 'Good, thank you. Can we camp there as planned?'

The man looked disturbed at the thought. 'No, Grandmaster. What is left is fouled with the dead, and not fit for man nor beast.'

'Of course, yes. Well, find us another site, and we will have to be ready to defend it.'

'The open ground before the walls will be sufficient.'

Hugues nodded curtly. 'Good man, tell the vanguard to start

marking out the site and make preparations. We must assume the enemy is still nearby, and that we will have to defend the camp.'

'As you wish, Grandmaster.' The knight bowed again and set off with his two silent companions in tow.

Hugues had seen battlefields before, and he would never forget the site of the battle outside Uppsala, but the scene in the destroyed fort disturbed him in a fresh manner.

The stunted, charred remains of the gatehouse were a horror of half-burned corpses, clustered in heaps and mixed with fallen logs and caked in ash. He could see that a vicious fight had happened there, and beyond the interior was strewn with the bloated, putrefying dead.

He looked around for as long as he could stand, one hand clamped to his mouth and nose, and saw that all the bodies he could see were Christians, there was no sign of the enemy dead, if the enemy had even suffered dead.

The sight that aggravated him most was the half-sunken barge protruding from the river at a drunken angle, and the dim shapes and posts in the river that showed him where the others lay.

The crossing was impassable without the boats, it was many miles upstream through wild forest to where the river was fordable, and he nor anyone in his force knew exactly where. They were trapped with their wagons on this side of the river until more barges could be brought, or made.

When he could take the scene no more, he turned and rode back to the camp, waving over his second in command, a competent French knight called Foissart. 'Brother Foissart, tomorrow we will need see if we can fashion a raft from what remains, to reach the other side and see what the situation is.'

Foissart dipped his head as he thought. 'It should be possible.'

Hugues grimaced. 'And we need to clear the camp of the bodies and bury them. Somewhere far enough away. This site will need to be rebuilt and it cannot be a graveyard. It will be a terrible job, but it must be done.'

Foissart sighed and looked away. 'The men will do as commanded, and without complaint.'

'I know. You have done a fine job with them in our time in the south, I wager these are the finest body of men in Christendom.'

Foissart nodded with quiet pride. 'The needs of the brotherhood demand the best, and my duty is to provide it.'

Hugues smiled at the Frenchman and felt the satisfaction of having outwitted Reinhard. Foissart was a devout man, but at his core he was a man of war, and he despised the ill-discipline and dishonour that had infected much of the rest of the Order, spread by Reinhard and his minions. In Foissart he had a leader who could get hold of the rest of the Order's soldiers and work them into shape.

The night was uneventful, and by noon the next day the men had cleared the bodies from the ruined fort and a group of the wagoners had constructed a small raft from the timbers, sufficient to carry half a dozen men across the river.

Hugues sent scouts across to check the opposing bank was truly in friendly hands, and then went across himself, with Foissart remaining behind to continue the work. The raft was unstable and terrifying to stand on while wearing armour, but they made it to the far bank eventually under the careful propelling of a pair of the wagoners, and Hugues disembarked.

Two of his men were waiting for him along with a number of nervous-looking soldiers that were not part of the Order.

'These are men from the garrison,' said one of the Order's men.

Hugues looked the sorry-looking soldier up and down and he tried to keep the distaste from his face. 'Tell me what happened here.'

'Yes, my lord. I was on watch on this side of the river, six days ago. A while after sunset, we saw that the other side had opened their gates, which was odd.'

'Odd? Why?'

'It was after dark, we weren't allowed to open the gates after dark.'

'I see, a sensible rule.'

'Indeed, my lord. Well, soon after the gates opened, fighting broke out in the entrance and then… well, it was all over before we could do anything. They were all over the walls and in the tents, killing all our boys.'

Hugues held up a hand. 'Wait, the fighting only broke out after they were through the gate?'

'Yes.'

'So why was the gate opened for them?'

'I don't know… perhaps they were bribed?'

'Bribed? Did any of them survive?'

'Two, my lord. They swam the river as the fort fell.'

'Where are they?'

'Gone, disappeared in the night.'

'Hmm.' Hugues thought about it and shook his head. 'No, bribery doesn't make sense. There would have been a fight around the gate immediately unless dozens of men were being paid, and they would not have stayed around to be killed. They must have been disguised.'

'Dressed like us?' The man looked suddenly horrified.

'I expect so?'

'Then how… how do we tell them apart next time?'

'By using more care. Now, they captured the far bank, but how did they defeat you? And why did you survive?' Hugues asked, with a pointed glare.

The soldier gulped and looked at his hands, rubbing his thumb over the back of his other hand. 'They used the barges.'

'And you didn't fight them?'

He looked up earnestly. 'We did, I swear, but they were too many, and we had nothing here to defend against them. No wall, no ditch.'

Hugues scowled. 'I don't see any bodies on this side, did you even try and fight?'

'Yes, my lord. We fought them, and a few men fell, but we returned the next day and buried them.'

'I see. Whose man are you?'

'Count Otto's.'

'This side of the bank is our lands, not Count Otto's. Why are you here?'

'I, uh… I don't know, my lord. We were told to be here, so we are.'

'Well, I will be replacing you. Take your men and whatever equipment survived and return to the other bank.'

'What shall we do there?'

'I don't care, garrison the far bank if that is still your duty.'

'But… there is nothing left to garrison.'

Hugues waved the soldier away. 'As I said, I don't care; just be gone immediately.'

The soldier looked distraught, but he saw more sense than to argue anymore and hurried away with his fellows.

## Chapter 25

# Silence and Shadows

IT WAS THREE days before ships could be brought from the nearest garrison that had them, and Hugues was finally able to get the column across. The wagons had to be emptied, disassembled, and carried across on the ships separate from their cargo, and the horses had to be swum across on tethers attached to the sides of the boats. It took a day and a half to do what flat barges would have done in a single morning, but eventually the labour was complete, and the wagons were re-assembled and re-loaded and ready on the road.

Hugues left a hundred men to garrison the town and start clearing the ground to build a new, stronger fort, promising workers, tools and supplies would be sent from Arbugæ to help construct it. Then he took the majority and set out on the two-day journey to the Order's headquarters.

Reinhard was out on the street in front of the now heavily fortified headquarters building talking to two men Hugues did not recognise when they arrived. Reinhard flicked a glance up as Hugues walked over to him, and Hugues saw a flicker of concern before the bishop managed to clamp down on it and look back to the two men, ignoring Hugues for the moment.

Hugues stood there, too tired to play Reinhard's game by getting annoyed at the rudeness, and waited until he was done with his discussion. Finally, Reinhard sent the two men away and turned to look at Hugues. 'What do you need?'

Hugues was taken aback. Reinhard usually played a game of mock politeness, fastidious in observing the niceties even if in name only, and to skip to the brusque question was entirely out of character. Hugues saw that the bishop looked more drawn, more sallow than usual. The normally calm exterior was subtly missing. Faster hand movements, fiddling and twitching of the fingers, eyes moving around more than normal.

Something was wrong with the man, he was not sure what it was, but he was intrigued. He too decided to skip the preamble. 'The fort at Karlsgrind is gone, overrun and burned to the ground, most of the garrison slaughtered.'

'Yes, I am aware.'

'Good, then what is being done about it?'

Reinhard's brows furrowed slightly. 'I don't know what Count Otto will do, I have not heard from him. We are doing nothing about it yet.'

'Nothing?' stammered Hugues.

'Yes, nothing.'

'Why not?' replied Hugues, aghast.

Reinhard looked confused. 'It is not our fort, it is Otto's responsibility. I have my own plans, but they do not involve sending my men to pointlessly search the woods for a hundred miles around.'

'By Christ, man, it is the main road back to the coast, the route our supplies and messages take.'

Reinhard bristled and wagged his finger at Hugues. 'Do not use our saviour's name in that manner. Not in front of me, not ever.'

'And why not? What will you do about it? Isn't it Christ's

responsibility to respond to me taking his name in vain? So then you won't do anything about it, on principle, not your responsibility?' Hugues asked, staring the man down mockingly.

Reinhard took several deep, calming breaths, which clearly did not calm him at all, and then shook his head with a sneer. 'You have no understanding of what is happening here.'

'Now on that matter we agree entirely. What, exactly, is happening here?'

Reinhard looked at him for a moment and then shook his head. 'I don't have time to explain to you, I have a service to take, and matters of the defence of this province to attend to.'

Hugues pursed his lips and whistled in frustration, putting one hand to his forehead. 'If only there was someone else whose responsibility that was, who would understand the task far better than you.'

Reinhard didn't rise to the bait, he merely scowled and stalked off, leaving the furious Hugues standing there, unsure what to make of it, or what to do about it. *The man has lost his wits.*

As he looked around, he saw a group of knights standing on the far side of the road, one of whom he recognised as Sir Hans. The knight gave him a long look and then a slight toss of his head, indicating down towards the riverbank, before saying something to his companions and heading off on his own.

A little confused, but assuming it was an invitation, Hugues walked after the Saxon knight, his small entourage following, and caught up with him a hundred paces down the road, just past a row of half-built stables that were being added outside the burgeoning Order headquarters.

'Sir Hans, good to see you again,' he said, drawing alongside.

'Ah, my lord Hugues, it is my honour,' replied Hans, stopping and giving a precise bow. 'How can I be of service?'

Hugues looked at Hans's earnest face, thinking he had misunderstood the situation, but then Hans flicked his eyes to his left, towards Hugues's men, and smiled politely.

Hugues finally got the clumsy message. He turned to his men and smiled. 'Go and find us some quarters, and see to the horses, I will be with you shortly.'

Hans waited until they were alone and then set off again, putting the stables between them and the Order's buildings until they were walking down the riverbank.

'Hans, I'm hoping you at least can tell me what is going on here. What madness has descended while I was away?'

Hans nodded. 'It is a good question, my lord.'

'Well? You are aware that Karlsgrind was sacked?'

'I am.'

'And nothing was done?'

Hans nodded curtly. 'That is the way of things here.'

'This has happened more than once?' said Hugues, aghast.

'Yes. There are raids and attacks, large and small, occurring all around the province, in increasing numbers. Karlsgrind was merely the largest.'

'And nothing has been done in any case?'

'Very little. The fortress here is strengthened, troops from far-flung outposts are brought in to increase the local force, there are some ill-targeted reprisals from time to time, but nothing substantive.'

Hugues put a hand to his forehead and squeezed it until it hurt. 'This is Reinhard's decision?'

'Yes.'

'Have you opposed it?'

'Vocally and frequently. But I can do nothing, this is not our province, my responsibility ends at the town's border, and frankly is very limited even inside it.'

'Why? You are Conrad's man here?'

'Yes.'

'And he has joint ownership of the town.'

'In theory. In reality, I have a dozen men, and the Order has many hundreds. Reinhard does not share any power he can avoid.'

'Have you petitioned Count Conrad?'

'Yes.'

'And?'

Hans looked uncomfortable. 'I cannot discuss my lord's private correspondence.'

'Oh, damn your honour, this is important.'

Hans looked deeply troubled but nodded slightly. 'I can say that I think he does not wish to risk attempting to interfere, which he believes will make the matter worse, knowing his brother the way he does.'

Hugues grunted, it made sense. 'But the trouble will spill over into his lands, surely.'

'It already is.'

'Then we must do something!'

Hans looked at Hugues, confused. 'That is exactly why I am speaking to you. I was of the impression that you would be able to act, given your command of the soldiers of the Order.'

Hugues gritted his teeth, embarrassed. 'That is another situation that is not as simple as it should be.'

Hans frowned and nodded, looking at the ground. 'I was concerned that was the case.'

'Has anyone spoken out against him?'

Hans tensed his mouth and nodded curtly. 'Some have stood against him, in one way or another.'

'And how did he control that?'

Hans looked up at the taller man, pain etched in every feature that gave Hugues a sudden wave of chills. 'They die.'

Hugues was too shocked to reply for a moment. Then he leaned in. 'Reinhard is murdering dissenters?'

'Yes.'

'How does he get away with that?'

'He has enough fanatics on his side, and very few are overtly killed by him. An alarming number of good, disciplined men drown in the river while drunk, or are killed in the dark while walking alone, supposedly by Norse raiders, that are never seen.'

Hugues paled, it was worse than he could have imagined. 'He is assassinating them in the shadows?'

'Yes.'

'Men of the Order?'

'Men of the Order, locals, even knights of the Crusade.'

'Surely not… this is an outrage… who?'

'Sir Dietmar,' said Hans, his temple pulsing with anger.

Hugues put his hand on Hans's shoulder. 'Dietmar is dead?'

'Yes. He tried to stop Hartung murdering a village full of innocent people, and they killed him for it, in front of me.' Hugues felt Hans shake under his hand, and felt the sheer strength of his anger.

'And the men of the Order accepted this travesty?'

'Not all, but the ones who did not are the ones who fell into the river, or were murdered in the dark, or who fled to avoid either fate.' Hans shook his head. 'There is nothing left in the Order here other than darkness and rot. The whole exists only to protect Reinhard and his grip on power, nothing else matters, no one is allowed to stand in the way.' Hans grabbed Hugues's hand, suddenly and violently. 'You must end this, Grandsteward, and I will help you, whatever it takes.'

Hugues tried to pull his hand away but the grip was iron. 'I… Yes, it must end, but I must think about how.'

'We both know how,' said Hans.

Hugues shook his head. 'No, Hans, I understand your anger, but no, it's impossible. Don't speak of this.'

'It MUST be done, or we are all lost, our honour first and our lives second. He has to die.'

'Hans, why is this so personal to you? I am sorry for Dietmar, he was a good man, and I know he was your friend.'

'Friend?!' Hans's face twitched slightly. 'He was the finest knight in the Crusade, a man of unwavering honour, and Reinhard corrupted Hartung, my lord's son, and the boy ordered him slaughtered in the street. Like an animal!'

Hugues finally wrestled his hand free and looked in shock at the figure of anger and hate that had once been the mild-mannered Sir Hans.

'Hartung gave the order?'

'Yes,' hissed Hans. 'But the words were not his, I know him. The boy can be saved if the man who whispers poison in his ear is removed.'

Hugues finally understood the depth of Hans's anger and resolve, and it scared him. 'I will think of a way, Hans. I swear it. I will find a way to end this, to free Hartung from his clasp, but we cannot... we cannot simply do what you suggest. We would all be dead men.'

'It is better to die with honour than to live without it. That is the lesson Dietmar taught us with his dying breath,' said Hans with a cold whisper.

Hugues backed away a step and shook his head. 'Do nothing, Hans, until I have made a plan. We can do this a smarter way.'

Hans furrowed his brow, fighting to control his anger, and then looked away. 'I will give you some time, and then, one way or another, I will finish this myself.'

Hugues nodded vaguely and turned, heart fluttering in his chest as he made his way hastily back towards the buildings.

He went into the headquarters and found an angry Sir Foissart remonstrating with a pair of priests. 'What is the matter?'

Foissart turned to him and shook his head. 'There are apparently no quarters for any of us in these buildings, except for you. The rest of us and the men are to find lodgings in the town.'

'Which lodgings?'

'None are prepared, we are to make our own.'

Hugues scowled. 'What about the buildings we had before we left?'

'Those have been converted into storage, or stables, or otherwise been re-allocated.'

Hugues felt like lashing out at the two priests, but they were merely mouthpieces for Reinhard's latest game of power. He was forcing Hugues to choose between being isolated and alone in the headquarters, or moving out into the town and symbolically out of the centre of power.

He gestured to Foissart. 'Come, it does not matter, we will find somewhere.'

The Frenchman looked outraged, but Hugues gave him a stern look and, with one more filthy look at the priests, the knight went with him out of the headquarters courtyard and into the street.

'We will really accept this?' asked the knight.

'No, of course not, but shouting at those lickspittles wouldn't achieve anything.'

Foissart perked up at that. 'So, what shall I do?'

'I am the commander of the forces of the Order, and I will immediately start acting like it. I think this is a bluff, he hopes I will go along with it as I often have in the past. But I do not think many of the men will refuse direct orders from me, especially with you and the rest of your men behind me.'

'So, what are your orders?'

'Find the buildings we used to occupy, and simply remove whoever or whatever is inside them, and find somewhere else for that to go. If there are problems, or refusals, avoid violence at all costs and simply call for me. I will test his lackeys one by one, and the first to refuse an order directly to my face will be dealt with most harshly, stripped of his position in the Order and banished. Reinhard will not be able to stop that, and the rest of them will fall into line. We will beat the men of this Order into shape and discipline, as we did with those who came south, and then we will regain control of this province.'

Foissart smiled broadly and nodded. 'I like it, the direct attack.'

'Is everything a battle to you, Jean?'

'This certainly is.'

Hugues laughed. 'Yes, yes, I suppose so. Good, then go and pick a dozen men you trust and we shall begin.'

Resistance to his attempts to regain control of the Order's soldiers was both more fanatical than he expected, but less overt than he had feared. His orders were almost universally complied with eventually, but only under duress, and with nothing resembling willingness or agreement. And he constantly had to override counter-instructions coming from the burgeoning fortress on the riverbank where Reinhard stayed in seclusion.

Reports continued to trickle in about attacks and raids and trouble in the villages, but Hugues was focused on securing matters in the town before embarking on the distraction of addressing the rebels.

After a week of work in trying to undo the damage Reinhard had done to Hugues's authority over the forces of the Order, some progress could be seen, and Hugues summoned Foissart to discuss countering the raids and violence that continued to plague the province.

It would have been more typical to summon Foissart to his quarters, but his quarters were temporary and unpleasant, and Hugues met the man outside in the street, walking with him through the town and down towards the river. It was harder, in any case, to eavesdrop on men walking and talking in the open, and Hugues suspected Reinhard would have men, possibly even some of his own staff and guards, bribed to listen to such conversations.

As they walked down towards the river, they and their escort were paid little attention by the soldiers, labourers and locals who went by. There was nothing remarkable about eight men of the Order moving through the town, and Hugues felt safe to discuss his intentions.

'Are you ready to begin countering the enemy raids?'

Foissart grimaced and curled the corners of his mouth. 'To some extent, yes. But this is a large province, with hundreds of villages, and we have a bit over a thousand men available, some of whom are not trustworthy, and some of whom Bishop Reinhard will not allow to leave.'

'And if we simply order them to leave?'

'We face the confrontation we have so far avoided.'

'Its result would still be uncertain?'

'Yes. I have swayed a few of the less zealous captains that you are in fact the true authority, but most of the rest see the bishop as the very messenger of the Lord, and would stand with him against us if forced to choose, and a large proportion of the men with them.'

Hugues sighed. 'I do not expect their zealotry to fade quickly, if ever.'

'No.'

'So, it is an unsolvable problem.'

Foissart shook his head. 'With enough training, and enough reminders, many of the men will be brought into line, and then I suspect you would have enough.'

'Having enough to win an open confrontation that I do not wish to have is not a good outcome. I will need to find another way to end this foolishness. We must confront these raiders, and we must have Reinhard's agreement to do so.'

'Well, I am only following my orders, to bring discipline to the ranks,' said the knight, sounding a little chastised.

'Oh, don't worry, my friend, I am not criticising your work, I just see now that the solution must be another path.'

'Well, if you need to persuade Reinhard, demonstrating your increasing control over the men cannot hurt your position.'

Hugues smiled and nodded. 'No, you are correct. So, continue, nibble away at the rot bit by bit, while I consider how to achieve some sort of accord.'

Hugues had not told Foissart about his conversation with Sir Hans. He did not want the knight to know disposing of Reinhard had even been discussed. Not only was it dangerous knowledge, but the Frenchman was an honourable man, and the mere existence of such a conversation might be a step too far for him to accept.

'Brother Foissart!' called a voice from behind them. Hugues and the Frenchman turned and saw three Order soldiers jogging past their escort.

'Yes, what is it?'

'Excuse me, my lord,' said the soldier to Hugues, before looking at Foissart. 'Sir, there is trouble at the horse lines. Some locals say it is their land, required for crops, and that Grandmaster Reinhard gave them confirmation it belonged to them. They are insisting we move the horses.'

Foissart frowned. 'They can insist all they like, they cannot do anything about it.'

'That is what we said, sir, not in so many words.'

'We told them to fuck off, pardon my language, sirs,' said the second man, bobbing his head to Hugues, who raised an eyebrow in distaste.

'But one of them went to go and complain to the Grandmaster, and some of his men came out. There are half a dozen of them there now, insisting we take the horses and leave. I told them to wait until I got orders from you.'

Foissart grunted. 'Good, you did well.' He turned to Hugues. 'I don't think this needs to trouble your time, Grandsteward, I will handle it.' He looked around them. 'Do you mind if I take four of your escort? It seems speed is essential, to get there before they try anything stupid.'

'Just four men? The bishop sent six.'

'Four men, but with these three here and me… it will be enough to prevent trouble.'

Hugues nodded. 'Good, we will finish our conversation once you have attended to it.'

'Yes. Thank you, Grandsteward.' Foissart bowed swiftly and strode off, four of the guardsmen peeling off to follow, leaving just Hugues and two men, suddenly feeling quite vulnerable.

He looked furtively around the street but saw nothing alarming. His caution overcoming his desire to continue his walk, he headed off back towards his makeshift quarters. When Foissart returned, they would finish making their plans.

'Well, where did he go?' Hugues gave the man an irritated and exasperated look. The Order soldier looked confused and then looked aside, as if he expected to see the man in question appear in the doorway.

But Foissart did not appear in the doorway to his quarters. It would have been an act of God if he had, because Hugues had already been inside to check for himself, and the knight was not there.

'You went with him to the horse lines.'

'Yes, m'lord.'

'And he resolved the argument there.'

'Yes, well…' The soldier paused, looking unsure. 'I believe it was resolved, the troublemakers left in any case.'

'And then Foissart left to return here?'

'I don't know, sir.'

'HOW CAN YOU NOT KNOW?' Hugues snapped, his tolerance collapsing and shouting at the man's cringing face.

'I was helping the lads repair the lines that the locals had cut. I didn't see when he left, m'lord, or where he went.'

'What of the others? Where are they?'

'Well, Thomas came back with me, and…' The man looked hopeless and shrugged.

'And you don't know where the others went.'

'No, m'lord.'

'And you haven't been able to find them.'

'Not yet, no.' The man stared at the ground, suddenly finding it very interesting. 'They must be close,' he added, lamely.

Hugues started an angry retort at the obviousness of the statement, but bit it back and shook his head. 'Go and fetch me his second. No, in fact, go and fetch me every senior man you can find. Now!'

The soldier scurried off and Hugues stood there in concerned and irritated contemplation. Foissart had walked to the horse lines with four men, according to several of the men there he had ended the dispute and dispersed the troublemakers, and then he and possibly two of his men had left. They had been on foot, Foissart's horse was still tied in its stall, just a few paces from where Hugues stood, aloof and unconcerned with the whereabouts of its master.

A few of his captains and sergeants appeared as he waited, and Hugues flicked his eyes between them, trying to read anything from their expressions. Foissart had only been missing for a few hours, most of them would not be concerned by that at all. Hugues was fighting with the thought of how humiliating his reaction would seem if the man was merely on an errand, or shirking his duties for a short time with one of the local women.

But no, his horse was here, and Foissart was not the type to sneak off when he knew Hugues expected to hear from him.

Another soldier ran into the yard, a second trailing in his wake. 'As you ordered, m'lord, one of the sentries from the eastern road.'

The town had no wall, but posts had been established on each of the roads into the settlement, to check and inspect any wagons or suspicious travellers, and to keep an eye on who and what was coming into town, or leaving it. The posts were manned by Reinhard's men, something Hugues decided at that moment he would need to rectify.

'You, did you see Brother Foissart return to the town this afternoon?'

The man shrugged and shook his head. 'I don't know who Brother Foissart is,' he said, with a lack of interest veering into insolence.

Hugues muttered under his breath. 'A French knight, tall, brown hair, a slim expression to his face, he had four men with him. He left around noon and would have returned later.'

The man's eyes flicked up as he thought it over, and then he shook his head again. 'Lots of brothers passed out and back today, that doesn't remind me of any of them.'

'Isn't it your duty to know who passes?'

The man shook his head vigorously. 'We are to check only the locals, and visitors we don't recognise. Men wearing the Order's markings are not to be hindered or questioned. Those are our orders.'

Hugues was dumbstruck. 'What? Who gave you those orders?'

'Brother Sighard.'

'Sighard told you that any man wearing the symbol of the Order is to pass without comment or record.'

'Yes.'

'So anyone wishing to enter or leave unnoticed, all they have to do is wear the cross.'

The man thought about it for a moment and nodded. 'Those are my orders.'

'Insanity.' Hugues looked at the rest of the gathered men, looking from face to face, trying to work out which of them he truly trusted, seeing anger, confusion, and embarrassment. He settled on anger as being the expression he was seeking, and pointed to one of the knights. 'You are now responsible for the entrances to the town. Gather fifty men for this purpose, only those who were with us in the south. I want four on duty at each post day and night, all those who pass will be identified. Replace whoever is there now and send them away.'

The insolent guard straightened and there was a mumble of protest, but he had the sense not to take it further than that.

Hugues pointed at another of the gathered leaders. 'You, take another fifty men, search for Foissart. Start at the horse lines and the road back and then the city, I want every building searched for him, and those two men he was with. Find their names, find where they slept, find where they went.'

'Yes, m'lord.'

'I want Foissart here before nightfall, or to know where he went. You will not sleep until that happens, understood?'

The man nodded firmly and Hugues dismissed them all, snapping at his squire to bring his horse.

It was evening, the sun setting and the shadows lengthening into darkness before the man who he had assigned to searching reported.

'Nothing?' said Hugues, aghast.

'No, Grandsteward. No one has seen him, he is not in the city, and there was no sign of him on the road. No sign of trouble, nothing.'

'The man has not disappeared into the air! Where can he be?'

'Well…' The knight looked nervous. 'There are two possibilities.'

'Yes?'

'We were not allowed to search the Grandmaster's quarters.'

Hugues waved the concern away. 'He is not hiding in the bishop's bedchambers.'

'Well, the Grandmaster did pronounce more than we were expecting as being his quarters.'

Hugues raised an eyebrow. 'How much?'

'The whole of the headquarters, as well as the stables, and some storage buildings.'

'He did what? He forbade you search storage buildings?'

'Yes, m'lord. The guards posted there refused to let us in, told us to ask the Grandmaster.'

'And did you?'

'He was too busy to receive us,' said the knight lamely.

'And you…' Hugues stopped himself, it was not the place of the knight to create a conflict with the master of the Order, if Reinhard was being so obstinate, he would have to deal with it himself. 'Never mind, you did the right thing. What of the second possibility?'

The man shuffled on the spot. 'The river.'

Hugues pressed his lips into a line. 'The river?'

'Well, if he's gone, he didn't go by road, no horses are missing. But he could have gone by boat, several left today, and the guards on the dock don't keep track of which Order men come and go.'

'By orders of Sir Sighard?'

'Yes.'

Hugues pinched his nose. 'Do you really think Foissart would have left, is that what you are suggesting? Desertion?'

The man shook his head slowly. 'No, not Foissart, not like this.'

Hugues nodded. 'Taken against his will?'

'Possibly.'

'But in the middle of the day? He was armed and had two men with him. How would anyone force him through the town without notice? Have you found either of those men?'

'No sign, they did not return to their quarters.'

'This is impossible, three armed men of the Order, disappearing from our midst. Impossible.'

'It is possible that he went into the river, rather than onto it. The road out of town is close to the bank.'

Hugues straightened, he had the same fear. He remembered what Sir Hans had said, that some opponents and dissenters had disappeared, some supposedly having drowned in the river. But someone as senior as Foissart?

There was the sound of voices outside, protesting and then

silenced, and Hugues looked up nervously as the door swung open and a large, surcoated knight came in.

'How dare you!' Hugues said, his voice trailing off as half a dozen fully armed soldiers filed in behind the big knight. Hugues gulped nervously as his man took a step to place himself between his lord and the threat, hand latched to the hilt of his sword.

The big knight stepped forward casually, his face coming into the light of the lamps around Hugue's table, and he saw that it was Sir Sighard.

'Sir Sighard, have you lost your mind? Forcing your way into my quarters, what are you doing here?'

If Sighard was chastened, he didn't show it. 'Grandmaster's orders.'

'Orders to do what?' Hugues looked at the six stonefaced soldiers and the fear gripped him. Reinhard had decided to make his move, it was suddenly clear to him.

'Investigating the desertion of Sir Foissart.'

'Desertion?' gasped Hugues.

'Yes.'

'And what evidence do you have of desertion?'

Sighard's brow furrowed. 'He was seen fleeing the town, with two accomplices.'

'Fleeing? How?'

'On horse, by the eastern road.'

Hugues slammed his fist down on the table. 'On horse! His horse is still in the stable.'

'No, his horse is missing, and two more were stolen. They killed a stablehand and fled. They were seen.'

That made Hugues stagger to a halt. It was the most brazen lie, but Sighard looked on impassively as Hugues struggled with what to do. The sense of threat was palpable. He finally stood up. 'You lie, Sir Sighard. I inspected his quarters myself, his horse was there, and no one was murdered.'

Sighard shrugged, as if the accusation neither surprised nor bothered him. 'It must have been after your inspection. Come, see for yourself.' The knight stepped to one side, and a corridor formed between him and the door. Hugues could think of nothing he wanted less than to step out into the dark streets with Sighard and his men, but he also had an intense desire to see for himself, and it did not look like Sighard was going to accept no as an answer.

Eventually, he decided to go of his own accord, rather than have the last vestige of his dignity stripped by being forcibly escorted to whatever fate awaited him. 'Sir Jean, gather four men and accompany me to Foissart's quarters.'

'Sir Jean will stay here,' intoned Sighard.

'I will do as the Grandsteward, not you, commands,' said the Frenchman, hand flexing on the hilt of his sword.

'These are the orders of the Grandmaster,' said Sighard, ushering a few of his men towards the knight, corralling him against a wall. The knight looked at Hugues for guidance, tense and on the verge of violence, but Hugues gave him a slow shake of the head.

'I will escort you, Grandsteward, you will be perfectly safe,' said Sighard, in the least reassuring way possible.

Hugues did his best to look unperturbed and nodded. 'Very well then, lead the way.'

Hugues looked in disgust at the butchered remains of the stablehand. Foissart's horse was indeed missing. And his quarters had been ransacked, his equipment was missing, along with some other possessions, while items of lesser importance were carelessly scattered around on the floor and on furniture.

Hugues stood there in shock as the very same soldier he had questioned earlier, who had reported not seeing Foissart, told him a breathless tale of the three men coming in and stealing three horses, of how the stableboy had tried to stop them, and of how he himself had been beaten to the ground.

The soldier was sporting bruises and a fresh cut above his eye, one that still oozed blood that trickled down the side of his face. The soldier couldn't meet his eye as he gave his story, and Hugues shook his head in disgust once the performance was over and the soldier sent away.

Sighard stood there impassively until Hugues could bear it no more. 'So, what now? What does the bishop order?'

'There is clearly a lack of discipline in the men who left with you. The Grandmaster doesn't blame you. The rot clearly starts with Foissart and must be burned out, one deviant at a time. I will be in charge of that, I will take responsibility for returning the men to the proper state of obedience and devotion to the Order.'

Hugues's shoulders slumped a little. He was alone in that yard with Sighard and Sighard's men, and could not bring himself even to make a pretence of resistance. In fact, he had decided that to appear completely cowed was to his benefit. 'You will report to me, on the progress, of course?'

'You will be informed as and when required.'

'Excellent,' Hugues said, trying to keep the wavering out of his voice. 'Then I will return to my quarters?' He had intended to make it sound like intent, but it came out as a question.

Sighard stared at him intensely for a moment and then nodded. 'As you wish, Grandsteward. My men will escort you.'

'Thank you.' Hugues staggered out of the yard with as straight a spine as he could manage and let two of the silent soldiers take him back to his quarters.

## Chapter 26

# Blades and Betrayal

HANS HAD HIS midday meal and spent some time talking to his squire about the care of the horses, or the lack of, to his eyes. The men were getting lazy, the months spent in the town with little to do had worn away at the good habits of care for horses, equipment, and their own bodies. Hans had been distracted by the situation with the Order and had not been driving them as hard as he should have been.

His squire, still bashful from the verbal lashing he had received earlier, appeared in the house and walked over to his knight. 'There is a man to see you, Sir Hans.'

'Who?'

'An Order soldier, he said he has a message just for you.'

'He won't give his name? Then dismiss him…' Hans looked up and thought about it. 'No, I will see him. Where is he?'

'He said he would wait in the stables.'

'Who else is out there?'

'At the moment, just a couple of squires and stablehands.'

'Good. Tell them all they are finished for the afternoon. Go and get some food.'

The squire looked pleased, the sun was barely falling. It was early indeed to be excused their duties. 'Yes, sir.'

'I expect the horses to be out for exercise at dawn, then looked after, properly this time. Don't make the mistake of leaving them in that state again.'

Chastened, his squire nodded and left the room.

Hans belted his sword and walked out to the stables, wondering if the soldier brought a message from Hugues or from the bishop. He doubted anyone else in the Order had cause to send him anonymous messengers in this fashion.

He walked through the yard and came to the small four-stall stable built against the wall of the next building. It was roughly built, low and dark, but he could see a man leaning against the back wall waiting, half hidden behind his horse.

Hans walked past the mare and stopped in surprise. 'My lord Hugues, I did not expect it to be you.'

Hugues looked uncomfortable. 'I did not know if I could trust any other with this message.'

'Oh, and what message is that?'

Hugues closed the distance between then, looking around to check the yard was truly empty. 'I'm ready, to take the action you intend. I will help you.'

Hans smiled mirthlessly. He had heard of the search for Foissart, the rumours that he had deserted, and known that it was much more likely the man was dead. Killed for causing trouble. 'It has come to that so quickly?'

'It has. Reinhard has gone too far, it cannot be allowed to continue. Do you trust your men?'

'Yes.'

'With your life?'

'Of course, these men would die for me.'

'Good, can we go inside? I can't be seen here by anyone else who happens to come calling.'

'Well, no one comes calling here, we are outcasts in this town. But yes, we can go in, we shall not be disturbed.'

'Good, events are disturbing enough already.'

Hans sat back and stared into his cup, taking it all in. 'What you are asking is very difficult. It will be hard enough to get to the Grandmaster, but to make his death look seem like the work of the enemy? That is very difficult indeed.'

'Well, it is essential. Anything other than a martyr's death will bring all the wrong questions, all the wrong outcomes. I need the whole Order, and all its supporters, focused outward for the killers.'

'We would have to draw him out, he would be guarded. No Norseman would get close enough to him in that fortress to slip a dagger into him as he sleeps.'

'No, and such an assassination would only rouse suspicion. No, it must leave no doubt that the locals are responsible.'

'I do not know if that can be done,' said Hans with a sigh.

'Then we cannot do it until we find a way.'

'Are you setting impossible conditions to simply ensure it is not done?'

Hugues pursed his lips in distaste and shook his head.

'Then why your sudden change of heart?'

'You know about Foissart?'

'Do you? I hear nothing but rumours.'

'Reinhard had him murdered, I am sure of it.'

'Why?'

'Because he was competent, and uncorrupted. But most importantly, because he was loyal to me, not Reinhard. He was going to regain control over the men, but now Sighard has seized control, and I don't have the means to prevent it.'

'You are the Grandsteward, isn't Sighard under your command?'

Hugues snorted. 'Reinhard's creature, he has bullied and threatened and bribed enough of the other commanders that few are left who would obey me. Reinhard has claimed that he needs Sighard to enforce the Lord's peace in this town, and that is that. They follow him now, not me. They all know that if Reinhard can make my senior captain disappear in the middle of the day, without so much as a cry of alarm, that there is nothing I can do to counter him. Not while he is alive.'

Hans nodded. It made sense. Reinhard had escalated the dispute beyond all reason. If Sir Foissart was indeed dead by Reinhard's order, it was an outrage without compare, even by the high standards the bishop had set in the last months.

'Well, you must find at least some who you trust, if you want to make some kind of plan work, you will need men inside the Order who will help us. Mine alone cannot do it, we are both unwelcome and untrusted here.'

Hugues looked worried but he nodded. 'There are still a few of my men who I believe would stand by me, no matter what. But I am avoiding putting them to any public test, lest they also "desert" in inexplicable circumstances.'

Hans studied Hugues carefully for a moment, thinking over how much he should say. But he sensed that the time was correct. 'I know of a few of Reinhard's men who do not agree with how the Order is being run.'

Hugues perked up, genuine surprise writ across his features. 'Men in his own ranks who would turn against him?'

'Yes.'

'How? How could you know this, why would they risk you knowing? How have they not been purged?'

Hans tapped the fingers of one hand nervously on the back of the other. 'Because they have been careful, and I have been careful. They are Saxon men, mostly, men I knew before they took the oaths of the Order, and who know me and my reputation. They trusted me in confidence, and we have had some, careful, discussions.'

'I see. And they are how you were hoping to get to Reinhard?'

'Yes.'

'But it was not enough? You needed me?'

Hans rolled his head slightly to the side and chewed his lip for a moment. He was still unsure about telling Hugues everything. They shared a goal, but some things should only be shared when absolutely required. 'It was uncertain, but with your help I believe the outcome is much more likely to be favourable.'

'I see. Well, with your friends as well as my men, it can probably be done, but how to do it cleanly, without bringing the blame down on us, that is the hard question.'

'We must take him outside of his fortress, with a small guard, or guarded by men we control.'

'Sighard goes everywhere with him, and he chooses the guards himself from his inner circle, I have no influence there,' said Hugues.

'Then we will have to bring overwhelming force.'

'The greater the force, the messier and less certain the result.'

'Then what, Hugues? This is your requirement, that we make it appear to be an enemy attack, you create this problem, how do you propose we solve it?'

Hugues put a finger to his mouth and chewed the problem over, his mouth tense and eyes flicking across the floor from one blank spot to the next. 'I don't know yet, but I have been here too long already. We need to bring in a few trusted men and make a plan, and somewhere more discreet to meet.'

Hans thought about that, bringing any of his men in filled him with trepidation. But he nodded. 'As few as possible.'

'And I will need to know the ones of Reinhard's men who I can use.'

Hans sucked a deep breath through his lips. 'That is a great risk.' But he nodded reluctantly. 'I will give you three names, the ones I am most sure of.'

'Good. And we must have a meeting place, I took a great risk of being spotted coming here, it cannot happen again. We certainly cannot have half a dozen of us sneaking into your stables, I am sure Reinhard could be watching.'

'Yes, somewhere outside town.'

'I will arrange for my men to be on guard at the east road three nights from now. Four miles down the road, beyond the camp your men use, is a small farmhouse, used to store spare wagons, tools and such things, no one lives there. It is guarded, but I can ensure the guards are my men. It is not an important place, so Reinhard will not be watching it.'

'I know the buildings.' Hans thought about it. The farmhouse was off the road, past a small copse of trees inside a small valley. It was a good location for a quiet meeting. 'So, we will meet there, sunset three nights from now. Bring a few men you trust, I will as well. Have them all go separately or perhaps in pairs, we must not draw attention. Even if the men guarding the road are yours, others could be watching.'

Hugues nodded. 'I will do it as you suggest, single riders of the Order leaving town will attract little notice.'

'Yes.'

Hugues smiled grimly. 'Then we are set on our course. From this moment, we cannot change our minds.'

'I understand.' Hans stood and Hugues followed suit. He stretched out his hand and the baron took it with a reassuring firmness.

'Three nights,' said Hugues, nodding and letting go of Hans's hand.

Hans let out a deep breath he had not realised he was holding when the door shut behind the Grandsteward. His belly was a jumble of nerves, but now that the time for action was finally upon him, he felt the sudden rush of excitement, the buzz of impending battle. He squeezed and relaxed his fist, trying to focus, to clear his mind. Then he made up his mind who he would speak to first, there were others who hated Reinhard almost as much as he, and now was the time to bring them inside the circle.

The guards on the east road leading out of the town studiously ignored Hans and his companion as they rode out on the appointed evening. Of all the parts of this meeting, this had made Hans the most nervous, that he and his squire would be questioned as they tried to leave town that late in the day. He had decided they should go armed and armoured, not disguising themselves. Very few people would stop or question a mounted, armoured knight. If they had gone in cloaks and concealed their identity, they were more likely to be challenged, and less likely to be able to talk their way through the questions.

If anyone had stopped them, he intended simply to brusquely brush the questions away.

But it was not necessary, no one paid them any attention, they were just two more armed men riding around in a town full of armed men. The road was not very busy this late in the day, and most were heading in, not out, but they passed out of the town and rode briskly down the road eastwards.

They rode until they were alone in the gathering gloom, out of sight of the town, before Hans stopped his horse, looking back along the road and seeing nothing. 'You go ahead,' he said to his squire. 'I am going to wait here a while and ensure no one was following us.'

He had been reluctant to bring the boy in on the plot, but it would be hugely more difficult to make the plans while keeping the young man in the dark, as his duty was to be with Hans at almost all times. He had decided it was better to bring him along than to try and sneak around without him noticing or asking awkward questions.

The lad had barely expressed a reservation. He looked up to Hans with an almost childlike devotion, hooked on the image of the great warrior; the idea that what Hans was asking him to do might be wrong did not seem to occur to him. Hans had framed it as a question of justice and honour and the boy had willingly, even excitedly, committed to help, and to keep it secret.

It made Hans uncomfortable how easy it had been to sway the young squire. Convincing the two other men he had sent ahead, both old comrades of Sir Dietmar, had been equally easy, but at least both of those men knew exactly what it meant to be doing what they planned, and they had their own reasons for wanting Reinhard to meet the fate they planned for him.

His squire nodded and set his horse off down the road towards the hidden farmhouse with a click of his tongue and some pressure from his heels, and Hans walked his own mount off the road into the blackness under a tree, settling in to watch the road. He stood there as the shadows faded into nothingness and the sunset became a glow behind the horizon, until it was clear no one was on the road behind them. Then he turned his horse and headed down the side track that led to the farm.

It was about a mile down the road into the valley, and Hans chewed over what he would say to the rest of the conspirators. The key was to get Reinhard alone with as few companions as possible. The precise method for doing that eluded him, but he had some ideas.

He passed through the copse of trees at the base of the valley, and emerged out the other side. He could now see the farm buildings tucked into the woods beyond on the right, the fields sprawling along the valley floor to his left. The darkness was deepening, but he could see a faint light from the roof hole of one of the buildings.

When he reached the buildings, which formed a hollow square around a yard, he saw his squire's horse tied up inside, along with three others. He dismounted and led his horse over to tie it up alongside them. As he entered the yard, he looked around in surprise, as no one was in sight. There was light spilling out from the doorway of the far building and everything else was in deep shadow.

Then a figure emerged from the doorway, and he saw it was one of Hugues's men, a surcoated brother of the Order. Hans started to move towards the man, but something was off, and he stopped in his tracks, hearing movement behind him and turning, seeing two more men appearing from around the corner and casually blocking the way he had come into the yard.

'Sir Hans, good of you to join us. I was starting to worry you wouldn't arrive.'

Ice gripped Hans's veins as the unmistakable voice of Reinhard called out across the yard. He put one hand on his sword and saw four more figures appear from the darkness of the half-open stables at the far end of the yard, a mere ten paces away. Reinhard walked out, flanked by two more knights, and a fourth figure resolved itself as two, a soldier driving Hugues before him.

He saw Hugues looking downcast, unable to meet his eye. *So, we are betrayed.* He looked beyond his dejected co-conspirator and Hans felt the crushing blow as he saw that, in the darkness behind Hugues, a cluster of prone figures were visible in the stable, a single foot spilling out from the shadows of a stall. His men, his squire, already captured – perhaps already dead.

'Plotting against the Lord's anointed representative in these lands? The master of the Order of Christ's Light? I am so disappointed, Sir Hans. So many others will be so disappointed, a man of your reputation, fallen so low. Come now, give up your weapons. It is *done*.'

Reinhard hissed the last word, the pure triumph of it dripping from his tongue.

Hans didn't move. He scanned the scene. Reinhard was close, so close. The yard was small, cramped, and Hans was already well inside its boundary. Two knights flanked the bishop protectively, he recognised the hulking figure of Sir Sighard to the bishop's right, and Sieur de Blanchant on his left, between the bishop and Hugues. The French knight was standing with his famous sword unsheathed, resting by his side, expectant.

Another knight, the one who had come from the building, was standing on Hans's left flank, watching him, but he seemed nonchalant, too certain of their overwhelming numbers. Hans didn't look behind him, but he knew the two men were still standing there, he had not heard them move.

The last of Reinhard's men was busy guarding Hugues, so he was not a threat. Hans ran through the situation in his mind, imagining how he could get to Reinhard. The men behind him would be too slow to react if he attacked, he could ignore them. The man to his left was the closest, but alone, isolated, and his sword sheathed. Hans could reach him before he was ready, he was sure of it.

'Come now, Sir Hans, don't make a fool of yourself. Surrender yourself to the justice of the Lord, you will be fairly judged.'

Hans did not reply, he made no move for his sword, he edged forwards as if in indecision, but measuring his distances, planning his moves. His left hand moved from the reins of his horse and toyed with the leather thong that tied his helmet to his horse's saddle. He hadn't worn it for the ride, it would be pointless in the dark, but he always had it with him. He knew it was a vanity, but men recognised the famous steel-faced helm, it was part of his reputation.

Hans considered his options as his fingers played with the simple knot, assessing the layout of the yard, the positions and the readiness of his opponents. *These men don't know me, they don't know what I am capable of.* They expected him to surrender, but they had overplayed their hand. Only three of them were a threat, the man to his left and then the two knights standing with Reinhard. He had faced worse odds and triumphed before. He would take them one at a time – the closest man first and Roland last, he was reputed to be a fine swordsman. Sighard was a simple brute, he would go down easily to a swordhand as skilled as Hans's. But he needed to buy time, he needed Roland to be distracted, just for a few moments. He could not face Sighard and Roland together, he needed to fight each man one at a time and win quickly, that was his path to Reinhard.

He built the fight in his mind, the progress of steps, the predictions of where he would face each man and how he would defeat them in a single pass. They would be reacting to him – he would dictate the flow of the combat, unpredictable, unexpected. They had numbers, but he would have surprise and sheer violence. *Yes, it can be done.*

Hans loosened the knot on the helmet. He needed a little time and distance on Roland, that was all. He needed to disguise his intent. 'Let Baron Hugues go, this was my idea, not his. Let him go and you can have me.'

Reinhard laughed, sickly and high-pitched. 'My dear man, do you really believe the Grandsteward would betray me?'

Hans baulked and looked over at Hugues, who could barely meet his gaze, and suddenly he understood; *Hugues's man was not a prisoner.*

*No.* The betrayal tore a deep gash in Hans's heart, and for a moment his fingers fell limp on the helmet and sword hilt as the scale of his defeat became clear.

'Come now, surrender yourself. You are beaten, this is not a game for men such as you, a blunt instrument of war,' mocked Reinhard, and the closest knight took a cautious step forwards, almost to within striking range.

Hans felt the heat of anger rise and his eyes flicked up towards the bishop, just eight paces away. *A blunt instrument of war?* These men did not know his worth, did not know what he was capable of. They thought he was beaten, but he could not be beaten so easily. Sir Hans Mettel, the Green Knight, was not to be taken down with words and mockery, betrayal and subterfuge. Hans felt the pure heat of anger dissipate, and the calm of the moments before combat enveloped him as he made his decision.

Hans hooked his fingers under the lip of the helmet and

stepped forwards with his right foot, lining up his body and closing the distance to the bishop by a pace. *Drive Roland back two paces, isolate Sighard.* Hans didn't put the helmet on, he simply launched it without warning, throwing the heavy steel object with his left arm and using the rotation of his body to help as he drew his sword with his right. He felt a twinge of pain from his old injury as he threw it, and he flicked his eyes towards his first victim. *Speed was everything.*

The knight closest to him was as surprised as Hans expected, and he had barely got his blade up to protect himself when Hans cut him across the arm with a brutal crossbody swing on his second step forwards. The wound wasn't fatal, but Hans didn't need it to be, he only needed to win six paces of distance. That cut won him two.

*Sighard next.*

He saw from the corner of his eye that the helmet had missed its mark, sailing past Roland and clattering off Hugues. His injured arm had let him down, the shoulder had never been the same since he was wounded at Helsingborg. He snarled but had no time for regret, he saw Sighard raising his sword and stepping towards him, rushing to meet Hans's charge, as he had expected the big brute would. *Predictable.* Being predictable in combat was a fatal error.

Hans's feet powered off the hard-packed dirt, four paces from the shocked figure of the bishop, thin mouth wide and painted in horror. Hans stepped to Sighard's inside and speared at him with an extended thrust, feeling Sighard twist away from the lethal blow with surprising grace, the sword barely punching into maille. The big man was uninjured, but he was unbalanced and stumbling past Hans, taking him out of the fight for a few precious moments.

*Three paces.*

He stepped to his right, away from the reeling Sighard, pulling the sword back to begin a cut towards where he expected Roland would be. The final two paces could be gained with it. He would kill or drive Roland back with this cut and then Reinhard was his.

As he stepped forwards and his sword started to come around, there was a blur of steel catching the firelight in the right side of his vision. *How…*

'Fuck!' moaned Hugues, one hand clamped to his nose. The flying helmet had slammed into his face, snapping his head back and re-breaking his already disfigured nose. Blood was pouring down his chin, dripping onto the mud where it mixed with the blood that still trickled from Sir Hans's motionless corpse.

Brother Roland was wiping the blood from his precious blade reverentially, inspecting the holy artefact and then carefully returning it to its scabbard.

Reinhard just looked on in mild shock, trying to make sense of what had happened, trying to shake the look of sheer murderous rage that had been on Hans's face as the Saxon knight had sprung towards him. Roland had cut the criminal down so close to him that blood from the terrible wound in the German knight's neck had sprayed his cloak and seeped into his shoes. Reinhard finally took a shaking step back and looked at Roland accusingly.

'You said you would protect me!' he whispered in a hoarse voice.

Roland raised his eyebrows and looked at the body and then back at the Grandmaster. 'You said you wanted to provoke him, that it was better to end like this than to have a trial.'

'Yes, but not to let him so close!'

Roland shrugged nonchalantly. 'I did not expect the helmet, that was a clever ploy. It could have worked.'

Sighard kicked the body, as if checking if it was truly dead. A churlish action to cover his own embarrassment, as Hans's head was nearly severed.

'I expect to be better protected in future!' Reinhard said with a scowl that tried to hide the fear that still shook his hands. Most of his men had the decency to look embarrassed, but Roland did not. He walked over to where the steel-faced helmet lay in the dirt and picked it up, turning it over and inspecting it.

'I had never seen him fight, only heard the stories, that the man behind this steel was unstoppable in battle, an angel of death. A shame. He was a fine swordsman, I would have liked to face him alone and truly tested myself against him. He faced six and still attacked? A true knight.'

Reinhard glared at the knight but said nothing, the more he complained the weaker he would look. He satisfied himself with looking over at Hugues, who had his eyes rammed shut and was leaning back, hand still clutched to his face. Reinhard couldn't help but feel a burst of satisfaction at the sight. He and Hugues might have come to an accord to end their conflict, but it was still wonderful to see the man laid a little low.

Hugues had proved to be a more formidable adversary than expected, to the point where he had considered disposing of him. But truthfully, it was never an option he took seriously. He enjoyed the man too much; having a good, controllable opponent was an excellent self-disciplinary tool. And when Hugues had come to him with an offer, to expose and hand over a ring of plotters, including brothers of the Order whom he trusted, for what were very reasonable concessions in returning the baron's powers, Reinhard had been happy to comply.

'You will live, Grandsteward?' asked Reinhard with deep concern in his voice, walking over so that the two men could talk unheard by the others in the yard except Sighard, who followed him like a surly shadow. Hugues may have warned him of this plot, but he still did not *entirely* trust the man.

'How is it always me that is injured by those attacking you?' Hugues said bitterly.

Reinhard simply curled his lip in a small smile. *God protected his own, according to their value*. 'It is as it is willed,' he said, ignoring the quiet curse he got in reply. 'So, I believe our understanding is complete?'

Hugues managed to lever his red, puffy eyes open to meet Reinhard's gaze. 'You are yet to uphold your terms in full.'

'Do not worry, I will. I will return Foissart, I believe Sighard is done questioning him.'

'And is he capable of returning to his duties?' Hugues asked accusingly. Reinhard swung a questioning look to Sighard, and the big knight nodded slowly.

'It is as you ordered, he is intact.' The way he stressed the word *intact* made Reinhard shudder slightly. Sighard was truly a terrifying man, and Reinhard was endlessly thankful to have him in his service, not in the service of a rival.

'Good, then the prisoner will be released. Clearly, he was not involved in this treachery.' Reinhard indicated the three bodies of Hans's men, lying in the stable where they had been quietly disarmed and then brutally strangled by Sighard one by one as they arrived, with no more remorse than a housewife might wring the neck of a chicken.

'And I will regain control over the Order's forces?'

Reinhard tapped his finger on his lips. 'Sighard will retain some men to be my personal guard, and to maintain the security of the Order's assets… one hundred or so should do. But yes, the rest will be returned to your authority, it is time to end the threat of these Norse raids, time to strike back against them, and I believe you will do so effectively.'

Hugues narrowed his already narrow eyes at the announcement that Sighard would retain a significant force outside his control, which he had not agreed to, but clearly the man saw that some unplanned concession was expected, and he nodded brusquely. 'So, I am free to start a campaign to end these raids? I will have your support?'

'All the support I am able to give, and more beyond. The duke will provide more resources to help.'

Hugues looked at him suspiciously. 'Why the change of heart?'

Reinhard waved his hand at the bodies around them. 'Hugues, good Christian men have been murdered! On our own doorstep! This is an outrage, it cannot be allowed to continue. They attacked this food store, killed the guards and brave Sir Hans and his men who attempted to intervene, and burned all the supplies into ash. An outrage, and a devastating blow to the people's food stores for winter. This demands retribution.'

Hugues looked around and then back at Reinhard. 'That is how you intend to present this?'

Reinhard inclined his head.

'But there are no supplies here.'

'Roland is already making arrangements, do not be concerned. A great deal of food was stored here, a great deal. Its loss is a serious problem, one we have to address, or we are likely to see a very hard winter, a very hard winter indeed.'

'I'm sure it will be less hard for some than for others,' said Hugues drily.

'Well, that is always the way, my dear Hugues, always the way. Let's return to my quarters, I have an excellent surgeon, he can help with your wound. Come, Brother Sighard, it is time to return to town.'

'Yes, Grandmaster.'

'Good.' Reinhard stepped carefully around the dead German knight, his terror at the man's assassination attempt far from forgotten, and headed for his horse which was concealed behind the building. He felt deeply satisfied with the results. More traitors within the Order had been revealed, a dangerous enemy had been disposed of and Hugues had been returned to the fold. Apart from nearly dying, it had really been an excellent evening.

## Chapter 27

# Shadows and Stones

'YOU DID WELL, Gjaldir.' Eric Firebeard thumped him on the shoulder genially and walked off towards his house with some of the other Norwegians he shared it with.

Gjaldir nodded to himself and smiled in satisfaction. The raid had gone well, a small Christian outpost near the road, a waystation for travellers and barracks for passing soldiers. When they had attacked there had been few people present, just twenty or so guards and some locals who worked there. Gunnar and his men had quickly overcome the defences at the simple gate and fought their way in, leaving Gjaldir and a dozen other warriors outside to keep watch.

It had been Gjaldir who spotted the men in the undergrowth first, moving through the treeline along the road, creeping towards the watchful Norsemen. He had shouted out in alarm, and suddenly the woods had been alive with Christians, rushing from cover towards the small Norse group.

There had been twenty, at least, and Gjaldir had acted on instinct, shouting at the other warriors and ordering them to fall back into a stout line in the open gateway. Within heartbeats, their short line was beset by twenty or thirty enemy, and if they had been in the open they would have been overwhelmed in moments. But compressed into the gateway, they had been able to hold until Gunnar finished off the enemy inside and brought his warriors to help.

The enemy, seeing their trap had failed, had turned and fled into the night, leaving few from either side on the ground.

Gjaldir had felt exhilarated and sheepish, the men had not been his to command, but he had felt what needed to be done, and shouted the orders while others stood in indecision and no one had hesitated to obey them. Gunnar had said little about it, as was his way. He rarely commended any man for doing simply what he should have done but Gjaldir had felt a heady rush that had taken a long time to pass.

Eric's words, despite being days later and so brief, filled him with that rush again. The respect of your fellows, to be seen as one of them. It was all he had really wanted, and so rarely achieved.

Still smiling to himself, he decided to walk down to the lake. He could go to the house first, but he would be dragged into the comfort and familiarity of Brunhild and Aeske, and first he wanted a moment alone, to think, to rinse his body in the cool, clear waters of the lake. He dumped his maille and weapons on the shore, he would deal with that later with sand and a brush and some oiled wool, and set about stripping his clothes.

The clothes went onto the shield lying on the ground, he would need to scrub the bloodstains and ingrained mud out in a tub, cold lake water would do little for three-day-old blood. He stood, stark naked, and looked out over the lake, sighing contentedly.

It was a simple place, and beautiful for it. The waters were often still and flat, blue and green like church glass. The far bank was wooded and jagged, a wild backdrop to the peaceful lake, hidden today in an abnormally late mist that hung over the lake, reluctant to give up the grasp that such weather usually relinquished in the morning. He hobbled down the stony shore and dipped his toes into the water, feeling the shiver that rushed up from his feet through the small of his back and then prickling the hairs on his neck.

He pushed through the feeling, walking out into the lake as the coldness worked its way up his legs, seizing his stones in an icy vice and then snatching his breath as he ducked down to immerse himself completely.

He shuddered and scrubbed furiously at his hair while he was under the water, crouched down on his heels on the lakebed, and then stood suddenly, breaking the surface and gasping from the cold, and from the crawling sensations that rippled around his exposed skin.

He pulled up handfuls of water and splashed them onto himself, rubbing at dirt and dried crud, working his way down to his feet and then ducking under once more. Shivering and clutching one arm to his chest, he decided he had had enough and carefully walked back to the shore, squeezing the water from his hair with his other hand and shaking it like a wet dog.

He reached the shore and looked up at his pile of things, and half-stumbled as he saw the grey cloaked figure sitting there a few paces away; Tormund. The seer, however, did not react, was not looking at him, and did not appear even to have noticed him. The weird little man was motionless, staring out over the lake, immersed in his own little world.

Gjaldir felt deeply uncomfortable. He had become accustomed to the Norse attitude to being naked. They rarely cared who saw them, lived communally with men and women in the same rooms, and the warriors would, when out on raids or trips, strip and wash together without a second thought.

But something about this was different, and he felt vulnerable and embarrassed emerging from the lake shivering and unclothed to find the seer sitting there, a solo audience. He realised in that moment he had never seen Tormund wash, or indeed seen him wear different clothes. He was always in what at least appeared to be the same grey tunic and strange cloak.

But the man continued to ignore him, so Gjaldir continued up the stones and rubbed the worst of the water from his limbs and torso, rushing to put his clothes back on. Once his trousers and tunic were replaced, he felt better, and was torn between going back to the house, or staying by the lake as he had intended.

Yet still the seer ignored him, and he decided the man would not force him to flee simply with his unsettling presence. Gjaldir turned to face the lake, his back to Tormund, and tried to calm his mind again. But the little man was like an itch in the back of his skill, infuriating with his persistence. *The lake shore is vast, why does he have to share this one spot with me?*

In an attempt to take his mind's focus off the seer, he bent down and rummaged through the stones until he found what he was looking for, a smooth, flat, water-worn pebble. He stood and went down the few paces to the water's edge, bending his knees and cocking his arm before flicking the stone across the lake's surface. The pebble bounced smoothly off the calm water, and then again and again half a dozen times until it lost its speed and disappeared beneath the surface with a splash.

He found another pebble, flatter, more suitable, and carefully lowered his body, getting his arm near the surface and flung it again. This pebble barely kissed the surface on the first touch and away it went, bouncing again and again, Gjaldir counting to ten before the stone's front edge dipped and caught the water, tumbling and splashing before sinking, almost fading into the wisps of mist clinging to the surface of the lake.

Gjaldir smiled to himself, satisfied. That was a rare throw to carry so far, with so many bounces. There was a cackle of laughter behind him and his smile evaporated, the corners of his mouth turning down into a frown as he stood to his full height and turned to look at the seer, who was staring right back at him.

'What amuses you?' he asked, with open hostility. Tormund was ruining his mood with his lingering presence, like a bad drunk on a fine day.

'I did not know why I was here, and now I do,' said the seer as his laughter died out.

Gjaldir sighed and decided to ignore the man, you could never get a straight answer out of him. He tried to pretend he was not interested and picked out another stone, but he rushed and his mind was still on Tormund. He could feel the stone had the wrong shape even as he stooped to make his throw.

The stone bounced once with a spray of water, careening too high into the air, and then fell back to the water, sinking on the second impact. Tormund laughed again, harder this time, and Gjaldir gritted his teeth, abandoning the pursuit and heading to collect his things and leave.

'Do you not wish to know?' asked Tormund with a disarming smile.

'I do not,' grunted Gjaldir as he sat to put his shoes on.

'Ah, a lie. A poor start to a conversation. Most conversations that start with a lie end with one too.'

Gjaldir did not reply, clamping his mouth shut because he knew that was true. He hated it, the man was infuriating, but he did find his strange pronouncements oddly fascinating.

'Well, I was drawn here, and I did not understand why until you threw the stones.'

'Let me guess, you saw me in a dream,' said Gjaldir, wearily.

'No, no. Not you.'

Gjaldir felt a fleeting moment of annoyance that it was not, in fact, about him. But he said nothing and Tormund carried on.

'I have dreamed of Odin skimming stones across a bright lake on a misty morning. Many times I have been shown this.'

'How do you know it was Odin?' Gjaldir wanted to stop

replying, but he found he couldn't. He wanted to stand up and leave, but he remained seated where he was, his curiosity rooting him in place.

Tormund laughed again, full of mockery. 'I recognise the All-father when he is revealed to me.'

'So, what does this have to do with me? I threw some stones, so what? Many people do.'

'Yes, yes, they do. But I am not drawn down to watch them do it.'

'And what drew you here?'

'Hah, well… That is hard to explain.' Tormund went silent and Gjaldir cranked his neck around to look at the man, seeing that his eyes were still fixed firmly on the lake, unseeing, his mind clearly elsewhere. 'Have you ever sensed the presence of something, perhaps a figure hidden in a dark doorway, or a shape in the night? You cannot see it, yet your eyes know it is there. You feel compelled to go to it, to know it, and find that yes, in fact, there was the thing there that you could not see.' He flicked his intense stare onto Gjaldir. 'Have you felt that?'

Gjaldir thought about it for a moment, remembering many such occasions, including just a few days ago when his eyes had been drawn to the forest, where the slightest hint of something amiss had given away the approaching Christian ambushers. 'Yes,' he said, reluctantly.

'Well, that is a fraction of what I feel. I am drawn to events, sometimes small and insignificant, sometimes of great magnitude. I can travel for days or weeks with this feeling, never straying from the path, or sometimes it blurs and fades after just a few steps.' He shrugged. 'I do not understand it, but I always follow it to see what I am supposed to see.'

Gjaldir nodded slowly, although he did not really understand. 'And that feeling brought you here, as I was washing?'

'Hmm?' Tormund chortled. 'As you were washing, gods no. I

have been in the trees up there for a day and a half, waiting. I was beginning to lose interest.'

Gjaldir gaped at him. 'You waited there for a day and a half, and you think me throwing some stones is what you were brought to see?'

'Yes,' said Tormund, with infuriating certainty in his voice.

'Why?'

Tormund thought about this for a moment and then answered with his own question. 'Tell me. Do you believe in the power of dreams?'

Gjaldir shrugged and then shook his head. 'My dreams hold no power.'

'Ah, do they not? Or is it only that you have never thought about it, never looked deeply enough into them?'

'I have better things to do than sit and consider dreams.'

'Ah, well, does it not confuse you that you can see in your dreams things that you have never beheld with your eyes? Or see events that you have never known about before?'

Gjaldir shook his head. 'I see many kinds of nonsense in my dreams, I have seen a wolf become a cow and climb a tree, I remember that vividly. Do you think that had some meaning?'

Tormund considered it carefully for a moment and then shrugged, a rare moment of uncertainty for the annoyingly surefooted seer. 'I do not know, it could just be the nonsense that fills young men's heads. It is possible you are not blessed with dreams that have been given to you; few are. But it is also possible, given how close I feel the gods upon you, that you have simply never considered them carefully enough.'

Gjaldir sighed and waved his hands in despair. 'And how would I ever know? You see meaning in a dream of a man throwing stones.'

'A god, a god throwing stones,' Tormund said, chidingly.

'So you say.'

'And the answer is a lifetime.'

'What answer?'

'You asked how would I know. Well, a lifetime of careful contemplation, of exploration, of delving into those dreams and considering their meaning.'

Gjaldir felt his interest wane. He did not have a lifetime to spare sitting and thinking about strange dreams. He remembered that the seer was full of clever nonsense and put a hand down to lever himself to his feet.

'Wait, give me a moment, let me show you,' Tormund said, holding a hand out placatingly.

Gjaldir sighed and rocked back on his buttocks. 'You have just the one moment. I have things to do.'

'Consider the dream I told you of. I saw Odin skimming stones across a clear lake on a misty morning. What meaning could this have? I know Odin is the Allfather, a great leader and a decider of men's fates. He sacrificed his eye for wisdom and to know what has not yet happened. So, I ask myself, why would he be skimming stones?'

Gjaldir rolled his eyes and replied, his voice thick with sarcasm. 'If he knows the future, then he knows where they will go.'

'Precisely! Excellent, that was my first thought too,' said Tormund excitedly.

Gjaldir was surprised, and looked at the seer carefully, trying to find mockery and seeing none.

'But then, if he knows exactly what will happen, the world makes no sense. Many stories tell of Odin intervening in the world of men, of his struggles with his family and other gods, if he knew all of the future, why would this be required? No, perhaps, like me, he sees clouded snatches of what is yet to come. I am sure he sees much more than me but perhaps it is not clear?'

'The mist,' said Gjaldir, with a little prickle of excitement.

'Yes! The mist. He sees, but his view is uncertain, obscured.'

Gjaldir felt a burst of curiosity he could not suppress. 'So, what is the secret? Why is he throwing stones into the mist?'

Tormund beamed at him and then shrugged. 'I don't know, but that is the right question.'

'You don't know?' asked Gjaldir incredulously. 'You came down here for days just to watch me skim stones, you babble about your dream, and now you tell me you don't know what it means?'

'Yes,' said Tormund, without a hint of disappointment.

'Well, what is the point of that?' asked Gjaldir, shaking his head.

'My boy, it is exactly the point.'

'What?'

'To consider it. To explore it. My dreams are not clear; their meaning is often hidden. Sometimes it takes days, sometimes years. Some dreams I am sure are important but I have never deciphered. Sometimes I am shown the meaning long after the dream, sometimes not at all.'

Gjaldir sat still for a moment and then shook his head vehemently. 'You are utterly infuriating, I don't know why I listen to you.' He stood and hastily collected his things, gathering them all in his arms and giving the seer an annoyed glare.

'Because you feel compelled to,' said Tormund with a sly look. That stopped Gjaldir in his tracks. *That is true.*

'How do you know that?'

'Because the stink of the gods is upon you, boy. You are in their grasp, they speak to you, whether you hear it or not, and you cannot walk away from the voice of the Aesir.'

'And what good has that done me?'

'Who said it was a good thing?' said the seer, now he was the one with the confused expression.

Gjaldir baulked. 'I... well, I assumed that it was a good thing to be in the eye of the gods, or whatever. You said I was important, that I would make a weapon with fire from the sky, and then I did.'

'Yes, but you can be important without it being good for you.

We are the playthings of the gods, and their attention can be very bad, very bad indeed.' This the seer said with a new emotion that Gjaldir had never seen the man express before. Regret. But it passed in a fleeting moment and his faint smile returned. 'They make their plans, and then they use us to carry out or help those plans, as they see fit, for good or ill of those of us so chosen.'

Gjaldir felt a slight shiver, and started walking away again, intending to get away from the seer and his confusing thoughts. But then he stopped as the thought came unbidden into his mind, and spilled from his tongue without his consent. 'The stones are Odin's plans.'

There was silence from behind him and then the sound of hands smacking together in triumph. 'Yes, you have it! Ah, it is so clear now. Odin casts his plans out into the world, but the mist of uncertainty clouds his aim, and he can never be entirely sure what will happen, or where the stone will go.'

Gjaldir turned to Tormund, who had stood and had both hands clasped under his chin. He furrowed his brow. 'No, that does not make sense. You said Odin uses us to control his plans, to guide them. Once he throws the stone, what control does he have?'

Tormund shook his head in wonderment. 'You ask the right questions.'

Gjaldir cursed himself for the curiosity, but it would not leave him. 'What else did you see, in the dream?'

'Well, it varies from time to time. I have seen fish jumping, and wind whipping the mist into a dance. I have seen the sun beating down and waves on the water sparkling the light into a thousand shards. I have seen trees and bushes and grasses and… well, I do not know yet what importance any of this has.'

Gjaldir put his things down on the ground again and went over to the shore. 'Have you ever cast a stone yourself?'

'No.'

'Well.' Gjaldir bent down and selected a good, smooth stone.

'You have to choose the stone carefully. It must be smooth and flat, but not too flat, otherwise it has no weight. Then you cast it, and the best water is on a still day, like today.'

'Why?'

'If there are waves, they will catch the stone and throw it off course, even small ripples can disturb it, and throw it left or right, or throw it up in the air to sink when it lands.' Gjaldir threw the stone out and they watched it bounce a half-dozen times before it sank.

'So, it is not true that once you cast the stone, its destination is assured?'

'No, of course not.'

'So, then Odin controls the ripples, and the waves. And thus he controls the path of the stone,' said Tormund triumphantly.

Gjaldir thought about it. 'Well, waves and ripples cannot appear from nothing; they all have a cause.'

'The wind,' said Tormund.

'The fish,' said Gjaldir at the same time.

'Yes… So, Odin casts his plans, as best as he can from what he can see of the future, choosing the best stone he has available. But it is not enough, he must guide those plans, each time the stone bounces, he must nudge it to correct its course. He can cause a wind to make waves, or send a fish to make ripples, or any other type of disturbance. He uses his wisdom and knowledge to understand the impact they will have, and ensure the stone goes where he intends.'

Gjaldir shrugged and shook his head. 'Or it means nothing, we are just giving meaning to a dream that has none.'

Tormund laughed heartily. 'As I said, a conversation that starts with a lie ends with one.'

'What do you mean?' said Gjaldir defensively.

'You believe it has meaning, I know you do, yet you lied about it.'

Gjaldir's cheeks flushed. 'I was just talking. It does not mean I believe all your babblings.'

'No, but you believe this one. I wonder, after you have thought about it, what part do you think you play? Perhaps you are one of Odin's plans, a stone cast across the lake of history? We will speak again, when you have had time to consider it.'

Gjaldir said nothing, the feeling that had compelled him to remain had fled, and he turned and stalked back to the longhouse, feeling like he had just somehow been defeated in some way. But his mind could not stop considering the stone, the fish, and the ripples.

# PART 3

## Chapter 28

# Rebels and Regrets

LEIF STEPPED INSIDE the room and saw that it was already half full. Gunnar was standing with Jarl Gustav, Knud, the leader of Vatnsborð, and Halla, talking in low tones. Gathered around them were Gunnar's men, Vidar, Harald and Eric, a few of Gustav's senior warriors, and Asel, Frode's man.

Halla flicked her gaze up and saw him, before returning to her conversation. Leif walked over, nodding to a few of the men and exchanging quiet greetings. Some of them had just come back from another raid. It had been difficult, they had lost half a dozen men. The Christians were learning from their disasters, and it was becoming harder to find easy targets. He had heard about Gunnar's men and the attempted ambush at the waystation. That was something the Christians had not done before.

He made it to the inside edge of the loose circle and looked on as the three leaders finished their discussion. Halla looked around the circle, checking who was there, and then nodded. 'Good, that is everyone. We have gathered you to tell you that we have decided the time has come for the great raid.'

Leif felt a rush of nerves and excitement at the proclamation.

They had all known it was coming at some point, everything they had been doing was leading up to this goal, to capture key Crusader strongholds and drive an uprising among the people, to overthrow the weakened Crusader forces.

'Asel tells me that he has prepared our people as best he can, weapons have been readied, gathering points and targets agreed. When we arrive in my brother's lands, hundreds of warriors will be waiting for us, important enemy garrisons will be besieged or already destroyed, and then we will raise a larger force from the rest of the people before the Christians in other parts can react.'

'And then what? We face them in open battle again?' said Harald sceptically.

'No, we know that does not work. We will disappear if they come in force, we will melt into the forests and countryside and appear wherever else they are weak. We will spread the story of this uprising, and encourage the rest of our people to follow suit. The Christians can beat our army in the field, but they cannot govern the country if all the people refuse it. They cannot stamp out a thousand fires of rebellion at once. No, we will not face them in a grand battle, we will confront them in small numbers. We will make every town a deathtrap, every road deadly, every supply convoy a target and make sure no Crusader can safely sleep at night behind their gates and walls.'

Halla bared her teeth as she looked around the room, and the passion and confidence rolled off her in waves. 'We will starve them, trap them, kill them one by one. When they gather, we will disappear, when they separate into small groups we will descend on them and tear them apart, one at a time. That is our strategy, and for it to work, we need the people to help us, and for the people to help us, we need to show them a great victory, show them it is possible.'

Gunnar nodded. 'And we will win that great victory at Arbugæ, the home of this band of white-coated soldiers that give us so much trouble these last weeks. Asel knows their ways, and where they live. He knows their weaknesses and their movements. With him and the men he has prepared inside the enemy lands, we will rise up and slay this monster from within its own lair, and then the people will see that we can be victorious, and they will join us.'

'And what of your brother?' asked Eric cautiously, looking at Halla.

She glared at him, tight lipped, and he shrugged. 'I am sorry to offend you, but it matters. Many will still follow him, will he join us?'

'He will,' said Asel with confidence.

'How do you know, have you asked him?'

'No, it is too risky to do so. But he still cares for the future of his people above all else, and if we show him that we can still win, he will join us.' Asel looked uncomfortably at Halla, but she nodded stiffly.

'My brother is misguided, but I know his heart is good. He will join us, when the time comes.'

Eric nodded. 'I am content then.'

'Good,' said Gustav, sticking his mangled thumb through his belt. 'Asel, you will go to convey our plans to your people?'

'I am sending two of my men, they will go as soon as we are ready to tell them the day of the raid.'

'You will not go yourself?' asked Gustav with concern in his expression.

'No, it is better that I am with you, and when my forces gather, that I am there to organise and lead them. They all know me, and trust me, without me their loyalty cannot be assured.'

Gustav hummed slowly, his discomfort obvious, but he acceded with a tilt of his head. 'You know them better, I will trust your judgement. Make sure those men you send know exactly what is expected of them.'

'I will, they are good warriors, they will not let us down.'

'When the time comes, we will sail downriver with all our ships, loaded with all the weapons and equipment we can.'

'How long will that take?'

'Three days' rowing to Karlsgrind.'

'And we can pass there?'

'Yes, the last report is that the fortress is still not rebuilt, and the river is not blocked. But we do not know how long before they block it again, and we must make the journey before they do. We need those ships to sail down the lake to land near Arbugæ. We cannot carry everything overland.'

'So, when will we go?'

Gustav looked at Halla and she nodded. 'Five days from now. We will be in Jarl Frode's lands in twelve to fourteen days.'

'So, Asel's men will go before us, give my people warning, and then we will arrive in two weeks,' said Halla. 'Does anyone object to this plan?'

There were mumbled agreements around the room and no one spoke against it until Harald spoke up. 'And what if Asel's men do not make it on time, or are stopped?'

'They will split up when they reach Christian territory, so even if one is stopped, the other can continue,' said Asel.

'And if one is stopped and tortured, our plans will be revealed.'

'They have both sworn not to be taken alive. They will die on their own blades before being captured.'

Harald shrugged. 'That is brave of them, but if they die, will the uprising fail?'

Asel looked uncomfortable but shook his head. 'It will be more difficult, but my people are already expecting this, all they need to know is when. When we arrive, they will know the time has come. It just means they will not rise before the Christians also are warned. It would be better if they could have that advantage of surprise, but it is not a disaster if they do not.'

'Yes, much better,' muttered Gunnar.

'Then we must hope they get through, and prepare as if they will not,' said Gustav. 'We go regardless.'

Harald nodded, appeased.

'Good. Then you all know what to do.'

'What will you do, Lady Halla? Will you come with us?' Leif asked.

Halla looked up and shook her head. 'No, I will remain here with our people.'

'I should remain with you,' said Leif.

'No, Gustav will need every warrior we can give him.'

Leif was deeply uncomfortable, it was not his sworn duty to protect Halla, but he felt responsible after not being there to fight at Ragnvald's side on the day he had died. Keeping his widow safe was his way of atoning for what he saw as that failure. Halla smiled at him reassuringly. 'We have seen no threat here, and the enemy will be too busy with your raid to be searching a thousand miles of forest for this little village. And anyway, we have weapons, and those like me with the will to wield them. We will be quite safe. When you have captured our lands, you will send word and we will come to join you.'

'As you wish, Lady Halla. But I will not send word, I will come with a warband to escort you,' said Leif with a nod, and Halla gave him a genuine smile of appreciation.

'You will do the right thing, as you always do.'

Gustav straightened his old spine and addressed the room. 'Then everything is agreed. Go and prepare. Gather your warriors, get every man the best arms and armour we can manage, and prepare for the journey to Vatnsborð in five days. We may never return if we are successful, and we will certainly never return if we fail, so leave nothing we need behind. Everything can go in the ships.'

'You will lead us, Jarl Gustav?' asked Eric.

Gustav grinned and shook his head. 'Gods no, Gunnar will lead. But I am indeed coming. This is one raid I will not miss. If you are worried I will slow you down, you can leave me in the ships with the rest of the cargo.'

There was a ripple of quiet laughter at that and Gustav stepped forwards, embracing each man in turn, sharing some words of encouragement. There was more to being a leader than being a good battle commander, Leif mused, and Gustav was a man who bore the weight of it easily.

The day before they left for the raid, Gjaldir was watching Aeske as the boy built a pile of mud. Gjaldir did not know why the boy was building the pile of mud, or what its purpose was, or even why Aeske was enjoying it so much. But none of that mattered. Aeske was having riotous fun with his mudpile, and Gjaldir was content to sit in peace and watch over him, giving his mind space to consider what lay ahead.

As he sat there, a familiar hand was placed on his shoulder, and he looked up to see Brunhild smiling down at him. 'You do not need to watch him all the time.'

'No, but I enjoy it,' Gjaldir replied, as Aeske spotted his mother and waved at her to come and inspect his increasingly impressive pile of mud. Brunhild motioned at him to wait a moment and the boy looked downcast, but continued with his labours anyway.

'You are afraid you will not see him again,' tried Brunhild.

Gjaldir looked up at her, taken aback. 'No, that is not it.'

'You are leaving tomorrow, and from what I hear, you will not return.'

Gjaldir sighed. 'You are about to make the speech.'

'What speech?'

'The one where you explain our fates are not our own, that we can be separated at any time.'

'Well,' said Brunhild defensively, 'it is true. I do not know where you will go, and I do not know where I will go.'

Gjaldir stood and faced her. 'No, you have always said this, and you have always pretended it is wisdom. But it is not true, and it is nothing but fear. Fear that you must learn to reject.'

Brunhild's face darkened in anger and her lips pressed together in a way that told Gjaldir that a verbal thrashing was coming. But he held his hand up and shook his head firmly. 'No. Not this time. You are wrong to fear that fate can separate us at any moment. It might be true, but what does it matter? How many times has fate brought us together? How many times could it have separated us, killed one of us, and failed to do so?'

Brunhild opened her mouth to spit an angry reply but stopped and closed it reluctantly, huffing and looking away.

'I know why you feel powerless, and I know why you feel fear about what will happen, but cast it aside. We are not powerless, we are not simple slaves. If fate separates us, I will come and find you.'

'And what if you die?'

'Then I will have lived my life, however short, even if it is just this day, with you and Aeske. Not in fear, but in joy. Yes, one day one of us will die, or both of us, but I will not spend the moments or months or long years between now and that day in fear of it ending!' He grabbed her gently by both shoulders.

Brunhild snatched back a sob and shook her head, refusing to meet his eye. 'It is so easy for a warrior, a freeman, to speak like this. It is the woman who waits at home, who worries, who buries you when you return bloodless and cold. A slave even more than most.'

'You are not a slave here,' said Gjaldir with a shake of his head.

'No one has freed me. I am given tasks and am not treated as one of the wives and mothers. Nothing has changed, not really. You only want to believe it has.'

Gjaldir furrowed his brows and felt a pang of regret. In his eyes, he thought the bonds of slavery had loosened and dissolved in their new settlement. It seemed pointless to keep such distinctions, of slave and master, when they were all working together to survive.

But perhaps that was only in his eyes, and not those of the other warriors and free men.

'I am sorry. When I return, or when I find you, we will resolve that.'

'You are making promises you cannot keep,' said Brunhild with a shake of her head.

'I have always kept them before. I love you, and I love Aeske, and I will either return to you or I will die. That I swear. Nothing but death will keep me from you again, and I do not intend to die.'

Brunhild's expression softened for a moment and she looked away, shaking her head before leaning in to bury it in his shoulder. 'You are still a foolish boy who understands nothing,' she said, but there was no sting in her words, and Gjaldir chuckled softly.

'And that is why I must return to you, for without you, I am hopeless.'

There was a high-pitched shout of excitement from behind them, and Brunhild lifted her head off his shoulder to look around him. Gjaldir looked back too and found that Aeske had climbed his mudpile, and was triumphantly standing atop it. It was about half as high as he was, and slowly collapsing under the weight of its builder, but Aeske was beaming. Whatever he had hoped to accomplish, he had clearly done so, and Gjaldir smiled back at him.

'Jaldir, look!'

'I see you, Aeske.'

'Come here!'

Gjaldir looked down at Brunhild, who was wiping her face and trying to compose herself. 'Go to him, let him know how proud you are of his… What is he building?'

'I have no idea,' Gjaldir said with a shake of his head and a broad smile.

Brunhild giggled, a sweet noise that shoved a warm hand of joy deep into his chest, and she playfully shoved him away. 'Well, go and find out!'

Gjaldir raised his hands in capitulation and walked off towards Aeske, whose mudpile had stabilised into a sort of squashed lump like a pile of dough that was about to be kneaded, only much larger. 'Well done, Aeske,' said Gjaldir, holding his arms out and moving in to pluck the boy from his muddy stronghold and swing him around.

Aeske squealed in joy as he was swung around, muddy hands grasping at Gjaldir's forearms. Gjaldir put the boy down, who immediately dismantling his mudpile with double-handed scoops. Gjaldir had no idea why, but… well, it just really didn't matter.

Gjaldir did not sleep much that night. He lay in the furs with Brunhild's head on his chest, and Aeske curled up under his right arm. He had spent much of his life knowing what he thought he wanted, and constantly finding his mind changed. First as a young swordsmith he wanted to be a member of the Bremen cutlers' guild, to travel to the big cities and work there for rich noblemen; a dream that felt so long ago as to be ridiculous. Then, as a man of the Crusade, he had wanted nothing more than to return home to Minden and leave the war behind him.

Slavery had taken him so suddenly and so brutally, and all he had wanted after that was freedom. As the time in bondage had passed, his old desire to be a respected smith had returned, but he had achieved it, the maker of weapons for kings and legends, and found it was not enough. The success was dry and tasteless in his mouth. He had set his heart on becoming a sworn man of Jarl Ragnvald, to finally be in charge of his own destiny, not a tool of others.

That notion, even as he lay there, seemed so foolish and vain. Why had he ever thought a warrior had more control over his fate than a smith? No, the only thing all these shifting ambitions had taught him was that all that had ever truly mattered to him was the thing he had never had, and never tried to have until so recently: people he loved.

As he felt the gentle breathing of Brunhild on his chest, and the still warmth of Aeske curled at his side, Gjaldir knew with the joyous weight of certainty that he had finally found the only thing that would satisfy him, and could not shake the cold dread that they were once again to be parted.

Brunhild's words clawed at him. She was right, as she usually was. He was not in control of his own fate. He could make proud boasts about his intent, but he was still just a tool for other men, a warrior committed to a war he cared little about compared to the family alongside him.

It was in that night, the last before he left, that he decided that, assuming he survived this campaign, he would spend the rest of his life focused on the people around him, not the vanity of his own ambition. He had learned that an ambition met is an ambition lost. Once you have it, it is no longer there. Family, friends... they were the opposite. Once you had them, the joy of having them only grew. All he had to do was survive this last great raid, and keep his promise to return.

Those were the thoughts that clawed at him, whirling around in the dark, fearful recesses of his mind. Nor could he shake the thought of the stone, the fish, and Odin the caster of fates. Perhaps the message was for him, he was the caster. He needed to make his plans to keep this fragile, informal family, and guide and protect those plans as Odin would guide the stone.

He was still wrestling with those thoughts as the darkness finally took him into its depths.

# Chapter 29

# A Hird of Heroes

'GJALDIR.'

The voice came to him from the dream, ethereal and distant.

'Gjaldir!'

It was more urgent, closer. He searched around for the source in the darkness.

'Oh, get up you dozy bastard. It's time.'

Something patted him repeatedly on the face and he blinked his eyes open, the dreamworld fleeing in an instant, to reveal Eric Firebeard's grinning face.

'Ah, there you are. Thought you could sleep through the war, did you?'

'What?'

'Sun's up, and you aren't. Get your kit, we don't have long. We are marching out. If you haven't got time to eat, tough shit, that will teach you not to sleep so long.'

Gjaldir blinked and levered himself up, confused, looking left and right and finding that the furs beside him were empty. *Fuck.*

Eric left, he was already dressed and wearing his seax, and

Gjaldir looked around the achingly bright room for Brunhild, but did not see her. Annoyed and worried, he got to his feet. *I am not leaving for war again without seeing her.* He felt a mild state of panic. The previous year he had been plucked away to go south as a smith while Brunhild was out doing chores. He had not seen her for eleven months, returning to find she had given him up for dead, and nursing another man's child.

He struggled into his tunic and looked at his equipment. Fortunately, he had had the presence of mind to collect, clean and pile it the night before, and everything was there waiting for him. His hauberk and helmet, both taken from dead Christian soldiers, his axe, given by another warrior to replace the one Dengir had given him and he had then lost in battle, and Dengir's old shield and seax. His spear was leaning against the wall at the back.

Satisfied that he could grab it all and leave at a moment's notice, he went to the door to go and search for Brunhild, nearly bowling her over as she came through it the other way at the same time.

'Ah, you are awake.'

'You did not wake me?'

'No, you were dead to the world. What, did you think I was going to let you leave without telling me again?' She gave him a sly grin. 'So, I took Aeske to wash and I made you some food. Here.' She handed him a wooden bowl he had not noticed she was carrying. He took it and saw that it was full of thick mashed and boiled oats, berries mixed in, with a little honey on top. He smiled, it was a rare treat, he did not know where she would have got the honey from.

'I stole it,' she said with a wink.

'Thank you,' Gjaldir said with a grin. 'I won't tell.'

'You wouldn't dare.' He nodded and put his free arm around her, but his grin faded.

'We are leaving.'

'I know, I can see the warriors gathering, and you are slow.'

'I…' Gjaldir looked down at the warm meal she had made for him, and tried to control his emotions.

'Sometimes it is best to say nothing,' Brunhild whispered. She put a finger under his chin and raised it, so that she could look him straight in the eye. 'You have made your promise to me, stupid Christian, and I expect you to keep it.'

'I will. Of course I will.'

'Good.' Brunhild smiled, a smile that carried to her eyes, and drew little furrows in their corners. 'Now eat quickly, and go. Don't embarrass me by making it look like I delayed you.'

Brunhild kissed him forcibly on the cheek and moved past him, heading into the longhouse to continue about her day, as if nothing was changing, as if there was no risk they might never meet again.

Gjaldir took his meal and his equipment outside. He could not bear to sit there watching her.

'I was about to come and drag you here by your arsehairs,' said Eric when Gjaldir finally went to find his place with Gunnar's men. 'Harald said you weren't coming, that you didn't have the heart for it.'

'No, I didn't,' replied the confused-looking huskarl.

'Well, I knew you were thinking it. I could tell from your dour expression.'

'You are full of nonsense, Eric.'

'Maybe – it is true that you always look dour, so perhaps it was just that. Never mind, the great warsmith is here, and all will be well. We have many Christians to kill, so it is good that you will be there to sharpen my sword after I am done with them.'

'You will be sharpening your own sword,' said Gjaldir, shoving the grinning red-haired man away.

'He is accustomed to sharpening his own sword, what woman would have a man with a face like that?'

Eric looked around in genuine shock. 'Harald, did you make a joke?'

Harald said nothing, but Gjaldir saw the hint of a smile cross his thickly bearded face before he turned away.

Eric looked back at Gjaldir wide-eyed, the wind taken out of his banter by Harald's intervention. 'I have known Harald for a dozen years, and I swear by the gods, he has never told a joke.'

Gjaldir put his best serious face on and stepped over to Eric, leaning down slightly and nodding. 'He was not joking, you truly are terribly ugly.'

Eric guffawed and tried to slap him, but Gjaldir was ready and too fast, whipping his head back out of range with a laugh.

'Everyone here?' A voice interrupted their playing, and Gunnar strode into the group.

'Yes.'

'Good.' Gunnar looked around the loose circle, some forty or so seasoned warriors, mostly Norwegians, with a few strays like Gjaldir and Vidar among them. He nodded at them heavily. 'It is time. We will lead, in this march and in all things on this raid. Remember who you are, remember where we came from. We are warriors of Norway, men of Sigurd Magnusson, men will look to us for example, and we will not disappoint them. This will be a long, hard fight. But we will free these lands that are not our own, that our king died for, or we will fall. If any of you is not committed to that, disappear before we leave, and I will forget you ever existed.'

Gjaldir swallowed hard, feeling that Gunnar's sweeping eyes had settled on him as he spoke, accusing, probing. The gnarled old champion stared them all down, daring any to flinch. But no one spoke or moved.

Whatever Gunnar was hoping for, he appeared satisfied, or at least not disappointed, and he broke the silence.

'We will be split between two ships. Half with me and Jarl Gustav, half with Eric. We go now.' The group of warriors divided itself and Gjaldir found himself in Eric's band, and followed him down to the lake shore.

The seven ships were already filled with weapons, shields, spare equipment, food, water and all the other material of war. Now over three hundred warriors would pile into them, leaving them heavily laden and slow.

Before the sun was even two handspans above the trees, the seven ships were ready, full of warriors of Gustav's army and the men of Vatnsborð, waiting on the calm lake waters.

'Rest here, we will wait for the rest of the ships,' Eric called as the lead boat unloaded. They had been rowing downriver for two days, along the lakes and down the river. They had just come around a wide bend in the river, and the ships, heavily laden and undermanned, were spread out on the water, leaving Eric's crew to arrive at the night's camping site first.

The other ships came in one by one, and their crews disembarked, the men unloading what they needed to make camp. Gjaldir saw Leif's crew disembark and he nodded at the Svear warrior.

Leif passed him, giving him a nod and a smile, and walked over to where Eric stood. 'Have the scouts returned from Karlsgrind yet?' the Swedish warrior asked, and Eric shook his head.

'No, I expect them today, I was hoping it would be earlier, but if we continue to follow the river, they will find us.'

'Hmm.' Leif looked concerned. 'We need to know if the Christians have blocked the river again, before we get there.'

'Yes, it is possible we will need to stop soon and wait for news. When Gustav's ship arrives, I will speak to him.'

'Shall I send some men out, to watch the land around?'

Eric thought about it for a moment and shook his head. 'In these woods? What enemy would be here anyway?' Then he paused and held up a hand. 'For caution's sake, send a few. Don't let them go far, it would be easy to get lost.'

Leif nodded and went back to his men, picking some of his warriors and sending them out into the forest to keep watch.

Gjaldir sat down on the riverbank, watching the water swirl lazily by. The river was broadening here, there was a small lake just downstream, and then the channel narrowed again as it headed south. The thickly wooded far bank was dotted with side channels and marshes as the river split and pooled just before it reached the lake.

He rummaged through his rough bag and found some dried fish. For years he had hated the tough, stinking food the Norse loved so much. But now he tolerated it, it was incredibly convenient when raiding, although he preferred dried venison, which was harder to come by.

As he sat there, chewing on the fish, the last of their ships appeared around the bend and sighted them, the steersman in the first turning the ship in to come towards the riverbank. Behind that ship came Gustav's, bringing up the rear. They headed towards the crowded riverbank, and Gjaldir saw that Gunnar was standing in the prow.

Gjaldir paid them little attention as they rowed along the placid river, but he paused mid-chew as he heard something, faint and uncertain, but he thought it was a shout.

He looked around and saw that some other men had heard it too. 'What was that?' he said to a warrior near him, who looked up and shrugged, returning to fixing one of his shoes. Gjaldir stood, and heard the sound again, clearer this time. Other warriors were standing, and Gunnar was looking back from the boat.

As Gjaldir stood there, straining to hear the sound again, he turned his left ear in the direction of the noise and his eyes were resting on the far bank, on an inlet to one of the heavily forested side channels. And he was still absently watching it when the first ship appeared from behind the foliage, rowing quietly, packed to the brim with soldiers.

Gjaldir did not react for a moment, too stunned to understand, and he was about to shout out in alarm when another man beside him beat him to it. 'CHRISTIANS!' roared the warrior who had been fixing a shoe, dropping it to the ground and pointing an accusing finger.

The bank of the river erupted in a maelstrom as resting warriors grabbed at weapons and jumped to their feet. There were more shouts and confusion as a second ship appeared, and then a third and a fourth, racing down the last section of the branch of the river and angling straight towards the two heavily laden Norse ships in the river.

'No,' said the warrior next to him in a defeated voice. Gjaldir shared his horror. The first enemy ship was only moments away from reaching the first of their ships, where the unprepared crew was in panic, torn between trying to row to the bank, and arming themselves to defend their vessel.

There was chaos in the river as the Christian boats, swift and fully manned, set upon the Norse transports like wolves onto newborn lambs.

The small Norse army on the bank were shouting and cursing but there was little they could do, fifty feet of deep water separating them from the one-sided battle unfolding in the river. Gjaldir stood there downcast, watching in silence as the first two enemy boats boarded the first Norse ship even as it tried desperately to make it to shore. The crew, mostly unarmoured and at their oars, were slaughtered by the rushing wave of boarders, drawing cries of fury and outrage and animal anger from those watching from the shore.

Men were already starting to man one of the ships that had been drawn up near the shore, rushing to go to the aid of the ships on the water. Then Gjaldir saw that Gunnar was urging his crew to abandon their oars and arm themselves, realising they wouldn't make the bank in time, and not wanting to be caught unarmed and unprepared.

'Archers! Anyone with a bow with me!' he heard someone shout and turned to see Eric Firebeard bending a bow, sending a shaft lancing down towards one of the Christian ships, and saw it thud into a shield. Then another man was loosing arrows, and another, and soon there was a steady hail of shafts raining down on the Christian ships, with a few thrown spears too, that checked the enthusiasm of the Christian attack, even as Gustav's ship drifted towards them with two Christian ships closing in to cut it off.

Gjaldir saw Gunnar standing in the bow, shield up, sword in hand, ready to defend his ship as the first Christian ship arrived. Gjaldir felt a burst of admiration for the man. Gunnar led his men from wherever the fighting was hardest.

As they watched Gunnar's ship close with the enemy, and as the Christians tried to shelter from the withering flurry of projectiles under their shields, Gjaldir heard a piercing cry of alarm from behind him, and a hundred heads in the disorganised mass on the riverbank whipped round to see what was happening.

A Norse warrior staggered through the treeline, just a few dozen paces away, emerging over the rise that marked the edge of the first, and concealed what lay beyond. The man stumbled over the crest and fell to one knee, struggling to rise, one arm hanging uselessly at his side, clutched by the other. He raised his one good arm and pointed behind him. 'Christians, they are here!'

Gjaldir scanned the crest as the wounded man staggered down the gentle slope, shouting and pointing, and he saw the first speartips and helmets appear, all along the crest, a forest of them against the true forest behind. And he felt his guts loosen and his heart flutter.

'SHIELDWALL!' someone screamed, and hundreds of Norsemen leapt into action, shaking themselves out of the shock that had frozen them in place. The different groups of the Norse rushed to form a wall, mixed up and split from their leaders, simply putting themselves in the line wherever they could as the solid ranks of the enemy surged off the crest and stopped as they saw their opponents.

'Odin protect us,' muttered the man next to Gjaldir as they saw the sheer number of enemy who were appearing over the crest. Then the enemy let out a great cheer, a raucous, excited, confident roar that perhaps only Gjaldir among the Norse understood. 'DEUS LE VULT!' roared the Crusaders, and then they came down the slope at a run.

It was too fast, too sudden, too unexpected, and the mixed Norse warbands, some in the process of manning the ships to join the fight in the river, had not even formed a single wall when the enemy attack crashed into them. Bands of warriors, large and small, stood together as best they could as the wave of Crusaders swept down the gentle slope and crashed over the mess of Norse defenders.

Gjaldir, in one of the largest groups, watched in horror as a solid block of white surcoated Crusaders crushed the first half-hearted attempt to stop them, scattering warriors in their path. At the head of the enemy formation a huge white banner was flying proud, the golden cross emblazoned upon it, the gold twinkling in the sun.

At the foot of the banner, a knight shouted orders, his sword raised and pointed at the sky over the Norse as his men cheered and the formation rumbled over the congealing forces of the Norse.

Then the enemy hit the wall in front of him, and the world turned to the thunder of battle as the Norse veterans met the advancing enemy head on.

Gjaldir put his spear overhand and jabbed it over the heads of the wall in front of him, bouncing the tip off a helmet and then swearing as someone grabbed the shaft and tore it out of his hand before he could react. He was too shocked and afraid, he had not been holding the shaft well enough, his jab had been weak and poorly timed, and now the weapon was gone.

He fumbled his axe from his belt but in the third rank, there was nothing he could do with it, so he simply set his shield against the back of the man in front and supported him with it, leaning in and taking the pressure of the enemy trying to push them back.

And push them back they did. The enemy had greater numbers, and they were attacking downhill. The Norse line was compressed down towards the river's edge, the ground getting less favourable as they went. Gjaldir's feet were on dry grass, and then stony foreshore, and then sand and pebbles. He looked around in panic, straining with all his considerable strength but helpless to stop the inexorable advance.

In a few moments, the Norse would be pushed back into the river, and it would be a slaughter.

Gjaldir looked to his left and saw that Gustav's ship, forgotten and alone, was in desperate trouble. Two enemy ships had put themselves alongside in the centre of the river, and dozens of Christian soldiers were fighting their way on board. He saw Gustav standing in the bow, shouting orders and imploring the few men who still had oars to pole the ship back to the bank, sticking the oar handles into the bottom and trying to drag the whole mess of ships to shore.

He looked to his right and saw another two Christian ships rowing for the bank where he stood, a hundred excited men lining their sides, ready to jump down into the back of the Norse formation. He knew with sudden certainty that the battle was already lost, and that when those ships arrived, the slaughter would be appalling.

He was not the only one to realise it. 'LEFT! PUSH LEFT, AWAY FROM THE SHORE!' Someone he did not know was shouting at the line, cajoling, physically shoving men left, towards where another large group of Norsemen were fighting their own battle, more successfully, further down the bank.

Gjaldir was indecisive, unwilling to abandon the heavily engaged man to his front, but a hand grabbed him and yanked him back and he saw Harald's thick black beard as the man grunted and pushed. 'Go, stupid boy. Go!'

He and Harald ran down the back of the collapsing line, grabbing and shoving at others, trying to save who they could. The first enemy ship arrived just beside them and armed soldiers splashed down into the shallows, and the attempt at retreat became a rout.

Gjaldir fended off an attack with his shield, not daring to stop running, dozens of other Norsemen running around him, all cohesion gone. Men were being cut down like standing wheat as the shieldwall disintegrated and every warrior fought to the death or fled for his life.

Gjaldir heard a low, keening wail of fear, and it was a few moments before he realised it was coming from himself and slammed his mouth shut, only to have to open it again to suck in a great lungful of air. Harald was still at his side until he wasn't, the black-haired man simply disappeared from his vision and he could not stop to look back.

Gjaldir muscled himself past a knot of whirling, struggling men, the two sides entwined in vicious and merciless combat, and he saw an opportunity to put his axe into the back of a white surcoated Christian's head, ripping the weapon free of his victim with the momentum of his passing, never slowing his run, hoping the man he had saved would follow him.

Then he was clear, other men running around him, as they sprinted towards the perceived safety of the main Norse line.

Gjaldir saw Leif at the back shouting orders and gathering the arriving survivors, forming them to face the direction they had come from, to guard the flank from the victorious enemy that would surely soon follow.

Gjaldir found himself once again at the back of the line and looked out over the water, seeing that the fight on Gustav's ship was coming to its end. The attempt to get the ship to shore had failed, just a couple of dozen paces from the bank, and Gjaldir saw the desperate combat inside the boat as the Norse were backed into the bow. He saw Gunnar and Vidar fighting side by side, and even Jarl Gustav hacking at the Christians with his sword.

Gjaldir jogged over to Leif and grabbed him by the shoulder, the huskarl turning with wild eyes to look at him. 'What?'

'Gustav, Gunnar!'

Leif's face contorted with pain as he looked out over the water. 'There is nothing we can do for them.'

Gjaldir shook his head and looked at the fight on the water again. *No, not Gunnar. The man cannot be killed.* Even as he watched, the first desperate Norseman jumped over the side, sinking like a stone in his maille. He saw Gustav hacking at a shielded soldier, but the old jarl could do nothing about the return blow other than raise his famous mangled hand in desperation.

The Christian sword cut through Gustav's forearm and bit deeply into his bicep, and Gjaldir could hear the jarl's howl of pain and fury even from the shore. He thought the jarl would fall, but somehow, with the enemy's sword stuck in his arm, the jarl found the strength to jam his own blade into the Christian's face, letting go of it as the enemy slumped dead to the deck. Gustav reeled back out of the fight, clutching his twice-ruined arm to his chest.

Gjaldir heard the sounds of renewed combat behind him but he ignored it, transfixed by the fight on the boat, by the sight of Gunnar and Vidar and half a dozen men making their stand in the bow, their blades bright and terrible, reaping the limbs and lives of the throng of enemy who came at them with too much bloodlust, and too little caution.

Gunnar was a god of war in the prow of that ship, an immovable barricade in a collapsing wall, and Gjaldir watched in awe as the old warrior worked with controlled precision. The enemies' advance along the narrow ship was choked with the bodies of dead Norsemen and their own soldiers, and for a moment a space cleared in front of Gunnar. The king's champion looked around him, seeing how few men remained, and saw Gustav slumped at the back, holding his arm.

Gunnar shouted something to his men, and then dropped his

shield, raising a hand to rip his helmet from his head as Gjaldir looked on in confusion. The huskarl leaned back and raised his sword, whipping his hand forward and flinging it at the shore where it thumped into the sand just a few paces from where Gjaldir was standing.

His confusion was allayed when Gunnar bent down into the boat and hauled Gustav to his feet, urging the wounded jarl over the side, half dumping him into the water and then jumping in alongside him. Gjaldir was rooted to the spot as he saw both men struggling against the weight of their hauberks, even without helmets and weapons. And then Gustav slipped below the water.

Gjaldir burst into action, dropping his axe and shield where he stood, ignoring the combat around him on the shore, and ran into the water, pounding through it until it reached his armpits and reaching out to where Gunnar was sputtering and struggling, desperately trying to drag Gustav's submerged body into the shallows.

Just as it looked as if Gunnar would go under with his jarl, Gjaldir managed to reach the two men, his feet barely on the bottom, his panic rising with the water as it lapped at his chin. He grabbed an arm and hauled on it, backing up with his feet, scrabbling at the bottom, his head going under several times as he dragged whoever he was holding towards the shore.

They got into the shallower water and Gjaldir risked a look back, seeing that the fight on the ship was ending, and the few last men were making their own jumps into the river, or staying to die on the deck.

He was up to his armpits now, and powering towards the shore, dragging the exhausted men behind him until they too got their feet underneath them.

Gustav was still alive, breathing in ragged, shallow, pain-filled breaths, and Gunnar gave Gjaldir a single thump of thanks on the back, and powered on up the slope for dry land, Gjaldir in his wake.

The escape of Gustav and Gunnar was a temporary relief at

best. The fight on the riverbank was a losing one, the numbers of the enemy too high, and the combatants had almost reached the place where Gjaldir was re-emerging out of the water. Gunnar managed to snatch his sword from the sand and headed off down the bank with Gustav, but Gjaldir could see his shield and axe were practically underneath the feet of the men still fighting.

Armed only with his seax, Gjaldir felt naked, and weighed his options. There were no discarded weapons to pick up, the Norse were being pushed back, and everything that fell to the ground, human or weapon, belonged to the Christians now.

Gritting his teeth, and unwilling to abandon his weapons, Gjaldir warily made his way towards the disintegrating wall, seax in hand.

He reached his weapons just as the fight fragmented into a vicious melee, and within a heartbeat of recovering his shield he was using it to defend himself against two enemies. His axe was gone, unreachable in the madness, and he jabbed with the seax and covered with the shield as he backed up, unable to touch the two men who were trying to crowd him in, spreading out with their longer weapons to get around his shield.

He was running out of room to retreat, and facing the choice of going back into the river, or trying a desperate attack to try to kill one enemy before the other got him, as Gunnar had taught them.

He was still in his maille, and knew he would not survive more than a few moments in the water, so he gritted his teeth and planted his back foot, ready to make a desperate attack.

The lunge failed before he launched it, and he knew it. The man he chose saw it coming, and stepped to the side, cutting at him with his sword. Gjaldir stumbled and ducked, all he had achieved was putting himself directly between two enemy, and he knew he was a dead man.

He shouted in fear and anger and drove forwards, trying to escape the unseen blade that he knew would be coming for his back, and he tangled with the soldier to his front, wildly stabbing with his seax, both men falling to the ground in a jumble of shields and blades and bodies. Gjaldir roared and struggled to wriggle his seax into his opponent, even as he attempted to roll the Christian on top of him, a desperate ploy to put his enemy between himself and the second soldier's blade.

He had no concept what he would do if this worked, if he managed to kill the enemy he was wrestling with and was left lying under his corpse. It was laughable, the other enemy would pick him off with ease. But it was a plan of sheer desperation, with no time to think it through.

Gjaldir got his surprised enemy on top of him and the soldier came up looking confused, suddenly straddling the Norse warrior. Gjaldir's plan fell apart further when the Christian managed to trap Gjaldir's seax under his shield, and then Gjaldir was helpless, disarmed, and staring up at the Christian as he brought his sword around to finish the fight.

He never had the chance. The air above the doomed Gjaldir was suddenly full of the body and fury of Eric Firebeard, who stepped into the enemy straddling Gjaldir and chopped off the top of his head with a brutal axe swing. The lolling, lifeless body collapsed down onto Gjaldir, the limp limbs freeing his seax, but the dead weight thumping down on his chest and fouling him.

Eric roared and pushed forwards, thumping into the second soldier and taking just a moment to shout at Gjaldir as he cleared space, 'GET UP!'

Gjaldir bodily rolled the corpse off, scrabbling to collect his shield as he levered himself to his feet. He was faced with a confusing whirl of action as he rose. Eric was still duelling the second soldier to his right, while on his left he saw that the second shield-wall was collapsing from the flank, one file at a time being ripped apart as the victorious Crusaders rolled around the edge. Their focus on that fight was the only thing keeping Eric and him alive, they were now almost behind the enemy line.

Eric finished his opponent and turned as several more came at them. 'Fucking run!' the red-haired huskarl wheezed, and Gjaldir didn't need any more encouragement, turning to get back to what remained of their force even as his legs and lungs screamed in protest. Eric was struggling too, gasping and staggering, and Gjaldir grabbed a handful of the man's sleeve and helped drag him along.

They pounded, unnoticed, past several Christians, who either didn't notice them coming from behind, or saw them too late, and finally they reached the ongoing battle, simply battering their way through a gap, Gjaldir taking a thumping blow to his ribs and a painful cut to his arm before they were back with their own warriors.

Eric gurgled and coughed and Gjaldir desperately sucked air into his own lungs, bending over and putting the edge of his shield in the ground, leaning on it while he tried to get his breath back. He looked up to see Bjorn, blood closing one of his eyes, helping another one of Gunnar's men back, dragging a ruined leg behind him.

'Bjorn!' Gjaldir called, seeing the warrior look up.

'We must go!' Bjorn started running towards them, waving agitatedly.

'Eric, come, it's Bjorn.' Gjaldir was still clinging to Eric, party to help, partly for his own support. But when he tried to go to Bjorn, Eric did not move. He turned to look at the huskarl just as Eric's legs started giving out. 'Eric!' he exclaimed, as the man stumbled and sank down against his chest.

Gjaldir half caught him and the Firebeard raised his head groggily, eyes unfocused and vague. 'My debt is paid,' slurred Eric, and Gjaldir let the man rock back onto his knees in confusion, and then saw that blood covered the side of Eric's neck, where the big man's hand was clamped to his skin, blood pulsing through his fingers and running in streams down into his maille.

'No, no, Eric,' Gjaldir moaned, but the Firebeard did not answer him. His eyes were rolling and his hand fell away from his neck, revealing a deep gash and a violent spurt of blood.

'Gjaldir, come, now! He's gone, Gjaldir. We must flee!' Gjaldir just stared at the dying man's face and his face twisted in agony as his friend's last lifeblood pumped from his opened neck. A hand grabbed his shoulder and wrenched him round. 'GJALDIR!' Bjorn shouted in his face, his own bloodied features twisted in grief. 'We must go, NOW!'

'He died for me,' Gjaldir choked, the strength gone from his mind and his limbs.

'Then don't disgrace him by joining him!' Bjorn shoved an arm under Gjaldir's and hauled, trying to lever the bigger man to his feet. Gjaldir might have stayed there on the ground, ready to give up, if it was not for that thought. He could not let Eric have died for nothing.

He forced his legs to straighten, and let Bjorn help him as they ran, along the back of the fight, where the last remnants of Gustav's army were dying in droves. There was no chance for them all to flee, no help that could come, and the men of the North stood and died in their crumbling ranks as a few dozen of their comrades fought their way clear with their jarl, Gjaldir's mind fading into a fog of shock and grief as strong arms guided him away.

## Chapter 30

# A Precious Few

LEIF SPAT BLOOD onto the ground and tried to fight back the feeling of nausea that threatened to overcome him. He held onto the small tree and just stared at the ground, trying to clear his mind.

He did not know how long they had run for, or when the Christians had stopped pursuing. He was not sure they had, in fact, stopped pursuing. That fear had driven them on until they could not go on anymore. Exhausted warriors were dropping to the ground all around him, Leif even saw Gunnar slump onto the grass after calling for the halt, heaving and coughing.

He swept his eyes over the exhausted warriors and could count no more than fifty men. Very few of the men around him were seriously wounded. The wounded had fallen behind quickly and no one had been able to carry them. Those that stopped to help had fallen behind into the grasp of the enemy.

Gustav had been an exception. The old jarl had been half dragged and half carried, a monumental effort by a dozen warriors taking turns. But the old man was as pale as a sheet, propped up against the tree beside Gunnar while another man tried again to re-bandage his mangled arm.

Leif staggered over to the two men, and Gunnar looked up with a desperate and drawn face, and gave him a slight shake of the head. Leif nodded sadly and lowered himself to the ground, seeing that Gustav was muttering and shaking, his eyes half closed, pupils unfocused. Leif grabbed the jarl's remaining hand and the fingers did not even try to press back against his.

'He is going, it will not be long,' said Gunnar with a pained voice.

Leif nodded, there was nothing else to say. Both of them had seen enough men bleed to death to recognise it. Gustav's mind was slipping away, and his body would follow soon after.

'We need to keep going,' said Bjorn, who came to crouch down beside them.

'I don't think we can,' replied Leif, looking around him. 'Most of these men would probably rather die than rise again. We need rest, I think the Christians stopped chasing long ago.'

'They will come, they always do. They will probably be ahead of us already, on the river.'

Leif and Bjorn looked at each other for a moment, the same realisation dawning on them. 'They might go to the village,' said Leif. 'Shit, where is Knud?'

'Dead, I think, but some of his men are over there.' Bjorn pointed to where a huddle of Vatnsborð warriors were gathered. Leif walked quickly over, his legs burning in protest, and he tried as quietly as possible to catch one of their eyes. One of the warriors looked up, Leif recognised him as Bekkr, and the man looked at him wearily and nodded, saying something to his men and coming to join Leif.

'I'm sorry, I'm sorry we led you into this disaster.'

Bekkr nodded slowly, his eyes bitter and distant. 'It was not your doing, we agreed to this, Knud believed in it.'

'I am still sorry, but it is not over.'

The warrior laughed bitterly. 'It is very much over, my friend.'

'No, I mean it is clear they knew we were coming, this ambush was no accident. And if they knew we were coming, they know where we were coming from.'

Bekkr tensed and looked up at Leif with renewed concern, and then his mouth curled in anger. 'I had not thought of it, but you are right. They could be in Vatnsborð the day after tomorrow, if they row hard.'

'How quickly can we get back?'

The Vatnsborð man swore bitterly. 'The day after that, if it was a few fast men, travelling alone. This ragged band? Four days?'

'Well, we must try, if the Christians wait a day, we could still get there first.'

'My people know what to do. We have a place to hide.'

'But will they have time?'

Bekkr looked at him and sighed. 'They will not have long. The men who would normally be watching the lake for ships are dead or here.'

'They we must try.'

'Yes, we will send our fastest to warn them.' He went back to his small group and there was a rapid conversation, and two men nodded, dumping what little equipment they had left, and set off without looking back.

Leif went back to Gustav and found Gunnar sitting with his head in his hands. Gustav was motionless, his chest still, his mouth sagging and open. It was over. Leif crouched down and put a hand gently on Gunnar's shoulder. 'I am sorry, but we must continue. We must get back to our people before the Christians do.'

Gunnar didn't move, didn't react, he just held his face in his hands and slowly breathed in and out. Finally, he leant his head back and dipped his chin just once, before dragging himself to his feet, and started collecting the tiny group of his Norwegians that still lived. Half of Gunnar's warband had been on Gustav's ship, and Leif doubted any of them had survived to reach the shore.

Leif moved among the rest of the men, quietly rousing them, pleading and imploring, trying to ignore the shattered expressions, the hollow eyes. He came across Gjaldir, flat on his back staring at the sky, and felt a small burst of pleasure that the man was still alive, a tiny mercy amongst the horror. 'Gjaldir, we must go.'

The big man's eyes drifted slowly over to meet his and he sighed, levering himself up. 'We are going back home?'

'Yes.'

'Good.' Gjaldir got to his feet and looked at him expectantly. 'Now?'

Leif smiled and patted the younger man on the shoulder, moving on to the next.

It was a fine autumn morning in their new village as Halla sat in a loose circle with a number of the older women, each occupied with repairs and restitching of various clothes and items of leatherwork. Halla squinted in the bright early light as she worked the bone needle into the hole in the tough leather. It was freshly tanned and strong, but her fingers were stronger, and she got the bone and its twine follower through the hole and pulled the slack until the twine was tight, crossing over the previous strand and going back towards the previous hole.

Perhaps other leaders would have had someone else make her a new pair of shoes, but she had the skills, and without the men in the village, everyone was busy. While the old women sat in their circle and gossiped and worked, the younger women were busy in the fields and forest, or fishing on the lake. So Halla made sure she was seen to help with many of the daily tasks even as she stayed in or around her house, being there so that her people knew where to find her, and could come to her with questions or problems.

She heard footsteps approaching and saw a small group of

women and thralls approach, with several children in tow. Apart from their repairs, the older women would keep watch over the younger children while their mothers went out and worked. There were few enough children in the settlement anyway, and it was not a heavy burden.

Her thrall, Brunhild, shuffled her son Aeske over to leave him with Alda and crouched down to give him a reassuring smile and a kiss on the head. Halla watched as Brunhild turned to leave, and the child promptly tottered after her, evading the outstretched hand of the woman.

Halla watched as the boy called after his mother and Brunhild stopped and tutted in annoyance, turning the boy around when he reached her and then pointing him at the older woman again. The boy shook his head and clung to her leg, burying his face in her skin.

Halla waved at the thrall. 'Brunhild, bring him to me.' She did not expect Alda would have much success containing the boy.

Brunhild nodded and picked the boy up, carrying him over, looking flustered and embarrassed.

Halla smiled reassuringly. 'Leave him with me, I have nearly finished with this, I will ensure he is well looked after.'

'Lady Halla, there is no need, I don't want him to disturb you.'

'It is no trouble. I am not very good with a needle anyway, I welcome the distraction. Where are you going?'

Brunhild looked at the two other women behind her. 'We need to collect firewood for our house.'

'Good, they need help in the vegetable garden too, once you finish.' Brunhild accepted the new task without a hint of complaint or disappointment. A lifetime as a thrall and a hard year in this new village did not make for slaves who openly resented work.

'Yes, Lady Halla,' said Brunhild respectfully, gently pushing her reluctant son towards the older woman.

Halla considered, as she often did, the promise she had once made to Brunhild, that she would one day be freed for her part in saving Halla's life during the treacherous attack by the warriors of Tora Hansdottir, the widow of Jarl Birkir, while they were guests in her home.

But those events were still a secret that she would take to her grave. She would never allow anyone to know that one of those warriors had nearly forced himself onto her, never bear the shame of her people whispering about what had happened. She would free Brunhild, as she had promised, but to do so now would only cause trouble with the other thralls in the village. It would appear to be grossly unfair to free one without an obvious reason and leave the others in servitude.

So she contented herself for now with treating Brunhild as kindly as she could, and looking after her child for the morning might assuage the quiet prickling of her guilt.

Halla picked Aeske up with hands under his armpits, marvelling at how heavy the boy was considering how small he seemed, and the child looked back nervously at his mother. 'Modir?' He reached out a hand, questioningly, imploringly.

'I will come back, Aeske. Stay here with Halla,' Brunhild said with a reassuring smile at her son.

Aeske did not seem at all convinced, and he wriggled in Halla's grip. Halla bounced him on her knee a bit and put one arm around his chest, reaching back with the other and untying the red strip of silk that bound her hair into a loose knot. It was one of a handful she had cut from a richly decorated but quite useless dress her husband Ragnvald had brought back from one of his raids. The dress might have been very valuable to some Christian lord's wife, but to her it had just been material for using in other ways. After her husband's death, she had kept it as a memento, one of the few things she still had that Ragnvald had given her, the rest lost to time and the Crusaders.

She held the strip out in front of Aeske, dangling it and waving it slightly. The hand that had been reaching out to his mother stopped as the boy considered the brightly coloured ribbon of material, then the boy grabbed at it, turning it over in his hand as he examined it, and relaxing as it distracted him.

Halla gave Brunhild a knowing look and the young thrall nodded happily and turned away, escaping while her son was preoccupied with his new toy. Aeske giggled to himself as he waved the red ribbon around, fascinated as it fluttered in the air, his shyness instantly forgotten. Halla let him play like that for a while, then gently put him on the ground beside her, watching to ensure he would settle as he played, and went back to her shoe repair.

Halla was nearly finished on the shoe, a process slowed considerably by constantly having to restrain or redirect the adventurous child, when there were running footsteps and one of the village's women came around the corner of the house.

'They have returned!' called out the woman breathlessly, and Halla looked around in confusion.

'What?'

'They have returned, our men have come back. The ships are coming down the lake.'

There were joyous comments from the women around her but Halla understood the implications and was deeply alarmed. If they had already returned, something had gone deeply wrong.

'Who, how many?'

'All of them, I think? We were washing clothes in the lake and we saw them coming. I ran straight to tell you.' The woman looked pleased with herself. 'I thought you should know immediately.'

Halla tensed, a prickle of fear growing in her chest. 'My girl, how do you know they were our ships?'

The woman's smile faded and she shook her head. 'Who else could they be?'

Halla stood and looked around. The women in the circle

looked at her, confused. Halla could not decide what to do. She desperately hoped that the girl was right, that this was indeed her own people returning early, or perhaps a small band of them.

She picked Aeske up and hurried over to put him in Alda's lap.

'Stay here, ladies,' she said to the group.

She hurried down through the village towards the lake shore, seeing the rest of the people going about their days. She considered calling out to them, telling them to arm or run, but what use was a panic if it turned out it was her people? And if it was so many ships of the enemy, what use was arming the old men and boys?

She pushed the fear aside. There was no reason to believe it was the enemy. They passed the last row of longhouses and reached the edge of the settlement, where she could see onto the lake. She stopped, peering out over the water, trying to see anything, but seeing nothing. The trees between their village and Vatnsborð obscured that part of the water.

Halla chewed her lip in indecision and then ran to the thin screen of trees, through the new vegetable gardens and ignoring the confused looks of those working there. She got through the trees and into the old village, finding other people relaying the news of the ships and heading down to the shore. There was a sense of nervousness in the air here.

She had just got through the last line of houses, into the area of the fish-drying racks and slipways for the small fishing boats, when she heard the shout from ahead of her.

'CHRISTIANS!'

Halla felt the word as a punch of panic, and her knees wobbled as she looked out at the approaching ships and began to make out the first details. They were indistinguishable from their own ships to her eyes, longships, but the number was wrong, there were too many, and she could make out the details of the men standing in them now.

Halla had never laid eyes on their enemy, but she saw their

shields were not round, and that they wore tunics of some sort over their maille, many of them white. She had never seen a Norseman do that.

Halla looked around in shock as the village burst into activity. Then she turned to run back to her people.

She ran back through the trees and into the vegetable gardens, waving and shouting at the people working them. One of them ran over in confusion. 'What is it?'

Halla grabbed the girl. 'Run through the village, warn everyone you see. Tell them to run for the eastern woods. The Christians are here. Go!'

Halla did not pause to see if the girl understood, they only had moments. She turned and dashed through the longhouses, screaming the warning at the top of her voice. But the sound of the Crusaders' warcries sounded behind her as their first ships reached the shore, and confused and terrified people were already dropping their tools, spilling from houses, or already starting to run.

Some ran away from the terrible sound. She passed two old men, armed with a pair of spears, grim-faced and pale, running the opposite way, towards the oncoming enemy. She did not even have time to share a word with them as they ran to the hopeless task of facing the Crusader invasion, but she hoped they could give others time to flee.

'What is it? What is happening?' said one of the women she passed.

'An attack, take everyone you can and go to the woods!' said Halla, stopping only long enough to say it, before running off again. She was breathless now, and she could hear the sounds of fighting from the few of their people who had the time and courage to put up a futile fight on the shore in Vatnsborð. Then a pair of ships came past the trees and rammed their bows into the stony shore among her own people's houses, and suddenly the enemy were among them. There were shouts of terror and panic, and also the hideous sounds of the terrified and dying, as the Christians caught up with those who had not fled fast enough.

Halla saw a stream of her people running for their lives away from the sound of the fighting and angled to go and join them. Some were clinging to possessions or weapons and one had a child in her arms. *Oh, no.* Halla stopped in her tracks, remembering Aeske.

She looked around towards where her house was, towards the north of the village, not yet reached by the enemy, and set off as fast as her burning legs and lungs would carry her. She ran past people going the other way, ignored shouted questions and cries for help. The village had descended into chaos, and she knew it was too late to do anything but save whoever could be saved, and she was not going to leave Aeske to the Christians.

She reached her house and found the abandoned remains of the circle where the women had been sitting, half-finished clothes scattered around. She looked around in panic, trying to see where they had gone, and saw that the door to the house was closed. She ran over and hammered on it. 'Let me in!' she shouted in a voice that cracked as she spoke.

There was the sound of the locking bar being pulled back and she shoved her way in, seeing the frightened face of Alda and then peering beyond her, seeing a dozen more. 'No, no, no. No, you must run, now! You cannot hide here.'

Alda looked around. 'Most of us can't run anywhere, lady.' Halla cursed and looked around the room.

'Where is the boy? Where is Aeske?'

A woman stepped through the huddle, Aeske held in her arms, looking utterly unworried, the red silk still wrapped in his fingers.

'Oh, thank the gods. Here, give him to me.' Halla rushed over and took the boy, holding him tight to her chest, and then looked around desperately.

'Those of you who can, run with me, now. East, into the woods. Those who cannot, I'm sorry.'

There was no time for anything more, Halla fought back a sob as she turned to leave, and Alda pressed an unsheathed seax into her head. 'You will need it, lady. Go.'

Halla mumbled her thanks and headed for the door, seax in one hand and Aeske clutched tightly to her chest with the other.

A few of the women followed her out, and then the door behind them slammed shut. 'This way!' she said, pointing with the knife and heading down the path that led eastwards. But no sooner had she said that than she saw armed men appear in a gap between the houses to their right, and the flight became a panic as each of them ran for their lives.

Halla ran for the gap in the buildings to the east, the child slowing her down as two other women got in front of her. As the first reached the building, a soldier appeared in the gap, shouting triumphantly as he saw them, and bodily checked the first terrified woman, smashing her to the ground and then darting after the second.

Halla pivoted and turned left, running along the back of the house and then between two storage huts, hearing the screams of her companions behind her but losing sight of them and their pursuers.

She passed another row of the turf-covered houses, passing a sheep pen and the haybarn, briefly pausing at the edge of it, looking both ways to see what she could see. On her right, to the east, she could see some of her people disappearing into the trees past their meagre fields, but she could see the backs of armoured men pursuing them.

She swore and huffed as she tried to regain her breath, knowing she couldn't follow them. She looked north, to where the treeline stood fifty paces away, she saw a few figures fleeing into it, but no enemy. Gathering her courage and looking around again, she broke from cover and started running towards the trees.

She didn't look back as she ran, not until she reached the first fir, staggering behind it to put it between her and the village, hiding her slim frame behind its trunk as she peered back. She watched as stragglers of her people were cut down by the rampaging Christians, tears of anger and loss rolling down her cheeks as she heard the screams of those who had been caught.

Then she saw a half-dozen of the invaders appear at the edge of the village, scanning the trees. Halla tensed and tried to shrink behind the trunk, hoping she could not be seen. For a while she stayed there, quietly whispering to Aeske to keep him calm, but a young boy, perhaps in his teens, who had been lying behind a fallen trunk a dozen paces from her panicked and stood up to run, and the soldiers shouted and gave chase.

Halla cursed and turned away, heading into the forest as Aeske started crying. She couldn't calm him and run at the same time, and her fear started to build as she heard the sounds of crunching undergrowth and crashing branches in the woods behind her growing closer. She could have left the boy and escaped. But Halla barely considered it, brushing the selfish urge away. She had failed, she had failed to protect her people, failed to act when this attack seemed obvious, failed to save them. If she could save this one boy, perhaps it would wash a little of that stain of shame away, perhaps it would settle a little of her debt to Aeske's mother.

So on she went, trying to manage the burden of the terrified child even as her body flagged. She splashed through a small stream and pushed through a bush beyond it, the branches lashing at her and Aeske, causing him to cry even harder in pain and fear, and she heard a foreigner's shout behind her, perilously close.

She risked a look back and saw two armed men reach the stream behind her and jump it, coming for her, panting and flagging, but catching her all the same. The last of the strength in her legs was flowing away, even as she willed them to continue, and her lungs burned like a hearthfire in winter. She passed a thick stand of trees, putting them between her and the enemy, and dropped to her knees, letting go of the seax and trying to put a hand over

Aeske's mouth even as he struggled and wailed, desperately trying to quieten him. 'Aeske, please, shuushh.'

The boy wriggled and protested but her hand stifled the noise as she crouched in her improvised hiding place and she kept her eyes locked with his, cooing and shushing him as he finally started to calm down, his little fingers wrapped tightly around the red silk strip.

'Good boy, be quiet. Good,' Halla whispered.

She tensed as the sound of crunching undergrowth came closer, and she heard a man speak, just the other side of the trees, perhaps a dozen paces away.

She held her breath and shrank into the cover of the bush as the sounds got closer, and then a man appeared through the foliage, sword pushing a branch aside.

The man's eyes locked with hers and he smiled, a voracious, terrible smile.

'No, no. Gods be merciful, no.'

The man whistled for his companion and advanced on Halla casually as she struggled to her feet. Halla took her hand away from Aeske's mouth and pressed her face to his. 'I'm so sorry, Aeske.' She lowered the boy gently to the ground, putting herself between the soldier and the child, recovering her seax from the ground. She stood up to face the Christian, mouth curled in hate even as the tears dried on her cheeks.

Halla shifted her grip on the seax, hefting it and feeling her weight as the man advanced confidently, his smile never disappearing. Halla lifted her blade and pointed it at the soldier's chest. 'You will not have the boy,' she rasped, 'you will NOT have him!' and stepped forwards to meet her killer.

## CHAPTER 31

# THE DEATH OF HOPE

THEY SAW THE smoke long before they reached the village. Several of the Vatnsborð men rushed off to see what they could see, hoping desperately that it was just the abandoned village burning, and not their families entombed within it. Leif wanted to stop and to check if the Christians were still there before they blundered into them, but no one heeded his calls.

Leif and those who would listen prepared themselves and headed after the local men, keeping an eye out for the Christians.

They didn't come across any of the enemy, and as they reached the outskirts of the village, a few figures trudged back towards them and came over to Leif, Bekkr at their head.

'It's all gone,' said Bekkr bluntly.

'And the people?' asked Leif, his heart sinking.

'Some... It looks like they tried to fight them on the shore. Some must have escaped but... there are bodies everywhere, in the village and in your houses.' One of the other Vatnsborð men was crouched down behind Bekkr, sobbing quietly. Leif averted his eyes from the broken man's misery, trying not to shame him by witnessing it.

'How long ago?'

'The fires are dying down, I think it was this morning.' Leif nodded. It was closing in on darkness.

'We should search for the survivors.'

'Yes.'

'How could they know to come here?' said Leif desperately.

'How could they know any of this? But they did. Perhaps they caught one of the messengers, tortured him.'

'They swore to die before capture.'

The man shrugged. 'It doesn't matter, somehow they knew.'

Gjaldir walked in a daze through the new village they had built. Bodies were scattered around, scorch marks showed where the soldiers had made half-hearted efforts to burn the greenwood and turf buildings, and smoke curled from smoking piles of charred wood where they had succeeded. He came across a woman and a child, curled together in death, and bent down to try to identify them, but he did not recognise either.

'Over here!' a voice called from his right, and he looked up, setting off at a run between the buildings until he could see who had shouted. Half a dozen of the warriors were waving and pointing, and he followed their gaze to see a group of people slowly making their way across the open towards the village from the forest.

His heart filled with hope as he saw how many people were there. The outpouring of relief from the group as they reached the village and met the returning warriors was overwhelming. Women embraced men they did not know, two children were lifted up by arms that were not their father's. A single armed man, twice Gjaldir's age at least, approached Leif, his head hung in shame.

Leif stepped over and greeted him. 'Do not be ashamed, Oddvar, you helped these people to safety, did you not?'

The man barely met Leif's eye but nodded quietly.

'Then you did the right thing.'

'I left while others fought.'

'And they died honourably, but it is good that you have survived. Are there others?'

Oddvar nodded, pointing back to where they had come from. 'They fled into the woods. I tried to keep as many with me as I could, but the enemy was everywhere.'

'Good, we will go and find the rest of the survivors. Where are the enemy?'

'They left, around noon. Gathered their men and left in their ships. You did not see them? I assumed you defeated them to get here.'

Leif choked. 'No. They found us first.'

The man nodded, and then his eyes narrowed. 'Then that is why I see so few of you.'

A few of the survivors were listening now, and Gjaldir saw Leif stumble, lost for words or how to explain the magnitude of the tragedy.

A gravelly voice spoke from behind them. 'We were ambushed and defeated, the army is gone, we are all that survive.' Gjaldir turned and looked at Gunnar, the huskarl's face drawn and dark, eyes lifeless.

'Defeated?' said a woman, and the group descended into fearful questions and cries.

'Enough! Yes, we were defeated, our settlement has been destroyed, the survivors scattered. This is the fate the Norns have woven for us, and there is no time to question or mourn. We must collect our people from the forest, before they too are lost. I want parties of six to go and sweep east and north, gather whoever you find, bring everyone back here.' Leif tried to get control of the situation before it descended into misery and hopelessness.

'What if the Crusaders return?' asked Oddvar.

Leif nodded slowly. 'It is a good point. We will prepare to leave if we have to. Collect all the food that can be found, warm clothes and tools also. Only the essentials. I will give you ten men. The rest of us, we will split up and search the forest.'

Gjaldir was given three warriors and two women and set off north-east, headed into the treeline. They did not call out, Gunnar had forbade it, but walked among the trees, looking for signs of life, stopping to listen as if on a hunt.

Immediately they found tracks in the soft forest floor, a confused mixture of trails that all led east. Some must have been survivors, some enemy. They followed the thickest gathering of them.

The first person they found was a corpse, an old man face down in the litter with a gaping wound in his back. They left him where he lay. The second they found was a girl, almost a woman, who surprised them by rising from underneath a rotting log, where she had been hiding. She was filthy, shivering and barely clothed, but she ran to the group and threw her arms around one of the two women.

'Mother! Oh, by the gods, Mother.'

The woman burst into tears and cries of joy, brushing the dirt from her daughter's face and kissing her on both cheeks and her forehead, wild with relief. Gjaldir could not help but smile at the joyous reunion of a family who had both thought the other was dead. The mother looked at him and gestured with her head back towards the village.

Gjaldir nodded and waved in that direction with his axe. 'Yes, go, take her to the others.'

The woman smiled gratefully and set off with her daughter, laughing and talking, one arm supporting the weakened and freezing girl.

The rest of them kept going, and passed a couple more bodies but no more living souls over the next few miles, as the trails diverged and faded, until they were left just following one. Three people, one of the warriors with Gjaldir reckoned. Small feet, not soldiers. They pressed on.

They reached a break in the trees and there was a field of knee-high grasses and wildflowers, and the trail became hard to follow and then disappeared in the waving plants.

'Bollocks,' said the warrior, after casting around for a while and finding nothing. Gjaldir looked around, and was about to tell them to turn and go back to follow a different trail when a voice called out to them in Norse from the trees. 'Are you blind? Here!' Gjaldir looked around, seeing a woman standing in the shadows of a fir tree, waving at him to come over.

They jogged over to the trees and Gjaldir saw that the woman was one of Halla's people, Sigyn. She recognised him too. 'Gjaldir?'

'Yes.'

'How are you here, why?'

'It is… difficult to explain. But we have come to find you, and take you to the others who have survived. Are you alone?'

Sigyn looked around and then shook her head. 'No, I have been watching you for a while, but I was not certain you were ours, that it was not a trap. Come with me.'

She led them into the trees for a way until they came upon a small group of people. A child, two young boys, and half a dozen women of various ages. Gjaldir smiled. 'That is good, Sigyn, I did not expect to find so many.'

'You did not find them,' she said acridly. 'You could have stumbled about in the forest all day without finding them if I had not found you.'

Gjaldir nodded. 'As you say. Either way, it is a blessing. Let us go and join the others. The enemy have left.'

'How many have survived?' asked one of the older women.

'Dozens so far.'

'No.' The woman shook her head firmly. 'Not us, the warriors. You have returned far too early, and you have blood on your clothes, damage on your shield. You have fought the Crusaders also, and been defeated by the look of it. How many of YOU survived?'

Gjaldir shrank a little and looked at her. 'Maybe fifty,' he said quietly.

The old woman said nothing, she just closed her eyes and put her head in her hands, muttering something to herself. Sigyn grabbed his arm, eyes searching. 'Fifty? FIFTY!'

'Yes.'

Sigyn ran a hand through her dark hair and looked away, at the huddled group of survivors, and then back at him. She shrugged her shoulders in defeat. 'Whoever it is, take us to them. I am too tired to bear more of this sadness.'

Gjaldir returned with his group to the lake shore and found where the survivors of the army and village were being gathered. He searched the other cold and tired clumps of people and shouted out as he saw who he was desperately looking for: Brunhild, sitting alone on the lake shore cradling a bundle, staring out over the water.

He ran over towards her, calling her name, oblivious to the people around, and dropped to his knees beside her, expecting to share a full-hearted embrace, to see Aeske. But Brunhild didn't move, didn't take her eyes off the water. The bundle she held was just a cloak, clutched forgotten in her left arm. Her right hand was pressed to her mouth, a patterned strip of red silk wrapped around her palm, her lips pressed to its surface.

'Brunhild?' he asked, seeing the mask of pain and feeling the fear swell in his chest. 'Brunhild, what happened? Brunhild!'

A hand firmly grabbed his upper arm as he reached for her, and tried to drag him away. But a dozen wild boars could not have held his arm, and the hand was like a spiderweb trying to catch a crow, and he put a hand on the side of Brunhild's head and brushed her hair away so that he could see her better.

'Brunhild... Talk to me, please.' Gjaldir felt the truth sink into him, and he shook it away, refusing it, unable to speak the name of it.

'Gjaldir, come away from her.' Another hand was on his shoulder now, insistent. Brunhild's eyes never wavered, she gave no sign that she knew he was there, the hollow, dry orbs just fixed on the water of the lake as her lips gently trembled on the patterned red fabric. Gjaldir's eyes moved to the cloth, and he saw that it was not patterned, it was spattered with blood, blood that made darker patches in the red, blood that was dried between Brunhild's fingers and ingrained into her nails.

'Come away!' the voice hissed, and the strength left Gjaldir's body and he allowed himself to be raised to his feet and led away, staggering and shaking his head.

He looked up and saw that Leif was the one guiding him away, and that the warrior's eyes were filled with tears. And finally Gjaldir understood. 'No, no… Leif, no.'

'I'm sorry, Gjaldir. I'm so sorry, my friend.'

'What… what happened?'

'We found her in the woods, searching for Aeske.' Leif looked away and took a deep breath. 'And we went to help her, and we found him with Halla.' Leif waved a hand futilely. 'She died defending him, Gjaldir. The blood of an enemy was on her seax, and her body was curled around his. But they didn't spare him… and they took her head.'

Leif shuddered and had to look away, and Gjaldir sat down heavily, staring at his hands and shaking his head. 'Why? How could they?'

Leif shook his head. 'It is the way of war.' It was all he could say before he walked away.

Gjaldir sat there until the light dimmed and the night fell. No one bothered him, at some point someone gave him food and water, but both were left untouched at his side. He sat there trying to remember what life had been before, and could not. He could not remember why anything had seemed to matter, other than what was now lost.

At some point he simply ran out of grief, his body hollowed by it, and he looked around dumbly, seeing the food and water and realising he was desperately thirsty, draining the wooden cup in one draught, but ignoring the food. The emptiness of his belly was indistinguishable from the hollowness in his chest.

He stood and looked around, and found the campfires of the survivors around him on the lake shore and in the ruined village, gatherings of mourning people, the sound of talking overridden by the misery of dozens who had lost as much as him, or more.

He suddenly felt ashamed, that so many others had continued to help, and he had succumbed to his grief. He wandered among the fires until he found Leif and Gunnar and a few others sitting around one. He slumped to the ground beside them and Leif gave him a sympathetic look.

'Why have we made fires?' he asked quietly, while drawing himself closer to the warming flames.

'Because no one had the heart to say no, nor stay in houses still full of the dead and their spirits. The enemy is gone anyway.'

'So, we can rebuild the village?'

Leif shook his head sadly. 'We cannot, not to live here. It will never be safe again. Tomorrow we will recover whatever we can, and then we will move.'

'Move? Where? For what point?'

Leif raised a hand to calm Gjaldir. 'We have had this debate, and I will not have it again tonight. We will go to join the survivors of Vatnsborð tomorrow in the place they have fled to, and decide then what to do.'

'The people of Vatnsborð will help us? After everything we have done?'

'We will,' said one of the figures around the fire, without looking up. Gjaldir saw that it was Bekkr, and acknowledged the man awkwardly.

'Why?'

'Because you are our kin, and the fewer of us there are, the more important that becomes. It is true that your coming here has led to our doom, but it is the gods who decided this, not you. We joined you willingly, and I have no reason to change that now.'

Leif nodded gratefully. 'As you say, we are kin.'

'So what…'

'Enough,' said Leif. 'Everyone here is exhausted, it can wait until the morning.' Gjaldir lowered his chin and was silent, brooding as he stared into the flames.

Gjaldir jolted awake and did not remember falling asleep, but he woke next to the cold ashes of the fire and Leif was gently shaking his shoulder. The warrior moved on to the next man and Gjaldir levered himself to a sitting position, feeling how cold his limbs were and rubbing his arms vigorously with his hands.

The weight of the previous day, for a few moments out of his mind, fell upon him like a felled tree, and he gasped for breath, looking around and seeing that it was as he remembered. He had not dreamed it. He stood and looked to where he had left Brunhild sitting by the lake shore, but she was not there.

'Leave her be, Gjaldir,' said Leif, coming over to stand with him. 'It is worse for her, worse than we can understand. Nothing will help but time, so give that to her. I know you want to try, but you cannot help her.'

Gjaldir looked at him in confusion, a hint of anger mixing with his pain. 'Leave her alone? How can I leave her alone now, after what happened?'

'Because you must,' said Leif. 'You will be a big, loud, living reminder of her pain. So give her time without that.'

Gjaldir looked away angrily, but felt there was some sense in what the warrior said. 'As you say then.'

'Good, now, come with me. We need strong arms and strong hearts to do what is needed in the village.'

Gjaldir did not look back, he knew what it meant.

They spent the day collecting the bodies of everyone who had died in the village and in the forest around it. There was not a single body of the enemy, although if that was because none fell in the unequal fights on the shore and between the houses, or if they had simply taken their dead away, no one could say.

Gjaldir saw them bring the body of Halla back to the growing pyre, and he saw them carrying a small, wrapped bundle along behind her, and he leant against a building and wept again. But he did not have the courage to go and see him, to see what cold, careless steel had done to that precious boy, so he busied himself with collecting the rest of those who had fallen.

By the end of the day, the huge pyre was finished. Nearly two hundred bodies stacked with timbers torn from the firewood stores and damaged buildings of the village. It was a grim and mournful task, and no one was unaffected by it. Warriors of a dozen seasons wept like children, until finally dusk fell and they could light the wood and send the souls out into the night.

The survivors gathered upwind of the stacked wood and corpses and watched as the flames spread, struggling to burn bright but eventually rising into a great column into the sky. Gunnar, Leif, Gjaldir and Bjorn stood a little apart from the crowd, or perhaps the crowd avoided them. He did not know.

'They will see that from twenty miles away,' grumbled Gunnar.

'It does not matter. We will be gone by the time they could get back here,' said Leif, staring deeply into the flames.

'And we will leave behind our people and our future in these ashes,' muttered the dark-haired man.

Gunnar had barely spoken since they left Gustav's cold body in the forest, unable even to bury him, but the despair in his voice was overwhelming.

Leif frowned. 'Gunnar, do not speak like that.'

'Why not? Eric is dead, Vidar is dead and thirty others of my warriors with them. They died while I fled. I abandoned my men to save Gustav and I left them to die in the ship and on the beach, and I still failed.' His words trailed away to nothing.

Leif recoiled from the old champion. 'It was not your doing.'

'No, but I should have died with my friends. I should have died with my king last year, I couldn't save him, I thought that if I helped Jarl Gustav to victory, protected him, I could somehow correct that dishonour... But now I fled while my men died and it achieved nothing.'

Leif leaned in closer, trying to get Gunnar to look at him, lowering his voice so that others beyond their small group would not hear them. 'There are men still alive who need your skill and your leadership, we have all lost almost everything but I know that you will not abandon them. Do not let them see you like this, do not let them hear you like this.'

Gunnar looked into Leif's eyes, his own bloodshot and hollow, but he gritted his jaw and nodded. 'I will do what I can, but I am not your leader, nor theirs.'

'Gunnar,' Leif growled in anger. 'Now is not the time for this, the men know and trust you, know your reputation...' Gunnar stopped him, holding up his hand.

'I have made my decision. I will fight for as long as I am able, but I will not lead into another disaster or failure. I cannot bear it.'

Leif glared at Gunnar but saw that it was pointless. Instead he stalked away angrily, and Gunnar muttered to himself and stumbled off too, the old man looking lost and broken in a way that would have horrified Gjaldir, if he had the capacity in that moment. Instead Gjaldir just looked back at the pyre, staring vacantly at the flames with Bjorn, silent for a while, until a question burned through him.

'Why are we alive, Bjorn? They call you the faithful, so what made you run? What made Gunnar run? Why are we alive, when so many good warriors died?'

Bjorn shifted uncomfortably and cocked a black eyebrow in the flickering firelight. 'That is a hard struck question, Gjaldir. A man might kill for such a question even being spoken.'

Gjaldir shrugged. 'I don't think I even care.'

'Then why did you run? Why did you not die on that beach?'

Gjaldir thought about it for a moment. Remembering Eric shouting at him, and then Leif dragging him away when the Fire-beard sagged to the ground and died. 'I was told to, and my friend died to let me escape. So I had to.'

Bjorn shook his head. 'Those are the lies you tell yourself.'

Gjaldir looked round angrily. 'I am not lying.'

'Eric did not die to save you, he had no intention of dying. I am certain he wanted to go with you. And you have never been one for doing what you are told.'

Gjaldir huffed and his knuckles worked together as he wrestled with the truth in the words, but he had to admit they were true. 'Eric stayed when he could have left, he may have wanted to live, but he risked his life to help me.'

'Yes, that is the truth. And he was an honourable man, paying a debt to you. But it is still not why you ran. I know why you ran, and it is nothing to be ashamed of. I'm sorry for you that what you sought to return to is no longer here. It is a terrible thing.'

Gjaldir grated his teeth together as Bjorn got to the heart of it. *Yes, I ran so that I could live to see them again.* But the truth did not assuage his anger. 'And what about you?' he spat.

'I was sworn to Halla, and could not help her by dying there in a losing battle.' Bjorn fixed Gjaldir with a steady gaze and then relented. 'That is my lie. That is what I tell myself when I am alone. The truth is… I didn't want to die by that fucking river.'

Gjaldir was taken aback by the admission, from the warrior most men held as a paragon of bravery and honour. 'And what if your oath had been to Gustav, would you have died to help him escape?'

'Yes,' said Bjorn without pause.

'Why? Why would that make enough difference?'

'Because my honour gave me enough of an excuse to live, and that is all men need. But it is true I would rather die than live in shame. People say that I am brave because of my loyalty, but it is nonsense. I simply couldn't bear to live with people thinking I was an oathbreaker or a coward.' Bjorn stared at the flames for a moment. 'I would rather die than face that shame. Perhaps that makes me the greatest coward of all.'

He looked at Gjaldir again, shaking his head sadly. 'The truly brave are dead, and they do not care what we think. They stood in line and died with their kin. Those of us who are left are the ones who can live with the decisions that kept us alive. All we can do is try to do better next time.'

'Even if that means being the ones who die?'

'Especially if it means that. If it is right, if it is the time, if it can do some good, then welcome it without fear. That should be the goal of every warrior. But until that day, you stay alive, you run, you fight, you do what your honour will allow you to do to survive.'

'And what if that moment never comes?'

Bjorn laughed bitterly. 'There is no point asking me, the last warrior of Jarl Birkir, how to recognise the right moment to die. You should ask my friends and my kin, but by the time you meet them, you will already be dead.'

Bjorn walked away and Gjaldir was left staring at the swirling flames alone, trying to make sense of the older man's words, and failing. His mind was too tired, too full of sorrow. He shook his head and walked away, off to their campsite. No one would spend the night in the village with the flickering shadows and the dead.

When morning came, the survivors packed up what they could carry and prepared to leave the village for good. Bekkr would lead them east, and then for a day's travel south-east to his people's hidden stores, where those that fled from Vatnsborð should be waiting.

As they were preparing to move out, Gjaldir heard a commotion and a bedraggled warrior appeared through the crowd, headed towards them. He was wearing a hauberk, but had no shield or weapon, an empty seax sheath was at his waist.

Bjorn's face cracked into a grin just as Gjaldir recognised the long-haired warrior. 'Vidar! By Thor's hairy arse.'

'Did you miss me?' said Vidar, half jogging down the slope, looking ragged and tired. He jogged straight into a full embrace with Bjorn, both men laughing and thumping each other on the back.

'Vidar?' a deeper voice called out nervously from behind them, and Vidar looked up. 'How the fuck are you alive?' said Gunnar, walking over, his face twisted in a rictus of conflicted emotions.

Vidar gave Gunnar an odd look, his eyes flicking to Bjorn and back to the old huskarl.

'I'm sorry I left you, on the ship,' said Gunnar, his voice cracking.

'You had to save Gustav, I understand. Where is he?'

Gunnar grimaced and Vidar opened his mouth and sighed. 'Ah, I see.'

'But how did you escape?' asked Bjorn, as Gunnar just stared at the man as if he was a ghost.

'Well, my friends, that is a long story, and I am desperately thirsty and hungry.' He eyed the half-ruined village around them. 'I had feared I would find this. How bad is it?'

'Very bad,' said Bjorn, the levity gone.

'Shit. Well, we are still alive.'

'There are over a hundred others,' said Gjaldir, somehow feeling defensive about the situation.

That perked Vidar up and he looked at Gjaldir. 'A hundred? Well, the war isn't over yet then, young Christian.'

Bjorn waved Vidar towards one of the buildings. 'Come, we have water and food, more even than we can carry. Eat what you want from what we are leaving behind. Gjaldir, show him.'

Gjaldir took him to one of the intact buildings and the discarded food that could not be carried, and handed him a leather bottle of water. Vidar emptied the whole in one and refilled it, tying it to his belt. Then Vidar looked at Gjaldir with a worried expression. 'What has happened to Gunnar?'

Gjaldir didn't know what to say. He opened his mouth, but the words would not form.

Vidar huffed and nodded in understanding. 'He has been through more than most men could endure. But everyone has their limit. Do not judge him for it.'

Gjaldir nodded dumbly.

'Come, let's go and join the others. I am tired, but I will manage another day's walking, somehow.'

The two of them headed out to follow the others, headed north-east out of the village, past the smoking remains of the pyre, which they passed in silence.

'So, it was pretty bad,' said Vidar once they had passed.

'Yes,' said Gjaldir sombrely.

Vidar stuffed some dried fish into his mouth, almost groaning with pleasure. As they reached the back of the column, rejoining Bjorn and the silent Gunnar, Leif came running back towards them from the front and saw Vidar, almost choking with surprise and then delight. 'They told me you had returned, Vidar! There is so little now to be glad for, but seeing you return fills me with joy. But how… how?'

'He was about to tell us,' said Bjorn pointedly.

Vidar cleared his throat with another swig from his leather bottle. 'I was one of the last in Gustav's ship, and I turned to follow Gunnar. The next thing I remember is waking up, still in the ship, with a sore head. Someone had hit me so hard my helmet was nearly turned into a bowl. I was stuffed against the side with a dozen other prisoners, with my hands tied to my belt.'

'You were tied up, on one of their ships, yet here you are.'

'Yes.'

'How?'

'Well, we were being rowed back down the river, towards Karlsgrind, and I know that river well by now, so I waited for a shallow spot and jumped out.'

'You just… jumped out,' said Leif. 'And they did nothing about this.'

'I had seen they let another man get up to piss over the side, and we were all wearing hauberks and had our hands tied. They must have thought no one would be stupid enough to jump.'

'How did you not sink?'

'Oh, I did sink, that was the plan.'

'Your plan was to sink…' said Leif incredulously. 'Vidar, this isn't a joke, we need to know the truth.'

'It is the absolute truth, I swear it. I sank, and then walked along the bottom.'

'You walked!'

'Yes. I knew the shallows were close, I drew in as much breath as I could, and then when my feet hit the bottom I stood up and walked up the riverbed, I think about a dozen steps, until my head reached the surface. The ship was already past me, and the crew were shouting and laughing. By the time they realised I wasn't dead, I was too far away for them to do anything about it. I walked out of the river and spent three days walking alone to get back here.'

Gunnar just stared at the man as if he was insane. Leif did the same and then burst out laughing, a noise that jarred Gjaldir with its levity, so out of place. 'Vidar the fucking cunning. You just…' Leif mimicked the steps with his two forefingers, 'walked out of the river in your armour.'

'Yes,' said Vidar with a satisfied grin.

'That is not cunning. Why are you impressed?' Gjaldir was appalled, looking at them all one by one. 'Any mistake and he would have drowned. The river might have been too deep, or he might had got turned around, or snagged on a branch, or run out of breath, or… well, anything could have happened!'

'Yes,' said Vidar with a smile, wrapping his arm around Gjaldir's neck. 'But none of those things happened, apart from the branch, that did happen… but I survived! And now I am here. And death would have been preferable to being a prisoner of your kin.' Gjaldir just shook his head.

'You are insane.'

'Maybe.'

'Did you at least learn anything on this boat, before you jumped off it?' asked Leif.

'Yes, Asel was there.'

Gunnar tensed and growled. 'He betrayed us?'

'What? No, no. He was a prisoner, wounded too. But we talked, he thinks one or both of his men were captured and tortured. And one of the prisoners understood a little of the Christian's words. We were being taken to the "bishop".' Vidar said the unfamiliar word slowly, tripping over it. But Gjaldir recognised it.

'The bishop?'

Vidar looked at him. 'Yes, what is the bishop?'

Gjaldir looked at him in confusion. 'Um, a holy man, a very important one. Usually they would be in charge of the churches in a whole county or town.'

'Hmm, and why would one be here, having prisoners delivered?'

Gjaldir shrugged. 'I don't know.' He thought about it for a while longer. 'Perhaps to have them baptised? Or forgiven?'

'Baptised? What is that?'

'Uh, it is how… well, it's how someone becomes a Christian.'

Vidar's eyes widened. 'Well, now I am even more glad I got out of that ship. So, where are we going?'

Leif looked troubled again, the burst of joy dissipating as quickly as it had arrived. 'I don't know, Vidar. I just don't know.'

## CHAPTER 32

# THE LORD'S WORK

'Your excellency, the ships are returning,' Brother Bertrand said, having slipped through the tent's flap a moment earlier.

Reinhard looked up and narrowed his brows slightly. 'When out with the Order, or in front of the men, you are to call me Grandmaster. You know this.'

Bertrand inclined his head. 'My apologies, Grandmaster, I misjudged the situation.'

Reinhard nodded, satisfied. Truly it did not matter, but he found it important to critique the fastidious Bertrand from time to time, in case he became lazy or complacent. 'Does it look like good news, or bad news?'

'There appear to be all of the ships that left, and they are loaded with men, the banners of the Order flying proud. I would certainly say it looks like a successful return.' Bertrand paused. 'Although, of course, I know little of military matters.'

'Your description certainly sounds like a victorious return.' The months of letting raids and setbacks plague them had worn away at the Order's morale. He needed to remind the rest of the provinces of the power of the Order, and the strength of his leadership. *And I need the men to remember that too.*

He had executed a dozen men of the Order for conspiring with

Sir Hans and his acolytes. Some of whom Hugues had named, some had been named under torture, a couple Reinhard had added to the list because they were troublemakers and he wanted rid of them. Bertrand was becoming terribly proficient with his questioning of prisoners. Reinhard never took part in the process, but the quiet priest and his assistant Gotfrit knew how to get results.

In any case, the executions had darkened the mood in the Order's ranks, and Reinhard hoped the victory, suitably attributed to his foresight and leadership, would raise the morale, and his own standing with the Order's soldiery.

He rose from his small travelling desk and stopped for a moment to say a short prayer, calming himself and clearing his mind before he strode out of the tent overlooking the riverbank. As soon as he had gone past the flap, which he suddenly regretted not having someone lift for him, the riverbank and the returning ships were laid out below him in the splendid sunshine.

Fourteen ships in total, full of Order soldiers in their white surcoats and Count Otto's men in their wild array of colours, were headed towards the docks at the riverside, where another hundred of the Order's men, dressed in pristine white emblazoned with gold crosses, were forming up to greet them. Reinhard breathed in hard and smiled. It was a glorious sight, and he felt the pleasure of the victory coursing through him.

Censuring himself a little for perhaps enjoying it too much, he flicked his fingers at Sir Sighard, and the knight, waiting patiently a few paces away with the Grandmaster's guard, trotted into formation behind him as he walked down the gentle slope towards the docks.

Reinhard stopped at a suitable distance, it was correct that they should come to him, not him go to the dock like a fishwife overjoyed to see her husband return from the sea, and he waited for the ships to unload. Ten ships had set out on the expedition, so Reinhard knew they must have captured the rest.

Hundreds of men started piling out of the ships, and Reinhard saw Hugues leaving the lead ship, his own company of Order soldiers around him. The Grandsteward drew his sword and raised it into the air triumphantly, the men around him joining in with cheers and declarations of devotion. A group of soldiers came from some of the other ships, arms loaded down with weapons, and dumped them on the ground at Hugues's feet.

Reinhard sighed and did his best not to react to the vain display with anything other than a patient smile. *The man could have his moment.*

Finally, Hugues was done with his self-congratulation, and he strode up the slope towards Reinhard, all smiles and pride.

'Grandsteward, we see you are victorious, and we raise a prayer of thanks to the Lord for making it so.' It was time to start taking away some of the credit for the victory, and giving it to the Lord was a sensible place to start.

'Yes, in the Lord's name we confronted and trapped the heathen, and in the light of his glory we crushed them, destroyed them utterly.'

Reinhard's eyes widened a little. 'Utterly?'

'Yes, barely a few dozen fled for their lives, the rest are dead or,' Hugues flourished a hand down at a ragged line of prisoners being coerced from one of the ships, 'captured for questioning and judgement.'

Reinhard smiled, genuinely this time. The total destruction of the enemy was more than he had expected, and it was good news for him.

'Their village was destroyed, their people turned out and put to flight,' Hugues continued. 'We bring back their ships, their weapons and their supplies, many of which were stolen from us so heinously.' The baron was enjoying himself, performing for the crowd of hundreds of soldiers, but Reinhard was too pleased to care too much or attempt a riposte. Hugues crossed the final distance between them and had the good sense not to come close enough to be offered the ring to kiss.

Hugues turned and waved at the men who had followed him up the hill, gesturing at them to attend to the ships, and with that, the display was over. Reinhard smiled through his teeth but nodded at his own captain, who dismissed the orderly ranks of soldiers who had formed up to greet the army.

When no one else other than Sighard and his men, and Hugues's entourage, were close, Reinhard looked at Hugues carefully. 'So, dear baron, is it really as good as you say? The rebellion is crushed?'

'Yes. Their leader escaped the battle at first, but we found his body. His men abandoned him. They are a broken force.'

'A few dozen, you say?'

'Yes, if that.'

'Excellent. Ah! Earl Frode, good of you to join us.' He looked at the Norse lord, who was walking over with his shoulders slumped, silent and gloomy, regarding the unloading of the ships with a grimace. Reinhard watched him for a moment before flicking his eyes to the right. Coming up the slope was a familiar figure, leading an escort and about ten bound prisoners.

'Brother Roland, I am pleased to greet you victorious.'

Roland stepped forwards as Reinhard gestured to him, and took a knee in front of the bishop, crossing himself while Reinhard gave a quick prayer of thanks, before dutifully kissing the proffered ring.

'Brother Roland led the forces of the Order valiantly,' said Hugues with unfeigned admiration in his voice. 'While I commanded the ships, he crushed their army against the river, and then went on to capture their village and scour their people from the land.'

Roland did not let a hint of pride mar his face, waiting in perfect neutrality. 'It was my honour to wield this blade against the enemy, and it did not fail me.'

'Good. I am sure that this is a sign of God's pleasure at our actions, to deliver so great a victory. With this sacred weapon, we will continue to cleanse the lands. All of the North will hear of it, I will make sure of it.'

Roland bowed his head. 'It is my honour to serve God's will.'

'It is. And you have brought prisoners, excellent. Brother Bertrand will be pleased to question them, perhaps some will confess their sins and be welcomed into our forgiveness. Bring them closer, let us see what manner of creatures they are.'

Roland gestured to the men escorting the prisoners and the glum group was herded over and forced to their knees a few paces from the Order's leaders. As Reinhard gazed along their lines, one of the prisoners looked up and exclaimed in shock, then tried to stagger to his feet, pointing at Jarl Frode and shouting at him in fury. Reinhard, surprised but intrigued by the sudden confrontation, saw Frode could not meet the angry prisoner's fury, and turned away, pained.

He gestured over his shoulder and Bertrand sidled over. 'What is being said?'

'Uh, your excellency, this prisoner is accusing the former Earl Frode of being a traitor, ah, an oathbreaker and… well, a number of insults of degrading and vile nature.'

Frode put a hand to his face and muttered something to the prisoner, who just spat and was finally wrestled to the ground on Roland's command, shouting and cursing all the way.

'Frode made some apology, I didn't quite catch it,' said Bertrand, as Frode turned, his face bitter and anguished, to walk over to them. Reinhard felt Sighard tense at his side, but held up a calming hand.

'So, Bishop Reinhard. It is done?' the Norseman said in a dejected voice.

'It is, indeed.'

Frode mustered some strength for his gaze. 'And will you keep your terms?'

Reinhard smiled, magnanimous. 'I will. Your people will be well looked after, and spared the results of this failed rebellion. Well, almost spared.' Frode's expression darkened at the last pronouncement and Reinhard chuckled under his breath. 'Those of your men who plotted to join the rebellion must be punished, of course.'

'That was not agreed,' Frode growled.

'Perhaps, but it is necessary.' *And what can you do to prevent it?* Frode should have expected some degree of diverging from the agreement, he knew who he was dealing with, after all. Reinhard enjoyed the moment he saw the fight go out of Frode's eyes, saw the shoulders slump fractionally, and the hands relax.

God forgive him, he enjoyed that moment. To take a man, to bend him to your will, to break him and control him… It was blasphemous to think it, but it gave a small taste of the Lord's power, and it was intoxicating.

To have broken his enemy to the point where the man had betrayed his own people's cause and engineered the destruction of the rebel army… It was glorious.

Reinhard fought to control himself, and chided himself for allowing the passing feeling to overtake him. *I must control myself, for self-control is dear to the Lord.* He looked up at Frode again, who was watching him anxiously. Reinhard put the mask on his face again and smiled, but looking at the man reminded him of another issue.

He turned to Roland. 'And what of the other leader, the woman known as…' He flicked his fingers at Bertrand. He knew her name, but he wanted to feign indifference.

'Halla, Grandmaster,' Bertrand said.

'Ah, yes. What of her?'

'She is dead, Grandmaster,' replied Roland.

Roland pointed at a man carrying a bag, and the soldier stepped forwards gingerly, then upended the bag, dumping its grizzly contents on the ground.

It was a pair of heads, a man's and a woman's. Discoloured and rank, but still recognisable.

Frode wailed in protest and agony as he saw the contents and turned away, a pained cry dying somewhere deep in his chest. Reinhard looked at the broken man, feeling a hint of sympathy that was quickly extinguished. 'I don't know what you expected, Earl Frode. This was the arrangement. Your sister had to die, or she would have taken your people down with her in her desperate rebellion.'

'I didn't expect to be subjected to this!' shouted Frode angrily, and the soldiers nearby stirred in anger and outrage at the Norseman shouting at their Grandmaster. 'And I didn't expect…' Frode paused and Reinhard raised an eyebrow.

'What? Didn't expect what?'

Frode drew in a deep breath and settled his sunken eyes on Reinhard's. 'I didn't expect to outlive my usefulness to you, to be humiliated like this.'

'Ah, I see,' said Reinhard. 'But I promised that your people would be safe.'

'Carefully worded,' Frode grated, 'to avoid making any promise about me. I am the last jarl of these lands, the last threat to your rule. I expected you to end that threat, not parade my sister's head in front of me. I bought my people's future with her life, do not torture me with it!' howled the broken jarl.

Reinhard finally understood. 'My dear Frode, I did consider it, yes. But I decided you had earned your life. You see, you really are no threat, not anymore, I was going to let you live out your days in peace. But I see it now, you wanted me to end it, didn't you?'

Frode swallowed nervously, but squared his shoulders slightly and nodded. 'I have no peace left to live in. I only want you to uphold your agreement to spare my people, my life has no purpose after that.'

'Well, if that is what you want, it can be arranged.' Reinhard looked at Brother Roland. 'Earl Frode requests an honourable death. Indulge him, if you would be so kind.'

Roland bowed his head without hesitation. Snapping out orders to a pair of men, who ran down the slope to where the captured weapons were piled. The rest of them chivvied the prisoners away, and cleared a space in front of Reinhard on the grass. Sighard positioned himself carefully right at Reinhard's side, and Reinhard did not send him away. He remembered the encounter with Sir Hans all too well, although he did not think Frode would try to kill him, because he knew the revenge Reinhard would take on his people.

The two soldiers came back up the hill with arms full of swords and a couple of shields. Frode was not wearing a hauberk, and Roland stripped his off to avoid displaying an advantage, putting the white surcoat on in its place, earning a muttering of admiration from the increasingly large crowd of soldiers that was gathering at the news of a duel about to take place.

Frode was given the choice of the weapons and shields brought up from the riverbank, and he picked a sword at random, not even bothering to check it. He had to have a shield put into his hand, but he looked at it in disgust and cast it aside. 'I only require a sword.'

Roland looked at him for a moment and then he too cast aside his shield, and the two men faced each other across the open space. Roland was nearly motionless, scanning his opponent, who looked barely aware of the waiting knight, staring at the ground morosely.

The watching crowd cheered Roland on, cries of cowardice raining on Frode, who did not appear to notice or care. Frode lifted the hilt of his sword up to examine it, a tear visible on his cheek, and men jeered him. Reinhard scowled. This was not the glorious moment he had anticipated, but a farce.

Roland clearly agreed, because he strode towards the slumped Norse lord and aimed a quick cut at Frode's head. Frode animated as if suspended on strings, taking a pace back and leaning away from the high cut, flicking his own blade across and catching Roland on the upper thigh as he passed, scoring a line clean through the knight's thick linen chausse, blood quickly showing on the plain fabric.

Roland looked down at the wound in annoyance, but it did not appear to hinder him, and he approached Frode again, more carefully this time, as the Norse lord stared him down without fear. 'You cut the heads from women, Christian. Is this your god's will?'

Roland refused to be distracted, lunging and forcing Frode to cover and step back, his own weapon raised in a counterguard.

'You brought my sister's head back as a trophy?' Frode snapped his own attack, feinting low and then flicking the point up, aiming for the underside of Roland's chin. But Roland was equal to it, and met the blade and pushed it aside, managing to cut Frode's arm lightly as he retreated.

The Norseman did not even look at the wound, if he noticed it at all. 'That sword belongs to Jarl Ragnvald,' hissed Frode, pointing at Ljós a Norðan with his own blade. 'You are a pale shadow of him, a coward and a killer of women. You are not worthy of wielding it.'

Roland glanced down at the sword in his hand, the golden runes shining in the sun, and he finally replied, 'You knew the man I took this from? If he was so worthy, why did I kill him so easily?'

Frode snarled in anger and jumped forwards, throwing a right cut that Roland parried, rolling his blade over the Norseman's as they bound, pushing it out of line, and then thrust Ljós a Norðan hard, driving the point into Frode's unarmoured chest.

The Norse lord gasped as the steel sank into his right lung, and Roland grabbed Frode's swordhand with his left. Frode staggered, but Roland held him in place with his hand and the blade, gazing curiously into the Norse lord's eyes. 'Yes, just like this, a thrust to the chest.' He leaned in, so that their faces were close. 'A little lower, though, through the liver. A painful and slower end.'

Frode struggled to breathe, and his left leg wobbled. Roland raised a foot to push his opponent off the blade, but Frode suddenly snarled, grabbing Roland with his spare hand, dropping his sword and grabbing the hilt of Ljós a Norðan with his right. Roland exclaimed in surprise, unbalanced as the Norseman pulled himself in closer, the blade sinking further into his chest, and then Frode opened his mouth and lunged, screaming in anger and pain, and clamped his teeth onto Roland's cheek.

Roland howled in agony, desperately trying to push the man away as Frode's strength faded and he finally slumped to the ground, taking the sword, and a ragged strip of Roland's cheek skin, with him.

Roland wheeled away, one hand clamped to his cheek, blood seeping between his fingers. One of his men stepped forwards to help him but he held out a hand, palm upwards, and angrily hissed at the man to stand his ground.

The Frenchman fought to regain his composure and glared at Frode, who was kneeling on the ground, wheezing and fumbling at the hilt of the Light of the North, which was practically touching his ribs.

Roland picked up Frode's discarded sword, his left hand still held over his wound, and bared his teeth at his dying opponent.

Reinhard watched in silent fury. Any glory the moment might once have had was gone. He fumed at the knight, imploring him to regain his composure and salvage something from this debacle.

But Roland was too angry. Instead of an elegant thrust, or clean cut, Roland bellowed and hacked at the kneeling man, again and again, until one of his knights pulled him away. Reinhard closed his eyes in fury. He had hoped the knight would have had more discipline.

Finally, Roland was separated from the ugly scene, ushered away, leaving the crowd stunned and muted. Reinhard turned to Sighard angrily. 'Go and recover that sword, it is not to be left like that, it is an object of veneration. And send Brother Roland to my tent as soon as his wound has been tended to.'

'Yes, Grandmaster.' Sighard trotted off to recover the sacred blade from what was left of Jarl Frode as Reinhard gave the ugly scene one final glare, before stalking back to his tent.

Reinhard had calmed down somewhat by the time Roland was brought to his presence. The knight's head was bowed, and his demeanour muted. Reinhard let him stew unaddressed for a good while, before finally speaking.

'That was ill done.'

'Yes, Grandmaster. I apologise profusely.'

'I do not care for your apology, it has no value. I wanted a display of your superiority for the crowd, and yet, despite killing the man, I and everyone watching was left with a distinct impression that he, in fact, won.'

Roland bowed his head a fraction more and Reinhard stared at the mess on his cheek. It was an ugly wound, ragged and shallow. It would leave a nasty scar.

'I chose you to wield the sword because I believed you had the skill and the temperament. Was I wrong?' Reinhard ignored the fact that, of course, Roland had more chosen himself by capturing the sword. It was a matter of no importance in that moment.

'I submit to your judgement on the matter, your excellency.'

'Hmmm.' The answer pleased Reinhard. Humility was a trait he liked in his subordinates. *For humility was dear to the Lord.* 'Tell me, what made you so easily angered?'

Roland wrung his hands and looked up slightly. 'I was reminded of the day I captured the Light of the North. This Jarl Frode, he knew the man who I fought that day, and that man killed my brother with that sword. The memory angered me, and I lost control.'

'I see. I knew from my past conversations with Frode that he had known the man for whom that sword was made, but I did not consider it important. Nevertheless, I shall take that fact into consideration. But remember, my child, control of oneself is the ultimate aim. Because only when you can control yourself can you perform the finest service to the Lord. And when you lose control, well… you displayed today how that service can fall short, even in victory.'

Roland bowed deeply. 'I understand, your excellency, and I will focus on this matter deeply.'

'I believe you, and I will give you the chance to atone. Grand-steward Hugues says several dozen of the heathen escaped. You will take a party back north and hunt them down. I will not have these troublemakers continue to hinder the Lord's work. Go, and finish them, and you will have my forgiveness.'

Roland bowed again, the relief clear on his face. 'Thank you, Grandmaster. It will be done.'

Reinhard let him stay there for a long moment and then nodded, satisfied. He raised his ring as a signal, and Roland knelt to kiss it, and then with a mere twitch of his fingers Reinhard dismissed the knight.

No sooner was the humbled knight gone than Bertrand entered.

'Grandmaster, shall I arrange to return to Arbugæ tomorrow?'

Reinhard put his finger to his lip and then shook his head. 'No. No, our work here is done, our enemies destroyed. I will go to Uppsala. The church is nearing completion, and I will not spend another winter in this backwater chasing a few bandits. No, I will go to where the power is, and that is at Uppsala.'

'But, your excellency, you told me that…'

'Don't question me, Bertrand. It does not matter what I once told you, it matters what I am telling you now. The Order must assert itself over all the lands, not just these ones. We will leave a garrison in Arbugæ, maybe even Baron Hugues will remain. It does not matter. I need to go to Uppsala before the great lords of the Crusade forget who I am, or what power I wield. For power forgotten is power lost.'

'As you wish, your excellency. I will inform Sir Sighard.'

'Yes, yes, you will. And draft a letter to be distributed to all the parishes about the victory here, how the Light of the North was carried at the forefront of our troops, and that the Lord saw this devotion and granted victory, praise be to him, and so on as usual. Make sure it is clear that devotion to God was the key to victory, and that the sword is its symbol.' Hugues may have preached to the soldiers gathered here that he had won a great victory, but Reinhard would have a different story read in every church and heard by every baptised citizen of the provinces within a week. He was building a power and a story that he could later use for whatever purpose he deemed fit.

'I will write it for your review.'

'Good. You may leave.'

Bertrand left and Reinhard scratched absentmindedly at his ear, deep in thought. *Yes, it is time. As it is felt here, the rest of the provinces will feel the full weight of the Order's heel upon their neck, and know my foot is within the shoe.* He smiled to himself and pulled out a fresh sheet of parchment. There was much to be done. It was time to execute Henry's order. Now the scouring of the North, and the imposition of the will and peace of the Church, would truly begin.

Roland, Sieur de Blanchant, went into his tent, his mind burning with the shame of his humiliation, and the raging pain in his cheek. His anger, which had ebbed and flowed since his brother's death, was never fully quenched. He looked at the sword Ljós a Norðan and tried to calm himself. Every time he saw that sword, it reminded him of his brother's death. He remembered the blue-eyed Norse lord plunging it into Guiscard's chest, remembered seeing the younger man fold around the steel as it stole his life.

He knew men regarded it as an honour to wield the blade, he even believed that it was the holy object that Grandmaster Reinhard had declared it to be. But it was not a privilege, it was his personal cross to bear, a heavy weight that reminded him every day that he had failed to get his brother home.

He gingerly touched the wound in his cheek. It had hurt life hellfire when his squire cleaned it. It would heal, but was just another reminder of his failings as a knight. Men would see it and see his disfigurement and know that he was unworthy, he was sure of it.

As Roland was brooding, his eyes were drawn to the corner of the tent, where the steel-faced helm that had belonged to Sir Hans Mettel lay discarded. He had kept it as a curiosity, maybe to try it one day, or maybe as a trophy. He leant down and picked it up, staring down at the empty eye slits, and seeing the blurred reflection of his wounded cheek on the steel. *What can show a fault can also hide it.* He turned the helmet over, and then carefully lifted it over his head, slipping the blank steel plate over his face until his eyes lined up with the eyeholes. The helmet was loose without his arming cap and maille coif.

He took his hands away and looked around, turning his head left and right, feeling at home in the emotionless metal mask. That was what the Lord needed him to be. Emotionless, cold, hard… unyielding. There was a noise at the tent's entrance and he looked up, seeing that it was his squire. The younger man stopped in confusion as he saw Roland in the helmet, but he recovered and bowed brusquely.

'Sir, Grandsteward Hugues has assigned a hundred men and a ship for the expedition to return upriver. We already have supplies and equipment here so we can be ready to leave in the morning.'

Roland smiled slightly inside the expressionless helmet. 'Today.'

'What?'

'Today, we will leave today.'

'Sir, the men are tired…'

'The men are soldiers, and they will endure. We have a quarry to run down, and every hour it will be getting further away.'

His squire knew better than to argue, and just nodded while looking disapproving. 'I will tell them.'

'No, I will. They will hear it from me, and any who cannot stomach my plans will be left behind, to answer for their refusal later.'

'As you say, Sir Roland.' The squire beat a hasty retreat and Roland picked up the scabbarded sword, fixing the belt around his waist and tightening it. The pain of the wound in his face faded as he set his mind to the task ahead. He had the Lord's work to do.

# Chapter 33

# Despair and Defiance

'WHERE WILL WE live this winter?'

'We should rebuild Vatnsborð.'

'We can't! The Christians might return.'

'You fools, we must give ourselves up, this fight is over.'

Leif held his arms up, trying to placate the crowd of angry and frightened people. It was eight days since the sacking of Vatnsborð, and they had gathered every survivor they could find at the hidden refuge that Bekkr had led them to. But now no one could agree what to do next and the arguments that had been brewing over days of inaction had broken into the open. The refuge was a hidden store under an overhang of rock in a gully, intended to be a temporary hiding place if the village was raided, not a home for the winter.

With Knud, Halla and Jarl Gustav dead, no one was the accepted leader of the remaining people. Most of the warriors looked to Leif for leadership, but few of the other people knew or cared who he was. Gunnar might have had the gravitas to take on the mantle, but the old huskarl was a shadow of his former self, quiet and withdrawn, his relentless spirit finally crushed by the losses he had endured.

Leif looked at Gjaldir, Bjorn and Vidar, who were standing behind him, trying to support him, and he gave them a weary shake of the head. The arguments between the group in front of them were on the verge of descending into violence, and no compromise or agreement seemed likely. The group was in danger of completely splintering and dispersing.

Leif turned from the crowd and walked over to the small group of his friends. He looked completely lost. 'What do we do?'

Gjaldir shrugged dumbly, Bjorn rubbed his chin, even Vidar seemed lost for ideas. 'Give them time? They need time to calm and grieve.'

'How much time? If we don't prepare for winter, we will not survive it.'

'Time spent here has only made it worse, it would be better to do the wrong thing than to do nothing,' replied Bjorn.

'We don't have time to build a new village, perhaps we should return to Vatnsborð, take our chances with the Crusaders returning?' said Gjaldir.

'Maybe we should leave, take those that will follow us and go to the coastlands,' said Vidar.

Leif rounded on the man. 'And give up on the people? Leave them to die?'

'Look at them, Leif!' Vidar said, pointing at the furious crowd. 'They don't want our leadership anymore. We cannot force them to accept it. Maybe it is time to look to our own future.'

'No,' said Leif with a growl. 'Those are our people, and we are not giving up on them.'

'Leif!' a voice called from behind.

'Wait,' said Leif angrily, dismissing the newcomer while he leant in towards Vidar.

'It cannot wait, the Chri...'

Leif turned on the man, furiously cutting him off. 'It can wait, look at what…' Leif suddenly stopped and saw it was Harald, who had been left watching Vatnsborð with two others. 'The Christians?'

'They have returned. Three ships landed in the village, about a hundred white-coated soldiers, with equipment and supplies. They look like they are prepared to be here for some time.'

'Fuck,' muttered Leif. 'And what are they doing?'

'I've left the boys watching them, but it looked like they were examining the tracks going out of the village.'

'Oh, shit,' said Vidar. 'We brought carts, a blind man could follow our tracks.'

'Yes,' said Harald glumly. 'I followed them easily myself. They will lead them straight here.'

Leif put his hand to his forehead and then laughed. 'Well, this is one way to settle these arguments. We must leave, now. Take everything we can carry, leave the carts.'

'Leif, there are two hundred people here, we cannot hide our trail.'

'Then we must move faster than them. Just outrun them until they run out of food and are forced to leave.'

'Two hundred people, including the old and the children, outrunning a hundred soldiers?' Vidar looked around the group with fear in his eyes. 'It is not possible.'

'We will have to make it possible, the Vatnsborð people know this land, and the Christians do not, we will use that to our advantage. What other choice is there?'

Vidar looked at Leif, and they all saw he wanted to urge them to abandon the people, but the long-haired warrior was smart enough to see he had no support in that, and he nodded briefly. 'As you say then.'

'Good, well, I better interrupt this mess to tell them. The rest of you, start preparing to leave.'

The news of the Christians coming ended the arguments with ruthless efficiency. No one argued that they would need to flee, although several small groups declared they would be going off on their own way, and Leif did not try to stop them. 'Splitting our tracks might be a good thing?'

'And we will move faster with fewer people,' added Bjorn.

They abandoned the carts and everything that could not be carried, including precious tools and supplies, hiding them a little distance from the gully and trying their best to cover the tracks. They debated burning them, but they held a slim hope of returning to recover the stores, and the fire would act as a beacon for their pursuers.

The two warriors Harald had left watching the village returned just before they left. 'They are coming,' the first man said simply, fear etched into his face, panting and red from having run to get to them.

'How far behind you?'

'Two miles? Three?'

Leif grimaced and looked at the column of huddled, frightened people who were just setting off with a dozen warriors at their head. 'Too close.'

'We will have to fight them, at some point,' said Harald, and no one disagreed.

'One hundred of them, sixty of us?' said Bjorn.

'We will find a good place, ambush them. We will have the advantages.'

'Even so, even if we win, the cost will be terrible.'

'Whatever the price to get these people safely away, we will pay. It is on our honour to do so,' said Leif. 'Come on, the last of them are leaving, we need to hurry them along. No stragglers.'

The main group of the warriors formed up at the back of the ragged column, pushing a determined and relentless pace, and making vain attempts to obscure their trail, or confuse followers with paths that diverged to later rejoin. But it was all futile. The forest floor was a delight for a tracker, disturbed needles and litter from the passing of hundreds of feet simply too obvious to conceal.

For the first day, there was no sign of their pursuit, apart from a single faint shout heard behind them. They were forced to leave two old men behind, who could not bear the pace and refused to be carried. Bekkr offered to stay behind with them for a time, and they all understood why. No one could be allowed to be captured, to reveal anything about them that would aid their pursuers.

They did not make camp that night, simply huddled in their blankets in groups, and the warriors roused them before the sun struggled above the horizon. On the second day, the relentless pace was starting to become unsustainable for about half of the miserable people. Children could not be prevented from crying, people slumped down beside the path and had to be forced back to their feet.

To make matters worse, the Christians were now close enough that they could be seen at the other end of one valley the group moved down, barely more than two miles behind. A silent, purposeful block of white-coated soldiers eating the distance between the groups.

Bekkr came to Leif as they left the valley, and Leif looked at him with dejected eyes. 'How much longer can they continue?'

'Not long, but I have an idea.'

'Tell me?'

'At the base of this valley two rivers join, and the area is all marsh. The trappers built a path through the marsh, including a couple of short, split log bridges over the deeper parts. I haven't been here for years, and I don't know if the bridges are still there. But if they are, we can cross them and destroy them, or defend them.'

'And if the bridges are gone?'

Bekkr looked ashen. 'Then we will be trapped in the marshes with nowhere to go.'

'How were the bridges last time you saw them? We risk everything going to them.'

'Old, rotten, still solid enough.'

'Anything could have happened since then. Do we have time to send someone to check?'

'No, if we aren't going through the marsh, we must continue this way, there will be no chance to turn and come back later.'

'How far is it to go around, upstream?'

'Four miles, maybe five?'

Leif nodded glumly and turned to the rest of the group around him. 'Do we risk it?'

'What is our other option?' asked Vidar. 'They are going to catch us, maybe this evening, maybe tomorrow morning. They know where we are, this ground is open, there will be no ambush or surprise. It will be a slaughter.'

'I agree,' said Harald. And others murmured their assent.

'Then the marsh it is. Bekkr, lead us there.'

The group reached the marsh and Bekkr led the column along the old path in single file. The path had once been a small piled embankment, wide enough for two men, but age and the water had broken it down in places so that they had to wade knee deep, and it was slow going.

As the head of the column made its way across the marsh, the rear waited in increasing concern as the time passed and the Christians closed on them.

By the time the first of the fifty-strong group of warriors at the rear were going down the path, the Christians could be seen coming out of the woods, less than a mile behind.

'We don't have enough time,' muttered Bjorn.

'We can't fight them here,' replied Leif.

'We may not have that choice,' said Harald.

The Christians took a little time to organise themselves for battle, which gave the warriors time to get onto the path, Leif and Harald being last in line. Their pursuers investigated the limits of the marsh around them, casting around for a way to get around their flanks, but finding nothing except chest-deep water and cloying mud.

Leif and his men finally reached the first of the two simple bridges and found to their relief it was still standing and the people had already crossed, and could be seen crossing the next one also. The head of the column was nearly over the marsh on the other side. The bridge was old and half rotten, and Leif used a spear to check the water either side of it and found to his despair that it was shallow, the channel there had silted up since the bridge was built, and it was barely necessary. A point emphasised when some of the warriors, too impatient to wait in the queue for the rotten old causeway, simply waded through the water beside it. It was a struggle, but they made it across.

'Cutting this down would be pointless,' said Leif.

'Perhaps the next channel is deeper. If it isn't, we can defend the far end of the bridge.'

'No,' said Vidar with a sad shake of his head. 'If we defend it, we are trapped. The Christians will send half their force upstream and come down behind us. If we retreat, they will cross in our shadow and be on us in moments. We have to destroy it.'

They reached the second bridge and found that the channel was indeed deep. But that was not the end of the problems. The bridge here was new, twice the length of a ship and strongly built from rough planks firmly set on thick posts standing in the current.

Leif looked back at their pursuers, who were now making their way cautiously along the path through the marsh, within range of a long bowshot. 'Can we destroy this in time?' he asked nervously.

'We have to try,' said Harald, dropping his shield near the start of the bridge and immediately setting to work on one of the thick planks. The warriors around him took his lead and started hacking with axes at the joints where the planks were firmly nailed into place. One warrior lowered himself over the side of the bridge and jammed his sword into the gap between the planks and the supports, trying to prise the sections apart, to no avail. Whoever built this bridge had built it to last.

Leif looked on with increasing concern as the Christians, who had seen what was happening, cried out to each other and increased their pace, jogging down the path towards the first bridge.

'Hurry!' shouted Leif, panic starting to tinge his voice. Beside him Gjaldir was hacking at a plank end with all his considerable strength, chunks of wood the size of apples flying from the end until the plank was free and Bjorn lifted it up and twisted it to one side, trying to rip it off the support the far end, where Harald hacked at it until it came loose, the two men throwing it into the slowly moving water.

The other plank was coming loose, and Leif motioned to Harald to come across before the bridge was cut, but the Norwegian just shook his head, not even looking up. 'One section isn't enough, I can jump that gap. Do another.'

Harald ripped the second plank from its remaining nails with a deep roar and dumped it into the water, then, without pause, started hacking at the exposed supports and the ends of the planks he was standing on, now separated from the others by a man's height of open water.

'Harald, don't be a fool!' shouted Leif, moving back with the others so they could work on the next section, men sweating and grunting as they demolished the bridge as fast as they could. But the black-bearded warrior ignored him, continuing to tear at the woodwork even as the first Christians got into spear-throwing range.

'He is not being a fool,' said Bjorn from beside Leif, where he was prying the end of a plank away with the wedge of his axe. Harald managed to destroy most of the end of the section he was standing on, but then the first Christians reached the end of the bridge and the Norwegian stood, picking up his shield and raising his axe, hammering it onto the boss of his shield and howling his defiance at the oncoming foe.

'JUMP to us!' shouted Leif, even as someone hauled him back, getting him out of the way so the section he was standing on could be removed. But Harald looked back briefly, saw that the bridge was still standing and shook his head. The two men were so close that if they had both reached out, they could have touched their weapons together. Leif knew what Harald knew. If he could jump the gap, the Christians could too. And they would be forced to defend the gap – trapping themselves, or retreat – allowing the Christians to cross.

Harald put his shield up and charged into the first Christian, not giving them the chance to knock him back into the water. The broad wooden boards covered the width of the bridge and only one enemy could face him at a time. Harald knocked the first man back into the next, nearly toppling them both off the planks, and then hammered at him with his axe in overhand cuts, landing on helmet and shield and upraised weapon.

The Christian withered under the vicious blows and crouched back from them, until Harald forced him to one side enough to simply put his big shield past the Christian's narrower one and lever him off the bridge. The armoured Christian shouted in alarm and fell from the planks into the water, disappearing with a splash and a flurry of bubbles.

The second man was no coward, and even as his compatriot was falling, he swung his sword overhand at Harald and landed a heavy blow on Harald's mailled shoulder, drawing a howl of pain and making the big man retreat a step to cover behind his shield as his weapon arm went limp.

Harald was driven back, closer and closer to the broken end of the planks. Now too far to reach with a jump. Harald looked back over his shoulder as the white-coated enemy tried to force his sword around the edge of the Norse shield, and he saw that the gap was now too wide to cross.

Leif's eyes met Harald's and the Norwegian smiled, the first time Leif had ever seen the expressionless warrior smile, and then Harald shouted at his opponent and dropped suddenly to one knee, causing the man to overbalance on top of him as he pushed, grabbing at Harald's shield for support. Harald let the man's momentum carry him, pivoting and letting go of the shield. The shocked enemy stepped forwards into thin air as he tried to use the unsupported shield to steady himself, and he pitched headfirst into the gap in the ruined bridge with a brief scream of surprise, leaving Harald kneeling on the bridge, axe dangling from his broken arm. The crippled warrior laughed heartily and took his axe in his uninjured left arm, standing and beckoning the next man to come.

Leif was dragged back to safety by insistent arms as the next section of the bridge underneath him was destroyed, eyes fixed on Harald as he squared up to his next opponent, a Crusader in the white, gold-crossed coat, wearing an unusual helmet with a steel faceplate. The enemy strode confidently towards Harald, putting his sword on his shoulder and lowering his stance as he closed with the Norseman.

Harald stepped forwards and lashed out with his axe, cumbersome in his left hand, and the Christian easily blocked his attacks, and then caught the axe shaft behind his shield on the final swing, bringing the two of them close together until Harald was roaring into the emotionless steel visage, spittle flecks spattering it as they struggled to shove each other over.

Then the Christian headbutted Harald viciously, steel crunching into flesh, and blood spouted from a shattered nose and rendered lip. Harald's head snapped back and he staggered groggily, losing the axe. The Christian soldier shoved Harald backwards, launching a lightning-fast series of cuts with his sword against the stunned and disarmed Norseman, cutting his hand from his wrist, then opening his face to the bone and spinning him around with a cry of anger and pain.

Harald staggered onto the broken end of the bridge, facing Leif, broken arm weakly fumbling for the seax at his waist, and the Christian stepped up casually behind him and raised a leg, kicking him square in the back with the sole of his shoe, sending Harald tumbling into the water below.

Leif shouted in fury and pain as the Norwegian disappeared beneath the water, and he stared at the faceless enemy who was now standing watching them, calm and immobile, from the other end of the destroyed bridge. Leif saw two men with bows shuffling past the queue of enemy on the narrow path and voices behind him called out in alarm. 'Shields up!' someone shouted, and another man pulled Leif back and got a shield in front of him as the first arrow was nocked and loosed at them, thunking into wood.

'We must go!' said Bjorn in his ear, and Leif gave the motionless enemy on the bridge one final look of hatred, a promise of death and punishment and merciless fury, before he allowed himself to be led away.

## Chapter 34

# A Moment of Destiny

THE DESTRUCTION OF the bridge and the sacrifice of Harald gained the exhausted survivors half a day of rest, but the respite was short lived. By the next day, the Christians had gone the long way around the marsh and were on their trail again, albeit further behind. The next morning, Leif called a glum meeting of the senior warriors. Gjaldir went to it, and no one objected. He was too curious to be left on the sidelines. All through the march he had kept to himself, trying to avoid Brunhild, who was being cared for by a group of the other survivors of Halla's people. He had marched mostly alone, in a tight circle of his own misery, punctuated briefly by the events at the bridge.

He sat on his heels at the back of the small gathering and watched Leif as he spoke.

'We have to fight them today in a place of our choosing, or be forced to fight when they catch us, wherever that is.'

No one argued. The death of Harald weighed heavily on them, both as a source of despair, and as an example. The man had died so that they could escape, and they all knew that they might have to do the same that day for the scared crowd of people they escorted.

'Bekkr, do you know anywhere?'

The man shook his head. 'I have never been this far down this path before. I do not know what lies ahead in the next valley.'

Leif nodded. 'Well, we will have to find something, and the sooner we leave, the more time we have to prepare. Rouse the people, tell them this is the last day of being hunted, one way or another. Make sure everyone who can fight has a weapon.'

'We will put some of those people in the shieldwall? It is only old men and boys and untrained women left,' Bjorn asked, concerned.

'No, but they will be needed if the wall fails.'

Bjorn nodded, his face drawn. 'I understand. And they will too.'

The group continued down the valley, following no discernible path through a landscape that looked like no man had visited in living memory. They were off the trappers' trail now, which headed north while they went east, towards the distant sea.

They had not gone far into the valley when Gjaldir saw it narrowed between an outcropping of rocks on the right, and the river on the left. The trees were sparser between the two, the ground rocky and uneven. Vidar pointed up at a large deadfall log on the slope above the gap. 'Look.'

Leif stopped to consider it, and then looked at the narrow gap and the steep slope. It looked to Gjaldir like it was terrible ground for a fight, uneven, rocky, sloped, narrow.

Leif nodded. 'It's perfect.'

Gjaldir considered it in confusion, but after thinking it through for a while, he thought he saw what Leif was seeing. It would be hard going for the Christians to move through it, and they wouldn't be able to use their numbers to stretch or envelop the smaller force.

'We make our stand here, and lure them onto the slope beneath that log, and then push it down,' said Vidar. 'It hasn't got far to fall. It may not do harm to many of them, but it might destroy their formation and we can use that to fall upon them while they are surprised and disorganised.'

'I agree. It is a good plan. Simple and violent.' Leif looked around at the warriors. 'This is what we will do, trust in the instinct of Vidar the cunning. It's always kept him alive, I hope the blessings of Odin will extend from him to us too.'

A few men laughed half-heartedly at that, the bravado of despair.

Leif looked around at the men as they formed a half circle around him. 'So here it is, the last battle. If we win here, we are free, we can go and find a place to live for the winter, and whatever else we want to do after that. And if we fail, well, it won't be our problem anymore, for we will be feasting in Valhalla. Will you all stand beside me on this shitty hill?'

The warriors howled and growled their agreement as a group and even Gjaldir felt his pulse rise. He was sick of war, sick of fighting, hollowed by grief; but this group of men who had suffered together, fought alongside him, gave him a sense of belonging. He knew he would stand with them through anything.

The men around him had lost everything, borne the pain of loss and defeat so many times that the prospect of a good death might have seemed a relief. The thought of inflicting that pain on their enemy before they died was perhaps their last comfort.

Leif's eyes landed on Gunnar, who had been so sorely absent from their leadership group for days. Men quieted and looked, stepping aside to look at the old huskarl, who nodded slowly. 'I will stand in the first rank, and no enemy shall pass me until they step over my corpse.'

Leif thumped his hand against his shield. 'I hope it does not come to that, but brother, I am happy to hear you say it. You will be in the centre of the wall. This gap is fifteen men wide. Forty-five will stand in the wall, with another fifteen behind, ready to help where needed. Vidar, you will command the fifteen behind?'

'I will.'

'And make that tree ready to fall, and when it does, be ready to come down behind it. We will have once chance at this, the longer we fight, the worse it will be. We need to break them quickly, or their numbers will overwhelm us.'

The warriors split up into groups, Gunnar appearing re-animated by the promise of battle, and personally organising the front ranks, carefully setting the line for the best position.

Vidar grabbed Gjaldir by the shoulder as he stood there, unsure where he should go. 'You are with me, I need a few strong men to push this trunk, and we need to prepare it, loosen whatever holds in in place, and make sure it is ready to fall. Can you do that?' Vidar asked, his eyes piercing Gjaldir's.

'Yes.'

'Good, let's go and see what can be done with it.'

Gjaldir nodded and followed the man up the slope the few paces to where the large fallen trunk lay in the shadow of the rocks above. It was straight and solid, a recent fall. It had tumbled down the slope from above until it lodged on an old rotten stump at one end, and jammed against a rock at the other. The two men considered it carefully.

'Do you think we can move it?' asked Vidar.

Gjaldir felt a burst of pride that his opinion was even being considered, but he had spent a lot of time felling and moving trees at Vatnsborð. 'I think so. We need to cut away a little from the end on the rock, and put something in place to hold it, a wedge perhaps.' He pointed at the nearer end. 'And we can cut away at this stump, lower it until the tree can be pushed over the top.'

'Can that be done in time?'

'I don't know, how long do we have?'

'No idea, so we'd best start now. Do we have any good axes?'

'I think we kept a couple.'

'Best go fetch them then. I'll gather some other men to help.'

Gjaldir sank down into the cover of the rocks with four others as Vidar peered carefully over the top, watching for the advancing Christians to get into the right place, in front of the Norse shieldwall.

Gjaldir listened as the Crusader soldiers moved steadily forwards, the dozen different sounds of shouted orders, metal on shields, crunching footsteps on the rocky slope gave away their movement.

He and the rest of Vidar's group were hidden behind the rocks, but the main formations of Norse and Crusaders could see each other clearly, the Northmen's shieldwall providing a target to attack, luring the enemy into the area where the precariously balanced log would roll.

Gjaldir waited, the tension burning in his limbs and chest, the time dragging on painfully as he waited for Vidar to tell them to move. Then there was a shouted command from the hidden enemy, and Vidar swore.

'What?' hissed Gjaldir.

'They have stopped.'

'Shall we push the log?'

'No, curse them. They have stopped too soon.'

'They will continue, surely?'

'I don't know. Their leader is looking this way, perhaps he realises the danger.'

There was another order shouted from below them and Vidar cursed again. 'They are spreading out into line and not moving further. They have sensed the trap. Fuck!'

'They won't wait there forever, they will attack eventually.'

Vidar ducked back down slowly and shook his head, his mouth pressed into a thin line of distaste. 'No, they don't have to. They can wait us out. As soon as we retreat, they can set upon us, or they can send men to climb the hill behind us and come down from the side.'

'Well...' Gjaldir was horrified almost speechless, he had thought the plan was sure to work. 'Why didn't we expect that?'

Vidar gave him an angry look. 'Because they aren't normally this smart. They attack everything they see, they always have. I expected them to attack when they saw the smaller force we have.'

'So, what do we do now?'

As if in answer, Gjaldir heard Leif shout out from the line below. 'Shieldwall! Forwards!'

'That,' said Vidar glumly. 'That is our only option.'

Vidar waited until he was sure the ruse was up, and the waved to his hidden men. 'Come, we will join Leif and finish this face to face.'

The men stood from their hiding places and they moved down the slope, past the log and headed for the back of Leif's line, which was moving under the shadow of the rocks to meet the Christians in the narrow gap, no room for either side to do anything but fight through their enemy to gain victory.

The Norse ranks were already three men deep, the Christian wall twice as deep, the white-coated, maille-armoured soldiers in the front, the men Gjaldir recognised as the knights and wealthy men at arms, and the more lightly equipped ordinary soldiers behind. Above the whole block hung the golden cross from a tall banner pole, both bright and foreboding.

The Christians let the Norse close most of the distance before a shouted command rang out and their own line advanced, and the two sides met.

At first, the furious exchange of blows favoured neither side, and men hacked and blocked and swore and bled, and died. But the Christians started, measure by measure, to push the Norse line back. In those tight confines, the heavy armour of the Christian knights, many mailled from head to toe, was telling against their more lightly protected opponents.

Gjaldir and Vidar's group threw themselves into the back of the wall, too far from the enemy to fight them, but trying to halt the loss of ground. But it was futile. As the Norse were steadily pressed back from under the shadow of the rocks, a few of the enemy spread a little to their right, clambering up the scree slope to press on the flank of the Norse line.

Vidar threw a few of his men into that dangerous flank, trying to stem the tide, but where Vidar saw danger, Gjaldir suddenly saw opportunity. He tried to push his way to Vidar, shouting his name. 'VIDAR!' But the man was deep in the fight and could not hear him over the cacophony of battle noise. Gjaldir looked around him at the men, saw their nervousness and fear, saw the inevitable end of this fight etched into worried faces, and he made his decision.

'Come with me!' he shouted at those nearest to him. At first no one moved, some gave him confused or angry looks, as if he was fleeing. Gjaldir had no time to argue or persuade, he just grabbed one warrior he recognised by the front of his maille and screamed into his face to be heard. 'We can use the log, come with me now!'

The warrior hesitated for a moment and then nodded, and Gjaldir grabbed a couple of others, and soon men saw that something was happening and joined him, until he had eight or so following him as he ran up the slope, past the fight, and went to the log. 'Push it!' he shouted at the men who had come with him. Many of them had been in Vidar's group and they understood, getting their shoulders behind the log and jamming spear shafts under it to lever it up over the remains of the stump that held it in place.

Gjaldir ran to the other end, where a hastily cut wedge held it against the rockface, and reversed his axe, hammering at the wedge to dislodge it. It started to give and he looked down the slope, making sure he had not made a mistake. He was certain he had not. The Norse line was shrinking away from the rocks, the Christian attack curling around it and pushing through, right into the space they had hoped to spring the trap. The Norse were also still in the path, but there were dozens of Christians between the log and his friends, and Gjaldir just prayed it would be enough.

As he was looking, an enemy knight in the formation below

was watching him, and he clearly saw the danger, because he started shouting orders and trying to drag men out of the way. Gjaldir felt a burst of savage bloodlust. *You're too late.*

He gave the wedge another heavy blow and it slipped out, tumbling away down the slope. The trunk shifted and for a moment looked like it would not move, but then the warriors gave it another heave and it slowly toppled off the stump, thumping into the rocky slope and bouncing, gaining speed as it rolled and slid down the scree-covered slope below.

Some of the Christians were already watching up the slope, and there was a sudden panic as the ship-sized trunk started slithering down the slope towards them. It caught on some rocks and bounced and jarred, but nothing stopped its progress and it bore down on the fighting men below with a deadly inevitability, and only too late did the mass of enemy try to flee from its path.

The slope was not as steep as it could have been, and the distance was not as far as would have been ideal, but the trunk hit the back of the Christian block with the force of a herd of cattle in full flight and men were knocked flat or thrown around like children's toys as Gjaldir watched, mouth agape.

The bottom end of the trunk did catch the left of the Norse line and Gjaldir's celebration died in his throat as he saw some of his own people thrown aside by the log even as it slowed on the flatter ground and the press of bodies hampered its roll, and then it rocked to a stop, half a dozen screaming Christians trapped beneath it, and fifty more scattered like a toppled pile of firewood.

There was a moment of stillness, as the shock of the impact registered on both of the small armies, and then a terrible roar of anger and triumph from the Norse line, who set upon the chaotic mess made of their opponents.

'With me!' shouted Gjaldir, because he could see that despite the shock of the trap, more than half the enemy were still standing, pushing and shoving to get themselves free of the new obstacle and back into some sort of line to oppose the re-invigorated Norse. Gjaldir pounded down the slope, slipping and scurrying and trying to keep his feet as he heard the others following around him.

As the slope levelled out and he and his small force reached the flank of the disorganised enemy, a dozen or so charged out to meet them in a ragged line, and suddenly Gjaldir was fighting.

The first man he reached, a spearman with a simple, cheap shield, he simply knocked over, using the slope and his size and strength to shove him to the ground, stepping over him and hammering his axe down into the man's skull. He saw his men ripping into the enemy around him and he pulled his axe free and looked for his next victim.

A white-coated knight of the Order was shouting orders at the men around him, turned away from Gjaldir, and he started to head towards the Christian, but then the man turned to look at him, and Gjaldir froze on the spot.

The faceless helm fixed its steely gaze on Gjaldir, the dark eye slits betraying nothing of the man beneath, but it stopped him in his tracks. He remembered with a gut-punching rush the day at the ford in Denmark, the horse and rider leaving him, of that same heartless steel gaze meeting his, and then leaving him to his fate.

And now that same gaze held his again, and the owner bore down on him, stopping to sidestep a clumsy strike from a Norse warrior and cut his swordhand from his body, barely stopping his advance as he bore down on the motionless Gjaldir.

Gjaldir looked at the man in horror as the knight stepped in to strike, raising the sword into a high guard and closing the distance rapidly.

'Sir Hans?' Gjaldir gasped in German, recovering enough sense to bring his shield up but feeling weak and disoriented as he was confronted with a shadow from his past life.

The metal-clad knight paused for a second, and if the steel face could show surprise it did, cocking slightly to one side to examine him, before bringing the sword round in a killing blow.

Gjaldir just managed to block the blow, deflecting it with the face of his shield and stepping back a pace, instincts and training taking over control of his body from a mind that was fixated on the blade that was trying to kill him, a blade that had hovered in indecision just long enough for Gjaldir to see what it was, and for his scrambling brain to recognise.

*That's Ragnvald's sword.*

Gjaldir desperately parried another attack, giving more ground as the relentless knight bore down on him, fast as a serpent, fluid and graceful. *Why does Sir Hans have Ragnvald's sword?*

Each thought nearly cost him his life as he desperately tried to keep the knight at bay with his shield and axe, which felt leaden and slow compared to the skill with which his opponent wielded his weapons.

He was forced to stop considering why Sir Hans was here, why he was trying to kill him with Ragnvald's sword, like some horrible parody of his past lives come to punish him. He tried to remember what Gunnar had taught him, tried to think what would work, but each defence was more desperate than the last, each blow survived required him to give more ground, making it only a matter of time until he tripped or stumbled on the uneven slope.

The panic rose as Ljós a Norðan scored his forearm, and then skipped off the brow of his helmet, a finger's span away from reaching his eyes. He started to panic as he realised he was going to lose, that his opponent was vastly more skilled than he was. He earned himself a half step of space by ramming the rim of his shield into the faceless helm, but it did nothing but make the knight re-compose himself.

Gjaldir tried to use the moment of space to attack, trying to push his opponent's shield into his sword arm to foul it and to strike with his axe over the top, as Gunnar had taught him. The knight sideslipped the attack and delivered a slithering thrust, impossibly fast, beating Gjaldir's defences and catching him an angled blow to the chest, spearing into his maille and driving the air from his lungs with a piercing burst of pain.

Gjaldir gasped and staggered back, his shield arm flailing as he tried to retain his balance through the sheet of pain in his ribs, and saw the knight step gracefully in towards him, putting his wrist behind Ljós a Norðan's broad pommel and lining it up for a finishing blow that Gjaldir had no hope of stopping.

In those moments between life and death, Gjaldir felt the cold wind of his fate blow over him and he felt the grip of a shiver, and the sounds of the battle closed off around him as the space between the tip of the sword he had forged, and his own body, become his entire world.

Somewhere above and behind him he heard a bird cawing, past the heavy beating of his own heart he heard the thumping of its wings as it passed. And then the tip of the sword was coming forwards, already inside the line of his shield, his axe wide to his right, impossibly far from the parry.

The knight planted his front foot as he thrust, lining up his entire body behind the blow that would pierce his target's maille and drive deep into the chest beyond.

And the foot landed on a patch of loose gravel, and as Gjaldir heard the raven's cry and felt the wind of its passage, the knight stumbled with a curse, his leg slipping out from underneath him, and the lethal tip of Ljós a Norðan skewed to the side and dropped, spearing into the ground. The knight started to topple forwards, completely off balance, his steel-faced helm angling upwards and his arms flailing as his foot scrabbled for grip that it could not find.

Gjaldir saw the man falling, and saw where he would go, and he stepped forwards into the fall, bringing his axe up and pointing its head like a spear, aimed directly at the head of the man who was falling so neatly into its path.

That expressionless helm, so immovable, so unreadable; but Gjaldir was so close he saw the eyes through those dark slits, and he saw nothing but fear.

The tip of his axe went under the steel faceplate and sank softly into the knight's throat with no more resistance than a spoon going into butter, and Gjaldir stepped into the knight and pressed him down into the ground, trapping his sword arm and pushing the axe deeper into the man's neck, hearing his gurgling and feeling his legs thrashing against the ground.

And then as quickly as the fight had started, it was over, and the body beneath him went limp, and Gjaldir's body purged itself of the tension and fear as his hands shook. He dropped his shield and axe and ripped the helmet from the dead man's head, confused and surprised not to recognise the man underneath, that it was not Sir Hans. He looked down at the sword he had forged for Jarl Ragnvald and picked it up, feeling its familiar weight.

Then the sounds of the battle returned with a rush and he looked up, remembering where he was, and what was happening, and saw the chaos of the battle around the fallen log on the slope below him was abating, most of the surviving Christians on one side of it, most of his people on the other, both sides exhausted and trying to recover.

The men who had gone with him down the slope had crashed into the side of the ruined enemy formation on this side of the log and they were reaping lives left and right, but they were horribly outnumbered and the enemy was starting to react. Gjaldir was about to go down to help them when one of the white-coated soldiers pointed up the slope at him. 'Roland is down!' the man shouted in German, and Gjaldir realised the man was shouting not at him, but at the helmet that hung loosely from his hand.

Other voices responded in panicked German and Gjaldir smiled wolfishly, remembering that the man he had killed had been shouting orders. He strode down the slope towards the enemy and raised the blood-spattered helmet to show to them. Then he filled his aching lungs and shouted in German with all the power he could muster. 'Your commander is dead, your god has no power here! Run, now, before I come for *your* lives too!'

Then he hurled the helmet at the crowd and raised Ljós a Norðan in the air as he gathered himself to charge down the slope.

But the Christians nearest him shrank from his advance, shocked to hear their enemy shout in their language, many unable to take their eyes off him and the sword.

'Back!' called one man nearest to him, and he started backing away, looking over his shoulder.

'The sword! Save the sword!' shouted another, and the man bravely came forwards, shield up and his own blade out, coming to meet Gjaldir.

Gjaldir would have laughed, if his lungs had not been so drained, because the tentative attack seemed childish, simple, obvious. The enemy thrust at him from behind his shield, as Gunnar had shown him the enemy did, and Gjaldir parried on the inside with his sword, turned it and pushed it aside, stepping into the parry and thrusting his sword into the throat of his opponent, as Gunnar had taught them to do.

The man sank to his knees and Gjaldir kicked him free of the bright blade, raising it again to confront the next man, cutting his fingers from his spearshaft in a spray of splinters as the Christian thrust it harmlessly at his maille, the impact coming as a dull thump, then he kicked the man to the ground, the joy of battle suddenly flowing through him.

And then there was no one else to fight. A howling, cheering wave of Norse warriors came over the fallen trunk and the enemy dissolved like dry mud in water, disintegrating and scattering, running back down the slope in clumps and alone, leaving their fallen around and under the tree, and the victorious Norse in control of the valley.

Gjaldir stood there, panting and drained, feeling the strength flow from his body in the way that it always did after a fight, and he saw Leif coming over with a strange expression, looking at him with an odd reverence and concern.

'Gjaldir?' said Leif, as Gjaldir stood there and panted, finding that his weakness was spreading, more than he was used to. 'Gjaldir, are you wounded?'

Gjaldir fought against the wave of nausea that was rumbling over him and shook his head. 'No, I am fine.'

'Gjaldir, your side.' Leif pointed at him and Gjaldir looked down, confused, to find the broken head of the spearman's weapon lodged in his armoured ribs, blood seeping out from around it. Panic gripped him and the sword dropped from his fingers as he looked up at Leif.

'Oh, shit!'

And then the world tilted and went black.

## Chapter 35

# Fate and Fortune

'LUCKY BASTARD, YOU are,' said Bjorn, inspecting the wound.

'I don't feel lucky,' grumbled Gjaldir, wincing at the pain as Bjorn's fingers probed the angry red wound.

'You took a spear in a rib and have no wound rot, no bone shards. A clean break that will heal. You don't know how lucky you are. A finger higher or lower and that spear would have been in your liver.'

Gjaldir mumbled through gritted teeth but Bjorn just shook his head and stood up. 'You'll be fine.'

It was three days since the battle in the valley, and the Norse had camped in the open valley floor beyond, resting and tending to their wounded. The surviving Christians had regrouped and then retreated. They had been followed until the marshes and the scouts had watched them continue, back towards Vatnsborð.

Gjaldir sat there, mouth and eyes screwed shut against the pain of the wound and the broken rib beneath, and tried to think about something else as he gently lowered his tunic back down over it.

As he was doing that, Leif, Vidar, Bekkr, Tormund Five-Bones and a few of the other men came over and the big blond Svearman gave Gjaldir a broad smile. 'I am pleased to see you up again. I have something for you.'

Leif beckoned to Vidar, who came up with a scabbarded sword. 'This belongs to you now.'

Gjaldir's eyes widened as he recognised Ljós a Norðan, still scabbarded in the same dragon scabbard that Dengir had made for it, the bone dragon ornament taken from the scabbard of Ragnvald's sword Drekkitunga before that. Gjaldir felt a sharp clutch of emotion well up at the thought of the two men he had both served and loved, and he reached out for the sword, hissing at the pain that caused in his side, pulling his hand back and clenching his fist.

'Probably best you don't use it yet, but when you recover, the sword is yours.'

Gjaldir looked up at Leif. 'It was Jarl Ragnvald's sword, not mine. You should take it, you were his huskarl. Anyway, it is sacred to your people, or so Tormund said.' He jerked his chin at the seer without looking at him.

Leif shook his head. 'It is sacred to *our* people. And you took it from an enemy killed in battle, so it is yours. That is our way. Now you can carry it.'

Gjaldir looked at the sword, feeling a desire for it, but afraid of that desire because of the expectations it carried. 'It is supposed to be carried by a Norseman, true and steadfast, isn't that what Tormund said?'

'It is, but as you are always telling us, you are a Norseman now. And no one here would argue that you are steadfast.'

Gjaldir croaked out a laugh and shook his head. 'No one has ever believed me when I said that I was a Norseman.'

'And no one would believe otherwise now,' said Leif, no longer smiling. 'Not after that battle. We all saw how you wielded this sword. We saw you charge an army with nothing *but* this sword, not even a shield. And we saw them cower from you, we saw you cut them down, take a spear in the chest and ignore it to defeat its owner. We all saw the power with which you wielded this blade, and the enemy saw it too and they ran from it. It is undeniably yours to wield.'

'This is no chance event, to recover this sword you forged in the key moment of the battle. This is the work of Odin himself,' said Tormund with a devout nod. 'It was his power you channelled in that moment, all here were witness to it.'

Gjaldir ignored the seer's claims. Everything was Odin's work according to the strange little man. Gjaldir knew better, he hadn't had the power of a god, he had had the luck of the devil. 'It was fucking stupid, charging in like that,' he said bitterly. 'A sword with no shield against a spear, a stupid fight to take. That is what Gunnar would say.' Then he looked around and narrowed his eyes. 'Where is Gunnar? He survived the battle?'

Leif nodded sadly. 'Yes, he did. Every man around him in the front rank was killed but he was unharmed and I think…' Leif paused, unsure what to say. 'Well, he has gone, he left in the night with nothing but his equipment and some food. I don't think he could bear it anymore.'

Gjaldir looked down at the ground, saddened by the news. Gunnar had always been a giant presence, an anchoring rock in the storm of hardships and defeats.

'So what do we do now?'

'That is what we gathered to discuss, but I wanted to include you in our discussions from now on.'

Gjaldir narrowed his eyes. 'Why?'

'Because you have earned it, Drengr,' said Bjorn with a smile.

Gjaldir blushed at the compliment, perhaps the highest one warrior could bestow upon another. To be called a Drengr was to be declared a man that others should look up to, and emulate. He thought perhaps Bjorn was mocking him, but he saw no jest in it, and the other men around nodded their agreement. Gjaldir did not know what to say.

'Well, I don't know what we should do,' he said limply.

'Well, neither do we, so that is the problem.'

'I think we continue, carry on the way we have been going, towards the coast,' said Vidar.

'And go where? Soon we will reach inhabited lands, and the Christians will be there,' replied Leif.

'So, we find somewhere to build a camp for the winter and we hide from them.'

'Winter is soon, we will be poorly prepared and there are too many people with us.'

'The people cannot continue fleeing from the Christians,' said Bekkr, shaking his head. 'We have pushed them to their limit. This battle was won, but how long before the Christians return? Either that band or another. One or two more fights like that and we will have no men left, victorious or not.'

'What else do you suggest?' asked Bjorn. 'We cannot go to a town or village with two hundred people and expect not to be noticed. Wherever we go, we will be hunted.'

Leif nodded. 'So we let them go.'

That took the wind out of Vidar and Bjorn. 'Let them go? Go where?'

'Wherever they can,' said Leif sadly. 'In small groups, spread out around the area to towns and villages, they have a chance to find somewhere to live. We give them silver and tell them to find somewhere to spend the winter. They will be more refugees amongst many, and the Christians will never find most of them.'

Bjorn looked punchdrunk. 'But we cannot go with them. Forty warriors, even disguised, will be noticed anywhere.'

'Yes, we will have to remain out here, in the wilderness. But we can take it, we can survive it. They cannot.'

‘We should not abandon them and call it anything other than what it is. Cowardice,’ said Bjorn in disgust.

‘And if we take them with us, and the Christians return, we just ensure their deaths!’

‘We defeated them, how are you so sure they will hunt us?’

‘Because we defeated them. They will not accept it. More will come, and no one with us will be safe.’

‘But if we scatter the people, this group that we have fought and bled for, we will never gather them again, this will be the end, the failure of everything we fought for, what so many have died for!’ Bjorn was animated now, aghast, looking around the group for support, his famed honour and loyalty not allowing him to consider that outcome.

‘They will be alive, isn’t that what we fought for?’

‘He’s right, Bjorn, and you know it,’ said Vidar. ‘Keeping the people together was Halla’s dream, and it failed, and she and so many others died for it. Don’t make the rest of them die for it too.’

‘And then what?’ Bjorn asked the group, arms outstretched. ‘When we scatter our people and survive in the woods all winter, us forty warriors, what then? What do we do after that?’ He looked around the group and received no answer, eyes were averted or looked at the ground. There was silence as he stood there glaring at them all.

‘Nothing, no one has an answer?’

‘I suggest we survive the winter first, what comes after that can be decided later,’ Bekkr said.

‘I agree, we do not need to decide here on this hillside, we need to focus everything on the winter ahead. Send the people away, let them find the safety they can, and the rest we can decide later,’ Vidar said, looking nervously at Bjorn.

Bjorn looked angrily around at them, his anger fading gradually to disgust. ‘Do it, but I will not take this upon my shoulders. If this is what you wish to do, to break apart what we spent so much blood keeping together, you will be responsible.' Bjorn turned and stalked away from the circle.

'Bjorn!' called Vidar. But Leif put a hand on his arm.

'Leave him, this was Halla's wish he is forsaking. It will not be easy for him.'

Gjaldir watched on uncomfortably in silence, clutching the sword that had been put on his lap, as the others left, downcast.

He sat there, alone with his thoughts for a long time, until he heard footsteps coming over towards him. He looked up and his eyes widened. 'Brunhild!' he exclaimed, then tried to control himself, putting the sword to one side and struggling to stand. He groaned his way to his feet and looked her in the eyes, searching for a trace of the woman he had known in them, but finding them cold and distant. 'How are…' The lameness of the question died in his throat and he looked down, not knowing what to say.

'I hear it was decided to send us all away.' The words pierced into Gjaldir worse than the spear had done, and he groaned. He realised the full truth, that finally what Brunhild had predicted all these years had happened. They were going to be separated, and there was little chance they would ever meet again.

Some small, shameful part of him thought in that moment that perhaps it was for the best, for the pain and loss they reminded each other of to be gone. A slim finger slid under his chin and pushed it up, forcing him to meet her unwavering eyes again.

'You have to go, I understand,' Gjaldir said. 'I'm so sorry, about it all.'

Brunhild's eyebrows furrowed slightly and then she shook her head. 'No. I will not surrender myself to the people who took away my son. I will not go and live in their villages, poor and afraid, until someone makes a slave of me again.' She let go of his chin as he stood there in confusion, and reached down to the sword that he had discarded, picking it up and pressing her hand into his chest as she held the scabbard, so close that they could have kissed, but without a fragment of the feeling that once would have encouraged them to do so.

'I want you to teach me how to fight. I will never be unarmed and vulnerable again. I will never be the helpless victim of the next man who comes with a blade and a desire to take what is mine. Take me with you, teach me how to use this, make the others accept me as a warrior, as you forced them to accept you.'

Gjaldir almost choked, but he saw the burning intensity of Brunhild's stare, and the utter conviction in her tone and expression, and he faltered, and nodded. 'I will.'

Brunhild took his hand and wrapped it on the hilt, taking a small knife out of her belt and running it across their entwined fingers, drawing blood from both and a wince of pain from Gjaldir.

'Good, then I will follow you to wherever it is you are going as a fellow warrior, and the gods or death alone can part us. On our blood we make these oaths. Will you swear it also?'

Gjaldir nodded slowly, still shocked. 'I do, I swear it. I will train you to be a warrior, and I will never let anyone prevent you from following that path, or any path you wish to take.'

Their blood mixed and trickled down the hilt of Ljós a Norðan and Brunhild held his hand there on it in an iron grip as her eyes searched his for any sign of falsehood, until she was satisfied and nodded. 'Then we are bonded.'

Then she let go of his hand and the sword and walked away, and Gjaldir looked down at his hand and the hilt of the sword in shock, feeling the power of the words that he had just spoken, and looking up at the disappearing figure of the woman he had loved but barely recognised, until she was gone from view.

Gjaldir hobbled through the trees of the encampment two days later, slowly and gingerly, as the people were preparing to leave.

Some people were headed for family or places they knew, some simply hoping to find a place that would take them in. All the silver the group possessed had been divided up amongst them, to help them secure a place for the winter. There were those who were relieved to go, and those who had refused to leave, preferring to take their chances with the winter. Some of the very few warriors who had had surviving family there chose to disarm and go with them, and no one tried to stop them.

After those who had died in the battle in the valley, and those who were leaving with their families, a bit under seventy people would be headed on into the wilderness to find a place to spend the winter, thirty-seven warriors among them. No one had argued with Gjaldir when he declared that Brunhild was going with them to train to be a warrior. No one laid claim to Halla's ownership of her, without ceremony she was considered a freewoman, and so it was her choice.

Tormund also insisted on going with the warriors. No one really wanted him to, but he simply couldn't be persuaded otherwise. They had the choice to kill him or let him, and no one would kill a seer who claimed the Odinsight, let alone one who had shown evidence he might indeed be under the eye of the Allfather.

Gunnar had not returned or been seen since the day after the battle and, reluctantly, they left without him. His loss was a hard one to stomach but they had no choice but to accept it.

The denuded group, stripped of the weakest and most vulnerable, set out north-east into the hilly country near the coast of Hälsingland, hoping to find a place to shelter for the winter, close enough to the coast to be able to raid for food from the Christian garrisons there when needed.

As they set out, Gjaldir dreading the journey with his wounded side, but determined not to delay the group, Brunhild came over to walk alongside him. She said nothing, and gave him no smile or sarcastic comment as she once would have done. There was no love or warmth in her presence. She had been clear; she was coming as a warrior, not his lover, and Gjaldir accepted that. After all that they had been through, it was a comfort merely to have her at his side.

She was carrying the shield and sword of a dead warrior, and a helmet and oversized maille hauberk were bundled up in a parcel strung over her shoulder. Gjaldir reached over and moved the strap, wrapping the end of her blanket around the rough rope sling as the other warriors did, so that the strap would not carve a groove in her shoulder as they marched.

She grunted her thanks and he nodded, setting off again with the barest hint of a smile. He was not looking forwards to the winter, but with Brunhild at his side, he could endure anything. Gjaldir hobbled along at the back of the column, Ljós a Norðan on his left, and Brunhild on his right, and for the first time since Vatnsborð, the two gave him a crumb of comfort and hope.

Grandmaster Reinhard was standing in the nave of the unfinished church outside the ruins of Uppsala, examining the work that was ongoing on spanning the roof of the structure. Winter would be upon them in a matter of weeks, and he wanted the roof completed before the weather turned bad enough that work would have to stop.

He pressed his lips more firmly into a line as the master carpenter came over, hands scrunched together in front of him, looking decidedly nervous.

'Grandmaster...'

Reinhard held up a finger to silence the man, not taking his eyes off the half-finished woodwork, wanting to forestall the tedious excuses and blathering. 'How much will remain unfinished?'

'It depends when the rains...'

Reinhard snapped his fingers and lowered his stare to meet the carpenter's eyes. 'How long until you expect to finish?'

'Four or five weeks, your excellency.'

'And everyone tells me we expect the rains in three.'

'Yes, your excellency.'

'So don't lie to me about depending on the rain. What will the situation be in three weeks?'

'The roof over the altar will be complete and covered, and possibly the transepts, but only about half of the nave.'

Reinhard's mouth turned downwards and his eyes narrowed. 'Which is as worthwhile as nothing, if half the roof is open, the building will be useless until spring.'

The carpenter bowed his head in defeat. 'Yes, your excellency, I apologise, I…'

Reinhard turned and walked away, there was no value in letting the man finish his grovelling. He was furious that the church, the centrepiece of his ambitions here, the grandest building north of Germany, would not be ready for so many months. It was not only a personal embarrassment, but could be seen as figurative of his power.

He stormed through the unfilled archway where the main doors would someday hang, Bertrand scurrying along behind to keep up on his shorter legs, and found Sir Sighard and his men waiting patiently to escort him back to his quarters. But Sighard was not alone. There was a messenger standing there with him, armoured and muddied from the road, a leather pouch slung across his chest. The man, perhaps little more than a boy, a page or squire seeking to prove himself by taking the dangerous job of message bearer, gave a crisp bow and opened the pouch, proffering a sealed letter.

Reinhard snatched the letter and looked at the seal. *Hugues*. 'Do you know what it contains?' asked Reinhard.

The squire started to nod and then caught himself and shook his head.

'Well, yes or no?'

'Grandsteward Hugues did not tell me its contents.' The man looked nervous. 'But I could guess.'

'Guesswork is a fool's method, young man, mark that and don't forget it if you want to continue in my service.'

The messenger bowed his head, chastened. 'I will, Grandmaster.'

Reinhard left him there looking at the ground as they both stood in silence for a few moments. 'Well? What is your guess?'

The squire looked up nervously. 'I… I am not sure.'

'That is why you should not guess, but you did, and I want to know. If your guess is wrong, I will dismiss you from my service, I do not tolerate stupidity.'

The squire started gasping, but he nodded brusquely and gathered his courage. 'I believe it carries news of Brother Roland, Sieur de Blanchant, your excellency.'

That cheered Reinhard up. 'Ah, excellent. He has finished off the rebels then.' He saw immediately from the squire's pained reaction that was not the case, and he was immediately furious. Not that the news was bad, but that he had just made a fool of himself by guessing incorrectly.

He ripped open the letter and scanned the first few lines, his scowl changing to a thin, white pressed line. Then he folded the letter carefully back up, not looking up at the messenger.

'You continue to be my messenger. Now go.'

The relieved man bowed deeply and almost ran away, desperate to get away from the wrath of the bishop.

Sir Sighard looked on with a downcast face, unusual for the impassive knight. Reinhard had chosen him partly for his even temperament, it was hard to fluster the man.

'Brother Roland has failed, he has fallen, and the sword is lost to the rebels.'

Sighard stiffened and his brows fell heavily onto his eyes as anger slowly burned through him. 'The sacrilege…' The German knight fought to control himself. 'I would gladly take his place, and hunt down these rebels and bring back the sword,' he growled.

Reinhard nodded. 'I know you would.'

'This loss cannot be tolerated,' the knight said, his voice full of barely restrained outrage.

Reinhard considered the knight and studied his reaction, the uncommon emotions pouring forth. 'Does it really make you so angry, Sighard?'

'Yes, your excellency! This is an insult to us all, a challenge to our Order and our entire faith!' Sighard swallowed whatever words he had been about to continue with and recovered back to his stiff pose. 'I am sorry for my outburst, Grandmaster.'

Reinhard smiled. 'No, do not be sorry. You are only blessed with an abundance of faith to God, and loyalty to the Order.' He studied the man carefully, all the implications being weighed in his mind.

'Thank you, Grandmaster. Brother Roland was a fine knight, and a faithful servant. And the Light of the North was a precious relic, a demonstration of the Lord's faith in us.'

'Yes, yes, it was.' Reinhard put his finger to his lip and tapped it for a while, thinking carefully, before coming to a conclusion. 'Brother Sighard, I think the rest of the men will take this news very hard, and it would be best if it came from you, not from whispered rumours spread through the camp.'

Sighard said nothing, but nodded gently once.

'So, I wish you to go to the men now, as fast as you can, before that messenger can spread his guesses first, and tell them of this outrage.'

Sighard nodded. 'As you order, Grandmaster.' The knight snapped out some orders at the escort, half of whom mounted and took off with him at a canter down the slope, headed towards the camp on the other side of the city, several miles away.

'Come, Bertrand, let us walk.'

Bertrand looked anything but thrilled at the prospect but followed Reinhard down the hill. When they were out of earshot of the soldiers who set off at a respectful distance behind them, Reinhard spoke to Bertrand without looking at him. 'I will need you to draft some orders for me, when we get back to my quarters,' he said, with a smile and a light tone.

'Yes, excellency. What orders?'

'Are you not curious at my mood?' said Reinhard, teasing his assistant.

'I confess that I struggle to follow its path,' said the man, already huffing from the brisk walk. 'It seems to me that losing Roland and the sword is a terrible loss.'

'Good. I am pleased that both you and Sighard think that, it means that almost everyone else will too.'

Bertrand seemed puzzled, although Reinhard couldn't be sure past all the huffing and heavy breathing. Reluctantly, he slowed his pace. He needed the man to be attentive.

'You see, in every disaster there is opportunity. We have been struggling to generate enough… zeal, in the repression of the local population, to achieve what Duke Henry wants of us. The locals are mostly compliant, and the new lords of these lands oppose every attempt to thin the herd. But now… well, I think every good Christian soldier will be horrified at the loss of the sword which we have spent so long insisting is so important.' Reinhard laughed to himself. 'The purpose of spending so much effort convincing everyone that it was a holy relic, the symbol of our victory, given by God himself, was to help force compliance, to demonstrate the power of our Order.'

'Your excellency, I still don't see how this is a good thing.'

'It is not your place to understand these things,' Reinhard said, without any venom. 'But I never considered that its loss might be useful, miraculous, almost.'

'Miraculous?'

'Yes, I feel the Lord's hand at work here. Come, Bertrand, you see it, surely?'

Bertrand huffed to a stop and ran his hand through the thin band of hair over his ear. 'This will make our people angry, and might incite the Norse to resist, or even rebel against us.'

Reinhard clapped his hands together once, startling the priest. 'Precisely! And we shall help them. These are the orders I want you to write. I want to increase our food collection from the locals, I want this to be a winter of shortages and famine. They are remarkably resistant to our attempts so far. They seem to always have more hidden food, and more ways of extracting it from the landscape. So, we must redouble our efforts.'

'Yes, excellency,' said Bertrand, showing no reaction to the notion, noting it with a nod as if it was an order for more candles.

'And when the locals are starving, and angry, I want raids, up and down the land, looking for these rebels and the lost sword. I want angry men of the Order everywhere, let their anger flow, let the locals feel the sting of it, and let them hear again and again how their own kind has done this terrible defeat to us. It will surely kindle the resistance in those with the spark of it in their hearts.'

'And what of those that are loyal to us? Those who are baptised and forgiven?' said Bertrand, with the first trace of what could be concern.

'Those will be spared, brought into our care, fed and sheltered. We will sort the wheat from the chaff. Yes, this sword will be the tool with which we root out every soul who still carries the hope of victory over us in their hearts, bring them out into the open, where we shall crush them.'

Reinhard looked at Bertrand with a wag of his finger. 'And you shall be the only person who knows how fortunate this event was. The rest of the Order, and the whole land, will see only our anger and anguish.'

'Of course, excellency.'

Reinhard smiled broadly. 'Our faith in the Lord has been rewarded, Bertrand. When we needed a symbol of victory, it was delivered, and when we needed the sting of defeat and shame to spur us to complete his work, was it not also provided?'

Bertrand nodded sagely. 'The Lord is good and wise. I am reminded of the sixteenth chapter of Proverbs.'

Reinhard thought for a moment and then smiled. 'Yes. The fourth verse is apt: "The Lord hath made everything for his own purposes, even the wicked for a day of disaster." Yes. Your understanding of the scripture is insightful, as always. The Lord has made this day of disaster as part of his plan, the wicked Norse to bring it about, and we are thankful for his wisdom.'

Reinhard looked wryly at the priest. 'And as you surely know, the next verse is dear to my heart.'

Bertrand nodded without smiling. 'The Lord detests all the proud of heart. Be sure of this: they will not go unpunished.'

'A timely reminder that I am often too proud of my work in the Lord's name. When we get to my quarters, you will take my confession, and then we will draft the orders.' Reinhard smiled, taking in the satisfaction of having the Lord's work so cleanly aligning with Duke Henry's demands. The loss of the sword would cause a renewed conflict in the northlands, he would ensure it, and then the winnowing of the people could truly begin. The sheep would be separated from the wolves, and the word of God and the rule of Duke Henry would be paramount in all of the North.

*And then*, Reinhard thought to himself with a smile, *the path to Rome itself will be open.* He grimaced as soon as the feeling of pride of that ambition washed over him. He must learn to suppress that, to continue his path and the Lord's work with humility, *for humility was dear to the Lord.*

# Chapter 36

# A Test of Faith

**March 1121**

GJALDIR FORCED HIMSELF to sit up and get out of the furs, shivering as the biting air clawed at his skin. The rough lean-to shelter up against the rockface kept the snow off them as they slept but the rough log and woven thatch sloped roof did not keep in the heat of the fire like a proper long-house would.

By the time they had found this place, it was too late to build more than these simple shelters, arranged in a line against the side of a low cliff, sheltered by trees from the worst of the winter winds. The snows had come soon after and the mud had frozen and building insulating earthen walls had become impossible.

So they made the shelters as closed in as they could and suffered through the early part of the winter, thankful that the only thing they were never short of was wood for the fires that hardly ever ceased burning in the simple earth-cut hearths inside each shelter.

For weeks they had lived off what they had brought with them and what they could forage and hunt in the surrounding forest, unwilling to leave their hiding place to venture out to the nearby coastal settlements to buy or steal more food.

Eventually the dwindling stocks and empty bellies had forced them to send a party out to raid a local Christian garrison. That raid had been laughably easy, the Christians in this area seemingly not expecting anything like the experienced warband of thirty men that had come out of the snow and the darkness.

The supplies they stole that night had lasted for weeks, but the Christians were alerted, and each raid became harder. There was the constant threat they would hunt for the source of the raiders and find the camp. It was a risk the group had no choice but to take.

Gjaldir re-started the fire, adding kindling and then larger wood to the smoking embers of the night's flames, sitting hunched over them as the flames grew, drinking in the warmth of their touch. Brunhild came to join him, hands out to the fire, eyes still untouched by its warmth, as they had been for so long now.

'Sword and shield today?' she asked, without looking at him.

Gjaldir nodded, keeping a sigh to himself. It was a ritual they followed every morning before they ate. Gjaldir would take Brunhild a little distance from the camp and he would teach her different aspects of fighting, passing on Gunnar's lessons, and what he had learned from his battles. There was no morning hungry or cold enough to dissuade Brunhild from the practice.

Brunhild was a natural fighter, fast and vicious, fearless to the point of recklessness, a trait Gjaldir was trying and failing to train out of her. She fought like she had no fear of pain or death, and Gjaldir worried that it was true, and that her first battle would be her last. Perhaps even that was what she sought.

'Good, I will get the weapons and meet you there,' she said, rising from the comfort of the fire. Gjaldir groaned a little and ducked out of the shelter, headed to the trees for his morning routine.

Gjaldir saw the blow coming, the same technique she often relied on, the blunt wooden stick appearing like a striking snake out from underneath her shield and lancing straight for his groin.

Brunhild had taken to heart Gjaldir's recycled lessons on where best to strike a man, and had no mercy in their training sessions in practising them. But the more she relied on them, the easier it was for him to defend himself. She was becoming too predictable. All he had to do was twist left and…

'Arghh… ooof,' Gjaldir exclaimed, as he went to parry the low blow and found nothing but air. Brunhild had deceived his parry, rising with a push from her knee to get her stick up and around his shield, turning the lunge at his groin into a thrust straight to his side, into the ribs near his healed spearwound.

Brunhild, as she had been taught, didn't waste a moment celebrating the hit, but got her shield behind his and twisted, opening him up to a cut to his thigh which connected with a painful thud, and then finally a thrust at his face, which he managed to parry, separating them.

'That was good,' said Gjaldir with a grimace.

'You are too focused on protecting your balls,' said Brunhild without a trace of amusement. 'It makes it easy to trick you.'

'Maybe, but I'd rather take a hit in the side than a sword in the stones. As Gunnar taught us…'

'Yes, yes, I know. Some wounds are fight-enders, and some are not.'

'Exactly, and a sword in my side, with maille on, isn't a fight ender.' He shrugged. 'I've proved that before.'

'I don't understand why cutting your balls off would end the fight, you don't need them anyway,' said Brunhild, delivering a knockout blow.

Gjaldir snorted and looked at her, first wide-eyed, and then with a little smile. 'Did you just make a joke?'

Brunhild wiped the smile from her face in an instant and scowled in return. 'No,' she said flatly.

'You did! You made a joke. There is hope yet.'

Brunhild's face turned the complexion of a brewing thundercloud and she pointed her wooden swordstick at him. 'Don't do that.' She turned away and stormed off. 'We are finished for today.'

Gjaldir sighed and rubbed his aching side. Brunhild was always a handspan from fury, and he and the others pretended to be unaware of the times she left the shelter at night, going off into the night and leaving the faint sound of weeping behind.

Gjaldir understood, he felt the raw pain every morning, every time he saw her. But also he did not understand, as she had made clear to him more than once: he didn't and he could never. He still held on to hope that the woman he loved would return, but Brunhild had made it clear that person was gone, dying in the fires and slaughter of Vatnsborð with her son.

He set off towards their camp, chastising himself for setting her off again. He had been too excited by her attempted humour, and he needed to control himself better.

When he reached the area, he found Leif gathering most of the warriors together and he jogged over in concern. 'What is happening?'

Leif greeted him with a curt nod. 'It is a fine day, spring is nearly upon us, and we are going out to raid that other outpost we saw in the third valley.'

'I didn't know we were planning another raid. I'll get my equipment.'

'No, stay. I'm not taking everyone. We need some to stay here and guard the camp, and your wound is not fully healed, however much you pretend it is.'

Gjaldir felt hurt, for it to be suggested he was unfit to fight. But he was unwilling to make a scene of it. 'Fine, I will stay. How long will you be gone?'

'Three days.'

'Good.'

Leif walked off and Gjaldir tried not to look aggrieved in front of the other warriors as they finished sorting out their equipment and walked away.

He headed over to the central shelter, bigger and better made, that housed all of their food stores. It was guarded all day and all night, because even in their tight-knit group, theft could not be ruled out. There were few rules in the camp, but one of them was that stealing from the communal supplies meant death. Two warriors guarded it in shifts, opening it only at mealtimes when some of the women, organised by Sigyn, carefully prepared and rationed out food, as they were doing now.

Gjaldir collected his portion of rough-ground fresh bread and old venison, mouth watering and stomach grumbling at the prospect of food despite its blandness, and went back to his fire to eat and sulk in the warmth.

'There are so many of them,' said Bjorn with a deep sadness in his voice, as he and Gjaldir greeted Leif and the returning warband four days later, and those who had come home with it.

'Yes. We encountered more than ever before. It is getting worse,' Leif replied as they watched the sad procession of ragged and half-starved people shuffling into their burgeoning camp behind Leif's warriors.

Each time they sent a band raiding, or risked going to local villages or settlements, the more desperate people they came across, and they all had the same story. They had been driven from their homes by hunger or threat of punishment for minor crimes or entirely imaginary acts of rebellion.

The Christians had spent the winter stripping most of the people of their food supplies and exacting terrible reprisals for the raids and violent resistance that continued sporadically up and down the land. Entire villages had been burned, young and old men taken for torture or maimed or murdered, women abused, livestock and seedgrain confiscated. All up and down the old Svear lands, the winter had been a misery for the Norse, and many had been forced to flee, joining the increasing numbers looking desperately for somewhere outside the control of the invaders, or simply searching desperately for their next meal.

Most disturbing to Gjaldir, and, he suspected, part of the reason why Leif rarely took him on the raids, was that the Christians were hunting for his sword. He had thought there might be more men sent after them, but he had not expected the scale of the reaction. Norse people were being taken away and tortured, even murdered, by white-cloaked soldiers searching for Ljós a Norðan, having their villages ransacked even on the suspicion they might be harbouring the fugitives, and Gjaldir could not help but feel the guilt of it.

At first, Leif had ordered that they be turned away. The group hiding in its hillside camp could barely feed itself. But as the number and desperation of the people they came across grew, even the hardest heart among them wavered in supporting that argument, and, without a specific order being given, the refugees most in need had been brought back to camp, and then finally anyone who wished to be.

There were few fighting men in their number to help with raiding for supplies, but enough that knew how to hunt and forage and fish that the burgeoning encampment managed to stave off starvation, even if it meant all of them were short of food.

The only blessing they had received was that the winter had been mild. A deep winter would have seen half the dispossessed perish from the cold and the lack of food, whatever efforts they put into helping them.

As Gjaldir watched the sad procession glumly, an older man, shepherding a woman and two small children, met his eye and then looked down to his waist, where Ljós a Norðan rested under his hand.

The old man stopped and raised a wizened hand, finger extended, pointing at the dragon scabbard. 'Is that...?'

Gjaldir sighed but nodded. 'Yes.' He had grown used to this. The stories of the recovery of Ljós a Norðan had spread through the people all winter, spread by the Christians in their search for it, and by the refugees, whispering of what it meant for their future. Many of those who came to the camp believed the stories they had been told, desperately clinging to the idea that the sword was the key to their future, that its recovery was a sign from the gods that there was still the hope of victory.

Gjaldir didn't believe that. He knew the truth, that he had regained the sword by luck, and that it was just a simple blade, but after a firm scolding from Leif, he didn't attempt to extinguish that small crumb of hope and comfort that people derived from seeing it. So he smiled at the man and moved his hand, letting the stranger see the hilt, and the figure of Odin staring out from the bronze pommel.

'Can I... can I touch it?' asked the man reverently.

'Of course.' Gjaldir stepped forwards and tilted the sword forwards, extending the hilt towards the man, who reached forwards with his thin fingers, shaking from the cold, and lightly rested them on the pommel, taking a deep breath and muttering a brief thanks to Odin. He took his hand away and smiled at Gjaldir, nodding his thanks. 'Gods watch over you, Gjaldir.'

Gjaldir mumbled awkwardly in reply, but saw another man shuffling forwards, eyes intent on the sword, and a woman behind him, and he held back a sigh of annoyance and beckoned them forwards, letting them touch the blade, showing one young boy the golden runes carved into the heart of the blade. More and more were drawn to the commotion until half the new arrivals were clustered in front of him like lost lambs in a storm.

Bjorn elbowed him gently in the ribs, leaning in to whisper to him. 'I think you can handle this.' And then the warrior walked off with Leif, Gjaldir trying not to show his annoyance as he was left with the crowd of newcomers.

When the last of them had finally moved off, Gjaldir was about to walk away when he saw that a single hooded old man was left a few paces away, staring at him. Gjaldir waved the man over but he did not move, just stood there as if unsure, so Gjaldir went down to him and peered at the hooded, hidden face, seeing something he recognised but not understanding until he was close.

'Gunnar?' he said, as the realisation dawned. 'Gunnar, what...' He looked the old huskarl up and down even as the Norwegian pulled back the hood of his cloak and looked sheepishly at the ground, he was horrified to see how the old huskarl had thinned and aged. The thick mass of his arms had been replaced with skin stretched over corded, wizened muscles, veins snaking under the surface and cheeks that were hollowed and pronounced.

But despite his reduced form, there was no doubt who he was. Gunnar could barely meet his eye, but nodded and looked at him uncertainly. 'I'm sorry for my absence,' he finally said, his voice still strong and full of gravel as it always had been.

'Sorry? We thought you were dead!' Gjaldir said, immediately regretting how harsh that sounded. 'Don't be sorry, I'm just glad you have returned.'

Gunnar looked awkward and ashamed, so Gjaldir grabbed his arm. 'Come, we must go to the others. They will be so happy to see you.'

Gunnar nodded stiffly and allowed the bigger man to lead him towards the centre of the camp, where Gjaldir could see Leif and Bjorn talking to Vidar, probably dealing with the challenge of where to put all these new arrivals.

Vidar was the first to see Gunnar coming, and he stopped in mid-sentence and his jaw dropped, then a smile cracked across his entire face. 'Gunnar!' exclaimed the long-haired warrior, pushing past a startled Leif and Bjorn and half-running to embrace his friend. Gunnar appeared reluctant but returned the fierce embrace from his fellow huskarl.

Leif and Bjorn came over, incredulous, and Leif looked at Gjaldir as Bjorn went to greet the old champion.

'Where did he come from?'

'He came in with the refugees, did you not see him?'

Leif looked at Gunnar again and shook his head in amazement. 'I did not recognise him, I can't believe it. There were so many of them, I just didn't notice, and he said nothing to me.' Leif stepped over to Gunnar as Bjorn released him and grabbed the man by both shoulders. 'It is good to see you, old friend.'

Gunnar's face creased with shame and he looked down. 'I am so sorry, my brothers, for abandoning you.'

Leif was taken aback. 'Gunnar… no, nonsense, it only matters that you are here.' He tried to get Gunnar's gaze but the man just stared at the ground. 'What happened to you, how did you come to return?' Then Leif stopped and looked around, seeing that they were drawing a lot of curious stares. 'Come, come inside and sit by the fire, tell us what you can.'

Gunnar nodded and the whole group headed for Leif's shelter, where a fire was already roaring. Bjorn went to get some food for Gunnar and he accepted it gladly as the others impatiently waited to hear what he had to say.

Eventually, Gunnar gathered the composure to meet their intent stares and he nodded. 'I went to see my king,' he finally said, and his voice cracked.

Leif looked confused for a moment and Gunnar shook his head. 'No, I did not lie, he is not alive. I went to visit his grave, to try and find some guidance.' Gunnar stopped, having difficulty speaking.

Leif's questioning look drew him on.

'And no, I did not receive any.'

'Well, where did you go, what brought you back here?'

'I spent time in the forest alone, then hunger and cold eventually drove me to seek shelter. I hid my weapons and equipment and went into a village, I thought I would be caught, but I was just one lost soul among many. I found a family kind enough to take me in and feed me a little in exchange for my help.'

Gunnar looked up at the roof. 'And then the Christians came and took all the food they could find, and I was unarmed and helpless, and forced to leave with dozens of others. And so it went on, all winter, moving from one place to another, seeing hunger and sadness killing so many of those around me.' He shook his head and sat in silence for a moment.

'And everywhere I went, they talked about the sword. The Christians came around asking their questions, but they never took me, just seeing an old man. And the people spoke of the great warrior Gjaldir and how he fought for them, and how the eye of the gods was upon him.' Gunnar gave Gjaldir a wry look.

'And I saw how hopeful they were. In a winter where the whole land was filled with misery and the sound of weeping, the only hope I saw in anyone was when they heard the stories about the sword, each more fantastical and exaggerated than the last.'

Gunnar shrugged. 'I realised in the end that leaving didn't save any of you from the fate that clung to me, so I decided to look for you, and eventually in my travels you came across the group I was with. And here I am.'

A half-dozen questions spilled from Bjorn and Leif and Vidar but Gunnar held up his hand, wincing. 'I know you will want to know everything, and I will tell you more, but not now. Please.'

Leif looked disappointed but he nodded. 'Fine, well, you are welcome to stay in this shelter. It will be crowded, but everywhere will be until we can build more.'

Gunnar looked out of the open entrance towards the rest of the camp. 'What is your plan for these people?'

Leif frowned and it was his turn to look awkward. 'We don't have one.'

That drew a raised eyebrow of disapproval from Gunnar that Gjaldir recognised well. 'These people came here filled with hope, but it is fragile, I spent the winter among them. That hope will quickly turn to despair with nothing to focus it on.'

Leif pursed his lips and nodded, looking around the group. 'I know, but we never expected to have all these people. I don't know what to do with them. At the moment, keeping them alive and sheltered is my only plan.'

Gunnar looked unconvinced, and Leif showed a flash of anger. 'You have been here for mere moments, we dealt with this all winter, this is not the time for your lectures.'

Gunnar's disapproval faded and he nodded, looking away thoughtfully, even as Leif cursed himself under his breath for his outburst.

The tense moment was broken when one of Leif's warriors came in and looked at him. 'We need you, there are not enough shelters for all these new people, and trouble is brewing.'

Leif closed his eyes and pinched the bridge of his nose as he tried to control his anger. 'I am coming. Fuck it, I am coming.' Then he stormed out of the shelter, leaving Gunnar looking glum.

Gjaldir watched the old champion, trying to gauge how much of the man he had once known was left. He was reduced, not only physically but in presence. His eyes were down and avoided contact, his hands shifted and fiddled.

Gunnar looked up and saw Gjaldir staring at him and the old man shifted uncomfortably and looked away again.

Gjaldir sighed to himself. There seemed little left of the old warrior's strength of mind, which had been more formidable even than his body. Whatever had happened to Gunnar over that long winter, perhaps it was a wound that could not be healed.

Gjaldir got to his feet, his joy at Gunnar's return slipping into disappointment, and he went to go and find Brunhild. They had practice to do, and Brunhild did not like to be kept waiting.

Two weeks passed and more people came in, until the swelling camp had nearly three hundred refugees in addition to the original occupants. As the first signs of spring came, the camp became restless. It was soon planting season, and if they wished to avoid another famine the coming year, they needed to find somewhere to get crops in the ground, or have another plan, but Leif was increasingly irritable and difficult to reason with, unable to decide what they should do. Everyone knew that if many more people arrived, it would become impossible to feed everyone. Their time in the camp was coming to an end, one way or the other.

The matter came to a head one evening as a spring storm brewed in the hills where their camp lay, peals of thunder dancing across the sky in the distance, and the smell of rain on the air. The dark clouds gathering on that otherwise bright moonlit night reflected the mood inside the central shelter as they gathered to discuss what to do.

Gjaldir sat in near silence as the others, Bjorn, Vidar, Bekkr and Leif, went over the old arguments. They could not stay where they were, as there was nowhere to grow food. They could not move to a village on the coast as the Christians would find them. They could not capture a town and hold it as they had too few fighting men.

The arguments descended, as they often did, into bitterness and despondency. Every avenue seemed closed to them. Gjaldir sat with his back against a post and listened, pondering over the issue himself and not coming up with anything worth discussing with the group.

'We cannot stay here!' said Vidar with an exasperated cry, as the argument reached its climax.

'Then what would you have us do!' shouted Leif, anger showing on his face. 'I have nothing for you, and you have no plan to keep these people alive for another year, no clever strategy to survive, no place to run or hide. What do you want me to do?'

'If you have no plan, maybe it is not you who should lead us,' said Bekkr with a grimace. 'We have followed you this far, but perhaps me and mine should return to Vatnsborð, perhaps it is safe there now.'

'Bekkr, I never had any intention of leading, if you don't think I should, why don't you try it? Take us back to your home. It would be a great relief to me.'

Bjorn nodded. 'Perhaps we should all return there, rebuild.'

Bekkr shook his head. 'You cannot.' He pointed at Gjaldir, who sat in the background in the shadows of the fire. 'Wherever that sword goes, they will follow. You cannot bring that destruction back to my home.'

Gjaldir nodded. 'Anywhere I go, they will hunt for it. Maybe I should just leave you so you can all return there without me.'

'No,' Bjorn said with a shake of his head and an angry scowl. 'We are not bowing to that fear, to the Christians' threats. And stop turning on each other, this is beneath our honour. We have been through too much together. Control yourselves.'

That admonishment cooled the frustrated warriors for a moment.

'Then what should be do? Still no one answers,' said Vidar sadly.

'We persist,' said a gravelly voice, and Gjaldir looked around to see Gunnar standing in the opening to the shelter, regarding them all with a scowl.

'Persist in what?' said Leif with a helpless shrug.

'The fight.'

'What? Gunnar, we cannot fight them, we have no more than fifty fighting men.'

Gunnar scoffed and stalked across the small space, towering over them as they sat. The weeks with them had returned a little of his old physique, and, Gjaldir noticed with a flutter of hope, more of his old confidence and force of character.

'I left you because I could bear it no more. Everyone dies around me, no matter how I try to save them. Yet I do not die, no matter how desperate the battle. I thought I could run from it, as I ran from it after King Sigurd died. But all that happened is I was alone and I was less than nothing, and it gave me no peace. The time I spent hiding among the people showed me there is heart in them yet, more than there was in me. They can be united once more, if they are given the right reason.

'There is nowhere left to hide. Nowhere the enemy cannot find us or where we can live in peace. You sent the remains of our people away to find shelter in towns and villages and farms before the winter, hoping they would be safe. But the Christians came for them anyway, and now even more desperate souls fill their places. What are we to do, us warriors, if not fight for them? If we send them to the vicious care of the invader, if we do not stand for them, who will?'

The old warrior stared them all down, his eyes no longer afraid to meet theirs. And they all felt the shame of it because it was true. They had scattered Halla's remaining people before the winter, and although some of them had returned, their suffering had been terrible.

'We have a nation full of people, all looking for deliverance, all looking for hope of a future. That is what we have to fight for, not a small group here or there, but for the whole of it. Halla was not wrong in her intent, she was wrong in her method. She tied us to one place and one group. You were not wrong in your intent sending our people away, thinking that, away from us warriors, the people would be safe from the Christian wrath.'

Gunnar held a clenched fist to his chest and he glowered intently at everyone who could bear to meet his eyes. 'But none of you understood or accepted the truth, the same truth that the kings of Denmark and Norway and Sweden failed to understand: that the Christians intend to destroy us all, and we must all stand together as one, or be defeated alone. That is the message Sigurd spread, and it is the one I will continue to give in his place, because we cannot give up, so much has been lost, so many have died. But so many more still live and are worth fighting for.' Gunnar stepped into the group and stared at them all, one by one, his old presence once again filling the space.

He pulled a roughspun bag off his shoulder and opened it, drawing out a tattered blue cloak. He brought it up and unfolded it, turning the faded material over in his hand tenderly. 'When Sigurd died, I knew that I would never wear this again. It marked me out as his protector, and in that duty I had failed.' Gunnar took hold of the corners of the cloak and threw it around his shoulders, fixing it together around his neck with the worn bronze brooch.

'I was wrong. My duty was not complete. Sigurd cared for nothing but his people, and I dishonoured his name and his sacrifice by forgetting that. From now on, as long as I have breath in my lungs, I will spend every part of it in the struggle to free them from this curse upon our lands. And I will be proud to do so with you, my friends and my kin, if you will go with me.'

Leif looked up at Gunnar with a glint of hope in his eye. 'So you will lead us, again?'

There was a pause as Gunnar met his eyes. 'No,' said Gunnar, shaking his head. 'I cannot. It is not my fate, or my place.' And Gjaldir felt the disappointment and turmoil that was written on Leif's face.

'Then who? If not you, if not Leif, then who?' asked Vidar. 'Bjorn, would you lead us to take back the North?' Vidar said with a half-mocking expression.

Bjorn scowled but shook his head. 'I have never been a leader.'

'Me, then? I am famous for my supposed cunning, but more for my jokes than for inspiring people to follow.' Vidar looked around. 'Bekkr? Who wishes only to go home?'

Bekkr only scowled and looked away, and Vidar gestured back at Gunnar. 'So, if not you, then who?'

Gunnar nodded and pointed across the space. 'He will.'

Gjaldir took a moment to realise that the finger was pointed arrow straight at him, and he straightened up and gagged slightly. 'What?'

All the heads in the shelter turned to face him. 'Gjaldir?' said Bekkr incredulously. 'A man who used to be a Christian, lead us against his own people? Don't be absurd.' Bekkr shook his head angrily. 'This is because of the stupid sword, isn't it?' He looked around the room for support, but found quiet faces ignoring him while they stared at Gjaldir.

'It's not actually the worst idea,' said Vidar finally.

Gjaldir gaped at him. 'What? Why?'

'Our people know you, and trust you. You have proved yourself a leader in battle.'

'And showed that you would fight for the people, even when you have the choice,' said Bjorn, rubbing his chin.

Gjaldir looked around at them all incredulously. 'Leif, this is madness, you are the leader, tell them!'

'Gjaldir, I have been a terrible leader, admit it. I was supposed to defend our people, and I sent them away to be ravaged by the Christians. And now here we are, about to run out of food, because I can't decide what to do next,' said Leif with a sad smile. 'And we have all seen the way the people look at you, how they believe you are blessed. No one outside this camp knows who I am. But they know you, and they apparently believe in you.' Leif nodded seriously. 'Gunnar is right. We have nowhere to hide, and if we are to commit to this madness and try and continue the fight, the people need someone they can believe in, and that will not be me.'

'Then Gunnar!'

'I am the past, not the future. A huskarl who has lost every lord he ever swore to, who fled his people when they needed him.' Gunnar shook his head. 'It cannot be me, even if I wanted it to be, which I do not.'

Gjaldir put his head in his hands and tried to calm his thoughts. *I can't do this.* The thought of it made him feel sick. *I don't know where to begin.*

He stood and looked at them, swaying slightly on his feet, and then a burst of anger overcame him. 'No!' he shouted, face contorted with the sudden strength of his fury. 'You are all cowards, too scared to take responsibility so trying to pile it on me with fine words and excuses.' He picked up Ljós a Norðan from where he had left it leaning against the wall. 'None of you believe it should be me, it's just because of this sword. I curse the day I forged it, it is nothing of what you all say it is, it's just steel and bronze and wood.' He looked around his friends' faces, seeing their disappointment and hurt, and settled on Gunnar, who looked at him impassively, unaffected by his outburst.

'My answer is no!' Gjaldir said, pushing down his feeling of shame, and pushing past them to get to the entrance.

'Gjaldir!' called out Leif, trying to stop him by holding out an arm.

'No, let him go. He must find the resolve himself, as I did,' said Gunnar, giving Gjaldir a firm thump on the shoulder as he passed.

Then Gjaldir was out of the shelter, stumbling in the moonlight as his mind swirled. He found he still had the sword clutched in his hand and he pulled his cloak around him against the cold night wind and walked towards his own bed. Others had left their shelters too, drawn by the shouting and commotion, and he swore and changed course, heading away from them all out into the woods where he and Brunhild trained.

## CHAPTER 37

# THE MAN ON THE MOUNTAIN

GJALDIR STRODE THROUGH the trees, looking around and seeking some shelter from the wind where he could be hidden and sit in peace. He looked at the hillside stretching out above him and started up it, headed for the shelter of a rocky overhang he had visited before, just a hundred paces away.

He slipped on a rock and swore, even as the first patter of rain started falling around him and then the first peal of thunder sounded overhead, rending the sky. He buckled his swordbelt on so that he could use both hands. He knew going up the slope in the dark was stupid. It wasn't very steep but in the night and the rain he could turn an ankle or worse. But the terror of going back and facing his friends again and feeling the shame of having run from them drove him on.

*All this for a sword.* He did not understand why the people cared so much about it, about the stories that were told about it. *Why should I be responsible just because I carry it?* He slipped again and shouted in anger and pain as the sword tangled in his legs. He stood up, hissing and clamping a hand to his knee, which had been torn up by some sharp stones, and howled his anger into the storm.

In a moment of impulse, he pulled Ljós a Norðan from the dragon scabbard and looked at it as another bolt of lightning streaked through his vision behind the hills across the valley. He felt the weight of the sword, and felt the far greater weight of the responsibility that came with it. The fury and sadness and loss combined into a foul beast of regret inside his heart and got the better of him. He looked out over the rocky outcropping to his left, high enough above the valley floor that the tops of the trees were lost somewhere in the darkness below him, and with a shout, hurled the sword out into the storm.

He let all his anger and frustration flow as the blade disappeared into the night, and then it was gone from sight, lost in the blackness, until finally he heard a faint crashing of branches down below as it landed. He stood there, panting and grumbling, feeling suddenly drained and foolish and unsure what to do. With the rain falling and the storm deepening, he pushed on up the slope towards the summit, to where the rock overhang sheltered a flat area that looked out over the valley over the cliff below.

He got into the shelter of the rocks and sat down glumly. The wind barely touched him in there, but he shivered and drew his legs in tight, wrapping his warm cloak around him as he stared out into the storm.

Thunder was ringing incessantly now, the storm gathering into the valley with incredible speed, its anger making his own look so very pathetic and small. Shards of lightning streaked down from the sky across the land in front, each bolt lighting the valley in a snapshot of brooding shadows and white light. The power on display made him shiver more than the cold.

His thoughts reeled drunkenly from anger to shame. Anger at the unfairness of the life he had been given. To be a slave, to be taken from his home, to lose the people he loved and be cursed by the meaning others gave to the blades he made and the responsibility they now wanted to pile on him.

Shame at the way he had ranted and run from them, petulantly thrown his sword off a cliff as a child would do.

But as he calmed down and his thoughts settled, his overwhelming feeling was simply that he couldn't. He couldn't do what they asked, he couldn't bear that responsibility. He would fail them, he would embarrass them, he would lead them into disaster or death.

All he wanted was to find somewhere safe to live in peace, with Brunhild and with his friends. But he had never been given that chance.

He sat there for a long while as the storm passed, the lightning and thunder moving slowly away, and the wind died down and the rain stopped. And he considered skulking back to the camp, but couldn't face the prospect.

As he sat there brooding, he was suddenly startled by the sound of footsteps on the stones, and he looked up to see a figure resolving out of the darkness, until he could see it was another warrior in a cloak, a large spear in his left hand, and he sighed. He had been found. Of course they would have gone out looking for him.

It was dark, so he didn't recognise the warrior, and to his surprise the man did not cry out or summon others, nor insist he come back, the warrior simply walked over, the butt of his gnarled spearshaft knocking on the rock as he trod, and then, with a sigh speaking of relieved muscles, lowered himself to the ground next to Gjaldir, sitting and looking out over the valley with him, not saying a word.

Gjaldir was perplexed. Now that they were closer, and in the returning light of the moon, he saw the warrior was an old man, older even than Gunnar. His beard was dashed with silver and well groomed, and as a bolt of lightning flashed across the valley, it revealed that his left eyelid was closed. The eyelid was sunken and scarred, betraying the missing eye beneath. Gjaldir wasn't sure he had seen the man before, he must have arrived with the newest groups of refugees.

The flash of the image was gone as soon as it came, and Gjaldir returned his gaze to the receding storm, the confusion slowly draining from his chest.

'Magnificent, isn't it?' said the old man after a while as a ripple of thunder boiled across the horizon again.

Gjaldir mumbled noncommittally.

'A good place to sit and consider things.'

'You couldn't sleep through the storm?' asked Gjaldir. The camp was only two hundred paces away, down the slope and huddled against the next outcropping, heavily overcrowded and stifling. The old man must have come up here for some peace too.

'The storm doesn't bother me,' said the old man with a smile. 'But what troubles you, Gjaldir?'

Gjaldir sighed. 'So you know who I am.'

'Of course.'

Gjaldir nodded bitterly. Everyone did.

'Why are you alone on this hillside in a storm? What brought you out in the wind and the fury of Thor's hammering?'

He thought about it for a moment, he did not want to discuss his problems with a stranger who might spill his secrets to others in the camp. But the man seemed almost fatherly, and he felt inclined to answer him.

'They want me to do things I am not willing to do, maybe not able to do.'

'Who?'

Gjaldir looked at the old man oddly. 'The others, Leif and Gunnar and the others.'

'Ah, and who are they to you?'

'I don't understand?'

The old man emphasised his words carefully. 'I mean, who are they, to you? What do they mean to you? Why does what they want you to do matter so much?'

Gjaldir nodded and thought about it. 'They are my friends.' Then he shook his head angrily. 'No, that is not fair. They are my brothers. They have stood in the shieldwall with me and bled with me.'

The old man nodded sagely as he understood. 'Well, that is a true dilemma, for there is no stronger bond. Is what they ask of you unjust?'

'Well… no.'

'Does it stem from selfishness or cravenness?'

Gjaldir had to think about that for a moment, because he had accused them of that very thing earlier. Then he shook his head shamefully. 'It does not, many of them have tried to shoulder this burden before me.'

'I see, well, is it unwise to ask you to bear it?'

'I… It might be. But they have their reasons, perhaps they are right.'

'So you do not know if you are capable, is that the issue?'

'Yes,' admitted Gjaldir.

'Well, I cannot help you with that,' the old man said non-chalantly, staring back out over the valley. Gjaldir looked at him reproachfully and the man chuckled, a warm, hearty chuckle, and continued. 'Your answers lie within yourself, and thus only you can find them.'

'How can I know?'

The man curled the corner of his mouth up and looked at Gjaldir square on, the shadow of his cheek hiding his missing eye. 'That is the hardest question. Some men must go to extraordinary lengths to seek hidden knowledge of the world, and of themselves. Sacrifices must be made, and some may seem unbearable.' The man smiled kindly and turned back to the valley. 'Tell me, Gjaldir, have you made great sacrifices in your quest to know who you are?'

Gjaldir clenched his hand and nodded. 'I have.'

'What were they?'

Gjaldir ground his fingernails into the palm of his hand as the losses of the last few years washed over him. 'I gave up my freedom seeking adventure, and then my desire for freedom seeking peace and respect. I gave up my respect to be a warrior, and then…' An unwelcome tear sprang into his eye and he cuffed it angrily away. 'And then lost my family while trying to fight to prove myself to others.'

The old man bowed his head slightly and nodded slowly, a pained smile creasing his lined face. 'Those are, indeed, great sacrifices. But…' The old man shook his head. 'Have you ever sacrificed for anyone other than yourself?'

That hurt. Gjaldir recoiled away from the accusation but had no good answer. 'Yes, I have risked death in battle to save others, taken wounds and saved friends.'

'That is good, and honourable. But honour is personal, and raises a man up. Have you ever sacrificed a great thing, without any gain of your own?'

Gjaldir glared at the man and then softened as he accepted the truth. 'No.'

The man's one eye searched his, as if weighing his soul, and Gjaldir felt himself shrink under its intensity. 'Do not be ashamed,' the man finally replied. 'Neither had I when I was young.'

Gjaldir looked out again into the darkness. 'What brought you here? What of your family? Are they…' Gjaldir faltered to a stop.

'They are not with me anymore,' said the stranger quietly, and Gjaldir felt the enormous weight of his sadness.

'Were they…' He did not want to bluntly ask if they had died. 'Were they lost to this chaos too?'

'Some of them are gone, others… well.' The old man gazed out across the valley, towards where the thunder was now a faint rumble and flashing on the horizon, and he gave a small smile. 'I hear from them from time to time, I see their work, although they have moved beyond my sight. Perhaps, one day, I will be reunited with them.'

Gjaldir nodded, he felt the same way about many of those lost from his past lives, their fate unknown. Then he tapped his fingers on his empty scabbard, feeling the weight of the sword's absence pulling at him. 'So, what should I do?'

The old man did not turn to answer, he simply tilted his head slightly. 'I am confident that you will know what must be done, when you ask yourself truthfully.'

Gjaldir shook his head. 'I will have to become someone I do not want to be, do things I do not want to do.'

'Yes. Sometimes fate requires that of a man.'

'And they all believe my sword has magical powers, but it is a lie. The sword is just steel like any other.'

'Perhaps. But perhaps belief is all that is required. Most power comes from belief in it. If enough people believe a thing has power, and believe strongly enough, then it does.'

'What?'

The old man chuckled again. 'Tell me, how does a crown have power? It is just a circle of metal or bone or wood, but people believe it bestows the power of a king, so it does. Even a god, what is a god if men do not believe in them? A shadow in the breeze, a word of no power. No, all power stems merely from belief in it.' The old man nodded. 'Perhaps, if they all believe Ljós a Norðan has power, then it does. All that matters then is to ask yourself: can you live with that?'

Gjaldir slumped, seeing the truth of the man's words, suddenly seeing the whole issue turned on its head and feeling foolish.

The old man sighed and levered himself to his feet, looking down at Gjaldir. 'This is a decision you can only make alone. I am sorry I could not help you more.'

Gjaldir smiled uncomfortably, still going over the man's words.

'No, thank *you*, you helped me a great deal.' He looked out over the valley again and sighed as the thud of the spearshaft against rock receded into nothing. He argued with the voice in his head for a while but the empty scabbard at his waist stared at him as if reproachfully every time he looked down at it. Finally he swore and got to his feet, rubbing his hands and stamping to get the warmth back into his extremities. 'Fine, I'll go and find the fucking sword,' he muttered to himself.

The climb down was harder than the way up, the slope down into the valley floor slick and treacherous in the darkness. Once he was down in the forest, he meandered around fruitlessly in the dark, barely able to see branches and stones, let alone find the sword. He slumped down against a tree and put his head in his hands, angrily remonstrating with himself, wrapping his cloak around himself and sinking into the dark depths of his thoughts and fears.

Something reached into the darkness and pinched him, and he lashed out in confusion, hand searching blindly to find it. There was a brush of feathers and a loud squawk and something pinched his hand again. He shouted in surprise and sat up, seeing against the pale light of the sky between the trees a dark shape flit away to sit on a branch on the tree opposite. A raven.

'I'm not dead, you carrion-eating bastard!' he shouted at the raven, which cocked its head and looked at him with curiosity.

'Fuck off!' he shouted at it, and then scrabbled around in the litter, finding a stone and then throwing it at the bird. The raven nimbly dodged the projectile, which clattered off the branch, and it hopped to a higher one, then looked at him again. The raven cried again, a croaking, mocking call, which infuriated him. He found a chunky branch in the litter and picked it up.

'I said fuck off!' And he launched it at the bird. The raven jumped out of the way and the stick bounced of a handful of branches, showering him with pine needles. Gjaldir raised a hand to shelter himself from the cascade of twigs and needles and then heard a crash and a thud and heard something larger falling towards him.

He stepped back half a step just as something lashed his face above his eye and thunked into the ground at his feet.

Swearing and clutching his eye at the sudden pain, he looked down and saw a glint of metal in the thin moonlight. Not believing what he saw, he blinked away the blood that was filling his left eye and squinted at the thing, reaching out carefully to grasp it.

It was Ljós a Norðan. He knew its hilt the moment he touched it, the familiarity of its shape instantly telling him. He looked up at the darkness of the branches above in amazement, he never would have seen it up there. He took his hand away from his left eye and winced, trying to open it and test it. But he could see nothing, and could not tell if it was because the eye was ruined, or because it was too dark and filled with the blood that was pouring from his sliced brow.

He pulled the sword from the earth where it stood, point down, and fumbled it back into his scabbard, even in that situation trying to clean it on his tunic before he did. When he finally had the blade clean and back in the dragon's throat, he turned and the raven cawed at him again from the darkness, sitting on a branch, just its shadow and one glinting eye giving away its presence. It looked at him and then took off, flying away through the trees in silence as Gjaldir watched it go with bemusement.

He found his way out of the forest and walked back to their camp, the bizarre sequence of events running through his mind. He wondered what the old man would say when he saw him again returning with the blade and the bloodied brow.

When he reached the camp, a voice called out to him and he answered, waving with his free hand. He could see little with his one good eye in the darkness, but there were a few people out of their shelters and a group of them rushed over to him, resolving them into the group of his friends and a few others. He saw Brunhild in the group, and the seer Tormund.

'There are a dozen men out there looking for you, don't just fuck off into the night in a storm,' said Leif furiously, arriving at their head.

'I'm sorry, but one of them found me, I thought he would tell you.'

'Who found you?'

'What happened to you?' Bjorn said, looking with concern at the blood coming out around his closed eye as Gjaldir reached the pool of light around one of the fires.

'Uh, that is hard to explain. I cut myself on something in the dark. I don't know if my eye is ruined.'

'Let me have a look,' he said in concern, ignoring the angry Leif.

Bjorn dragged him over towards the fire and took a proffered skin of water, washing the blood away from Gjaldir's eye as he grunted with discomfort. 'Umm, it's just your brow, you lucky bastard. The eye is fine other than being filled with a fool's blood. What did you cut it on?'

Gjaldir looked around sheepishly. 'My sword.'

'What?'

'Never mind, who found you?' said Leif. 'No has reported finding you. Damn you, boy, they might be lost or hurt out there, who was it?'

'It was…' Gjaldir suddenly realised he had never asked the warrior's name. 'Uh, an old man, wearing a cloak, carrying a long spear.'

Leif paused and looked at him in confusion, then at the others. There was a procession of shrugs and shaken heads.

'The old warrior with a missing eye, his left eye.' He looked around the others as they stood in silence, exchanging looks that verged from confusion to annoyance.

'This isn't funny, Gjaldir,' said Leif with a scowl.

'I'm not joking! Why would I joke?'

'Because there is no old warrior in this camp with a missing eye,' said Gunnar.

Gjaldir looked around them, suddenly uncertain. 'There is, he was there.' He saw Bjorn giving him a very strange look, saw the others looking at each other uncertainly and then several men were shoved aside and Tormund appeared in front of him, his eyes pinned wide.

'Tell me everything about this old man,' the seer said hoarsely.

Everyone was silent now, even the ones Tormund had barged past, and Gjaldir had never seen the seer look the way he looked then. He felt a chill. 'He was tall, perhaps almost as tall as me, and old, older than Gunnar.' He looked at the huskarl, who stared back intently. 'He carried a long spear, and wore a cloak with a hood over his head.' Gjaldir thought about it carefully. 'His left eye was missing, and he had a silvery beard and black hair, I think, although it was hard to see in the storm.'

'What was he doing?'

'He came and sat with me, he talked to me, gave me some advice about what to do.'

There was a ripple of murmurs in the dozen or so people who were standing around listening and Gjaldir looked around nervously.

'Tell me about the spear.'

'What?'

'The spear, boy. What about the spear?'

'The spear, well…' Gjaldir thought about it, and for the first time realised that the spear the man carried had been a bit unusual. 'Well, the shaft was not smooth, it was gnarled, old, maybe carved with runes. And it was big, longer than others we carry, with a broad head… Why does it matter?'

'Gungnir,' said Gunnar, almost as a whisper. 'A one-eyed traveller bearing an ancient spear, who comes offering advice to those in dire need. The spear was Gungnir.'

There was a gasp of shock behind the huskarl. Tormund just

stared at Gjaldir as if his mind had ceased turning, his head shaking ever so slightly.

'What? I don't understand,' said Gjaldir. He looked at Leif, seeing the big Swedish warrior was wearing a look of deep concern.

'Swear what you are saying is true,' growled Leif, even as the others muttered and Tormund shook and mumbled to himself.

'It is, it is! Why would I lie?'

'Because if what you say is true, the old man w…'

'Because Gungnir is the spear of the Allfather,' said Tormund in a deathly whisper, the breath rushing from his tense chest as he formed the words. 'You were visited by Odin himself. Even I have never… not in person, never.' The seer's words faded away into shock. 'You are an Odinseer.' He shook his head slowly, almost in misery. 'I thought it would be me.'

Gjaldir recoiled, and then looked around the circle, seeing shocked and confused faces. 'No, this is stupid, the old warrior must be new, you just don't recognise him.' He stretched his neck and looked around, hoping to see the stranger in the slowly gathering crowd.

'No, I've met every man who has joined us,' said Leif, perhaps the only one of them not awestruck to one degree or another by the revelation. 'There is no one here like that.'

Gjaldir shook his head and stuttered, but several of the people from the back of the crowd broke away, rushing off towards other shelters, calling out to friends and companions, telling them what had happened.

'Come with me, now,' hissed Leif, shoving Gjaldir and shepherding Bjorn, Gunnar and Vidar towards the food store, Brunhild following in their wake, leaving Tormund stone still in the space behind them, shaking and muttering.

Gjaldir was roughly pushed into the large shelter and the others came in behind him. Some of them still looked in shock. Leif grabbed Gjaldir by the neckline of his tunic. 'That story will have spread to everyone in the camp before dawn, that Odin himself came to you, that you were chosen by him. You must decide, now, what you will do.' Leif's eyes flicked between his intently, desperately, begging him.

'I don't… I don't believe it was Odin!' he said, exasperated. 'I don't even know if I believe Odin is real, or if he is a man who can walk around!'

Gunnar hissed at that offence, but Leif was unaffected. 'It doesn't matter, the people will believe it, and they will expect you to lead them out of this nightmare, they will expect Odin to have shown you the way. Gjaldir! You must decide!'

Gjaldir stood there, his mind churning, as all of them looked at him, thinking about what the old man had said about sacrifice and fate. He shrugged helplessly. 'How can I do this? I do not know how to lead so many people! I do not know how to manage an army or organise this camp or any of the things that you have been doing.'

'We will advise you. Every good leader takes advice and help from those he trusts. I will tell you how to manage a settlement, what I know of it, anyway, and I will help you do it,' said Leif with an earnest glare.

'And I will train the warriors, and teach you how to go to war,' said Gunnar with a growl and a nod.

'And I will advise you on strategy, and amuse everyone when we are sad,' said Vidar with a childish grin.

Gjaldir shook his head as they all spoke in turn, trying to stop them with a futile wave of his hand.

'And I will stand by your side, and guard your right in battle,' said Bjorn, nodding to him.

Gjaldir wilted under their stares, unable to make the leap to accepting the fate that was pressing down on him, but then he saw Brunhild, standing behind them all in silence, and his eyes met hers, and she gave him a single nod.

Gjaldir looked around the group and swore as his last defiance crumbled. 'Shit.'

'Good man,' said Gunnar with a proud nod. 'I knew you would come round to it, even if it took the Allfather himself to persuade you.'

Gjaldir looked at them all with pursed lips. 'I don't know how to begin.'

'The people will need to see you rise to this, you need to give them confidence and hope. We will swear our oaths to you, and then they will follow.'

'I would offer my word first,' said Bjorn, moving to stand in front of him and kneel.

Gjaldir shook his head vigorously. 'No, no you will not kneel to me, my friends, I am not a jarl.'

'Yes, we will, it is our way and it matters. But not here,' Leif said forcefully. He gestured to Bjorn. 'Outside, where the people can see us do it. We will swear to you, and they know our commitment. You have seen it before, do you remember, in Ragnvald's hall, how this is done?'

Gjaldir nodded, and put a hand to his face and looked around at them, overwhelmed. 'You would all swear to me, follow me, I who used to be your slave?'

'To the death, Gjaldir Odinseer,' said Bjorn, clasping his hand reassuringly. 'Come outside, and hear us say it in front of the people.'

Gjaldir went out of the shelter in a state of shock with his friends around him, and looked up, seeing that hundreds of people were gathered in the open space beyond, more appearing all the time. Tormund stood at their head, waiting. Behind them, the glow of the dawn was peeking out from behind the clouds, red and angry after the storm, bathing the whole scene in an eerie glow.

He moved out into the space, trying to look confident and

feeling like he would fall at any moment as he saw the sea of faces whose lives were about to become his responsibility.

He stopped when Leif gently tugged on his arm, and then his friends all moved in front of him to stand at the head of the crowd. Bjorn stepped forwards, a broad, warm smile on his face. He came to within a few paces of Gjaldir and waited, flicking a helpful eye to the sword at Gjaldir's waist. Gjaldir brought the dragon scabbard forwards, tugging on the hilt of Ljós a Norðan so that it was halfway unsheathed, the golden runes glowing in the soft morning light.

He proffered the hilt to Bjorn, who stepped forwards and put one knee to the hard ground, placing his hand on the hilt and then he spoke, loud and clear.

'I am Bjorn, son of Lendir, freeman of Svealand, who some call the Faithful. I was a sworn man of Jarl Harnsted and Jarl Ragnvald and Jarl Gustav after him. I pledge my service to you, Gjaldir Odinseer, and our people, the last oath of service I will ever take. I will guard your side and give my blood so that you do not bleed, and my life so that you may live. The next blade that comes for you will have to pass through me. I will stand with you until our people are freed, or death claims me. My word is my bond or may the gods curse my name.'

Gjaldir fought back the emotion as the man spoke, trying to remember what Jarl Ragnvald had said when men swore to him, and coming up with nothing. There was a deathly silence and then he finally found the elusive words.

'I accept your oath, Bjorn the Faithful, as my friend and my brother. I will never betray the faith you put in me today, I will never give up on you, or on the people who need our support. We will fight not for glory but for an end to this war, and the reign of peace in our lands. I will hold to this oath until freedom or death reward us.'

Bjorn smiled and took his hand off the hilt, standing to embrace him. Then he turned aside and took up his position on

Gjaldir's right, and Gjaldir saw Leif step forwards, the grin and joy that had so long been absent from his features returned. The big blond warrior dropped to a knee in front of him and put his hand on Ljós a Norðan's hilt.

'You've come a long way, boy, since the day we met on a river-bank,' he said. 'Well, look at us now.'

Gjaldir choked back a laugh and tried to retain his serious expression as Vidar and Gunnar came over and knelt either side of Leif, placing their hands on top of his. 'Thought it would be better to get this done quickly,' said Vidar with a grin. 'Before anyone thinks about it too much and sees the madness of it.'

Bjorn waved at the group of warriors standing in the crowd, and the men looked at each other, before coming forwards in ones and twos and then groups. Some looked at Gjaldir uncertainly, others with reassuring smiles, but very few refused to come at all. Gjaldir saw Bekkr and the last of the Vatnsborð men standing off to one side, and felt a pang of sadness when they walked away, headed to their shelter. Bekkr had clearly decided to take the last of his people home, and Gjaldir couldn't blame him for it.

But as the last of the other warriors came and knelt in a huddle, each placing his hand on the back of the man in front, Leif nodded and looked up at Gjaldir and smiled.

'Are you ready?'

Gjaldir's eyes swept over the crowd of expectant warriors, and came to rest on Brunhild, near the back, who knelt with her hand on another warrior's shoulder. She gave him the faintest half smile, and he swallowed to clear a catch in his throat and smiled back, feeling confidence in his answer for the first time that day. 'Yes, Leif Leifson. I am ready.'

## Epilogue

# Lundjen, Spring 2016

THERE WAS A strident knock at Halfar's office door. It surprised him, and he nervously jumped, despite the fact that he was, of course, expecting it.

He turned round to invite whoever it was in, but the door opened before he could say anything, and Professor Hallsson came in and closed the door behind him.

'You've seen it then?' said Halfar innocently.

Hallsson snorted in laughter and nodded. Halfar opened the webpage that he had minimised on the taskbar, a link to a page on the Oslo-based Norrland News site. The Norrland News was a left-leaning site, broadly aligned with the loose range of Nordic and environmental parties that held the minority in the national parliament.

'Government cover-up alleged over medieval royal tomb find,' said the news article.

'An anonymous whistleblower has given Norrland News exclusive access to government documents showing that an archaeological dig this spring may have uncovered the remains of the Crusade-era king of Norway and Sweden, Sigurd Magnusson.

Government officials have refused to comment so far, but an official release at the time said that the site was empty, revealing only animal bones. Our in-house expert, Jans Andersson, explains.'

'Jans Andersson is far from an expert,' Halfar grumbled as they read it.

Hallsson chuckled. 'Well, at least he knows the difference between animal bones and a body.'

'He calls it a tomb!' said Halfar indignantly. 'It's not a tomb, it's merely a grave.'

'Well, it was under a rock.'

'Put there in modern times!' protested Halfar.

'A distinction the news company does seem to have missed,' agreed Hallsson. They both stared at the screen for a while longer, going over the article, which laid out some key facts and photos from the documents, and which were, at best, poorly explained. But the overall picture was enough, the proof of government lying was damning.

Hallsson sighed and straightened up.

'Well, I wonder what happens next,' said Halfar.

'I pack my office up,' said Hallsson sadly.

'Really? You think they will trace this back to you?'

Hallsson shrugged. 'It's the only logical answer.'

'Well, nothing says you are guilty like packing. I suggest you do nothing until they accuse you.'

Hallsson nodded slowly. 'Yes, I suppose you are right. I will attempt to continue as normal. Although my name is all over those documents and my inbox is already filling with requests for comment.'

'Have you given any?'

'No. I'm under NDA,' said Hallsson with a wry smile. 'It would be inappropriate to answer any questions.'

As they stood there, there was another knock on the door, and both men looked towards it. 'Yes,' said Halfar.

The door opened and one of Hallsson's research assistants came in, who had been with him at the dig site. 'Professor?'

'Yes, what is it?'

'Uh, something you should see.'

'We already know,' said Hallsson, waving vaguely at the screen.

The assistant peered at the article briefly and then shook his head. 'No, not that. May I?' he asked, indicating the computer. 'I saw this live on the news, but there is a clip you should see on the live page.'

Halfar backed away and let him get to the keyboard, where he brought up the main news page, clicking on a breaking headline. A video popped up in stream of updates on the topic, with the words SCANDAL in all caps. Halfar's eyebrow rose.

The video started playing, and Jans Andersson was sitting with a presenter. 'Jans, we are hearing that, in the last hour, more information has come out about this government cover-up scandal. Can you tell us more?'

'Yes, I can. We have just been given more documents that were not previously sent by the whistleblower. They show that the government conducted radiocarbon and DNA analysis on the body recovered in the royal tomb, comparing the recovered DNA to a known descendant of King Magnus's daughter, who fled to Iceland and settled there.'

'Grave,' muttered Halfar in annoyance.

'And the government kept these results secret? What do they show?'

'They show, beyond almost all doubt, that the remains in the grave are those of Sigurd Magnusson, the King of Sweden and Norway, the so-called "Northking" or only king of all the Norse.'

Halfar gave a little yelp of joy and banged his fist on the table, startling the assistant.

'He is spoken of in fragmentary sources and in the Icelandic sagas, but not mentioned in the supposedly more reliable Christian historical record,' said Jans, with a beaming smile.

'Really? And is that significant news?' asked the presenter.

'It re-writes that part of our national history. It's hard to overstate how much this throws open the established story of how this nation came to be, and of the resistance to the Northern Crusades of the early 12th century. This proves they were indeed unified under a single king. It opens the entire narrative for re-examination.'

'Remarkable. Well, we will hear more about the historical implications from you in due course, I'm sure. Thank you, Jans, for coming on the show.'

Hallsson leaned back and sighed in surprise as the clip ended.

'That's what I thought you should see,' said his assistant. 'What will happen now? We will be able to talk about what we found, yes? And recover the artefacts?'

'I don't know,' said Hallsson. 'I hope so, but it remains to be seen how the government reacts.'

They were drawn back to the live feed when a new video popped up, titled 'SCANDAL FALLOUT CONTINUES', and Halfar leaned over and clicked on it.

'I have been told while we are on air that the man responsible for this cover-up was the deputy assistant minister for culture, Bertrand Lang, a junior member of the ruling party. He has resigned and an investigation has started. A government spokesman says that he was acting alone, and without the permission of the ministry of culture. A remarkable state of affairs indeed. I think we can connect to our political correspondent in Lundjen. Maya, are you there?'

A video popped up of a journalist with a microphone, standing with a backdrop of the National Parliament in Lundjen. 'Hello, Johan. It's been a chaotic afternoon here at the national parliament. Early denials have swiftly changed to silence and now to backtracking and attempts to distance themselves from the alleged culprit, as the government tries to contain the fallout from this scandal.'

'Is this such a serious matter for the government, do you get that sense?'

'Absolutely. This is a sensitive political subject at the moment, and this evidence that a government minister, however junior, has been hiding a key piece of national history is embarrassing and politically damaging. The Nording parties are already demanding a full investigation and apology, along with demands to allow wide access to the finds for proper and independent scientific examination. On top of the discovery of the supposedly mythical sword in Røros last year, this is proving to be an awkward time for a party that claims the Crusade-era Norse history of this country is mostly folklore and fiction.'

'Fascinating. Do we have any word on who the whistleblower is who revealed all of this yet? Or are there two whistleblowers? As I understand it, the documents came in two sets.'

'Yes, we have been informed that the whistleblower has been identified, and they have made a statement.'

Halfar gaped at the screen, as Hallsson looked around at him in confusion.

'In fact, I think you can put up a feed of his statement now,' said Maya.

A slightly grainy video popped up on the side of the stream, and Halfar gasped at the familiar face that was waiting to speak, unable to understand what was happening.

'Good afternoon,' said the soft voice. 'My name is Felix Meyer. I was Bertrand Lang's assistant, and I decided that I could not remain silent about this cover-up, no matter the consequences. So I have released the evidence related to the archaeological dig that was suppressed by Mr Lang.'

Halfar looked at Professor Hallsson, who was staring at the screen in incomprehension. He shook his head as his friend turned to meet his eye with equal confusion.

'Well, that's rather a surprise,' said Hallsson, his eyebrows half-way up his forehead.

'Yes, I can't believe he would do this!' said the assistant, beaming. 'I would never have thought he had it in him.'

'No. I don't believe it either,' said Halfar, staring back at the screen as Felix spoke to the camera in a monotone and finished his brief statement. 'I would love to talk to ask him to explain,' he said, dryly.

'Well, sounds like you will get the chance,' said the assistant, scrolling through the live feed as it updated. 'Apparently he is replacing Bertrand Lang at the ministry. The government are giving him their full support. Desperate to distance themselves from the affair, looks like he won't be punished at all for the leak.'

Hallsson's eyebrows only rose further. 'Well, that is… good news.'

He reached for his pocket as his phone rang, and he looked at the screen before answering it.

'Yes?' He listened for a moment. 'Of course, I'll be in my office.' He put the phone down and looked at Halfar with a wicked grin. 'You'll get your opportunity sooner than you expect. That was Felix's people. He will be here in an hour.'

Halfar beamed at Hallsson, and he smiled mischievously. 'I hope you don't mind if I attend that meeting, to… bring some questions.'

Hallsson laughed. 'No, Halfar. I wouldn't miss that conversation for anything.'

# Afterword and Historical Note

The penultimate book of this series goes out into the world in a very different situation for me than the first one did. I was but a hopeful, bright-eyed writer with a dream of getting my book out there and having some people actually read and enjoy it.

Now there are thousands of my books out there in the great wide world, and my lovely readers have encouraged me, reached out to talk to me, left me nearly a thousand ratings and reviews and just been incredible. It has been quite wonderful, and despite the end of this particular journey now coming into view, I now have the platform to continue publishing, and new series and ideas I want to put on paper. So thank you all, so very much. Each sale, rating and interaction pushes the wagon a little further down the tracks and makes the journey easier.

The experience since launching has been beyond my expectations, and then over the hill beyond that. The confusing, exhausting whirlwind of debut self-publishing has somewhat fallen into a comfortable rhythm. There is still a huge amount of work to do for each book, but familiarity breeds efficiency and comfortability, and I am enjoying the writing more than ever before.

I am, however, becoming ever more weighed down with the day-to-day admin of marketing and editing and a hundred other jobs, and it is for that reason I have taken up the opportunity to split off half my work to a professional publisher, Boldwood Books, with whom I have a contract for a new four-book series. I believe they are a fantastic home for my historical fiction work, they publish a lot of great authors in that genre and really know what they are about.

This move comes with good and bad news for readers, mostly good. My next series may be slightly delayed while it goes through the longer publishing process, but handing over half of my work means I will have more time for writing, and will mean I publish more books per year.

This also means my previously announced schedule of releases is no longer valid. My debut series with Boldwood is a four-part historical fiction about the life of Harald Hardrada. It is a story I have been working on for a while in the background, one I am very excited about, and will continue in the vein of Norse adventure but as straight historical fiction, with no fantasy elements. The first book in that series is already written, and is due to publish in autumn this year, only a short time after this book.

So that new contract delayed this book and for that I apologise, but, in the meantime, I have already started writing book five, *A Burning Blade*, the final entry in this series, and I will get that out into the world as soon as I can!

The historical notes for this entry in the series are quite limited, as most of what I have said for the previous books still applies. I have tried to keep the behaviours and actions of the various factions, leaders and ordinary people logical for what they might have done from a cultural and political point of view. I have tried to represent the weaponry and tactics in a realistic way, although I have taken some liberties for the purpose of the story, of course.

Some of the main locations in this book are fictional, for the first time in the series. The river and series of lakes that the Norse follow north and hide on is real, it's called the Kolbäcksån, you can look it up on the map and probably follow my description of their first journey to find where the fictional village of Vatnsborð clung to the lake shore in a hidden bay on the eastern shore of what is now called Norra Barken lake. If you want to see it, go to Google Maps, and look at the north-eastern side of that lake; you will see a series of bays and narrow inlets. In the first large one from the east, with a narrow entrance and a wider internal bay, there is a small farm or hamlet on the north shore in a clearing. The south side of that bay is the exact spot where I decided Vatnsborð was, and how I pictured the surroundings when describing it. You can see how it would be invisible to any passing ship except from a very narrow angle, and how it would be difficult to find and approach from the land.

Karlsgrind is also fictional, but lies in my mind where modern-day Kolbäck is, straddling the river on the direct road from Västerås to Arbugæ (today called Arboga).

The reason I have started including fictional settlements is simply that the names of the settlements of that size were not often recorded. We know the names of most of the big 10th-century Swedish cities and towns, but only a scattering of the smaller ones. So, I placed some where I needed them to be. There would almost certainly have been a settlement near Kolbäck, and perhaps near Vatnsborð, but their names are probably lost to time.

And so, the scene is set for the final book, the conclusion to the saga of Ljós a Norðan. The Norse, driven by inspiration and desperation, will attempt to preserve their shattered people, and the Christian lords, already feeling certain of their victory, will risk everything to jostle for control of the vast new lands their conquest seems to have delivered them.

I have had a couple of readers question if I meant to 'spoil' the ending of the whole story in book one, where Halfar tells the story of the Northern Crusades and how the Christians eventually took over much of the North. But no, it was quite deliberate. This is an alternate history, and as with most historical stories, you know the end result before you start.

The eventual end of the conflict is supposed to be known, in broad terms. The point of the story is not to reveal the final result, but to tell the tale of how it happened. It's about the story of the people swept up in the broader events, how they shaped them and were shaped by them, and focuses on their fates and legacy.

It is, to borrow a phrase, more about the journey than the destination. The ending is fixed, in geopolitical terms anyway, but the way there is unknown, as is the fate and influence of the characters within it. It's a theme of the whole series, the question of fate and a person's role in deciding their own life's course. Jarl Ragnvald said in the second book: 'A man is nothing but his word and his wryd (fate). The Norns may decide how his journey ends, but he alone decides how he walks the path to get there.'

So, the legendary warband of Gjaldir is assembled, his four heroic followers oathbound to his side, and the fate of a people lies on the edge of his sword. Their saga will end in the fifth and final book of the series: *A Burning Blade*. To be published in 2024

James C. Duncan

April 2023

## WANT A FREE BOOK?

If you want to be kept updated on new releases, discount deals, or become a beta reader, join my readers' club, 'The Warband'. It's completely free, I don't do spam emails and for joining you will get a free prequel novella for this series titled *Steel in the Morning*, a punchy Viking adventure exploring the backstory of one of the main characters of the series.

So, to get your free book and an inside line to all my future work and discounts and giveaways, just visit my website and sign up.

www.jcduncan.co.uk

# ABOUT THE AUTHOR

Hi there! I'm James Duncan. As an author I am fascinated with history and fantasy. I write historical fantasy/fiction based on our world, but in an alternate timeline, past, present, or future. Each book or series asks and tries to answer a question of 'What if?' My debut series, the Light of the North saga, asks the question 'What if the Norse didn't convert to Christianity, and instead the Viking raids continued?' And posits the answer, which you will have to read the rest of the series to find out! I do not create new worlds, I mess with the history and future of ours, grounded in our own past and the laws of our universe, but tweaked in events and often adding a soft sprinkling of the divine or fantastical, resulting in relatable historical and future fantasy.

Outside of authoring, I am a professional engineer, and split my spare time writing, reading, and being an amateur bladesmith. My bladesmithing work, and more information about my life and authoring, and the ability to contact me and talk to me directly, are available on my website. Thank you so much for reading until the last word of this book.

Printed in Great Britain
by Amazon

53801776R00297